PRAETORIAN III

Eagles of Dacia

by S. J. A. Turney

For Alun

Greatly appreciated,
greatly missed

I would like to thank those people instrumental in bringing Praetorian: Eagles of Dacia to publication and making it what it is: Jenny for her initial editing and Sallyanne Sweeney, my agent for a tremendous amount of work on the manuscript and support in general. Also to Leo Bacica for helping grow my fascination with Dacia enough to push me into sending Rufinus there. Ciprian Dobra for guiding me around Alba Iulia and supplying me with in-depth information that has seriously added to the tale. Last but not least, my wife Tracey for managing to get me to and round Romania without disaster and keeping me on track throughout.

Cover design by Dave Slaney.

All internal maps are copyright the author of this work.

Published in this format 2017 by Mulcahy Books

Also by S. J. A. Turney:

The Praetorian Series

The Great Game (2015)
The Price of Treason (2015)

The Damned Emperors (as Simon Turney)

Caligula (March 2018)

The Marius' Mules Series

Marius' Mules I: The Invasion of Gaul (2009)
Marius' Mules II: The Belgae (2010)
Marius' Mules III: Gallia Invicta (2011)
Marius' Mules IV: Conspiracy of Eagles (2012)
Marius' Mules V: Hades' Gate (2013)
Marius' Mules VI: Caesar's Vow (2014)
Marius' Mules: Prelude to War (2014)
Marius' Mules VII: The Great Revolt (2014)
Marius' Mules VIII: Sons of Taranis (2015)
Marius' Mules IX: Pax Gallica (2016)
Marius' Mules X: Fields of Mars (2017)

The Ottoman Cycle

The Thief's Tale (2013)
The Priest's Tale (2013)
The Assassin's Tale (2014)
The Pasha's Tale (2015)

Tales of the Empire

Interregnum (2009)
Ironroot (2010)
Dark Empress (2011)
Insurgency (2016)
Invasion (2017)
Jade Empire (2018)

Roman Adventures (for children)

Crocodile Legion (2016)
Pirate Legion (2017)
1
Short story compilations & contributions:

Tales of Ancient Rome vol. 1 - S.J.A. Turney (2011)
Tortured Hearts vol 1 - Various (2012)
Tortured Hearts vol 2 - Various (2012)
Temporal Tales - Various (2013)
A Year of Ravens - Various (2015)
A Song of War – Various (2016)

For more information visit http://www.sjaturney.co.uk/
or http://www.facebook.com/SJATurney
or follow Simon on Twitter @SJATurney

Simon is represented by Mulcahy Associates of London.

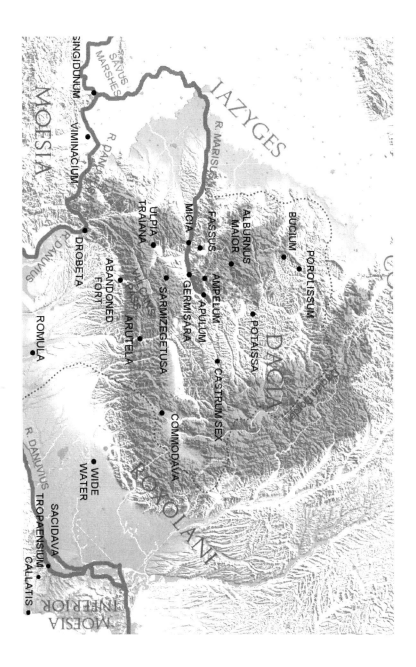

I – The road

Rufinus sighed and looked about with weary, dark-ringed eyes. A month, they had been given for the journey, and it had seemed ample time over that first leg with Gordianus and his entourage, as far as the thriving city of Aquileia. Then they had moved out of Italia and into the wilder lands of Noricum and Pannonia, and Rufinus had realised how complacent he had been with timing. He had ridden such distances, even many of these same roads, during the campaigns of the old emperor, but the judging of both distance and timing had proved to be much different when travelling with a woman in a carriage. How did civilians ever get anywhere?

Thank the gods for good Roman roads. The wooded hills east of Aquileia that rose and fell like ripples in the blanket of the world were hard enough work and he could scarce imagine what it would have been like across rough turf and shale without the road. But the constant struggle up the slopes with plodding beasts that stank worse with each passing day, and the muscle-rending effort of holding the brake pole steady as they descended each far side had left Rufinus feeling as though he had been soundly beaten with sticks at the end of every day. Of course, he had muttered complaints over the woman's need for the carriage, but only quietly and to himself. He knew better than to protest to Senova. She had a way of making you feel guilty and small without you realising they had said anything.

Gone was the servile and meek Senova he remembered at the imperial villa all those years ago. This Senova was a force of nature, headstrong and opinionated. She exasperated him, and the one real argument they had endured, somewhere in the hills above Neviodunum, had ended with him loudly and fervently wishing she was still that slave he'd first met. It had taken a week to heal that particularly idiotic wound. And the truth was that he *didn't* miss the old Senova. This Senova was wonderful. Infuriating, but wonderful. Even her Latin had changed, her halted misunderstandings and weird Northern accent all-but gone, replaced by the rather haughty tone taught by her tutor at Pompeianus' villa.

And so they had pressed on, down into the Pannonian basin, through bustling Siscia and across the damp flat ground to Aquae Balissae, then over more hills. More arm strain. More stinking beasts, More complaints, though even quieter now. Down once more onto the plains of the Iazyges and into the metropolis of Sirmium – a barbarian shit hole that had been given Roman civic buildings, faced with marble and fresh paint, and expected to look like Rome. It failed. And it smelled much like the beasts that pulled the carriage.

Rufinus had been glad to get out of the place until he discovered what lay between there and Singidunum. They had endured twenty three days of hills, woodland and plains, and on this, the twenty fourth: marshes. The Savus River they had been following for days split into multiple channels as it meandered on to join the great Danuvius. And each of those unnamed channels repeatedly broke and flooded, leaving a great flat wetland that oozed and hummed and stank. Almost as much as Sirmium. The great Roman highway cut through the Savus marshes like a pilum through the air, one long causeway that stood proud above the murk and reeds most of the time, occasionally sinking beneath the mire where repairs were clearly long overdue. Rufinus quickly became used to the new land's symphony.

Each terrain had its own melody, always played along to the percussion of the carriage. The marsh was a new and interesting one, albeit somewhat unwelcome. *Creak, groan, squeak. Creak, groan, squeak* – the wheels kept their rhythm, with the *clonks* and *thuds* of the various arcane mechanisms that gave the carriage its vaunted suspension – a facet of the vehicle that Rufinus could not feel making any difference. And with the *creak, groan, squeak,* and the *clonk* and *thud* were the snorting of the beasts and the occasional nickering of Atalanta, who clopped along patiently at the rear, tethered to the carriage.

And behind all that: the melody of the marsh. The beating of a million tiny wings and the occasional battering of greater ones as sparrowhawks swept over the flat landscape and occasionally great powerful ospreys, hunting fish in the pools. The calls of those birds and many others sawing out across the land. The scuttling of marshland animals, including the fearless small lizards that bathed in the sun on the stones at the roadside, unblinking as the strange entourage passed by. Water buffalo grunted and groaned, slopping and sploshing through the marshes. And more disturbing was the sound of the wetlands itself: a sort of background buzzing hum with occasional plops and gurgles. Not appealing noises at all.

'How far is Singidunum now?' Scnova asked from the carriage behind him, nestled somewhere inside surrounded by a thousand cushions. Rufinus scratched his head and wafted away the insects as he frowned at the road ahead. It was hard to judge distances in this godawful land. Guesswork was the only answer. The man at the gates of Sirmium had said two days across the Savus marshes, and the sun was sliding down the sky now, so...

'About this time tomorrow,' he replied over his shoulder.

Theoretically, there was a small private hostelry that doubled as a state mansio halfway between the two towns at a place called Bassiana. He'd been keeping his eyes open for it, though the view was more than a little restricted. The marshes may, by their very nature, be utterly flat, and in theory his vantage point atop the carriage seat on the causeway should grant him a good view. In practice, the entire Savus Marsh was a maze of high reeds, knots of trees, shrubs and lumps of land that looked like small hills until you prodded them with a foot and they bobbed off across the water, disturbing things that lived underneath and looked like they should inhabit nightmares rather than swamps.

Bassiana was not the only settlement on the road, of course. A forty mile stretch of road inevitably passed through other 'towns'. Each had been less impressive and murkier than the last, and of the various small conglomerations of huts, only Fossae had been built up enough to be said to have a centre.

Something bit Rufinus on the back of the neck and in a panicked moment as he swatted and rubbed and flailed at his skin, he let go of the reins and the dumb animals at the end of them started to veer off towards the rippling pool at the side of the road, perhaps fancying a drink. Rufinus yanked on the reins and brought them back into a straight line, still twitching at his neck, worrying what it had been. Some insects carried plagues. He'd heard that more than once from medici and capsarii in the field. When Rufinus had been a young boy the legions had been devastated by just such a plague brought back from Parthia.

He reached down and fished his wineskin from his belt, unstoppering it and taking a small sip, feeling the guilt wash over him on two separate counts. Firstly, of course, he had sworn never to indulge in drink again after those dark days when he had suffered in the grip of dependency, first on poppy juice, and then on wine. He had soon come to believe that he could manage it and stay sober, though he never allowed himself more than one cup in a day, just in case.

But there was also the guilt over the libation.

Senova had asked him to use the small portion of wine he had left as a libation in the small temple of Mercury at Sirmium. Rufinus had refused. He had seen and smelled the stuff they seemed to drink in the town, and had instead bought a small flask of local muck and poured that to seek the favour of Mercury on their journey. He was sure Mercury couldn't possibly actually taste all the many thousands of libations he received every day, so it probably didn't matter. And that way Rufinus could savour the last of his Surrentine in peace. But now the wine tasted sour with the knowledge that he had denied Senova and fed cheap shit to a god.

Another sip made it feel a little better, mind. He went for a third, but remembered himself and lowered it.

'Do you intend to hit *every* pot hole between Rome and Dacia, Gnaeus?'

What happened to that slave girl again?

'Driving this thing is not as easy as it looks. There's not a lot of road to weave about on.' Not true, really. There was room for two vehicles to pass in most places, but he was damned if he was going to own up to the fact that he had been experimenting recently, using bumps and pot holes to test whether the suspension in the vehicle actually existed at all.

'You woke Acheron.'

Rufinus made a noncommittal grumbling noise, trying not to voice his feelings over his faithful hound's current attitude. Far from trotting alongside and keeping him company, the great black Sarmatian hunter lay curled up, snug in blankets and cushions inside the carriage with Senova. Pampered animal. Rufinus was starting to suspect that Acheron would have trouble hunting an apple the way he was softening up under the woman's ministrations.

His attention was drawn to the road ahead. Two travellers on foot, heavy cloaks wrapped around them to keep out the damp and the insects, had emerged from somewhere at the side of the road and walked toward the carriage. His senses alert as always, he watched the two men carefully – both were middle-aged and scruffy in local drab clothes and with walking sticks. They nodded a greeting as they approached and one murmured a 'good day' in a thick Pannonian accent, and then they were past and moving on toward Sirmium. Rufinus let his guard drop again. Perhaps he was over-cautious, but life in these past few years had taught him never to underestimate a situation. The men had moved on, and so had Rufinus's carriage. And now he could see from whence the pair had emerged.

Off to the left of the road was a pleasant green space, surrounded by neatly-tended trees. At the centre stood a large altar in a ring of low stones. The grass had been trampled flat by the feet of travellers worshipping at the shrine.

'Good.'

'What's good?' called Senova from inside the vehicle. Gods but that woman had excellent hearing.

'There's a small shrine coming up. I've still got some of the Surrentine left. Perhaps I can seek the favour of a more local god?'

'So your wine is too precious for your own gods but expendable on a Pannonian one?'

There was no point in answering that. That way further arguments lay. 'I'm going to pull in and stop. You coming out?'

He could sense her shaking her head inside. 'I would rather avoid being bitten to death by insects, thank you, Gnaeus.'

His lip curled in irritation as he reached up to rub that latest bite on the back of his neck. It felt huge. He wondered if it was bleeding. Maybe it was a bat or something? Did you get flying wolves? Still grumbling about women, dogs, flies, and women again, Rufinus pulled the vehicle off the side of the road and onto the lush green grass of the shrine site. Insects still hung in the air as they did everywhere in this benighted region, but they were fewer here. The surrounding trees on three sides cut out the sight of the marsh and made it seem more peaceful and normal here, though the reeds and pools were still visible on the far side of the road.

'Send Acheron out. He could do with the exercise.'

Senova's reply was muffled but sounded faintly sarcastic, yet a moment later the carriage door swung open, the net-like curtains Senova had hung to keep out the insects flapping as the dog lazily dropped to the grass and began to pad around and stretch. Rufinus clambered down and crouched and rose a few times, loosening up his knees. Rolling his shoulders, he strode over to the altar. The depression in the surface was stained from past libations, and small offerings lay around the edge, gifted by hopeful travellers. Rufinus bent and peered at the altar's front.

Adsullata. Never heard of her. Must be a local swamp deity or something. Still, she was clearly worshipped and her blessing sought in this place, and Rufinus knew better than to ignore local custom in such matters. With a sigh, he straightened, brought up his wineskin and poured the remaining contents into the dish at the surface. Holding up his hands in ritual form, he cleared his throat.

'Divine... err... Divine. err... Adus... *Adsullata*,' he remembered suddenly. 'Grant us your protection and blessing on this crossing of your delightful swamp.'

He paused. It seemed weak, but what else was there to say?

'Don't do anything stupid,' called a gravelly voice, and Rufinus turned instantly, his hands dropping. Three men had emerged from the trees at the edge of the shrine. All three had gleaming, if pitted, blades unsheathed.

Damn it. His senses had not been playing him up after all. There *was* danger. He took a step to his right and was not at all surprised to see the two travellers in cloaks coming back along the road toward him, walking sticks discarded and replaced with blades. To complete the situation two more emerged from the trees at the far side.

'"Something stupid" like fight for my life, you mean?' Rufinus said quietly, his hands dancing along his belt. He had his pugio dagger there and small knife he used for eating, but his sword was in the carriage. Can't sit on a driver's seat with any level of comfort if you have a sword at your side. Poorly-armed and seriously outnumbered. Damn it.

'We're going to see who and what are in the wagon, lad. And we're going to take it and them. If you leave us to it, we might let you live. But you might get thumped a bit. Titus here likes thumping legionaries, since he got kicked out of the Fourth Flavia Felix. Not so *felix* for a man caught napping on duty, eh Titus?'

The indicated thug sneered. 'Might make it a quick death for you, though,' he said.

Rufinus began to plot and calculate. Senova must be able to hear what was happening. With luck she had burrowed down under the seats and gone into hiding. Acheron was standing close to the carriage, snarling, drool dripping to the turf. Seven men. Two on the road, with Acheron and the carriage between them and him. Three off to the left. Two to the right.

Appraisal time. The two he'd met on the road were nothing unusual, he remembered. Not especially big or lithe-looking. The apparent leader was mouthy enough, but he had let the two with him step out slightly ahead, so he would clearly be happy to let his men do the fighting. He was like a legionary legate: directing and controlling. One man with him was not too worrisome. He was Titus, the bulky ex-legionary. He looked big and scarred, but a man who fell asleep on duty was a careless and lazy one no matter how big he looked. The other one with them though could be trouble. He was shorter and narrower but moved with sinuous grace, like a dancer.

The other two men were both big and heavy, overhanging brows and muscled arms like sacks full of melons. They would be big and dangerous, but slow.

Rufinus toyed with the idea of lying about the carriage, claiming it was empty and that he was returning it to Singidunum, but that was pointless. They would still want to search it for valuables, and they might well have heard him talking to Senova anyway.

'Listen, lads,' he said equitably as he spread his arms in a peaceful gesture, 'I'm not looking for trouble, but trust me, if you are, you've found it. I'm no green recruit, and Acheron there has killed more men than the bloody flux. If you just step back, we'll move on and no one need get hurt.'

'Piss off, little legionary,' snorted Titus.

Ah well. It had been worth a try. Rufinus mapped it out again. Acheron could handle the two on the road. Leader would wait. So Rufinus was facing four. He had to even the numbers quickly. The two big mono-browed thugs first. They were big and slow. Don't waste time killing them. Just drop them out of the fight as quick as you can. Then move to the left. Draw the dancer to him. Get him between Rufinus and Titus so there was only one opponent at a time. With luck he could work this. He hoped Adsullata was watching and appreciated his sacrifice of the good wine.

'Take him, lads.'

Rufinus glanced off to the side. Acheron was snarling and looking this way and that between the various enemies. Rufinus pointed off toward the road. 'Kill.' A simple command, and one Acheron knew only too well. The great hound launched himself off toward the two men approaching on the road, snarling and slavering, muscles bunching as he ran. One of the men shouted a curse and turned, running. The other braced himself, raising his sword. Acheron hit him like a runaway wagon smashing into a straw dummy and Rufinus counted that particular fight as over before it began.

Turning his attention to his current predicament, he ripped the two blades from his belt. A pugio less than a foot long and a three inch eating blade. Could be better. He was even tempted to use his fists, they being his preferred weapon in many circumstances. But he needed to be quick and brutal. The two heavily-built men were closing on him, little more than a foot apart. Both wore native-style trousers with a thick woollen tunic over the top. No armour. Both men held their blades up before their torsos, ready to lunge with or swipe. Neither were prepared for the sort of fight Rufinus intended to give them. He reversed his grip on both knives, holding them blade-down.

Moving toward them he ducked left, then right. Predictably, the two men followed his movements, their blades staying ready to foil any coming strike. Good. Keep expecting it. Left. Right. Left. Right.

Spin.

Suddenly he was close enough for them to go for him. Their blades moved slowly, confusion mounting as their target whirled, putting his back to them, inviting the coming blows. But as the swords lanced out hungrily, already Rufinus was dropping into a crouch. Both his hands lashed out and back, stabbing with each blade, perfectly heighted and angled. He felt them strike and winced at the sheer violence of what he'd just felt. The pugio had been precisely on-target and had slammed into the tiny gap between knee-cap and femur, slamming down inside the joint, crippling permanently with one well-placed blow. The other, smaller knife was not large and strong enough to achieve the same goal and glanced off the patella, sliding down the inside of the knee and drawing blood. But Rufinus' backup plan was already there and he simply twisted his hand and altered the knife's trajectory. The blade sliced through the tendon behind the knee and Rufinus heard it snap.

He was back on his feet before the two men hit the ground, howling their agony and clutching at their ruined legs. Briefly he glanced over at the road. Acheron's first victim was nothing more than a twitching heap of meat and the great black hound was already diving at the man who had run. Four down. Three left. That was more like it.

He grinned at the trio.

'Regretting things yet?'

'Piss on you,' replied Titus the failed soldier.

'Oh, and for the record, I'm not a legionary. I'm a praetorian. And a veteran of Aurelius' Marcomanni battle. And I'm not letting you have our carriage.'

The lithe one was shifting slightly, and Titus was coming toward him too. With a certain dismay, he noticed the boss moving for the carriage. Perhaps he should shout a warning for Senova? But then perhaps the man would not look inside and instead try to deal with Acheron, in which case drawing attention to a lady within might be a mistake. Damn.

Back to his original plan, he danced left and then a little more and a little more so that the thin one was between him and Titus. The man's sword was at hip height, ready to strike or parry high or low as required. This one was worth his salt. Wasted on simple banditry. He bunched his muscles, ready to react. He had limited time, but still would much prefer to let his opponent strike first and display any weakness or bad habits. He was rewarded finally as the man lashed out, snakelike and quick. The blade almost reached Rufinus, but he leaned back slightly. His retaliation blow was deftly parried and Rufinus noted instinctively a slight turn of the head to the right as he did so. As the man straightened again, Rufinus caught his eyes and affirmed his suspicion. The man was partially sighted in his right eye, a milky film slightly discolouring the blue iris. Testing, probing, Rufinus took a half-step left. Sure enough the man turned slightly to adjust.

He was so busy probing the man's capabilities he almost came to grief there and then as the thug slashed out and Rufinus had to drop to the side at the last moment to avoid a vicious cut. His response was quick and yet carefully planned. Both hands shot out, but he made sure to move the right fractionally before the left and a little higher, dominating the man's field of vision. The brigand fell for the move, swiping down to block the pugio in the right hand as the left came round, sweeping in at his blind side and stabbing into his middle. The blade sank into the deep soft tissue and Rufinus felt a moment of elation before the knife was torn from his left hand. Even in sudden pain, the man had reacted, slamming his arm against his side and trapping the knife.

Hissing his pain, the man lashed out and Rufinus was not far enough back to entirely avoid the strike. He leaned away but the sword carved a long red line across the back of his right hand. His fingers felt like they were burning suddenly and the pugio fell from his grip.

Rufinus threw himself forward, realising that he was suddenly in real danger of losing this fight. He hit the man full in the chest and the two went down painfully in a tangle, onto the turf. The man's hand hit the ground and sprang open reflexively, his sword falling away.

Rufinus reared up and began to punch the thin brigand. Nothing subtle or sporting – just repeated blows to the head, determined to put him out. In mere heartbeats he had pulverised the man's face, mashing it into an unrecognisable tableau of blood and torn flesh. He leaned back, suddenly aware that he was open to attack and that Titus was now on him. He could see the big ex-legionary already lunging, his wicked blade coming for Rufinus' life. Prone, unarmed and unprepared. Bollocks. What a way to go.

And suddenly the man was no longer there, the sword seeking Rufinus' end gone with him. All the young praetorian saw was a blur of black, a smell of foul breath and blood, and a sound like a bow saw cutting through hardwood which he realised with a start had come from Acheron's mouth as it closed on the sword arm. Rufinus lurched up, staggering, to see Acheron standing over the body of Titus. Having mangled his arm with one bite, he was now at work on the neck. Titus was dead, though still moving, his eyes rolling, his voice soundless through a torn throat as he screamed silently for a quick end. Acheron gave it to him, though the manner of it still made Rufinus wince.

With a start, he turned, remembering the one remaining danger. He was just in time to see the brigand leader fall. The man had pulled aside the carriage curtains and spotted Senova, but even as a victorious and malicious grin spread across his face, she hit him in it with the pommel of Rufinus' still-sheathed sword. He staggered back with a broken nose and blood pouring down his face, blinking in surprise, and Senova swung the reversed sword like a club, the hilt smashing into his head and felling him instantly.

Rufinus stared as he ran toward her. The leader was starting to rise again groggily as Rufinus closed on the carriage and he stooped, grabbing the man by the hair and smashing his face into the carriage wheel. There was a satisfying crack and the bandit leader fell unconscious. Rufinus frowned, looking past him at the blood smeared wheel.

'Ah. I think I see how this suspension thing works now.'

Senova was rolling her eyes as he straightened. 'Have you finished playing with your friends now?'

'Damn it, Senova, this was serious. Dangerous.'

'That's why I grabbed your sword, Gnaeus.'

'Next time, try taking the scabbard off and using the pointy bit.'

'Yes, dear,' she replied in an infuriating tone, and disappeared back inside. Rufinus looked around at the bodies. Gods, but he was getting good at this. Perhaps it was not a talent to be proud of, like a poet or a sculptor, and certainly his father would not approve of such base violence. But he was *good* at it, and because he was so good at it, he was still alive.

'Who were they?' Senova asked. Rufinus looked around, watching with distaste as Acheron made certain they were all dead in his own special way.

'No one special. Just bandits. At least one of them's an ex-legionary from the Fourth at Singidunum. Probably the others are deserters and retirees too.' He bent over one of the bodies and noted a tattoo on an upper arm. A lion above a 'IIII'. Yes. Another ex-soldier from the Fourth.

'Are you wounded?' Senova called. 'I saw blood on your hand. Yours or theirs?'

Rufinus shrugged. 'Just a scratch. A big one, but still a scratch. It'll heal in a day or two.'

'Go and see the legionary surgeons when we get to Singidunum.'

'Senova, it's just a scratch. No harm.'

'That much blood is not a scratch. And even a scratch can get infected anyway. When we get there, you go and see the medicus.'

He sighed. There was no point in arguing right now. Mind, he had to admit that it did sting rather badly. Maybe she was right, but he couldn't tell her that. She was insufferable enough already. While she went about whatever business occupied her in the carriage and Acheron made sure he wouldn't need an

13

evening feed tonight. Rufinus went through the belongings of the bandits. It was distasteful work, but they had no need for anything now, and whatever they had up for grabs was Rufinus' by right of conquest.

A quarter of an hour later, with two more irritating insect bites and a hand rapidly going numb, Rufinus was the proud owner of ten blades that had seen better days and needed a good polish, a few coins, some salted pork rations and a set of dice, one of which always came up a five. The rest was all unusable or undesirable, or both.

He spent an unpleasant half hour then dragging the bodies across the road to the pool and throwing them in. Three of them floated on the surface, while the other four sank, and Rufinus frowned at them. One day he would have to ask a medicus why that happened, though he suspected it might lead to a number of strange and awkward questions in return. Also, he noted with interest, of the three that floated, two had rolled facedown, while the lithe one with the milky eye was face up still. Weird. There was something strange about this place. But at least Adsullata seemed to have heard his prayer, and he had removed the corpses from her shrine glade so as not to offend her. There was little he could do about all the blood, but someone in Sirmium had told him it rained at least every fourth day around here, so it would soon wash away.

'Time to move on,' he announced loudly as he returned to the carriage.

What in Hades am I getting myself into? Rufinus asked himself, and not for the first time. Dacia was the very edge of empire, every bit as much as those dark northern forests where he'd fought the Marcomanni. Dacia was supposed to be a civilised province, and yet it had only been part of the empire for eighty years. There might even be people still alive who remembered Trajan's armies coming, intent on conquest. It was said to be a rugged land of mountains and forests, peopled by rebellious barbarians who resented Roman rule and with a climate as confused as the population. And now supposedly a Sarmatian incursion to add into the mix.

And here, where he was now, was Pannonia, a land that had been Roman for near ten generations. And even this place was a marshy shit hole with drab barbarian towns and roads in need of repair and plagued by bandits. How much worse could Dacia be?

With a sigh and an imperious command from the lady in the carriage, Rufinus climbed up once more and settled in the seat. 'Off we go, then. To Singidunum.'

II – The Moesian Governor

In the event, Singidunum had proved something of a relief after Sirmium. It felt less barbaric, perhaps due to the efforts of the Fourth Flavia Felix based on the hill above the town. A well-presented forum had offered them quality goods and a sizeable bath house of recent construction helped soothe away the weariness of the journey. Rufinus delayed there longer than he had intended, in order to report the deaths of a number of deserters and ex-legionaries-turned-brigand in the marshes. The centurion to whom he spoke brushed the details aside, uncaring of men who had shown themselves insufficient for his legion. He did probe as to who Rufinus was, given his impressive survival of the attack, though he lost interest on the discovery that his visitor was a praetorian. Never the most popular unit among the provincial armies.

They set out again on the twenty sixth day, following the great Danuvius River that formed a thousand miles of border for the empire. Dacia, Rufinus kept thinking as he looked across that great wide flow. The only province that lay beyond that river. What lurked for him there?

Still, their first proper port of call – their immediate destination – was not in Dacia at all, but in Moesia. The seat of the governor of Upper Moesia: Viminacium, two days' journey from Singidunum. There, they were to rendezvous with the armies of Pescennius Niger and Clodius Albinus. And they should be there with two or three days to spare of the month they were given. That, at least, was a relief. Rufinus had his own ideas about what sort of reception an itinerant praetorian was going to receive, and if he'd been late too…

He had enquired of Pompeianus – who always knew everything about everyone in Rufinus' considered opinion – as to the nature of the two commanders he was to meet.

Pompeianus was acquainted with both, which came as no surprise. Albinus, it seemed, was currently serving as the governor of what Pompeianus called 'the three Dacias', based at Apulum and with direct command over the Thirteenth Gemina. Niger commanded the Fourth Macedonica at Potaissa and was therefore officially under Albinus' command.

'But what of the men?' Rufinus had probed. Pompeianus had snorted derisively. 'They are politicians and soldiers. That means that by nature they are untrustworthy and hard. Oh, I'm generalising. Niger seems decent enough, and he's clearly good at his job. He cleared Gaul of bandits last year, in conjunction with Albinus as governor, funnily enough. Albinus has achieved slightly higher office. He always seems to be one rung further up the ladder. But again, his record shows him to be eminently competent and I've heard nothing untoward about him. Neither has been implicated in any of the manoeuvrings of the court over the past decade, and neither has been dragged through legal proceedings.'

So that was that. All Rufinus had to work with. That and the fact that the frumentarius Vibius Cestius was a friend of Niger's. That, at least, stood the legate in good stead for Rufinus. It suggested a trustworthiness, since Cestius appeared to be a good judge of character.

Why the two most powerful men in Dacia were gathered in the capital of Moesia, three days march from the nearest feasible military crossing, was beyond Rufinus. But then he was a soldier, not a general.

They arrived at Viminacium near the close of their twenty eighth day. The sun slid down into a watery sky that had threatened rain all day yet failed to deliver, sinking into the low lands behind them while ahead, somewhere beyond that flat plain through which the Danuvius roared, lay the Carpates, the mountains that more or less defined Dacia.

Viminacium was a huge place, hemmed in by waterways and lying on a low rise. The fortress of the Seventh Claudia stood at the high southern point, with the walled town stretching northwards below it, alongside a small local river as it flowed into the Danuvius. Yet another area of unpleasant marsh lands lay between it and the Danuvius, though the lesser river carried craft from the main flow to the town's harbour.

Vehicles and their animals being banned from the town's streets on all but market days, they were forced to skirt the walls to its northern side and leave the carriage at a livery outside the gate there. Having paid his fee – higher than he had expected in the provinces – and received a chitty in return, Rufinus transferred the important gear to Atalanta's saddle bags and they moved into the place on foot.

The wealth and size of Viminacium surprised them as they passed through the grand gate and into a well-appointed Roman town, though the reason for its grandeur became clearer at the dock-side nearby. Ships unloading not only grain, but ingots of copper, iron, gold, lead and silver from the Dardanian Mountains were watched carefully by members of the Seventh Claudia.

Rufinus, Senova and Acheron meandered through the town, aware that they were well within time, and it would serve him well to gain some level of familiarity with the place, even if they were to be here only a short while. But as they moved through the streets, taking in the forum, the great baths, temples to the gods of half a dozen different cultures and a vast market, two things struck Rufinus. Firstly, he had seen no evidence of any troops other than the Seventh Gemina, and secondly the attitude in the town did not reflect that he had seen in other settlements that played host to visiting legions. Something odd was going on here, and Rufinus already suspected that the legions of the Dacian legates were not here after all.

What was going on? Had Cleander sent him on some wild chase to be rid of him? Was there something more sinister at the root? They moved around the city, Senova taking in the surroundings with the fascination of a new visitor, Acheron padding alongside and causing something of a circle of open space between them and the locals, Rufinus' suspicions building as they travelled.

Finally, they found themselves at the provincial palace, rising high above the city at the upper edge, close to the walls of the legion's fortress, a great complex of red-roofed structures. The place was old but with more recent rich ornamentation. Rufinus remembered standing and examining all he could of Trajan's funerary column in Rome, trying to familiarise himself with what he might find in Dacia, and remembered now that that great emperor had based himself here at the start of the campaign. Trajan himself may have had this building constructed, perhaps even with his famous architect, Apollodorus of Damascus.

Legionaries of the Fourth stood beside the grand doorway with its architrave portraying the slaughter and subjugation of the natives by some big-nosed officer and his cavalry.

'If someone put something like that up in Isurium,' Senova grumbled, pointing at the grand frieze, 'the locals would pelt it with rotten fruit daily.'

Rufinus fought through his instinctive disapproval of such a display of anti-Roman sentiment. Spending time with Senova was changing his attitude, he realised, and he wasn't sure whether it was for the better. He'd been subjected to endless lectures about slavery, which had diminished not one jot when he pointed out that the tribes of Britannia had a long and glorious history of enslaving one another long before Rome came along. And the idea of not offending barbarians would never have occurred to him a few months ago, but he had to admit that plastering the seat of local government with images of Romans standing on the necks of locals was perhaps not the most politic approach.

'Maybe they're *not* locals?' It was possible – likely, even – that the local tribe were not the ones being trodden down in the image, but perhaps Dacians during the war, or Iazyges from across the river. Rufinus honestly couldn't tell the difference between most of these tribes, though he'd never risk telling

Senova that. He'd be listening to a diatribe about the aloofness of Rome for a week.

'Hmph,' was his companion's final word on the subject and Rufinus, peering up at the architrave as they strode toward the gate, decided that perhaps it was time he paid a little more attention to the divisions between Rome's subjugated peoples. It might stand him in good stead in Dacia. And if not, it would certainly go down well with Senova.

Rufinus took Atalanta off to one side and tied her to the hitching rail, returning to the grand door to find the legionaries eying Senova suspiciously and deliberately not looking at the hulking black shape of Acheron who sat patiently, a puddle of drool growing on the floor beneath enough fangs to fill a bucket.

'Will my gear be safe there?' Rufinus asked. *In particular the silver spear*, he thought. He hated the idea of leaving such a thing out of his sight, but there might be trouble if he tried to seek an audience with powerful governors while carrying a spear, no matter what it was made of.

'We'll watch it. You have an appointment?' The legionary had a thick, weird accent, reminiscent of the native voices of the area. Rufinus couldn't place it, but it was distinctly eastern. He smiled. It was he and Senova that were the oddity here, of course.

Rufinus dug into his satchel and found the hardened scroll case containing his orders and documents from the imperial administration, bearing the dual seals of Cleander and the emperor himself. The fact that Cleander had permission to use the imperial seal rankled, but that was just a footnote in the catalogue of Cleander's crimes, to Rufinus. The seals were snapped, of course. The documents had been required to secure mansio lodgings along the journey from Rome. Still, the two men eyed the seals with interest as Rufinus slid out his orders.

'I've been sent here by the imperial chamberlain to meet with the governor of Dacia.'

The two men exchanged grins. 'Imperial bureaucracy. Always a month late,' snorted one, confirming Rufinus' suspicion that Albinus and his legion were not in Viminacium at all. 'You'd best see Capella, anyway.'

With no further explanation, the guard turned and waved into the darkened archway. A moment later a miserable-looking slave in a grey tunic and rough sandals appeared, head lowered.

'Take these visitors to the governor.'

The slave bowed deeper and gestured for Rufinus and Senova to follow, turning and padding back through the arch. Rufinus tried not to catch the glower on his companion's face. This was neither the time not the place for another *discussion* on the evils of slavery. He whistled to Acheron and the three of them moved toward the gate. The two guards lurched back, one's hand going to his sword pommel and the other wagging a finger toward Acheron.

'You can't take that thing in.'

Rufinus frowned. 'My dog goes where I do.'

'That's a *dog*? The governor hunts bears sometimes, but even them buggers are a smaller than *that* thing.'

Rufinus smiled maliciously. 'Well I can leave him with you...'

The soldiers looked at one another. The one still gripping his sword shrugged. 'A mandate from the imperial chamberlain overrules our orders, Oppius.'

The other soldier shook his head. 'His orders don't say anything about the dog.'

'They don't say anything about the woman either, but I'm not stopping her going in.'

'Good point.' The soldier waved at Rufinus. 'Keep that thing under control.'

'He'll be good,' Rufinus promised with a wicked smile as the three of them passed beneath the arch and hurried to catch up with the slave who was waiting quietly in the shadow.

The disparity between rich oppressor and poor oppressed was rather driven home as they emerged from the archway. The governor's palace seemed to have been constructed around a square, with a portico of red and white columns on all sides and a rather grand looking stair case opposite. At the centre of the wide courtyard was a pool with two fountains shaped into nubile nymphs, jetting water high into the air with splosh and a gentle trickle that reminded Rufinus he hadn't been to the latrine for some time. Hanging baskets of flowers gave a pleasant, colourful edge to the place, and the red-tile roofs had been scrubbed clean recently. A rich young man in a ridiculously expensive tunic and cloak sat on a marble bench in one corner while a slave polished his sandals.

The slaves were everywhere. They moved silently, gravely, with heads down, gazes locked on the floor in front of them. They were all clad in drab grey, which matched their skin tone as though they were dead already. Rufinus could feel the disapproval radiating off Senova and tried to concentrate on the matter in hand. Capella, the guard had said. Governor of Upper Moesia. An important province, even if the border had largely moved with the creation of Dacia. Governors of this level would probably be ex-consuls and men with heroic records as generals. Men of power and value. Men of whom to be wary.

Acheron trotted ahead to the glorious fountain and stopped there, dipping his head and drinking from the crystal water, noisily. A blue-tunic'd functionary started to scurry across the square, shouting at Acheron to stop, but as he came close and the great Sarmatian hound raised his soaking head and turned a mouth full of huge white teeth at the man, the functionary fell silent and instantly found something more important to do in a different corner of the courtyard. The flow of grey slaves in the square changed their silent, miserable flow with simple ease, leaving a wide space around Acheron, like a line of ants discovering an obstacle in their path.

The slave led them across the square and up the grand white steps into another great doorway with another pediment showing heroic Romans battering the wits out of snarling, wild-eyed savages. This one had no guards, but a man in a toga made a dreadful strangled noise and hurried out of the way as the dripping form of Acheron trotted up and fell in beside Rufinus. Inside, doorways led off to both left and right, and Rufinus realised oddly that most soldiers would feel overwhelmed to be in such a place. Not he, though, who had been in the palace of Vindobona when Aurelius died, in the palace of Carnuntum with the Pannonian quaestor, and in the imperial palace itself on the Palatine more than once. The number of slaves seemed to diminish inside the building to be replaced by clerks in military red, rushing this way and that with armfuls of documents. Rufinus and Senova were led directly ahead to a third door, manned by soldiers of the Fourth, and out into a second courtyard. The legionaries made to stop Rufinus and his great black hound, but either the sight of a scroll case bearing the imperial seal, or more likely the Tartaran rumbling coming from the dog, decided them against it, and they simply let the animal pass through. This court looked even richer than the last, with a floor of chequered black and white marble, a single fountain displaying four water-spurting dolphins, and delicate columns all around, draped with hanging flowers.

The governor's private area of the complex, he realised. Neither clerks nor slaves. Just an empty courtyard with trickling water. A sudden explosion of noise startled Rufinus as Acheron spotted two pigeons pecking at the marble floor and set off at a run in a tangle of legs and snorting. The guards behind them peered through the door in shock at the appalling noise and watched, horrified. Rufinus disliked pigeons on a number of levels – they were stupid and docile, seemed to be everywhere all the time, and took the greatest delight in crapping on everything – but despite that, he felt faintly sorry for the two birds as Acheron hit them like a ballista bolt at a pomegranate. The birds were too lazy, slow and fat to take off swiftly, though one bought time for the other with its life. The lucky plump bird, flapping madly and cooing, managed to reach a gutter as Acheron sent a cloud of grey feathers up into the air.

Oh good. Leaving that mess in the governor's courtyard would make them popular. The noise of snapping bones was gradually replaced by the sound of the fountain. Rufinus winced. *The latrines.* Damn it, he should have gone before attending to anything important.

Another set of steps led them up to a door. The slave rapped lightly on the wood and it was opened by a man in an expensive blue tunic and a face that not even a mother could love. The functionary listened to the slave's brief introduction, sniffed as though the visitors smelled like dead horses, which they probably did, and then beckoned. The slave disappeared and the two found themselves in a small chamber facing ornate bronze doors. The functionary was about to shut the door again when Acheron, still with feathers protruding from his muzzle, pushed through and stood beside Rufinus. The ugly man stared in horror.

'What is that thing?'

'This is my dog, Acheron,' Rufinus replied sweetly. 'He gets edgy when I'm not around, so for the good of all concerned I brought him with me.'

The functionary stared at Acheron, his face working through a gamut of expressions. Finally, he nodded and moved slightly so that Rufinus and Senova were between the dog and himself.

'Governor Quintus Naevius Capella has finished his work and was about to retire for the evening. Since you apparently have documents from the capital, confirmed by the guards, I will admit and announce you, but you must be brief and to the point. The governor is enjoying the company of the provincial procurator, Titus Sicinius Cilo, and may or may not wish to dismiss him first. Be quiet until you are spoken to and respectful with your gaze, and make sure that animal is quiet and well behaved. Your names and positions?'

'Gnaeus Marcius Rustius Rufinus of the praetorian guard, formerly of the Tenth Gemina, on the business of the imperial chamberlain, and the lady Senova of Isurium, my travelling companion.'

The effect was slightly spoiled as Senova let out a tiny snort of humour at the grand manner in which he introduced a Brigantian captive and former slave. The functionary gave her a suspicious look and rallied. 'It is customary for visitors to the governor to bathe before audiences, and not with the horses, for that matter. Still, time is short. Wait for your cue.'

With that he opened the door and stepped through.

'Domini, may I present the praetorian guardsman Gnaeus Marcius Rustius Rufinus and his companion, the lady Senova, bearing orders and documents from the imperial chamberlain in Rome.'

There was a pause, and Rufinus realised that had been the cue, so entered the audience chamber and bowed. Senova did the same just behind him, Acheron padding in and keeping pace at the other side.

The room was large – as large as the emperor's own *aula regia* in the capital, and almost as rich. Trajan's temporary palace, he remembered again – suitable for an emperor on campaign. Two men sat in large chairs on a dais at the far end, one slightly higher than the other. At this distance, they were visible only as a thin man and a fat one. Rufinus realised one was beckoning and strode into the room, closing on the chairs.

As he and Senova came to a halt some ten good paces from the governor, Rufinus became aware of two men lurking in the shadows at the rear. They were not legionaries from the Fourth, but were armoured in leather and had the look of professional killers. Private guards for the governor's person. Both men unslung small but powerful recurve bows and drew an arrow. Neither nocked the missile or stretched a bow string, but both had their eyes locked on Acheron. Seemingly, Rufinus was innocuous enough, but neither guard was going to let the hound move without loosing at him.

The governor – the one in the higher chair had to be the governor – was thin and reedy, like a man half-starved to death, his elbows and joints protruding from bony limbs. The toga hung on him like a cloak on a rake. His face was shrunken and cadaverous and Rufinus found it hard to look at the man without his eyes watering. By comparison, the procurator in the lower seat seemed as though he might well have eaten all the meals in Viminacium for several months. Parts of him overflowed the seat and the toga was seriously put to the test containing him. His neck looked like a sack full of melons. His lips were wide and rubbery beneath small, piggy eyes. Rufinus disliked all financial officers on principle, but this one shot to the top of his list for some reason.

Both men had a built-in sneer, as though the gods had forged their bodies to know they were better than everyone else. In fact, Rufinus disliked them both. The governor's left eyebrow rose in a series of jerks as though some slave somewhere were hauling on a tiny rope. Behind Rufinus, Senova made another faintly amused sound and he willed her to shut up and not get them in trouble. Both men looked at Acheron with a faint twitch of nerves, and made sure the archers were paying attention, before returning their attention to the man and the woman.

'Cleander has sent me a praetorian? Pray tell me why, and why he brings savage Sarmatian hounds into my presence,' rasped the bony one, his eyebrow now impossibly high.

Rufinus cleared his throat. 'Governor, I was led to believe that the governor of Dacia and his fellow legate – Clodius Albinus and Pescennius Niger – were here, preparing to deal with a Sarmatian incursion into Dacia. I am to join their retinue on the orders of the imperial chamberlain. The hound here, Acheron, is my companion and protector.'

The two men looked at one another, and the fat one let out a strange, girlish chuckle. The cadaver turned back to Rufinus. 'Niger and Albinus – the *black* and the *white* – are not here, young man. Niger never was, in fact. During the recent

26

troubles, he remained in the north with his Fifth Macedonica. In my understanding, the Sarmatian incursions have been dealt with and Dacia begins to settle once more. Albinus *was* here with the Thirteenth Gemina a while ago, but he returned to his own lands almost two weeks hence, after stripping Upper Moesia of its manpower.'

Rufinus frowned. 'I do not understand, Governor.'

Capella sighed, a sound like wind rustling papyrus. 'Albinus came here to replenish his legion, which was seriously under-strength.'

Still, Rufinus frowned. 'To Moesia?'

Again, a shared look and a girlish giggle, and the mobile corpse with the impossible eyebrow that still sat atop his forehead, susurrated an answer. 'Young man, Albinus could hardly trust recruits from his own territory when half of them were running from Sarmatian raiders and the rest were taking the opportunity to rise up and complain at their rightful masters. Dacians are untrustworthy at the best of times, and after the recent troubles? No, Albinus came to somewhere with a loyal source of manpower to recruit.'

'That seems unusual, Governor,' Rufinus said, in carefully blank tones. He had met more than one governor in his time, and none of them in his experience were likely to offer a wet fart for one of their opposite numbers, let alone such a grand accommodation.

'Albinus and I have... an arrangement.' It was said in an oddly mysterious tone, and elicited yet another squeaky giggle from the procurator. Rufinus was starting to wonder how long he could remain in the presence of these two without punching someone.

'Might I ask where Clodius Albinus is now?' Rufinus said, through grinding teeth.

'Dacia somewhere,' the governor said dismissively with a wave of a skeletal hand. 'I would suggest Drobeta. That is his nearest sizeable fortress. The nearest place that can support a legion.'

Drobeta. The place Trajan had constructed his great bridge and begun the conquest of Dacia. It seemed oddly appropriate to enter the province there. 'Thank you, Governor Naevius Capella. We shall make for Drobeta first thing in the morning. I shall inconvenience you no longer. Many thanks for your time.'

'For the emperor and his chamberlain, there is no inconvenience,' Capella replied, loading the words with enough dripping bile to suggest that he would rather eat his own foot than help Cleander. Rufinus might not like these two, but he had to agree with them on that point at least. With a bow, he turned and gestured for Senova and Acheron to follow. His heart jumped in his chest as he saw Senova opening her mouth, a quizzical look on her face. Oh, turds...

'What sort of arrangement?' she asked the governor. Rufinus' eyes widened. Gods, that woman!

'Come on, Senova.'

But she resisted his jerking at her sleeve. The governor and the procurator shared a conspiratorial look, and then the bony face turned back to face her. 'That is none of your concern, young lady.'

Senova kept her unblinking gaze on the governor long enough that eventually he looked away in discomfort, and finally she relented and allowed Rufinus to lead her away. The sound of the two bows being lowered and the arrows returned to sheathes in the shadows filled Rufinus with relief. He'd rarely been more grateful to leave a room as they emerged into the light of the inner courtyard, where two slaves were scrubbing pigeon remains from the marble.

'What in Hades was that?' he snapped at Senova as they strode back across the courtyard.

'He is up to something. Something illegal, I think.'

'Of course he is, he's a governor. Can't trust any of them further than you can shit a cobble stone,' he snapped angrily, slipping into the sort of language legionaries use and which he'd tried to stamp out of himself since his move into more delicate circles.

'You wanted to know what the arrangement was. I could sense that.'

'But I'm smart enough not to ask him directly.'

Senova simply snorted. 'Romans are too indirect sometimes. You dance around the subject too much.'

He fell silent for a moment and finally chuckled in a relieved voice. 'Well, we're out and moving without an arrow in my nethers, so no harm done. And did you see the look on their faces when you asked them? Like two young kids caught by their mother with all the honey cakes.'

Senova nodded. 'Children. That is what they are.'

'Still, please learn to be a little more circumspect.'

'Circum-what?'

'Careful,' he sighed. 'Some of these people are powerful enough to have us killed without blinking an eye.'

'Try being a slave for half a decade.'

He sighed. Somehow it always came back to that.

'Let's find the city's mansio and book in for the night. We still have the documents, and we don't want to set off 'til morning. The sun's nearly down now. What do you make of that, though? Albinus and Niger not being here?'

Senova sucked on her teeth as they passed through the palace office area and down the steps to the first courtyard, space opening around them and Acheron once more.

'I think we can go back to Rome.'

'What?'

Senova gestured with open palms. 'Your job is done. You were sent to join the legions here and they aren't here. The legions were supposedly putting down an invasion which has been repelled. Surely we can go home?'

Rufinus shook his head. 'I was sent to join the legions of Dacia. Doesn't matter where they are. And it doesn't matter that the fighting is over. Cleander wanted me well out of the way and wanted a report on the loyalty or otherwise of the local commanders. If we go home without even meeting Albinus and Niger, I will not have obeyed Cleander's orders. We have to go on to Drobeta. After that, we will see how the land lies.' There was a long silence as they exited the building and made for the hitching rail where Atalanta waited with their gear.

'He will be fine, you know,' she said suddenly, apropos of nothing.

'What?'

'Publius. He will be fine. He is too important to endanger.'

Rufinus nodded absently. He'd tried not to think on his young brother too much, languishing in the grip of Cleander at court. Senova was correct. As long as Publius was safe and in Cleander's grasp, Rufinus was no threat to the chamberlain, so he would be kept well.

'I will find a way,' Rufinus replied, 'to get Publius out and safe and to bring that snake bastard down. Maybe Pescennius Niger can help? Maybe even Clodius Albinus. If Cleander distrusts them and Vibius Cestius likes them, then they might be just the right men. I think I learned this past year that there is no way to effect true change on my own. I need the help and support of good men.'

There was an oddly loaded silence as he tucked the scroll case back into the saddle bag, and he chuckled. 'Yes, and good women.'

A low growl issued near his hip.

'Yes. Good dogs, too.'

III – A legion diminished

R ufinus had to admit to a certain level of awe and excitement at the journey onwards. There had been a number of people in the mansio in Viminacium that night, and it had not taken Rufinus and Senova long to fall into conversation with one of them. Minius Strabo worked for the *cursus publicus*, carrying letters around the region for the Roman administration. He had been a veteran of the Fourth Flavia Felix in that very city, and between his military history and travels in his new career – he told them in confidence that he had left the army and married a woman that had turned out to be a bottomless pit into which his pension went – he had an unparalleled knowledge of the area and its geography. Strabo had told them many stories of the road from there to Drobeta, and each of the man's effusive tales made Rufinus more interested in where they were going. Better still, even Senova was enthusiastic enough that she never blinked when Strabo told them he was saving for a new slave for his wife.

So they had set off in the carriage once more from the north gate of the city with Atalanta tied to the back and Acheron curled up in cushions near Senova. There was no bridge across the smaller river, due to the low-lying levels and the need to keep the channel free for ships, and so they paid – over the odds in Rufinus' opinion – a ferryman to take them across and there picked up the road east. Senova now kept the carriage windows open, peering out as they passed. The first day was nothing special, passing through the last of the lowlands, the terrain much as it had been for the past few days. That first night, they stopped at a small rural inn recommended by Strabo, had one of the better meals and best night's sleep on their entire journey, and cursed the imperial way stations and their blandness.

The second day, however, the scenery changed, and the glory Strabo had promised became a reality. They reached the foothills of the Carpates, and the Danuvius no longer meandered across a plain, but carved a path through high hills and then wooded mountains. Senova spent so much time peering out of the windows and moving from side to side in the carriage that eventually she gave up, brought a cushion with her, and joined Rufinus on the driver's bench. Just after noon on the second day the road, constructed by the legions of Trajan eighty years ago, became the wonder of which they'd been told. The great river entered a long, sheer gorge known as the 'Iron Gates', where the riverbank disappeared and gave way to high, grey cliffs. Rather than find some distant way around, needing to keep to the river and that all-important border, the great emperor's fine engineers had provided an ingenious solution. Here, the road was carved directly into the cliff-side: a great hollowed out highway following the Danuvius, which became unnavigable in places here due to rocks and obstacles. To widen the initial construction, a wooden walkway hung out over the water, trestles supporting it dug into the cliff-side below. It was a work of engineering the like of which Rufinus had never seen, and the carriage only just fit beneath the rock-cut ceiling. Still, he kept to the right as they travelled, Senova making nervous squeaking noises every time they moved out onto the wooden boards above the water.

The second night they stopped at Taliata and found adequate lodgings in the mansio there. The next day brought new and breath-taking views of the Iron Gates, and toward the end of that third day, they passed a neat canal that had been carved through one of the rock impediments in the river, allowing boats to pass between two of the larger towns, and for a time the road became an ordinary riverside highway, though still with magnificent views of grey mountains and green-blue water. The third night they stopped in a small town opposite Tierna, which sat heavy and brooding on the north bank. More marvels filled the last day, and as the sun began its descent they came within sight of Drobeta and its famous bridge.

It was hard to imagine how any human being had looked at the huge expanse of water between where Rufinus now stood and Drobeta on the north bank and decided it would be a good site for a bridge. Yet Apollodorus – and his master Trajan – had conceived here a bridge longer than any in the empire. Oh, Caligula had built a longer one, yes, but it had been a temporary structure made mostly of boats. This was a permanent timber and stone span, allowing access to the lands of the Dacian kings for the legions of Rome. Here a world had been conquered – or at least here that conquest had begun.

Rufinus' father had always upheld Trajan as the paragon of all that it meant to be Roman, as had much of the empire. Beneath Trajan's guiding hand the empire had reached its greatest extent – in fact, since his day it had actually shrunk a little. Trajan had built many of the architectural wonders of Rome and the empire. He had been a soldier, a leader, an administrator, an innovator, even taking a personal interest in the running of the empire at its lowest level, or so it was said. Of course, Rufinus took everything his father said with appropriate levels of scepticism, but there had to be more than a grain of truth to it and, looking at this bridge, which spanned almost a mile of water, it was hard not to be impressed.

The bridge, on powerful arches of stone, marched across the Danuvius, linking the world of Rome proper with this odd trans-Danuvian province in the mountains. Drobeta sat on the far bank, a fortress of stone on the highest point, beside the bridge, the civilian town stretching out west from there, down to the riverbank sixty feet below the bridge, where the port stood.

The carriage rumbled out onto the timber boards and crossed one of the empire's greatest rivers with a rhythmic thumping which finally made Rufinus aware of the value of the vehicle's suspension. The sun finally dipped behind the mountains to the west mid-crossing, and Rufinus was surprised by how swiftly the shadows rose to encompass the world even as he heard the watch calls ringing out over Drobeta's fort. By the time they passed beneath the grand monumental arch that marked the bridge's northern end, it was most definitely evening.

A mansio stood close to the bridge, off to the left, and beyond it in every direction the town of Drobeta spread, a surprisingly large place considering its relatively recent foundation. A small amphitheatre rose beside the mansio, built of the same dark stone as the bridge. But the town and its facilities were not their destination, and Rufinus drove the carriage on past the mansio and amphitheatre, making for the high walls of the fortress on the bluff above the water. In the gathering gloom, lights were springing up along the walls.

His suspicions rose once more at the sight of Drobeta. The fortress was large enough, and strong, but whatever the Moesian governor might have thought, it would not be large enough to hold a legion. The west gate stood impressive and powerful, torches burning above and men on guard at the parapet. It was something of a relief to see a banner displaying the lion of the Thirteenth Gemina. Given the size of the place, Rufinus had begun to worry that the army had moved on again and he'd once more missed them. Perhaps the bulk of the legion who would not fit in the fort were camped beyond, out of sight.

He rattled the carriage along the road and toward the gate. The doors had been shut for the night, and the legionaries atop the wall called for him to halt away from the walls. Rufinus hauled on the reins and craned to see the top of the wall.

'Who goes there?' called the soldier above in a thick regional accent.

Rufinus cleared his throat and shouted back up at him. 'Imperial guardsman Rustius Rufinus, direct from Rome on the orders of the imperial chamberlain. I am to present myself to the commander of your legion. I have all the appropriate documentation.'

There was some discussion atop the wall. Rufinus caught only fragments of it, but surmised that they were trying to decide whether to admit him after dark or tell him to stay in the mansio until morning. In all honesty the latter path sounded infinitely preferable, granting them food and the chance to relax rather than a meeting with important officers, but that was up to the Thirteenth. Finally, the gate creaked open and two legionaries emerged. Rufinus was surprised at how young they looked and almost chuckled when he remembered that he'd been much the same back in Vindobona not so long ago.

'Documents?'

Dutifully, Rufinus retrieved the scroll case, fished out the appropriate paper and leaned down to pass it across. The legionary propped his pilum against the wall, took the paper and examined it. His brow raised in surprise, probably at the imperial seal attached and what it suggested, and he showed them to his friend and they came to a mute consensus.

'Come in. Leave your carriage and animals with us and we'll put them in the stables. I'll have someone escort you to the headquarters.' Behind him, more legionaries opened the doors fully to grant them access, and Rufinus slowly drove the carriage across the threshold and into the fort of the Thirteenth Legion. Inside, he and Senova climbed down and he was grateful for a display of courtesy as one of the legionaries helped the lady from the carriage. There was a collective intake of breath as Rufinus opened the carriage door and Acheron dropped to the ground, stretching and huffing irritably at being disturbed.

Briefly, Rufinus considered gathering the most important gear – particularly the silver spear – but decided against it. He was simply presenting himself to the governor and did not need to be fully equipped. With Senova at his side and Acheron padding along at his heel, Rufinus followed the beckoning, wide-eyed legionary as he led them along the main street to the arch of the headquarters building, where two more soldiers stood guard. An escort had hardly been necessary for the simple journey – walking forward sixty paces from the gate – but there was something oddly formal and naïve about the whole thing. Everything here was being done so 'by the book' that it seemed out of place. No fort was ever quite so formal. As if to compound that impression, at the headquarters the legionary escort stopped, saluted to his peers and rattled off every morsel of information he had on Rufinus. The legionary beside the arch announced that he would show the visitor to the commander.

Rufinus rolled his eyes.

'I know a fort and a headquarters, man. I can find the office myself.'

The soldier stared at him as though he'd sprouted a tree from his head, frowned deeply, and then repeated that he'd show him to the commander. He turned with parade precision and marched into the complex. Rufinus shared a strange look with Senova, and they duly followed. The other guard at the arch took a single pace back as Acheron passed. Another thing that struck Rufinus as odd was that, though people were surprised and possibly dismayed at the sight of Acheron here, none of them were leaping away from him as seemed to be the norm. He reminded himself that he was currently about as close to the homeland of Acheron's breed as a Roman ever got. Perhaps the Sarmatian hound was common here. Perhaps Acheron was not frightening because they were used to seeing his kind.

The legionary led them through the principia's courtyard, with statues of Mars and Minerva and the emperors Trajan and Commodus, and into the basilica hallway. The chapel of the standards was well guarded, though it looked a little bare. A few flags and signa stood there, but no eagle or embossed image of the emperor. Rufinus' suspicions returned in force as he was shown to the office and announced with every bit of formality the legionary could muster.

Finally, ceremony over, the legionary bade him enter and then returned to his station. Rufinus strode into the office with Senova and Acheron close behind.

'Close the door,' said the man at the desk in a refined, cultured voice, carrying tones of Campania. Rufinus had never met Clodius Albinus or Pescennius Niger, but it was instantly clear that this was neither of them, for he wore the broad-striped tunic of a tribune. Rufinus clicked the door neatly shut and straightened to attention as he examined the man before him.

The tribune was not old, perhaps in his mid to late twenties. He was pale and smooth-skinned, with a neat blond beard and short, naturally curly white-blond hair. His nose was a little flat and his eyes sharp and a piercing ice blue. Long, expressive fingers drummed on the desk as he looked up.

'Gnaeus Marcius Rustius Rufinus. Sent by Cleander of all people to join the legions of Dacia on detached duty from the praetorian guard. An odd situation, if I might say.'

'I agree whole-heartedly, Tribune,' Rufinus replied. 'Might I ask after the governor, Clodius Albinus? It was to him that I was ordered to report.'

The tribune leaned back in his chair and folded his arms. 'I am Appius Iulius Celer, senior tribune of the Thirteenth Gemina, ranking officer and interim commander of this vexillation of the legion.' He smiled, and something about that smile put Rufinus at ease. It was a surprisingly friendly smile. 'I am afraid you are out of luck, Guardsman Rustius Rufinus. The governor has moved north once more.'

Rufinus' spirits sank. Missed him again. Was he doomed to chase Albinus around the province? Tribune Celer tipped water into the wine krater on the table and poured a cup for himself. He gestured to the visitors and Rufinus and Senova both nodded hungrily. The tribune poured a cup for each and slid them across the desk. 'Please, sit. You are both clearly tired and travel-worn and the lady should rest.'

He took a sip of the wine. Senova noisily gurgled hers down in one go, raising another smile from the tribune. Rufinus sipped slowly and sparingly at his, relieved that it had been well watered.

'How much do you know about the situation in Dacia?' Celer asked.

'Not much,' admitted Rufinus. 'I had heard that there was an incursion of Sarmatians that had caused a lot of trouble, but the governor in Viminacium suggested that the troubles were over.'

Celer snorted. 'In Dacia, the troubles are *never* over. It's just a matter of what troubles are going on at the moment. The Sarmatians crossed into Dacia, and when they did a number of Dacian peoples began to rise in revolt alongside them. The memory of Dacia as an independent kingdom is never far from the local's minds, you see. Dacia has not been a settled province for decades, if it ever was. The Marcommanic Wars drove tribes east and south into Dacia repeatedly over the years. It's not just the Sarmatians – *everyone* has a go at the border. It's a constant rolling threat. Anyway, Pescennius Niger and his Fifth Legion set to securing the north, and we – the Thirteenth – drove out the bulk of the invaders and put down most of the risings further south. But the legion was so heavily depleted in the process we moved into Moesia to recoup the numbers and rebuild the Thirteenth.'

'Yes, I'd heard that in Viminacium. It seems strange that the governor there was so agreeable to such a thing?'

Celer nodded. 'You know how governors are with scratching each other's backs. I have no doubt Legate Albinus had to make some laden promises in return. Anyway, we recouped the numbers but it has left us with a lot of green recruits. We returned to Drobeta to train them, but news came to the governor of another local rising up near our home fortress at Apulum. Well, that's close to the gold mines, and we can't allow such a rising to threaten gold production, so Clodius Albinus took the best part of the legion, including almost all the veterans, and marched off to Apulum. I was left in command of a cohort of men mostly only two or three weeks into their career. You have stumbled upon a little more than a training camp, master Rufinus.' His wry smile looked weary. Rufinus found himself feeling for the man, left in charge of new recruits while his commander marched off north to the *real* fight.

'You paint a worrying picture of Dacia,' Rufinus said quietly.

'Dacia is one long headache, Rufinus. It's a thousand square miles of trouble. And because we keep having to deal with incursions and put down the rebellious elements, those natives who remain loyal are beginning to lose confidence in our ability to protect them. That, in turn, makes *them* rebel. And so on, ad nauseam. We lose troops in Dacia on a weekly basis. Never in huge numbers as you do in a war, but there is a constant nagging rate of attrition. And Albinus cannot trust the natives enough to recruit them. Hence the deal with Moesia.'

'So how long are you in Drobeta, then?' Rufinus asked.

'As little time as I can possibly manage. The troops here have had three weeks of training now. Some of them can just about hit the side of a granary with a pilum. Some can march twenty miles without falling apart. Some even know the difference between *triplex acies* formation and a latrine ditch. They're months from being an effective legion, but I'm planning on giving them one more week of basic training and then moving out. My senior centurion reckons they'll be able to manage on the march by then.'

'And then you return to Apulum?'

Celer made a noncommittal gesture with his hand. 'We have been left the task of clearing out the few remaining noted pockets of resistance on our journey north, at places like Sarmizegetusa and Micia. The governor left them to us to deal with to avoid delaying his return to Apulum. Might I see your documents?'

Rufinus nodded and withdrew the scroll case, emptying the papers onto the table. Celer slid them toward him and sipped his wine as he looked down the documents.

'I see you are a veteran of the wars in the north?'

Rufinus nodded. 'With the Tenth.'

'Our sister legion. Good. Have you any command experience?'

A shake of the head sufficed. Celer huffed. 'Yet you seem to be extremely competent and experienced. I'm afraid this is the end of your journey for now, Rufinus. It would be remiss of me in the extreme to send you and your lovely lady, even with that monster behind you, up into the Dacian mountains, through rebellious territory, on your own. And I cannot spare the men to escort you, sadly. I have only one veteran century and five more of green recruits. You will have to stay with us until we move on. You can then accompany us to Governor Albinus at Apulum.'

Rufinus nodded. It made sense, and given Celer's fairly stark appraisal of the province, he had no wish to wander deep into its wilds unprepared. Albinus could hardly argue with any further delay when it was caused by his own tribune, after all.

'But I have no space for passengers, Rufinus,' Celer said seriously, rapping his elegant fingers on the table. 'I need your arm and your experience. Even my officers here are for the most part green and untried. Most of the centurions are former optios who have only been in that role for months at the most, and the optios are very much inexperienced themselves. My senior centurion, Caius Cassius Proculeianus, and his second are the only veteran officers I have. So, short of good officers and loaded with untested youths, I shall put you in command of one of the centuries.'

Rufinus blinked. 'Sir, I've never even been an optio. I've never commanded men at all.'

'But you have ample experience of being *commanded* by them in both peace and in war. You know what's required and have lived through hardships.' He gestured to Rufinus' left hand, where it rested on his right arm, folded. '*Many* hardships, I would say.' Rufinus was so familiar with the old wounds now that he was rarely self-conscious about the scars that marred him, but at the tribune's gesture he reflexively tucked the hand with no fingernails from sight.

'Captured by barbarians?'

'Captured by traitors,' Rufinus said in a small voice.

'They paid for it?'

Rufinus nodded and Celer leaned back.

'I would rather have in command a veteran who can handle himself than a part-trained youth with no experience. I shall have a crest and a vine stick made available by the morning, as well as a good russet tunic. Anything else you need, you can draw from the quartermaster tomorrow. Report here at first watch and I will give you your orders and documentation. In the meantime, get out of those praetorian whites, even if you have to dress like a peasant. I might have a certain grudging respect for our overpaid cousins in the capital, but you'll find little love for the praetorians among the veterans here. Your white tunic might land you in the mire rather fast. Then there is the troublesome subject of quarters. I cannot countenance putting this lady – she is your... consort?' he asked delicately. Rufinus nodded, flushing hot as he did so and cursing the fact that no matter how old and hardened he became, the subject of women always turned him into an adolescent.

'His woman,' Senova confirmed in a straight-forward tone.

Celer chuckled. 'Your *woman*. Yes. I cannot put your *woman* in ordinary legionary quarters. It would be cramped and unseemly to jam her in at the end of a barrack block with you. Equally, I cannot really put you somewhere other than with the men, Rufinus, if you are to work as an effective centurion. You will take the appropriate quarters once I have assigned you a century, but for the lady here I will have to make other arrangements. I have a workshop that is idle. I can have it converted to temporary quarters for you, my lady. But tonight it is too late to begin sourcing all the materials. You will both

41

have to find accommodation in the mansio in town. I will have all made ready tomorrow. When you go to the mansio, tell Drasda that I sent you. He will make sure you get the best room and meal available.'

Rufinus nodded his thanks and took another sip of his wine. It was a nice wine. Sharp, but with a spicy-sweet aftertaste.

'I have to say I'm pleased at this unexpected arrival,' Celer smiled. 'You have no idea how difficult it is to train a whole cohort with only two experienced officers.'

Rufinus chuckled. 'I suspect I will have, shortly, Tribune.'

'Good. Then I shall see you at the first watch tomorrow, Centurion Rufinus.'

Centurion Rufinus. There was something about the sound of that which gave him a warm glow.

He rose and saluted, and Senova did the same, raising another smile from Celer. As she stood, she looked at Rufinus. 'Are you not drinking that?'

Rufinus shook his head. 'You know me and wine. Moderation is essential.'

Senova shrugged. 'I hate waste,' she said, and tipped the rest of his wine back, smacking her lips appreciatively and replacing the cup. Tribune Celer chuckled again. 'Thank the gods for good company. Drobeta was starting to tarnish my soul. Oh, and one more thing,' he added, pointing behind them. 'I would ask you to keep your hound in your quarters or with the lady here. I am not a lover of dogs, and they reciprocate in the dislike. I prefer cats.'

Rufinus turned to look at Acheron, who was scratting absently at his ear and then sniffing his paw and licking it. Delightful. Putting forth a good impression as always.

'Yes, Tribune.'

'Good.'

The three of them retreated from the room and out into the basilica, shutting the door as they went.

'What do you make of him?' Rufinus said quietly as they passed through the long hall.

'Seems pleasant. I thought tribunes were all supposed to be untrained posh boys.'

Rufinus laughed. 'That's *junior* tribunes. There's five of them in each legion. Their tunics have a narrow stripe. They're usually nobles doing a term in the legions just so they can qualify for political office afterwards. They're not much use for anything other than running errands and delivering messages. But every legion also has a senior tribune with a broad stripe. *They're* veterans and usually very competent. Along with the legate and the senior centurion they pretty much run the legion.'

'He is good at his job, then, I think,' Senova stated, then frowned.

'You are a nobleman. Why are you a legionary and not a tribune?'

Rufinus sighed. 'I'm not a legionary. Not any more, anyway. And I'm not a nobleman. either. I mean, I have good blood – *patrician* blood, even. The family goes back centuries, and branches of it are quite important in Beneventum. But *our* branch of the family fell from grace under Antoninus Pius and we are little more than Roman citizens now. We're not counted among the patricians or even the equites now. My father does nothing but grumble about it and plot his return to importance and fortune, even though it was him who ruined the family in the first place. *Our* branch of the family languish in Hispania in self-imposed exile.'

Senova sniffed. 'Then you will make a good centurion and from there climb back to being noble again.'

'If only it were that easy, Senova, my father would have done it years ago.'

The three of them strolled out into the courtyard and Rufinus, first through the door and concentrating on the conversation with Senova, walked straight into the man coming the other way. As he staggered back, surprised, the other man stepped aside in a jingle of armour and accoutrements. Rufinus' eyes widened as he took in the figure and he almost let out a gasp of dismay. The man was a centurion. His helmet was surmounted with a black crest, his chain shirt overlaid with a leather harness covered in medals, a vine stick jammed under one arm and a sour expression on his face. There was a one in six chance of any centurion Rufinus bumped into – *literally*, in this case – being the veteran one, but there was no doubt in his mind that this centurion was no raw recruit. You could tell from just one look at his swarthy face.

'My apologies, Centurion,' he managed, straightening. He wasn't sure whether to salute. The etiquette was rather vague since he didn't currently belong to any legion, let alone this one and probably outranked him by virtue of being a praetorian, though it was unlikely the centurion would see it that way.

The officer looked him up and down, taking in the praetorian elements of his gear. Thankfully, the sight of them didn't seem to label Rufinus as the enemy, as he expected.

'You should be more careful,' the centurion murmured, his accent different from any Rufinus had heard thus far. Smoother, more eastern, he thought.

'Yes, sir.'

Damn it. Why had he called him *sir*? That had just unconsciously defined their relative statuses and probably for good. Rufinus found himself saluting, too, before he realised what he was doing. The centurion simply raised an eyebrow and nodded, marching past, into the basilica. Rufinus hurried out into the courtyard, then became aware as he walked that he and Senova were alone. He stopped and turned. To his astonishment, Acheron was in the doorway behind him, the centurion crouched and ruffling the hair of the great animal's head. Acheron was never that accepting of strangers. Except with Vibius Cestius…

'Your dog?'

Rufinus nodded.

'A magnificent specimen. I had one for a while. Lost him on campaign against Roxolani incursions. Keep him safe.'

Rufinus nodded again with a smile as the centurion gave Acheron a last rub behind the ear and then rose and strode off toward the tribune's office. 'This place is full of surprises,' Rufinus muttered as Acheron padded over to join them once more.

'I do not wish to live on my own,' Senova said, suddenly.

'What?'

The tribune. He will make a workshop into a home for me, and I will live there for a week while you stay with your legionaries. I do not wish to be alone in a place that smells of tools and timber for a week. I will go mad with boredom.'

Rufinus smiled. 'I doubt that. I've never seen you stop long enough to get bored. But the tribune was right. If I'm to command men I can't share the room with you. It would undermine my role. Besides, it's illegal. And you really don't want to stay out in the town. Anything might happen. At least here you'll be safe.'

'And bored.'

'Better bored than knifed or raped in an alleyway,' he said, trying to put an air of finality to it. They walked on.

A centurion. He was going to be a centurion. His father would be proud. He sighed. No, he wouldn't. His father would always disapprove of anything less than a tribune. Still, he was going to command soldiers.

Suddenly he couldn't recall anything a centurion was expected to do.

IV – A new career

Rufinus stepped out of the centurion's quarters – a larger room at the end of his century's barrack block – and took a deep breath of cool morning air. The sky was a pale blue and there was the promise of a warm day ahead. Good weather for his first day as a centurion. His first day in *Dacia* too, for he was now north of the Danuvius and had arrived in the province that had hung heavy in his thoughts this past month.

He had left his gear in the room, still in bags. He would have time to put it away later. Senova would be busy settling irritably into her new quarters now, her own bags unpacked. Rufinus had taken only his boots, weapons and personal effects from the bags. The rest of his equipment had been thoughtfully provided by Celer and had been awaiting him in the room. He wore a good red linen tunic, with a padded subarmalis over the top and then a fine chain shirt. A red cloak hung down behind him, pinned at the shoulders to the shirt. His helmet felt heavier than usual and a trifle unwieldy with the great black crest across it, but he'd admired the effect in his reflection in the dented bronze mirror and been more than satisfied. Celer had also supplied him with his *vitis* vine stick, a pair of bronze greaves and a medal harness to wear over the shirt. He had foregone this last, feeling it might be silly to wear the harness with just one medal. He still had the phalera embossed with a lion's head that had been passed to him on a dais in Vindobona half a lifetime ago, but a whole harness for one metal disc would be a laughable sight.

Instead, he had jammed the vine stick beneath his left arm as he'd seen centurions do many times over the years, and unwrapped the gleaming silver spear he had received from the hand of the emperor, gripping it in his right.

There was a slow, almost sarcastic clapping of hands, and Rufinus looked sharply to his left to see a man in an optio's crest, a great bull of a man with muscles like melons and a face that suggested he made a habit of running into walls. The man was giving him the slowest clap he'd ever heard. Rufinus felt anger beginning to rise up in him, but it had the unfortunate effect of colouring his cheeks, which was not what he wanted right now.

'Optio Daizus! Fall in, you horrible weasel,' snapped a voice that carried so much authority Rufinus found himself straightening automatically. The optio snapped to attention, turned and marched out toward the via praetoria. Rufinus spun to the source of the authoritative voice and was hardly surprised to see Caius Cassius Proculeianus, the veteran centurion into whom he'd bumped the previous evening. Cassius held his vine stick low and tapped it thoughtfully on his greaves.

'Now you look like a soldier. Not in that godsawful praetorian kit. I have a few words of advice for you, Centurion…?'

'Rufinus,' the younger man replied, trying not to stand so rigid.

'Rufinus. Firstly, lose the silver spear. I and many of the veterans know what that is and how much you must have fought to earn it, but most of these lads are new and haven't a clue. They will only see a king's ransom in silver and a man trying to lord himself over them. You'll win no respect with it. A vitis is all the symbol you need. Secondly, never stand around as though you're taking the air or enjoying yourself. A centurion needs to be in command at all times. Even if you feel like taking the air, make it look like you're examining something. Go find someone working. Watch them and nod approvingly or tell them what they're doing wrong. The men need to be constantly reminded of what you are. Thirdly, if someone is insolent like Daizus was just then, you need to leap on that and put it down straight away. You give them room to move and they will use it against you.'

Rufinus sighed. It was all good advice. 'Daizus is my optio, I suppose?'

Cassius nodded. 'And don't sigh and sag like that. You look like a woman at court. With a build like that you're a fighter. Act like one. Daizus could be a real asset to you. He's fairly new but one of the strongest and most confident of all the men in your century. If you get him on side, he will be the best optio you could hope for. But he had just been given word he was to command and take the centurion's crest. Then along you come and slip in ahead of him and he's dropped back to optio again He'll harbour a grudge until you sort it out one way or another.'

Again, Rufinus nodded. 'What's first?' he asked.

Cassius frowned. 'You know your legionary training, yes?'

'Well, I went through it, but it was a while ago, and I don't know where you are with it all.'

Cassius tapped the vitis again, rhythmically. Rufinus wondered how long it took a centurion to pick up habits like that.

'They have marching down reasonably well. We have them doing a run every morning and afternoon, a complete circuit of the camp. Each century's fastest man gets an extra wine ration that night. Each century's slowest gets to clean the latrine. It's a good incentive. We've been getting them jumping from the rampart's earth bank in armour. They're not so good at that, but I intend to have them ready to jump from the parapet by the end of the week, so you might want to concentrate on that physically. We do swimming in shifts. The currents of the Danuvius are far too dangerous for swimming, but there's a small tributary river a mile east of here, and that's fine for it. We're at varying degrees of success there and in a perfect world I would have them all swimming before we moved, though it's a lesser concern since we'll be faced with mountains and forests more than rivers.'

He gestured with his vine stick at Rufinus' sword, hanging beneath his right armpit.

'That, by the way, is on the wrong side. You're still thinking like a legionary, but you won't be issued with a shield. Get the sword on your left so you can draw it quickly. As for weapons training, we're making good progress there. Many of these men were drawn from the Scordici and have a history of fighting the Iazyges across the river. Most of them could already handle a sword. Some are good archers and a few can use a sling. They can throw spears pretty well. We're just working on giving them better judgement of the three vital targets, the use of a stabbing weapon, and breaking them of a lot of bad habits. We've tried pila many times, and they're getting better, but they still all throw like individuals. They seem resistant to the idea of throwing together, so that's probably your best martial focus this week.'

Cassius rubbed his neck and waved his vitis in a sweep. 'Other than that we're not bothering with too much. Things like entrenching and engineering can wait. I just want them fit and working as a unit, able to fight like one and unlikely to break in the face of the enemy. Has the tribune told you what we have in store?'

'Yes. Clearing some minor pockets of resistance on the way north.'

Cassius's lip curled. '*Minor pockets*. The master of understatement. Try not to be overconfident. There may be rebellious Dacian peoples here, but I doubt it's them that we'll face. What we will definitely be dealing with are Sarmatians who have found something good enough to cling to that it's worth fighting for and not going home. They will be hard men, and determined. And be careful not to lump all tribes in together. I know you are a veteran of the Marcomannic Wars, and there was a tendency to see all non-Romans as the same people then. Try to avoid that here. Not all Dacians are the same, and none of them are the same as the Iazyges or the other

Sarmatians. They are a proud people and easy to offend. And they have not always been best-treated by their governors.'

'You sound as though you respect them.'

'I do,' Cassius replied. 'If you're here long enough, you will too. Dacia is not some backwater hole. It's not swamps and forests like the northern lands or choking sands like the south. It is a beautiful province full of wonders.'

Rufinus frowned. 'Who are the Roxolani?'

'What?'

'You said your dog died in campaign against the Roxolani. I've not heard of them.'

Cassius tapped the vitis on his greave again. 'The Roxolani are a people on the steppe and the plains east of Dacia, between the province and the Euxine Sea. They're part of the confederation we know as the Sarmatians, but with Dacian influence. For a few years parts of their land were nominally Roman territory, but Hadrian let it go back to the Roxolani. We have occasional issues with them, but for the most part they are quiet neighbours, despite being more or less Sarmatians. Still, given the current Sarmatian trouble, the emperor had a new series of forts built along the eastern border recently just in case.'

'I have some trouble with all this. When we left Rome I had heard of Sarmatians invading Dacia, and I've heard of them before, of course, but I always thought of them as a tribe. Now it seems that the Sarmatians are more than just a tribe.'

'Think of Rome,' Cassius said. 'Even in Italia, while everyone is Roman, some are Sabine, some are Samnite, some Oscan, and so on. And then Italia is just one region in the empire full of Romans, which also includes Gaul and others. You see? The Sarmatians is just a name for all the steppe peoples, including the Roxolani and the Iazyges, and the Costoboci and the Carpi to the north. There are others too. And each of those tribes is really a name for a dozen smaller tribes under one king.'

Rufinus shook his head. 'So who was it who invaded and started this current problem?'

Cassius pursed his lips. 'The Costoboci came south across the border. They do it regularly in small raiding groups, but this time they came in force. Couldn't tell you why, but the Iazyges had either made a deal with them to join in the fun, or took advantage of our distraction, and they came east from their flatlands at the same time. The Thirteenth drove the Iazyges back across the border, barring the few groups we're now facing. I presume Niger and his Fifth Macedonica have secured the north against the Costoboci. Fortunately, we'd just had to kick seven shades of crap out of the Roxolani for causing trouble, so they wisely stayed out of it this time.'

Rufinus nodded, now uncertain that he would know a Sarmatian if they came up and bit him. 'Shall we?'

'I shall leave you to your men, Rufinus. I have to oversee two other centuries at swimming lessons. You can take your lads to the river in the afternoon.'

With that, Cassius turned and was gone. Rufinus returned to his quarters for a moment, replacing his silver spear and transferring his sword to the left. It felt odd there and would take some getting used to. Soon, he emerged once more and marched out onto the via praetoria. Eighty sullen looking men in red tunics awaited him, with optio Daizus standing to one side, looking superior with the butt of his long staff of office dug into the dust.

'Third Century, attention!' snapped Daizus as Rufinus appeared, and the men straightened almost in unison.

Rufinus strode across to stand in front of them and gripped his vitis in both hands.

'I am Centurion Rufinus, your new commander. Centurion Cassius Proculeianus has updated me on your position with training. This morning we are going to concentrate on weapons practice. This afternoon we will be swimming and I shall lead an eight mile march in full kit. I see you each have your gladius. We shall start with sword training, then, and collect the pila for missile drill thereafter.'

Sounded good, he thought. Confident.

'Optio Daizus, where is the parade ground?'

'Out of the east gate, sir, but the Fifth and Sixth centuries are using it now.'

Rufinus sucked on his teeth. 'Is the amphitheatre free?'

'I believe so, sir.'

'Good. Collect ten palus stakes and a mallet and assemble the century in the amphitheatre for sword practice.'

Daizus glowered at him, then turned and detailed men to collect the equipment. Rufinus left them to it and marched to the west gate. There he gave the daily password and exited onto a surprisingly busy scene. Carts and animals were crossing the great bridge already and the town was bursting into life. Rufinus strolled across to the amphitheatre. Three of the gates were shut and locked up and he had to almost circle the place to find the one open entrance. A man in a brown tunic with a solid-looking club stood just inside.

'I need to requisition the arena for legionary training,' he told the man.

'Fair enough, Centurion. But the lanista has training sessions on too.'

'He will have to desist for a while,' Rufinus said firmly, wondering silently whether the legion had priority or whether the lanista might have first call. Confidence. It was all about confidence. He strode past the man and along the tunnel, past various side-passages and stairways, and out into the arena itself. It was a small amphitheatre, especially for a man who had spent time in Rome's great venue, but would be adequate for training eighty men.

Or at least it would be when the lanista went away.

Over at the far side of the oval space, a man with a long stick was shouting commands at four big, heavy men. Two were armed with sword and shield and were attempting to find openings in their opponents' moves to strike, while the other two fought and struggled unarmed, fists bound in bandages. Rufinus smiled and wandered over toward them, tapping his vine stick absently on his greave as he went and chuckling at the realisation that he was doing it already. He came to a halt near the trainer.

'Your one with the dark hair is going to lose,' he said to the *doctor* – the trainer of gladiators.

The man turned a quizzical look on Rufinus. 'With respect, centurion, this is no legionary fight. This is boxing.'

Rufinus laughed. 'He's going to lose. He's got a weak left hook and the bald one has noticed. He keeps edging round to get on that side.'

The trainer frowned. 'You might be right.'

'I am.'

'Think you know boxing, Centurion?' called a gruff voice. Rufinus turned at the sound and felt slightly deflated to see optio Daizus striding toward him across the grimy sand. The men of the Third Century were emerging from the tunnel behind him, carrying stakes.

'I *do* know boxing, yes, Optio.

'Many an officer thinks he knows things and proves to be less than capable in the event,' Daizus said insolently, though Rufinus was grateful he'd said it quietly and the men had not heard.

'That's dangerously close to insubordination, Daizus.'

'I heard you came from the praetorians,' the optio said, almost sneering. 'All shiny armour and posh food. Overpaid and undertrained. Wouldn't take one of your praetorians over him,' he said, gesturing at the black-haired boxer.

'He is about to lose,' Rufinus said confidently.

'Maybe. If I were him I'd be forcing the bald one back to the right.'

Rufinus eyed his second in command. 'You are a boxer?'

'Damn right, Centurion. And if it were you and me there, I'd show you a bloody thing or two.'

Dignity. Confidence. Command at all times. I am a centurion.

'Be grateful that my rank prevents me from taking you up on that, Daizus.'

Dignity. Confidence. Command at all times.

'Likewise, Centurion. An officer sat on his arse and licking a split lip looks poor.'

Rufinus could feel himself starting to get riled. *Dignity. Confidence.*

'I have half a mind to knock that insolence out of you, Daizus.'

Dignity…

The legionaries had all entered the arena now and were lining up, watching their two officers with interest. Damn it. Both his and the optio's voices had risen in anger. Had the soldiers heard much of the exchange?

'Frankly, Centurion, I would wipe the arena floor with your pretty, white, praetorian arse.'

Dignity…

Rufinus realised he was tapping the stick on his greave so hard and fast now it sounded like a drum roll. Damnit, but the optio was getting to him.

'If I were a…' his voice tailed off. 'Fuck it.' A moment later he was undoing the cloak and draping it over his arm while he removed his helmet. Handing them to the surprised gladiator trainer, he removed his sword and belt, peeled off his chain shirt with some difficulty and dropped it to the sand. He then removed his subarmalis and tunic and placed them on the chain shirt to keep them clean, retrieving his helmet and cloak and adding them to the pile. By the time he straightened and turned, Daizus was similarly stripped to the waist, just breeches and boots.

Something odd passed through the optio's expression and Rufinus was suddenly acutely aware of the scars he bore and the fact that they were displayed now for all to see. Burns and scratches, lines and patches of shiny skin. Nails missing. Brand marks. Scars from the 'emperor's largesse'. His back was marked with white lines that carried their own tale of insubordination and punishment. At least the brand marks were no longer legible. Those that could have been identified, he had long since taken a hot knife to, making them illegible.

He could hear several of his legionaries whistling through their teeth, though whether in derision or respect, he couldn't tell. In accepting the challenge and stripping down he had ruined all hope of dignity and professionalism, the respect of his rank. But confidence, he did not lack. And if he could not instil authority with his voice, then he'd damn well do it with his hands.

'You were beaten,' Daizus noted, rather unnecessarily. 'Fell asleep on duty?'

'Killed a man,' replied Rufinus in dead tones. The legionaries went silent. Even the gladiators had stopped sparring, their trainer standing back and watching the two officers.

'How do you want to end this?' the optio spat, 'On your back or on your face?'

'Do your fists work as much as your mouth?' Rufinus replied and stepped out into the open space, away from his pile of clothes and armour.

Daizus came for him quickly. Rufinus was impressed with the speed and power of the attack. The optio kept his head low and stormed forward, both arms jabbing with a slight swing as though he were restricted in space, both aimed for Rufinus' solar plexus. The centurion dropped his arms just in time, taking the flurry of blows on his forearms as he gave ground. Then, in a move he had used time and again, he took an extra-large step back and danced to a halt as his attacker almost fell forward, deprived of his target. Rufinus swung, once.

His fist, bunched and hard, connected with Daizus's cheek and sent him sprawling out to the side. The optio recovered quickly, but Rufinus was dancing from foot to foot, waiting, anticipating. With a sudden roar, Daizus was coming again, this time with his arms up and ready. Rufinus put all his weight on his left foot and readied himself. The optio came at him and made to swipe, but Rufinus had pivoted on his left and simply swung out of the way with the grace of a dancer. As Daizus lurched past, Rufinus gave him two neat jabs to the side.

The optio staggered to a halt, shaking his head.

'You're strong, Daizus, but you're slow. And predictable.'

The optio turned and started to advance once more, this time slowly and with care. Rufinus watched him come. There was no sport in this. The only question in Rufinus' head was whether to be professional and end this quickly, or to draw it out and hurt Daizus to make the point. No. Dignity. He could regain that in the way he ended this.

'Stand down and accept defeat and I'll let you walk away with some self-respect.'

Daizus made to jab with his left hand and Rufinus almost fell for it. His feet were automatically positioning to duck him to the left, away from the blow, but he could see the muscles bunching in the man's right arm, too. He'd told the optio he was too predictable, and Daizus had taken that to heart. In trying to be unpredictable in response, however, he was simply being predictable again. The jab and the cross was a common combination in legionary boxing, though Daizus had clearly learned to fight in the civilian world. Rooting his feet instead of moving out of the way, Rufinus knocked aside the jab with his right wrist, feeling the sharp pain of the blow but hearing the snap of one of Daizus' fingers in the process. Even as the man's right cross came, Rufinus' left arm had come up to block, taking the painful blow on the forearm.

He gave Daizus no chance to recover. Without even taking the time to draw back his arm, he jabbed with his right fist and punched the optio square between the eyes. There was an odd, almost comical moment of complete silence and stillness, and then Daizus toppled backward, stunned. The optio collapsed onto his backside, shaking his head. Rufinus knew the effect of such a blow well, as both deliverer and recipient. The fight was over, and all he had to show for it would be a few bruises that would come up on his arms later in the day. But it would be some time before Daizus recovered his wits enough to stand.

Rufinus left the man sat in the sand and crossed to his equipment, dressing himself once more. He was aware that eighty five men were watching him in silent surprise, and he nodded at the trainer once he'd shrugged into his chain shirt and begun to settle it correctly. 'Tell your black-haired one to strengthen his left.'

The trainer nodded, eyes wide, then waved his charges away, sending them toward one of the doorways out of the arena. Rufinus finished dressing himself, pinning his cloak in place with some difficulty. The men of the Third Century were still watching him in silence.

'Alright, you lot. Get those stakes into the ground, evenly spaced, one palus to each tent party. Then you have one hour of sword practice.'

Once the first stake was in place, Rufinus produced a piece of chalk from his pouch and drew three lines on it. 'Groin, armpit and neck: the three kill points you can reasonably go for even with an armoured opponent. Every man makes all three blows and them moves to the back of the line and makes room for the next, and so on. The contubernium cycles through the training for one hour. How fast or slow you are is up to you, but I will give you added incentive. The stake with the most accurate damage at the end of the hour earns that tent party an extra denarius each in their pay this month. The one with the least damage earns an extra shift of night guard duty. Get to it.'

He stepped back and let the legionaries get to work, his eyes straying across to Daizus, who still sat, slumped. There was a very good chance he had ruined any hope of a good working relationship with his second in command, but he'd had to put the man in his place, and at least that had surely gained him the respect of the rest of the century.

Daizus recovered slowly, and by the time the sword practice ended an hour later, was dressed and leaning on his long staff of office, a yellowing blotch emerging on his forehead. He glared daggers at Rufinus, though there was no more insolent talk. The winning tent part of the training jeered at the losers, who defiantly shouted their anger in return. Rufinus stepped in, telling them there would be plenty of opportunities to get their own back.

And there were. The day passed surprisingly quickly for Rufinus, pilum training on the river bank proving, as Cassius had suggested, their weakest skill as a unit. He singled out three men who could consistently throw well and offered them an extra pay bonus if they would take the others in hand and help improve their own skills. The swimming earned a different tent party extra wine and another one the task of scrubbing the barrack veranda clean.

By the end of the day, he felt that the men were starting to show some level of improvement, though it was hard to tell over just one day. Throughout the experience, Daizus worked precisely to rule, his voice respectful but his face insolent beyond words. Rufinus' main worry, though, was whether he had taken Cassius' system of incentives too far. By the end of the week, at this rate, every man in the Third Century would have half a dozen rewards and punishments to his name, and Rufinus was already running out of ideas. He would have to become very inventive to keep going with this.

That evening, once he had seen the men back to barracks, he was leaning on the window sill of his room, when Cassius passed. The senior centurion paused and smiled. 'Tired?'

'It's been an interesting day.'

'I heard. Heard you laid your optio out in the sand.'

Rufinus nodded. 'I don't know whether it was a good idea. What do you think?'

Cassius shrugged and strode through the door into the room, where they could talk a little more privately. 'It wouldn't have been my solution, but only time will tell what effect it has. You're making waves here, though. Try to think like you belong in the role, Rufinus. It's a matter of familiarity and belonging. I see it all the time: new men come in from the central provinces and they think like an outsider. The Thirteenth has been in Dacia since the province was founded. The legion is connected to the land and most of its recruits are of Thracian or Dacian blood. They're a family, bound by ties of culture as well as martial brotherhood. It's the same with governors. They come in from Rome and see Dacia as a stepping-stone, a quick rung in the ladder to higher office, and a lucrative one at that. None of them think in terms of the good of the province. That's why it's always so unsettled.'

'I'd never realised things were so complicated here.'

'If you think *this* is complicated, wait until we go north and you meet the *real* Dacia.'

'Care for a drink?' Rufinus asked.

'Thank you, but I'm heading for the bath house. This next hour is reserved for officers. You might want to make use of it yourself.'

Rufinus smiled as Cassius left and wandered off, then slipped his boots back on and strolled out into the camp. Two corners and fifty heartbeats brought him to the door of Senova's temporary quarters in the former workshop. He knocked gently and the door was opened by a boy of perhaps six or seven in a drab tunic with downcast eyes.

'Gnaeus,' greeted Senova from across the room, where she sat on a pleasant couch next to a low table bearing a bowl of fruit. 'Good. Let him in, Luca.'

The boy stepped aside and then closed the door behind him before scurrying off through one of the two temporary partition walls.

'You have a *slave*,' Rufinus said with a grin.

Her expression hardened. 'How would you like a kick somewhere delicate, Gnaeus. I tried to argue against it but the tribune seems to think the idea of a lady without a slave unthinkable. I argued him down from three to one, at least. I keep trying to get Luca to sit down and stop working, but he won't.'

Rufinus chuckled and sank gratefully into another seat opposite, grabbing a large juicy peach from the bowl. Over in the corner, on a pile of blankets, Acheron opened one bored eye, then closed it and went back to sleep.

'How did your first day as centurion go?'

He took a bite of the peach and smiled. 'Up and down. Had to strip half naked and concuss an optio, but other than that it was easy enough. They've got potential. I think they're actually better warriors than my own intake were when I started with the Tenth.'

'With luck you'll be able to get through the rest of the week without having to punch too many people.'

Rufinus chuckled. He was fairly confident about the next few days, in truth. The men would do as he told them without complaint now that Daizus was in his place. And they would improve with all the incentives he offered, he was sure. He realised, as he reached for another peach, that the fruit bowl was sitting on something, and lifted the container, peering at what it had covered. A map of Dacia.

'Where did you get this?'

'The tribune. He has several. I enquired as to where we were to go, and he showed me. I thought I would like to keep the map and familiarise myself with the province.'

'Good idea. Show me where we're going, then.'

As she leaned forward, Rufinus caught with interest the name of the Roxolani off to the east, between Dacia Province and that part of Moesia that bordered the Euxine Sea. He could see a small line of dots, recently added to the map in a north-south direction: the new system of border forts the emperor had decreed. It made him smile to see one called Commodava. Perhaps one day he would be important enough to have a fort named after him. Rufinava? He chortled, then concentrated as Senova's delightful finger touched the map.

'This is Drobeta, here. We head this way and across a place called Vulcan's Pass here, where the mountains rise. Here,' she tapped the map at a black dot among some hills, 'is Sarmissomething-or-other. It was the capital when Dacia was a kingdom. Apparently Sarmatians now hold it. Then we head to Ulpia Traiana, which was the Roman capital for a while.' She slid her lovely fingertip to that next spot, off to the west, then north again. 'Then to a place called Micia. Then to Apulum, where the governor will be. She gestured to the capital. Rufinus tore his eyes from her finger, which was giving him very unmartial thoughts, and concentrated. His gaze strayed north, to the edge of the civilised world. There, beyond Roman territory, the word Sarmartii was sketched. Not far south of the border, a dot was accompanied by a 'V'. He pointed to it.

'That will be Pescennius Niger and the Fifth Macedonica.'

'You need to get your men ready. We're departing next market day, the tribune tells me.'

Rufinus smiled and sat back.

They would be ready. *He* would be ready. Despite Celer's stark description of Dacia, the way Cassius talked about it painted a very different picture. Likely the truth lay somewhere in between. For the first time since he had been ordered to Dacia by that sleazy bastard back in Rome, Rufinus found he was looking forward to pushing into this new and fascinating land.

V – Into Dacia

The week of training had gone by swiftly, though Rufinus' initial exhilaration at his success soon faltered and died. Optio Daizus was a perfectly acceptable second in command in military terms, obedient and competent. But he was far from forthcoming, did not provide any support beyond that sought verbally or demanded of his position, and spent every waking moment glaring daggers into Rufinus. The young centurion had the constant feeling that the man was biding his time, waiting for some way to redress the balance as he saw it. The fact that his forehead had come up in a lump between the eyes and had gone purple-yellow did not help, for it was a constant reminder of his humiliation that he could hide from no one.

Initially, the rest of the century seemed to be taking to their new centurion well enough. That first day they'd been enthusiastic. The second day there had been less satisfaction on display, though Rufinus had put it down to exhaustion caused by his new regime. Day three it became clear that this was not the case and, though he could not prove it, he was fairly sure that Daizus had been poisoning the minds of the men against him. Periodically he would stumble across the bruised optio with a group of legionaries and they would fall silent and glare until he passed out of earshot.

Day four was worse still. The weather changed and a chill filled the air, accompanied by regular rain showers that kept everything damp. He'd promised yet more wine as an incentive on pilum practice. Then, when he'd gone to draw the wine for the victors that afternoon, he had been refused and sent to the tribune, who informed him in no uncertain terms that he had to stop giving away supplies to the men. The wine store had shrunk alarmingly. Rufinus had had to go out into town, wrapped in a cloak against the rain, find a native merchant and buy expensive wine with his own diminishing funds. He'd given it to the men and they had waited until they thought he was gone and then burst out laughing. Apparently his upbraiding by the tribune had already become a joke.

Day five brought a new low. A full contubernium of men reported sick, pale and waxy, vomiting like mad as Rufinus gathered his men in the chilly, torrential rain for training. It came as no surprise to find that they were the men who had achieved the extra wine ration. The medicus had pronounced a mild case of poisoning, and Rufinus had gone to see his wine merchant only to be derided and refused a refund, even under hollow threat of prosecution. The tribune had dragged him in again and been scathing over his solution to the wine problem. The men had turned a little further against him. He heard through Cassius that his nickname was now Locusta, the name of a woman a century ago who had risen to infamy as Rome's worst poisoner.

Day Six was sullen and wetter and colder still. The men did as they were told, but took every tiny opportunity to misread or misunderstand what they were told, to the very edge of insubordination. Rufinus slogged through the days now, rather than leaping into them hopefully. Day seven brought him ever lower. Two men had fled the fort, disappearing into the wilds of Dacia or Moesia. Deserters. *Two*. The only two in the whole cohort, and they were his men. The call to the tribune's office had been no surprise. He felt the officer's comments to be a little harsh and unfair, but it was impossible to argue with the facts of them. Day eight was something of a relief, since the preparations for departure occupied the whole cohort all day and there was little time for rebellion or trouble, and the rain left off for the whole day despite a lead-grey sky.

The only real relief that week came at each day's end, when he developed the habit of twin visits.

First to Cassius to share wine and stories. Somehow, telling the veteran centurion of the successes of his military past somehow suppressed his current failures. Cassius continually tried to dole out advice, but there was little he could suggest that would make any real difference. In Cassius' opinion, Rufinus had set the whole decline in motion when he floored Daizus. Whether there could have been a way to get the men on side before Daizus worked on them they would never know, and was now a moot point. Rufinus had asked Cassius in desperation what to do, but the veteran centurion's only contribution was that he needed to find a way to bring the men back on side. Daizus was being careful. There was no evidence of wrongdoing, and so there was no way to take him officially to task for his evils. And to deal with it on a personal level would only expand on the trouble that had started it all. If Cassius had had control of the cohort, he'd have split the century up and transferred them into other units, bringing new men into Rufinus' command, but the tribune would not countenance such a thing, especially with such new and untried legionaries. Rufinus would simply have to work it out, and in the meantime impose as much order as he could.

After a brief relaxing but unfulfilling drink with Cassius, he would visit Senova. This, he knew, was another aspect of his current situation that did not sit well with the men. A soldier could not legally marry and, though many soldiers kept a woman against the day they retired and could marry, those women had no official status and had to make their own life beyond the fort walls, travelling as a camp follower. Of course, since they were only in Drobeta temporarily, any women the veterans kept would have remained at Apulum. Rufinus having a woman who lived in the camp did not please many. But somehow in Senova's company and with the comforting presence of Acheron, Rufinus actually relaxed for a time and maintained the vague feeling that things might still turn out right in the end.

He thought long and hard on how he could turn the men back to him, but in this situation there seemed no chance. If the opportunity ever presented itself, it would be on the journey.

Perhaps in the battles to come? He did, after all, have a history of heroically saving people in war...

The cohort prepared.

Then came the ninth day – market day. The cohort rose at sunup, broke their fast and made everything ready, then moved out. To Rufinus' relief, the men had neither the time nor the opportunity to cause trouble on the march. Better still, Rufinus could see a tiny grudging light of respect creep into the occasional face as they slogged along under the weight of their kit, while Rufinus, long-practiced, marched strong and steady alongside them. Most of the centurions were unburdened, leaving their kit in the carts at the rear. Rufinus had opted to carry his, partially due to the valuable nature of his personal effects, and partially due to the fact that he knew he could do it easily, and felt that setting an example might go a little way to repairing the damage done by Daizus' tongue. It seemed he was right.

Perhaps Acheron, trotting along beside him with a lolling tongue, helped a little too.

Either way, after a noon break on the first day, Rufinus tested the water by starting up an old marching song from the Tenth that he believed was common across the legions. Half the men joined in straight away, then the rest as the ripples of song moved along the column, bringing the other centuries in.

That day heralded an end to the bad weather and the sky came out blue again, the sun sizzling and bringing out the hum of bees and the buzz of crickets. Birds sang. A positive mood infected the entire cohort. The column travelled slightly east of north and Rufinus pictured Senova's map as they marched, counting off what landmarks he could spot.

The tribune knew his stuff, clearly, for the column was laid out in proper war form. Half a dozen scouts rode up to three miles ahead, repeatedly reporting back. Cassius Proculeianus and half his veteran century made up the vanguard, followed by Tribune Celer and his few staff on horseback. The rest of the centuries followed on, with the eight wagons and Senova's carriage, driven inexpertly by the slave boy, Luca, behind. A rear-guard of the other half of Cassius' men marched under their optio. From scouts to rear-guard the column was four miles long.

Since Drobeta the column had marched up into rolling hills. Rufinus had not appreciated how much they had climbed on the journey until noon when they'd stopped on a hill and he'd looked back to see Drobeta far below and behind, a small splat of darkness next to the turquoise Danuvius.

Some time in the mid-afternoon, the scouts announced that they had located an appropriate spot for the night. Rufinus had pondered their current position in relation to the map he had memorised and frowned. 'Why here? Is there not a fort nearby?'

Cassius had nodded. 'Ad Mutriam is a few miles to the south, but there was a large native settlement there. As soon as the troubles began the fort was slighted and the unit sent north to join the army there. Ad Mutriam is little more than a native town now.'

The senior centurion's men moved on and began the task of fortifying. Once the other centuries had arrived shortly thereafter, the veterans had already marked out the site and begun work. Shovels and picks were drawn from packs across the cohort. The new recruits may not have been trained yet in engineering works, but they could still dig where they were told. Rufinus twitched at his perceived need to join in. He was not used to watching while other people worked, yet he forced himself to march up and down as his men dug and heaped soil. He tried to ignore the occasional mention of Locusta as he passed.

The scouts had chosen well. This place, chosen for their first night, was at a meeting of small, seasonal rivers in a wide, shallow valley. One of the rivers had dried to barely a trickle, though the other was still a clean flow of water some eight feet wide. Where they met, though, the torrents had carved deep gulleys, providing natural defences on two sides and leaving the cohort only two ramparts to create.

By late afternoon the camp was fortified, the wagons had arrived and the rear-guard moved in. Hunters had been sent out and forage brought in to supplement the supplies in the wagons. Tents went up, latrines were dug and evening meals cooked.

The evening was sweaty and warm, and Rufinus retired once his men had dispersed to their tents, the last being Daizus who bade him a desultory good night and managed to hold off his sneer until Rufinus turned his back. The young centurion slept badly, sweating and uncomfortable in the stifling heat, the hills sheltering them and removing all possibility of a breeze.

The next morning as the men made ready to move again, Rufinus stood beside Cassius and watched in the burning light of the early sun.

'Does Dacia ever make its mind up? Is it still spring, or is it summer?'

The veteran laughed. 'Wait until we get into the mountains. It's likely still winter there.'

Senova drifted through the camp as though she had every right to be there, drawing hungry leers from five hundred men as Luca carried her wash things. It looked to Rufinus as though, despite her stance on slavery, she was starting to look mighty comfortable having Luca around. Rufinus, determined to build on the slight improvement in morale, made sure that Daizus was kept busy with tasks that morning, while he took personal control of the men packing their gear. His belief that the optio was the poison in the unit was confirmed since the men worked well and even laughed as they toiled without the evil bastard around to infect them. For a brief, unpleasant, moment Rufinus wondered how it would change things if Daizus suddenly disappeared for good. Then an image of Scopius falling back with a cry into the aqueduct tank slid into his brain and he shook his head. His days of dealing with bullies like that were over. Never again. He would simply remove Daizus' power over the men by trying to keep him busy and separate. His spirits rose a little when Cassius nodded his approval at the change and the tribune, out on his morning rounds, complimented Rufinus on his men's work.

The second day's march brought more of the same, weather-wise, and the cohort continued to climb in the sizzling sunshine. Even had he not had access to the map, Rufinus would now have been under no illusion that they were doing anything other than march into the lower reaches of the Carpates. The hills rising to either side of the valley they travelled were getting ever higher. At noon that second day they passed a spur that held a tiny fractured tower. Even from this distance, Rufinus could identify an old Roman signal station. Along with the slighted fort at Ad Mutriam, it stood as mute evidence of Trajan's grand army passing this way some eighty years ago.

Throughout the morning, Rufinus continually found ways to keep Daizus occupied and out of the way, though he could see the frustration and irritation building in the optio as this went on, and knew that at some point it would have to come to a head. During the afternoon, he was running out of reasons to send the man away and things began to sour once more. Rufinus tried to keep up the mood with another marching song but barely had he managed half a verse before Daizus blithely overrode him with a different song. Rufinus opened his mouth to object, but it was too late. This song was one of native origin, including Dacian words Rufinus did not know, and was picked up instantly by all centuries and belted out. Rufinus walked silently alongside, unable to join in. Occasionally, again, he heard the name Locusta bandied about with a snigger, though he'd yet to catch them at it.

That afternoon they arrived at the small fort of Stegara, which sat in low arable land at the head of an enormous shallow valley that ran south as far as the eye could see, delivering fresh water into the Danuvius far away. The fort was occupied by an auxiliary unit from somewhere in Arabia, and

Rufinus was one of the small party who accompanied the tribune to pay their respect to the fort's prefect as the cohort set up camp on the river bank beyond the civil settlement. The auxiliaries were dark-swarthy skinned with suspicious brown eyes. They spoke in some eastern language, occasionally dipping into what Rufinus now recognised as a local Dacian dialect. Not once did he hear them speak intelligible Latin. The prefect, who was from Ravenna, was a sour man, unhappy with his posting, polite but otherwise unhelpful.

The night was once again warm, and Rufinus began to feel that strange prickling sensation in the muggy evening that suggested thunder on the way. How appropriate as they made for Vulcan's Pass. He spent the evening with Cassius, who was fast becoming a good friend, and Senova, who had a number of blunt opinions on the legionaries around them and on the Roman tendency to consider themselves above whoever they happened to be encamped among. Cassius took the comments in good spirits, stroking the ears of Acheron who lay curled on a blanket, though Rufinus could see how easily a Roman officer could take offence at them.

'Romans never make an effort to learn the language of a region,' she said, taking a sip of wine.

'Respectfully, Senova,' Cassius replied, 'more than half this cohort are fluent speakers of the Dacian tongue.'

'Because they are *from* here,' she pointed out. 'But find any soldier who has come from the west or from Italia itself and see if they can speak the language beyond ordering beer and seducing women.'

'Why would they *need* to know anything else?' laughed Rufinus, and then fell silent under Senova's hard gaze.

'You should teach your men to use extra vocabulary of their own language, anyway,' Senova said, loftily. 'Then perhaps they would not have to refer to faeces or genitalia in every sentence.'

Now, Rufinus laughed again. Trying to clean up the legionaries' bad language would be a sure way to sink relations to an all-time low. Senova glared at him again. 'Slaves have to learn to be polite. They cannot speak out of turn, lest they be beaten. Legionaries could take a lesson in politeness from even the roughest slave.'

Now, Cassius sat up in interest. 'You have the tone of a knowledgeable woman, Senova. Have you owned many such slaves?' Rufinus' eyes slid to the figure of Luca, who scrubbed the pots quietly in a corner.

Senova turned to the veteran and Rufinus realised she was about to launch into her life story. Thus far he had not spoken of her status as a freedwoman to anyone, and the lack of brand marks on her made it impossible to tell. Moreover, her Latin and the accent that carried it had improved so immeasurably over her time with Pompeianus that she could easily have been a Roman matron from Campania rather than a slave from Britannia. Rufinus was not at all sure how Cassius and Celer would take the news that the woman they had been so accommodating for was an ex-slave. Moreover, one who had belonged to a *traitor*. Certainly if that information leaked back to his century, the men would never respect her or him again

Before Senova could speak, Rufinus dived in. 'Senova is from the rough world of northern Britannia and spent time at court in an imperial villa. She has seen the best and the worst of slavery.'

And lived it, but there was no need to admit to that right now.

As Cassius nodded his understanding, Rufinus could feel Senova's glare boring into his skull. He would pay for that at some point and would have to try and persuade her to keep her secret. It would be tough. Senova was a plain and simple thinker. She would not understand how being a former slave could carry any baggage. To her she had been a slave. Now she was not. Rufinus, however, know just how much that information would colour the Roman world's view of her.

The third day, Rufinus was torn. Somehow, his interference and opposition in the previous night's conversation had angered Senova again, and he could feel her disapproval radiating all morning as they prepared to leave. He could spend time travelling with her and try to explain the problems and why she needed to be more circumspect. But to do so would mean not marching with the men, and that would give Daizus full rein to trash him in his absence. In the end, he decided that Senova could wait, and concentrated on trying to stop the spread of the optio's attitude rot.

He was at best half successful. As the afternoon wore on, the heat never once abating and the promise of thunder remaining just that, Rufinus realised that, almost unnoticed, the Carpates were upon them. Though the valley they were moving north along seemed huge and thoroughly flat, he could now see the blue grey lines of low mountains stretching out ahead and to both sides. They were moving toward the pass at pace now.

They arrived at the evening stop-over half an hour later. An auxiliary fort rose on the bank of a narrow river, though it had been abandoned for a long time, by the looks of it. There were no gates in the archways and the walls had tumbled in places.

'Strange,' he commented, gesturing at the fort as the column halted and the centurions gathered.

Cassius shrugged. 'It hasn't been manned since Trajan's wars, but it has never been levelled. It's too useful as a stopping point when crossing the mountains, so it's kept in a semi-liveable condition.'

As they moved into the fort and began to disperse the men, Rufinus could see what Cassius meant. The defences were still easily the match of any temporary camp, and would require no effort to put in place. Assigning guards would be enough. And the buildings were not in the best of conditions, but there were good roofs on them all.

'Are the baths still working?' he asked hopefully, but Cassius shook his head before moving off to settle his men. Further along the column, Luca drove Senova's wagon forward, following a pointed gesture from another centurion.

Rufinus found one of the barrack blocks and assigned his men to it, checking out the centurion's room at the end. It had a door and a bed. That would be enough. He unpacked his kit and used his blankets and cloak to make the bed, arraying everything carefully. He then dropped in to the barracks to check on his men and was dismayed when what sounded like ribald conversation stopped the instant he entered, and Daizus, his forehead lump now receding and the bruise fading to pale yellow, glared at him in a most unfriendly manner.

Leaving the place, he wandered off to find Senova. They had not spoken all day, and now he would have to try and make things right. He found her carriage by one of the granary buildings and strode to the door, knocking.

Luca opened the door and admitted him. Senova was making a bed on a temporary cot from one of the supply wagons. The table nearby showed evidence of a half-prepared meal where Luca had been at work.

'I think we need to talk,' Rufinus said in a conciliatory voice. Somehow whenever he was with Senova he seemed to be apologising for something, though he was rarely sure what for, and even when he was, he often thought it nothing that required an apology.

Senova straightened and threw a look at him that carried so much dissatisfaction it almost knocked him over. 'I thought I was not supposed to talk. I believe you have started doing it for me, now, like a good Roman.'

'For the love of Jove, Senova, stop rubbing my face in it. I only ever have your good at heart.'

'Hmph.' She turned and went back to the bed-making.

'Where's Acheron?' he said, his gaze playing around the room.

'Isn't he with you? He's *your* dog,' she added in a tone that clearly put him at fault again. He sighed. 'I thought he was in your carriage. I'd best find him. Try not to be angry for ten breaths when I get back so we can talk.'

Turning, he stepped out of the granary door and strode back toward his century's barrack block. Calling in at his room to see if Acheron had made his way there, he was assailed at the doorway by a stench of ammonia that made his eyes water. Holding his breath and entering to investigate, he located his bed and discovered a lake in the centre had soaked his blankets and cloak and dripped through to create a puddle on the floor below. Anger flooded through him. They had *pissed in his bed*. On his *kit…*

Furious, he left and walked to the next door, where many of his century were gathered, bursting into the room in a rage.

'What animal has pissed in my bed? When I find out who it was, I will string the bastard up from the roof.'

There was a silence from the room. Some of the men looked distinctly uncomfortable, but many were suppressing smiles. Daizus was the picture of innocence, though Rufinus was under no illusion as to who had been the ringleader. This was as bad as the bullying when he'd first joined the praetorians, but it wasn't supposed to happen now. He was a *centurion* for gods' sake.

'When I get the names, and it has to have been more than one of you unless you've been saving it up for a week, I will drag you before the tribune and have you flogged. Do you have any idea how that feels, because you're in for a treat?' Again, many looked distinctly uncomfortable, and now that number outweighed the smiles. They had gone too far and some were starting to realise it. Perhaps this was the beginning. He could start to break Daizus' hold on them.

'Until the names of the guilty are given to me, this century is on one quarter wine rations, on latrine duty each night, and will cycle through guard duty with no free time. Daizus, because you are such an important man, I want you there for all latrine duties and all watches bar one.'

The optio's lip curled into a sneer.

'I think it's probably feral cats, Centurion. They're everywhere and they pee a lot. Bastards, they are.'

'I think it more likely rodents masquerading as soldiers,' snapped Rufinus. 'Now go strip down my bed, requisition fresh kit from the wagons, clean and fumigate the room and put it all right before I need to sleep. Any man who shirks this duty goes on the flogging list.'

Without waiting for a reply, he turned and stormed from the room. He was back out on the via principalis before he began to breathe even remotely normally. He had almost lost it back in that barrack room. He'd actually been tempted to hit Daizus again, and if he did that it would end any hope of putting things back together. In fact, though, having seen the change in the men's expressions when they realised they had taken it too far, he was content that this unfortunate episode had been the best thing that could have happened. In pushing things to that extent, Daizus had lost support. And in responding in a formal, authoritative manner rather than merely knocking out the optio's teeth, Rufinus had further turned the legionaries away from the man.

He stood for a moment, still trembling, and started with surprise as someone called his name. He turned to see Cassius Proculeianus strolling toward him along the street, Acheron pacing faithfully alongside. Thank the gods.

'Cassius, thank you. I've been looking all over for him.'

'Except the one place he shouldn't have been, Rufinus: in the tribune's rooms. Celer walked into his quarters to find Acheron curled up in his spare tunic. You might want to avoid the tribune for the next day or two. He hates dogs. He was so angry he couldn't properly form words.'

Rufinus sighed. What next? What else could go wrong today? Then he remembered he said he'd be back shortly to Senova. That answered that question, then.

'Fancy a drink before we turn in?' Cassius asked.

'At your quarters maybe. Mine smell too much at the moment.'

Cassius frowned in incomprehension, but Rufinus waved it aside. 'I have to go see Senova for a while, then I'll come along. Shall I bring wine?'

'Most certainly,' smiled the veteran, and was then gone about his business. Rufinus turned back to the granary and strode across. Luca opened the door to him again, and now Senova was sitting eating quietly. Rufinus urged Acheron in and followed, taking a seat opposite Senova as the dog curled up on a pile of spare blankets.

'I'm sorry,' he said. 'I know that you are free and of value. And for all I know you might have been royalty back among the Brigantes. But having *ever been* a slave still carries a stigma in Rome. I'm trying to save you from the trouble such knowledge will bring.'

Senova gave him a piercing look. 'You are trying to save *yourself* from it.'

Bollocks. Should have seen that one coming...

'Yes. To some extent, yes. I'm having a hard enough time being accepted here, and that would add a nail in the crucifixion of my reputation. But I truly do want to save you, too. Oddly, Cassius might not care. And I don't. But Celer would see you in a totally different way, and would stop treating you well. And the soldiers? Some among them might see you as fair game. Right now you are thought of as important and noble, so you're untouchable. But remember you're trapped in a fort with five hundred sex-starved soldiers. Consider the ramifications of everything you do.'

There was a long silence, and then a nod. 'Alright, Gnaeus. I concede you might be right on this occasion.'

Rufinus almost fell off his chair. An admission of defeat? This would be an evening to remember.

'I see you found Acheron,' she said finally.

'Actually, Cassius found him. He'd gone to see Celer. I might not be popular for a while with the commander. If you see him can you use your 'lady' status to try and smooth things over for me?'

'Cassius is a good man,' Senova said. 'Acheron likes him, and Acheron is a good judge of character.'

Rufinus nodded. 'Pompeianus once likened Roman politics to a great game. I thought he was over exaggerating, and believed that when Lucilla fell, the game for me would be over. But then Perennis and Cleander happened, and it began again. And this game won't be over until Publius is free and Cleander dead. So given the advice Pompeianus gave me years ago, it might be time to start building my collection of playing pieces. I am hoping that Albinus and Niger, who are both powerful men, will be such pieces in the game. They can surely help me, since Cleander does not like them.'

Senova nodded. 'Cassius is on your side, I am sure.'

'He is. How much use he can be in the game at Rome I don't know, but right now he is invaluable. Tribune Celer seems good too. Hopefully, he will be of aid. I've never needed allies like I do now, Senova.'

'You've got me,' she said quietly. And oddly, it was the most comforting thought he'd had all day.

VI – Fire and Ice

Rufinus was swiftly developing a love/hate relationship with the Carpates. As a mountain range, they were beautiful. Very different from the arid mountains of northern Hispania where he had lived as a boy, and different again from the areas of the Alpes he had encountered on journeys to and from the Danuvian frontier during the wars. They were more reminiscent of the Apennines of central Italia, though again loftier and somehow more rugged. The Carpates were green and grey, the green of endless forests and the grey of the rock bones of Dacia.

Vulcan's Pass followed the line of a river that snaked through the heights, climbing steadily and following a deep, winding gorge carved by the ice-cold, crystal clear water. The valley was wide enough in most places for the column to move in full, eight men abreast, though the tribune kept the column at half that to avoid constant adjustment for terrain. The river meandered back and forth around the valley floor, green swards and shale banks the ground beneath their feet. On occasion they were forced to cross the river, where it moved from one side of the valley to the other, and there, the locals had constructed low, rickety timber bridges that slowed travel to a crawl as men backed up waiting to cross.

The river was a gods-sent thing, though, for it provided beautiful clear water for the column. Forays into the hillsides each evening brought plentiful meat in the form of birds, rabbits and occasional deer. Cassius had warned them of the likelihood of wolves and bears too, but as yet none had been encountered. Firewood was abundant, too. Moreover, given the terrain, fortification of a camp was almost impossible and largely unnecessary, so the setting up of evening camp was a swift and easy task.

However, other aspects of the journey were less pleasant. The weather was clearly changing as they moved north into the higher mountains, and Dacia had apparently decided to abandon spring and summer altogether and move once more into winter, just as Cassius had predicted. The narrowness of the gorge cut the sunlight hours down to a minimum, and they spent much of the march in shade. Clouds had gathered from their first evening in the Carpates and had congregated every day thereafter. Rain had not yet fallen, but the temperature had steadily dropped such that each morning Rufinus was now shivering as he emerged from his tent.

But the real worry, and the hate side of his love/hate relationship with the mountains, was the constant feeling of lurking danger. For the three nights they had travelled along the snaking mountain pass, they had been watched. Rarely did they spot the figures watching them from the hillsides, but even when they couldn't, everyone could feel those eyes upon them. Guarded. Unfriendly.

Rufinus had brought his concerns to Cassius, unwilling as yet to attempt social contact with the tribune after the incident with Acheron.

'It feels as though we are trespassing on unfriendly lands.'

Cassius had simply brushed it aside. 'Mountain men.'

'That doesn't help.'

'The mountain men are a different breed. Insular. Fragmented. They don't congregate that well. They live in small villages and rarely see other human beings. Even in the days of the Dacian kings they were barely part of the kingdom. And they *are* a little unfriendly toward outsiders. But they're not stupid. No matter how much they might resent a Roman column camping in what they consider their valley, they're not daft enough to attack a whole cohort of men. I've heard of small patrols having trouble, but anything above a century will be perfectly safe. Try not to let them bother you.'

Rufinus nodded uncertainly. Whatever the veteran said, he continued to be unsettled by the watching eyes of the mountain men, and every time a forage party disappeared into the woods to hunt animals or gather dead wood for the fires, he half expected them to disappear without trace.

Then, on the fourth morning, when Cassius announced they were pretty much at the top of the pass and the cohort was taking down their tents and packing up, Rufinus strolled off into the trees beside the camp to urinate in private. The latrines were being backfilled, and he felt safe enough in the woods with Acheron at his heel.

Finding a nice space with a small dip that would carry away the stream without washing it back down into the camp, he leaned his vitis against a tree and hoisted his tunic, pulled aside the subligaculum, and began to urinate with a sigh of relief.

'Almapa,' announced a gruff voice. Rufinus turned sharply, the spray arcing out gracefully across the pine needles and narrowly missing the speaker.

'Kapas una!'

Two men stood a few paces away, blessedly just out of the range of his urine, which clamped off and dried up instantly. Mountain men, clearly. Both were tightly wrapped in furs, with hair bound in braids and beards that hung down to their chests. They wore colourful hats with blunted points that sagged, and held axes that looked strong and sharp.

'I'm sorry,' Rufinus told them in slow Latin as he tucked himself away and flushed slightly, 'but I don't speak Dacian.' His confidence grew a little as Acheron stepped in next to him.

'Rabo ne kappa.'

They did not look happy. On an impulse, Rufinus looked around to make sure he'd not pissed on someone's shrine or vegetable patch or suchlike, but it appeared no different from any other part of the forest.

'I don't understand.' Senova's accusation about Romans failing to learn about their subjugated peoples leapt into his memory rather unhelpfully.

'Rabo! Rabo!' The speaker lashed out sideways with his axe repeatedly, and despite his lack of comprehension, Rufinus knew instinctively that the man was telling him to go. The axe's direction, as best he could tell, was upstream to the north.

'I will,' he nodded, trying to make placatory gestures with his hands. 'I will rabo as fast as my legs will carry me.'

He backed away and scurried down to the camp, keeping his eyes on the two locals who did not move, but stood, watching him leave.

At the edge of the camp, he hurried over to his own men, who were assembling ready to leave. As he approached, he slowed and tried to calm his appearance. The faster they left this area the better, in Rufinus' opinion.

His nerves started to relax a little as they moved off and the morning march took them on up the pass. His straying gaze briefly caught sight of the two axe men watching them from a low bluff, and Rufinus vowed to learn a little of the language if he could. Misunderstandings might be dangerous with axe-wielding mountain men.

Striding alongside the column, Rufinus felt more confident. He'd not heard the name Locusta bandied about since that night with the bed incident, and the men no longer fell silent as he passed by. There were perhaps half a dozen legionaries who still glared at him and clung to Daizus, and he had taken note of who they were. Seven unhappy men out of eighty no longer concerned him, though. Daizus had fallen into a sullen inactivity, making no further moves or comments to his centurion. Likely he had realised how his plan had fallen apart and set his own men against him. He would realise that any such further stupidity would only make Rufinus look better and he worse.

And so things had settled for now.

Late that morning they came across a landslide. They had seen the evidence of several such events on a small scale as they climbed the pass, but this one proved more of an obstacle, since it had brought down a huge tree that lay across the valley, blocking any potential passage for the vehicles. The tribune called for sappers, and Rufinus picked out the half dozen biggest men in his century and sent them forward with axes. Alongside similar men of other centuries, they set to work on the tree, and Rufinus was impressed with the speed and efficiency with which the soldiers demolished the great obstacle, gathering the pieces they hacked off and depositing them in one of the carts to use later as fire wood, and swinging the remains of the heavy trunk out into the river. In short order they were moving again.

As noon approached, they came across a settlement where the valley widened, the river winding in a wide loop. A score of houses, surrounded by paddocks, orchards and animal pens sat beside the rough trail. Rufinus almost laughed as the cohort approached, for the opportunistic salesman in the natives suddenly came to the fore. Far from the axe-wielding unfriendlies he had met that morning, these locals hurried from their houses, setting up quick, makeshift trestle tables beside the road. By the time the vanguard reached the first house, the tables were laden with fruit, honey, vegetables, meat and various other goods, right down to woollen hats and heavy native trousers.

Rufinus decided it was time to risk speaking to the commander, and hurried forward.

The tribune turned as Rufinus appeared beside his horse. 'Yes?'

'Respectfully, sir, the men are due a meal break soon. It might do the cohort's spirits good to allow them some free time here and the liberty to purchase goods?'

Celer frowned for a moment, then nodded. 'Very good.' He turned and waved at Cassius and the rider with the vanguard. 'Call the rest of the scouts back for an hour and pass the orders. We halt here. The men can rest on the grass and are at liberty to trade with the natives.'

Cassius smiled and hurried off to pass the orders on.

Moments later the column was halting and men were drinking from flasks, retrieving bread from their packs, and flooding the tables, purchasing various goods. Rufinus crossed to one of the trestles and recognised two of his own century there. They were haggling in what sounded like the Dacian tongue he'd been hearing.

His gaze picked over the table. He peered at the hats, scarves and trousers. Remembering the cold of the morning, he wondered whether Celer would be relaxed enough about uniform to allow him a pair of those woollen trousers. They looked a great deal warmer than the thin breeches he currently wore. No. He'd not get away with that. A scarf, though…

He pointed at a scarf that was a sort of russet-orange colour with a thin yellow check thread throughout that he might get away with in uniform. The villager said something sharp and unintelligible and held up six fingers. Six what? Rufinus frowned and watched as she turned to serve one of the legionaries, who handed her three copper ases and walked off looking happy with a new drinking cup.

Fishing around in his pouch, Rufinus retrieved six copper coins and held them out hopefully, pointing at the scarf. The woman smiled and nodded, taking the coins. Rufinus lifted the scarf and left the stall, feeling the material as he pulled it through his fingers. It was an excellent piece of work and would certainly make cold mornings more bearable. Briefly, he again considered the trousers, but then pictured the tribune's face when he saw them and decided they were not an option.

Acheron made his presence known with a rumbling, and Rufinus paused at one of the stalls, purchasing some non-specific meat. He asked what it was but was no wiser when answered, and decided that Acheron was not a fussy eater, since he would happily munch on bandits given the opportunity.

Two stalls along, he bought a jar of honey, a loaf of fresh bread and a small pot of butter. They were not cheap, as he'd expect to pay in a town market, but they were fresh and clearly of good quality, so he let the locals fleece him with good grace. Back on the grass, he found a protruding rock and sat on a corner of it before deciding it was too cold and uncomfortable. With a smile, he took his prize over to the carts and found Senova and Luca sitting on the carriage bench. Luca had purchased some fruit for his mistress, and Senova offered Rufinus strawberries, cherries and slices of melon from a wooden bowl. He gratefully picked at them as he shuffled onto the bench and sawed at the loaf with his eating knife, spreading butter and honey on a slice and passing it to Senova. He then repeated the process for himself. As he ate happily, he gradually became aware that Senova was looking at him. He turned into the hard glare and frowned a question. Her eyes dipped to Luca.

Ah yes. The slave. Now Rufinus the centurion had been lowered to preparing food for a slave. With a sigh, he cut another slice and spread the butter and honey on it, passing it to Luca, who took it with surprise and delight.

He turned at the calling of his name and saw Cassius Proculeianus strolling over toward them, a bottle in his hand.

'Rufinus, here. Try this.'

Rufinus frowned. 'I try to save wine 'til evening these days. I'm sparing with it.'

'I noticed,' Cassius replied. 'One day, you'll tell me why, I imagine. But try it anyway.'

Rufinus shrugged and reached out, taking the heavy, earthenware bottle. He unstoppered it and lifted it to his lips. Before he could think of taking a drink, a sharp, acidic smell assailed him and he felt his nose hairs curling away from the scent in protest.

'What the shit is this?' he breathed, moving it away from his mouth.

'Try it.'

'You wouldn't be trying to kill me for any reason?'

'Try it, Rufinus.'

Wincing, the young centurion lifted the bottle and took a tiny, experimental sip. The contents of the bottle appeared to be a slightly fruit-flavoured liquid fire that seared the inside of his throat and burned off his taste buds. His eyes widened and he made a choking sound as he thrust the bottle back at his fellow centurion. Beside him, Luca looked hopeful.

'Trust me,' he rasped to the slave, 'you don't want to.'

He turned back to Cassius, who was grinning. 'How much did they pay you to take that stuff away?'

The veteran laughed. 'You get used to it. It's pretty much the only way to get through a Dacian winter with your wits intact. It's plum spirit. The locals all make it in their gardens. It's said that one of the Dacian kings had some liver complaint and couldn't drink wine, so he burned all the vineyards in Dacia so that no one else could enjoy it. His people couldn't face life without booze, so they made it from other fruit. They've been making it ever since. Puts hairs on your chest.'

'And burns them off other places, I reckon,' Rufinus replied, running his sore tongue around the inside of his seared mouth.

The cohort tarried for an hour at that unnamed village, and Rufinus could almost feel the goodwill growing between the troops and the locals as they traded. Finally the calls were put out and the centuries rose, gathered their kit and assembled by tent party. The locals cleared away their unsold goods and began to take apart the temporary tables. A quarter of an hour later the cohort was moving on and there was little evidence that the village had ever played host to them. The afternoon brought them, as Cassius had promised, to the heights of the pass, the valley still deep, but the climb levelling out. There they camped for the night in the lee of a craggy cliff, Senova's carriage pulled up with the horses and her, Luca and Acheron safely nestled within.

The tribune had graciously allowed the setting of camp without the usual fortifications once again. The ground was too hard to contemplate a ditch and a rampart, and they relied instead on a double watch all around, covering the northern and southern approaches where they nestled between the cliff and the river.

Barely had the tents gone up before the weather finally made its presence felt. The clouds that had been gathering ominously for the past few days began to drop snow. Not the fluffy, light snow that delighted children, either. This was wet, heavy sleet that battered the ground and felt like a slap when it hit you in the face. The wind began to howl down the valley and carried the wet snow almost sideways, making it very difficult to find shelter outside, and the men retreated to their tents early, eating cold food inside, in the absence of cook fires. Cassius dropped in to Rufinus' tent with his bottle of liquid magma, but Rufinus declined, sipping cold fruit juice from a skin while the veteran repeatedly assailed his body with his bottle of spirit.

'We should go and see Senova,' Rufinus said eventually. 'Check on her. I've not seen her since we made camp.'

'You go outside now and you'll be drenched,' Cassius said. 'I got soaked in the twenty paces between our tents.'

Rufinus nodded. He felt for the poor bastards out there on watch, wrapped tight in cloaks that would only take a dozen heartbeats to become sodden in this weather. It was hard now to picture the weather less than a week ago when he'd lay sweating in his tent, half naked and wishing it were cooler. Where was that benighted sun when he actually needed it?

'What's in store for the next few days then?' asked Rufinus.

'We're on the plateau now. We drop a little once we leave the river, and pick up the local trade trail from the east. The road will get better then as we move out into the hills. We'll be near the true Dacian heartland by the end of tomorrow, close to their ancient fortresses. Depending on what pace the tribune decides to set it's one more day, maybe two, across the hills to Sarmizegetusa. Then, we face the Sarmatians and hope that what we've taught this lot is enough to get us through without too much blood lost.'

Rufinus nodded. Three more days, then.

A sudden crash cut through their conversation and Rufinus' heart leapt. The din had been close and like nothing he'd ever heard before. Like a mountain falling over. Cassius was on his feet within a heartbeat and running out into the darkness and the snow. Rufinus exited moments later and his stomach churned at the sight awaiting him.

A section of the camp was a scene of utter destruction. A small area of hillside above had slid from the cliff and dropped on the cohort, bringing two medium-sized pine trees with it. Rufinus realised with dismay that the landslide had struck the tents of two different centuries, and that some of them had been his.

Men were rushing toward the carnage now as legionaries staggered from the rubble and earth, clutching broken limbs and swaying wildly. Rufinus ran over to the nearest, recognising the man who had bought a new cup that very morning, now clutching an arm than hung at an odd angle. Rufinus checked him over briefly. His head was drenched in red from a large cut on his scalp, and his arm had been dislocated rather than broken. He would live, and probably be fine with adequate ministrations from a medicus. Fortunately there *was* a medicus, as well as a couple of orderlies and at least four capsarii among the unit. He'd seen them back at Drobeta when he'd inadvertently poisoned his century.

Leaving the man to wander to safety, Rufinus reached a collapsed tent and could hear moaning from inside. A branch as thick as his leg lay across the tent, anchored there with the weight of the tree to which it was attached, pinning down the trapped legionaries. A soldier was running toward him, a saw in one hand and an axe in the other. Rufinus grabbed him as he passed and swept the axe up, rushing over to the tree's trunk. There, he began to hack at the join. Cassius took the man with the saw and ran off to another beleaguered tent.

Rufinus chopped and cut repeatedly at the offending branch, his muscles burning with the effort even as the freezing sleet battered him, soaking him to the skin and plastering his hair to his forehead. Finally, after what felt like hours, he felt the limb separate and hauled on the heavy branch, shoving it from the tent. Moments later he was at the leather structure, dragging it and lifting it to relieve the weight on whoever was trapped. Two figures emerged, dazed and staggering, from the tent. One had a broken arm and the other was covered head to foot with blood. Neither was in good condition, but they were both walking. More than could be said for one of their tent mates, whose legs Rufinus could see amid the mess, motionless.

Three legionaries arrived from somewhere and began to help lifting the debris from the tent and searching inside for others as a capsarius turned up and began to examine wounds, directing them to various locations depending upon the severity of their injuries. Rufinus moved on. The same tree's heavy bole had struck three tents directly. The men inside had stood little chance and he couldn't imagine there being survivors there. Further on, he found another tent, half-intact, half crushed by the fallen earth that rose above it in a mound. A legionary he did not recognise arrived and began to push the mound of earth away with a mattock. Two more were there a moment later, joining in, and Rufinus took the opportunity to push his way into the half-intact tent.

Two men lay inside, one face up, the other face down. For a moment he assumed they were dead, but then he realised that at least one of them was groaning. Swiftly, he dropped and examined the groaning one. He appeared intact, though his head was badly bruised and one eye welded shut. Rufinus lifted him with some difficulty in the tent's confines and struggled out into the cold with him. The man's head lolled in battered confusion, and Rufinus collared a man rushing past. 'Get this one to a capsarius.'

Leaving the man with his charge, he ducked back into the tent and crossed to the other body, which lay face down. A suspicion crept over him at the man's shape and as he tested the limbs and then turned the body over, his notion was confirmed. It was Daizus. The optio's bruising from the fight had almost gone, but now he had a fresh, huge contusion above the left temple and blood smeared his face.

Rufinus felt the neck and found a gentle throb there. He wasn't entirely sure how he felt about that. The optio's accidental death in a landslide would have made things a lot easier. Wicked Ideas assailed him for a single moment and then, sighing, he lifted the optio with difficulty and staggered with him out of the tent.

Two legionaries from his century, one with a nasty gash on his shoulder, were there suddenly, helping him with the optio. He left his second in command with the two men and hurried off to the next tent, seeking further survivors.

It took more than an hour in total, working in freezing sleet and howling winds, wet earth beneath the fingernails, splinters everywhere, cuts and abrasions from the fallen material. Finally, the trees were dismembered and removed to the riverside, the tents freed from the worst of the fallen earth and rubble. Rufinus' initial panic began to subside a little. Miraculously, the epicentre of the fall had been largely clear of men, for the ground there was too rocky to drive in tent pegs, and so a true catastrophe had been averted by pure luck. Rufinus vowed an altar to Fortuna when he was finally settled somewhere, in thanks.

A head count, repeated three times to be certain due to the appalling conditions of night-time weather, revealed the damage. Fourteen men dead or irreparably injured, eight of them men of his century. Another thirty three men injured but expected to pull through fully, twenty in total that would need moving carefully. It was not perfect by any means, but it could have been so much worse, and Rufinus was relieved beyond measure that the damage was as minor as it was.

The medicus and his staff had set up near the river for the presence of good clean water, and their tent, hastily erected, was a scene of horror. Rufinus passed by and winced at the sound of sawing and screaming. He found Cassius in conversation with the tribune and another centurion nearby.

'We can't just leave them,' Cassius was saying.

Tribune Celer shook his head. 'I'm not pleased with the idea of leaving twenty men to die, Centurion. But we cannot afford the delay that would be caused by tailoring our journey to the requirements of the injured. We are expected to do our duty and overwhelm these pockets of resistance, rendezvousing with the legion at Apulum at our earliest convenience. That was the governor's precise phrase, Cassius. *At our earliest convenience.* I will not delay unduly.'

Rufinus frowned. 'Can we not take the wounded in one of the carts, sir? That's standard procedure.'

Celer rounded on him. 'I am well aware of standard procedures, Rufinus. I am not entirely new to this career, you know? But if we take the wounded with us, their very presence – the need to move them gently and seek the smoothest path, the regular pauses for the attention of medics and so on – will slow us by days. Not even *one* day, but *days*. I cannot accept that.'

'But to leave them to their own devices, sir,' began Cassius.

'Enough!'

'Sir, can we spare two carts and a capsarius? And perhaps four men?'

Tribune Celer frowned. 'I might contemplate it. What do you propose?'

'Where is the nearest safe place?' Rufinus asked Cassius.

'Normally I would say Ulpia Traiana, but that's one of the places we're headed to deal with. The safest Roman installation from here would probably be all the way back to the ruined fort below the pass.'

Rufinus huffed. 'There's the village we passed through. They seemed friendly.'

'What are you planning, Centurion,' the tribune repeated.

'Twenty men will fit comfortably in two carts. With a capsarius to look after them and a small escort of four men they could make it back to that village by nightfall tomorrow if they push hard. They can convalesce there until they are mobile and then make for either Drobeta or Apulum. That way they have the chance of recovery and re-joining the unit, and yet they do not slow down our advance.'

Celer nodded slowly as he considered it.

'I don't particularly like losing a capsarius, especially after this, which has starkly illustrated how important they are. But neither do I particularly wish to lose twenty men unnecessarily. Your plan is approved, Centurion Rufinus. Make it happen.'

Rufinus saluted and turned. As he moved away to find the medicus and discuss it, Cassius fell in alongside him. 'Good job. They should be comfortable at the village.'

'We'll have to make sure they have coin with them. The villagers will be very helpful to paying guests, I suspect.'

And then, Rufinus could lead his men on and into war finally.

Outside the medical tent, he found the men of his century sitting and nursing their various injuries. Three of them looked up and nodded an appreciative greeting, and Rufinus recognised the relieved face of the man with the new cup and the dislocated arm. Daizus was there too. The man looked up at Ruifinus, his gaze full of spite and hate.

Should have hit him with a rock and left him there, Rufinus thought sourly. The optio was clearly less than thrilled with being indebted to his centurion. Still, there would be plenty of opportunities in the coming days for Sarmatian raiders to relieve Rufinus of his ongoing problem.

VII – First blood

Since the cohort had passed over the high point of Vulcan's Pass and traversed a gentle descent onto the plateau of central Dacia the scenery had changed, for sure. Rolling hills filled the next morning, giving way to a flat, grassy plain which then began to climb again into hills once more. The weather changed with the terrain, too. The snow continued into the hills but then began to falter and fade, giving way to crisp cold and blue skies, which accompanied them across the flat land, the grey clouds and threat of blizzard greeting them once more at the next hills.

The passage through the forested peaks was a nervous one for the whole column. The fact that they were approaching the first real trouble they could face sat heavy upon every brow, leaving the legionaries, both veteran and new, with the constant fear that every side valley or village or crest of a hill could hide a howling, slavering enemy. Given the additional constant threat of new snow and the fact that they still watched every slope nervously for falling trees, it was a tense journey for all.

In the event, all they had actually encountered were dour natives who regarded them with passing interest at best as they went on with their lives. The hills gradually increased in height and gradient over the next day until Rufinus was beginning to think of them as mountains, and started to wonder how long it would be before travel by carriage was no longer viable. Fortunately, this place for which they were bound had been important since long before Rome arrived, and so there were good routes through the hills, worn flat by centuries of traders and locals.

They reached their first goal in the middle of the second afternoon. They had climbed high enough again now that they had passed the snow line, and the trees formed black skeletal fingers pointing up to the white-grey sky in a thick forested mist, patches of white and slushy brown around the ground. The land seemed to be warming and the snow melting away, but for now it was still cold and wintry up here as the cohort climbed the great trade road to the fortress.

Sarmizegetusa was Dacian, and yet in some ways it was Roman. It was certainly impressive. Rufinus had seen fortifications constructed by trans-Danuvian natives before, during the wars against the Chatti and the Marcomanni – great turf banks, sometimes with timber palisades, sometimes with good stone revetting. Some had good towers and crenulations. Gates were well fortified and the terrain used to its best effect.

Even seen from a distance through the trees as they approached, Sarmizegetusa forced him to reconsider how he'd naturally lumped the Dacians in with other tribes he had encountered. They were not the same.

The great fortress-town that had once been the capital under the Dacian kings rose on a roughly rectangular prominence that sloped down from north to south, creating a high city and a low city within the walls. Rufinus had been told a little of the history of the place by Cassius on the journey, and could see that history written into the architecture. Rome had made its mark since taking control of the province. Some of the buildings within the walls, just visible thanks to the slope within, showed signs of Roman styling, and a bath house lay outside the southern gate. There was Roman work in the walls, clearly, where they had extended the original native square on the hill to enclose the lower slopes. But Rufinus could see the walls on the higher section and they were, he had to admit, every bit the match of the Roman work, and possibly more powerful still. High and thick, the walls were constructed of huge stone blocks that were perfectly flush-fitted together. Towers rose at intervals around the circuit, and these were not the rough towers of the Marcomanni. These were great square, roofed edifices of that same stonework, with apertures for missiles.

Trajan and his armies had laid this place low in his first campaign, sweeping it clean of life. The Dacians had rebuilt it after the emperor and his men left, and when they returned for their second war of conquest a few years later, the Romans had been merciless. The Fourth Flavia had been stationed here for a short while – it was they who had extended the circuit of walls, added building and put the imperial stamp on the former capital. Then, finally, they had pulled out and moved south and the Dacians had reoccupied their territory, putting their own mark on the Roman work.

The occupants had then been peaceful subjects of Rome until the Sarmatians came and drove them out, a year or more ago. The cohort had encountered those same ousted Dacians in the valley below, where they were living like refugees in temporary villages. Rufinus had not been sure what to expect of them. He doubted they would welcome the cohort, even if the Roman presence represented the only chance for them to reclaim their lives. In fact, the Dacian exiles had seemed too miserable and impoverished to care. Many of them had lost loved ones to the Sarmatian raiders. Others cursed former friends and neighbours who had thrown in their lot with the invaders. None of them seemed overly impressed to see the Thirteenth Gemina put in an appearance

As they now moved onto a wide terrace below the city's eastern walls, Rufinus noted with interest great geometric shapes in the grass, formed of stone and timber, yet not rising above ground level. Gutters and channels ran between them, as well as overgrown paved paths, carving through the slush and the snow. Off at the edge, where the black shapes of trees crowded in, the snow burning off created a white mist among the woodlands that was truly an eerie sight.

'What is this place?' Rufinus murmured to Cassius as the centuries fell into formation across the strange site, the wagons and carriage struggling up the road and groaning onto the flat ground behind them, the veteran rear-guard still a quarter of a mile back down the slope.

'It was their most sacred district. Sort of the equivalent of the Capitol in Rome, I guess. Temples and altars and so on.'

'What happened to it?'

'*Lucius Appius Maximus* happened to it,' Cassius replied darkly.

'I've not heard of him.'

Cassius nodded. 'He's a well-known character in these parts. He was one of Trajan's generals. He claimed to have found evidence here that the Dacians were sacrificing children the way the Carthaginians did, and in response he completely razed the whole complex. All their temples and altars were swept away and the capital given a new Roman face.'

'Children,' Rufinus breathed, his gaze playing across the site, picturing the horrors it had witnessed.

'It's all rubbish, of course,' Cassius replied. 'I've never heard of such a thing here outside Appius Maximus' words. When you get to know the Dacians you'll discover that they're actually pretty civilised. I do not for a moment believe that such a thing went on. It was just Appius finding an excuse to obliterate that of which he did not approve.'

Rufinus nodded again, though his imagination was still furnishing him with horrific images.

Tribune Celer, sitting astride his horse close by, had clearly caught their conversation.

'Do not let yourself be fooled, Centurion. You have a soft spot for the Dacians, but these are a different people, on whom we have stamped the trappings of civilisation. The rough, barbaric Dacians Appius Maximus found were probably quite capable of such abhorrent acts. Remember that the Sarmatians that serve among the auxilia in parts of the empire have become civilised through necessity, but remember the atrocities for which they are known. We shall no doubt see them in the city above. I for one laud my *ancestor* Appius Maximus for stamping out the Dacians' child-murder here, and I would do the very same myself.'

Rufinus had failed to connect the two names, and felt a flush of embarrassment as Celer sighed and straightened in the saddle. 'Come,' the tribune called, gesturing to the two of them and the other centurions. The optios took control of the men, keeping them prepared and in formation, while the six centurions joined Celer and his staff and then moved up toward the fortress. A perfect paved road, wide and smooth, led up from the destroyed temple region to the east gate of the fortress.

'While I open negotiations,' the tribune said quietly, 'study the enemy and the fortress itself close up. Learn what you can.' Passing between the tall, narrow, dark boles of the trees to either side of the road and the enveloping white fog they contained, the Romans followed the climbing, curving road.

Rufinus felt a touch of bile rise into his mouth as they turned the corner. The great walls were worthy of study, of course, as were the figures moving atop them, above the firmly closed gate. But the sight that really gripped him and turned his stomach were the heads.

A score or more spears had been driven into the ground outside the gate, making a grisly approach to the fortress, for each held a mouldering head, some almost down to the bone already. If Rufinus had been unsure as to who the heads were, the Sarmatian occupiers had made it clear by leaving the native pointed hats on a few of the victims, nailed on, Rufinus noted with distaste, hoping they'd already been dead when that happened. Dozens of sightless eyes stared at them. He tore his gaze from the heads and concentrated on the fortress-town.

The walls would be a tough proposition for sure. The height of five men, with towers here and there that provided a good range for arrows. Along the parapet they could see the head and shoulders of warriors in glinting armour with intricately-designed helmets or wild hair, long spears held tall.

The Roman party came to a halt, unpleasantly right in the midst of the heads and Celer, atop his white steed, motioned to his signaller, who blew three short blasts on his horn.

'I am Appius Iulius Celer, Tribune of the Thirteenth Gemina Legion. Who is your leader?'

There was an extended pause, and Rufinus wondered if they perhaps had not understood. There was no reason to expect them to have a good command of Latin, after all. Finally, three figures arrived at the central section of the walls, above the gate.

'I am Ouaras,' said the central of the three figures in thickly-accented Latin. 'I am Iazyges king in this place.'

Rufinus examined the king and those either side of him with fascination. All three had yellow or red-gold hair and were tall and muscular. One was clad in a coat of bronze scales, another in a chain shirt, while the king himself was tunic'd and wrapped in a leather jerkin of some kind. They wore their hair long and wild, not braided as many tribes tended, and two of them had great impressive beards pulled down by beads tied into the bottom, though the third figure – the one in the chain shirt – had shorter hair and no beard, for she was a woman, yet dressed for war. In an oddly inopportune moment, Rufinus found himself picturing Senova dressed for war, and the image was unsettlingly attractive. The surprising sight of a female warrior seemed to be fascinating the others too, though Celer cleared his throat and concentrated on the task in hand.

'I have no wish to waste good Roman lives,' he said, loudly and slowly. 'You are raiders and invaders. You have dismembered, killed and burned, stealing, torturing and raping your way into Dacia, and while most of your people retreated back across the border in the face of legions' retaliation, you few resist still. By all the rights of the civilised world I should condemn you to death here and now. However, I give you this offer, and only once. Take your people and leave. Travel west until you pass the last Roman mile marker and into your own land of hovels. If you do this, I will not be forced to butcher every last one of you.'

Ouaras leaned on the stone parapet.

'Invade, you say? Raid? No. Settle, it is called in Roman tongue. Our town, now.'

Celer swept out a hand, indicating the grisly poles to either side of them. 'I suspect the locals do not see it that way. And these are not from when you first came here. These are a month old at most. Who are they? Townsfolk who tried to take back their city? Traders you took a dislike to?'

A memory flashed into Rufinus' mind, tales of Trajan's soldiers putting Dacian heads on spikes in that very same manner during the great war. It might be barbaric, but it was a little hypocritical to condemn the Sarmatians for what was a common enough practice in war.

'General Appius Maximus,' the tribune continued, 'levelled a Dacian sanctuary here because of the barbaric murders they practiced. But the Dacians are Roman these days, their barbarism gone and forgotten, and it is you Sarmatians now who torture and maim, burning men alive in the veneration of your gods. As was Appius Maximus to the Dacians, so shall I be to you.'

'Talk or fight. Not both. I am getting bored.'

'Then you refuse my offer and I shall offer no mercy.'

Celer turned his steed, moving away from the walls, and the centurions and staff followed. After a few heartbeats, Celer cleared his throat. 'Tell me how we take Sarmizegetusa.'

There was an uncomfortable silence. Four of the centurions were new and untried, the staff were little more than clerks. Rufinus had, in truth, been too busy fascinated by the Sarmatians and their decapitated victims to pay much attention to the defences.,He upbraided himself for that.

'I did not see much evidence of bows,' Cassius said quietly, 'only spears. A sensible defending force would have had arrows trained on us during that meeting and, given the reputation of Sarmatian warlords, I am surprised we were not under attack even during your negotiation. We can assume they will have bows, of course. The Sarmatians are noted for them. But I think they are too nomadic by nature for this kind of

97

fight. They are horsemen, used to open battle, not sieges. I do not think they've planned ahead, but simply react to threats as they see fit. We have the advantage over them simply in the fact that we know what to do.'

'So that lends weight to the notion of a direct assault,' Celer mused.

'Quite, sir. This approach is also the simplest, given the access of the wide road and the easy slope. The other sides are much steeper, though the western approach is not too bad.'

'You are advocating a direct assault from this angle?'

Cassius nodded. 'It is a calculated risk. But given the apparent lack of enemy planning and the relatively gentle slope, it represents our best chance.'

The tribune mused, scratching his chin as they reached the lower end of that paved road once more and found the cohort assembled ready. 'There is no need for lengthy planning or preparation, then, gentlemen. How high would you say those walls were?'

'Around thirty feet, sir,' Rufinus said, picturing them and the angle at which they'd looked up to the Sarmatian defenders.

'We have lengths of siege ladder in the carts. In an ideal world we would have good siege engines, ballista and towers, but we are a part-trained cohort without a full complement of engineers and artillerists. It would take too long to construct machines, and I would not be comfortable relying upon their efficacy anyway. Let us avoid the time and effort of manufacturing. Have the carpenters take the ladders and peg them together. Improvisation is the watchword today.'

Rufinus fought the urge to argue against it. It might be an unacceptable delay to manufacture siege machines for the tribune, but then he wouldn't be the one trying to climb a ladder into a spear thrust. And while he knew that the siege ladders they carried were made to be pegged together into longer articles, he had also heard plenty of horror stories of such rickety combinations falling apart under men's feet.

'We will move in two centuries at a time,' the Tribune decided. 'The Third and Fourth will make the initial assault.'

Rufinus' mouth was working before he had chance to overrule it this time.

'Sir, it would make more sense surely to put the veterans in first?'

He could see Cassius nodding his agreement and felt bolstered by the understanding that he was not alone in his opinion.

'No,' Celer replied. 'I have only one veteran century, and there are several sites we must overcome on the journey north. I will not risk losing the core of my force in the initial engagement. The First Century are the backbone of the cohort. They will follow up the initial assault once the wall-tops are ours, and will take the fortress from there with the others.'

Rufinus saluted, though his pulse was thundering now. Untried men and a rebellious, untrustworthy second in command, committed to the initial assault. Rufinus searched his soul for a shred of confidence over what was coming, and came up entirely empty-handed. As the engineers and carpenters began to retrieve and alter the siege ladders from the carts, Rufinus peered over at Nicostratus, the centurion of the Fourth Century, who had been assigned the duty alongside him. He'd not spoken to the man a great deal, but he looked solid enough. Perhaps thirty years old, muscular and bearing a few scars, he looked the part. He certainly must have served as optio for a while.

Let's hope the men are up to it...

Rufinus and Nicostratus came to a halt, peering up at the walls beyond the lines of sightless heads. The number of figures along the walls had increased heavily, though still no arrows came, and the young centurion was sure they must be within bowshot now. He felt odd, after the past few years, marching into a fight without Acheron at his side, but he'd reluctantly left the dog with Senova at the carriage. The animal could hardly ascend a ladder and would just by impotent and at risk below the walls.

'Perhaps they just don't believe we'll attack?' the other centurion mused. 'They are too complacent for my liking.'

'Maybe Cassius is right and they're out of their depth without horses and open terrain to fight in. Either way ,the time has come. Best get to it.'

Nicostratus nodded and gestured to his signaller, who stood to one side with the standard bearer. The great curved horn let out three blasts in a rising cadence, and both Rufinus and the centurion of the Fourth placed their whistles to their lips and blew once, stomping off up the hill. The tramp of one hundred and fifty pairs of boots on the paved road behind them fell into perfect timing for only moments. Rufinus winced at the increasingly common sound of hobnails scraping and skittering on the paving. A slope of smooth stone was absolutely the worst terrain for Roman boots, and he'd almost have preferred to climb through the trees. He forced himself to pay attention to the task ahead and not shout angrily at the men behind him occasionally falling out of step and struggling not to fall. Years of experience taught a good soldier to walk a certain way on flat stone, pressing on the inside foot to give the best grip. He was relieved to see Nicostratus with that same slightly odd walk. The man was a veteran.

As they rounded the corner in the road and the walls came into clear sight past the trees, Rufinus risked a brief glance backward. What he saw gave him at least some hope for his untested men. They had begun to use the four long ladders they carried overhead to anchor themselves to one another against slipping on the stones. Mutual support. Excellent.

Rufinus returned his gaze to the walls, and for the first time saw an archer. One warrior rose above the parapet with a curved, eastern-style bow, drew back the string and loosed. The arrow flew straight and true and slammed into one of the men from the Fourth. Fortunately, it struck the double-thickness chain at the man's shoulder and, with the distance it had flown, all it did was rip out a number of links and bruise the man, knocking him back slightly.

Rufinus cursed their lack of shields. Not one of his men carried one, and that put them at serious risk from missiles, but it was impossible to climb a ladder with shield in hand, and each man carried his defence strapped onto his back, where he could retrieve it swiftly once they were inside. More arrows began to come now. Men cried out here and there as the shafts slammed into them, some harmlessly, but others with horrible results.

'Double pace,' bellowed a voice, taking Rufinus entirely by surprise. In a rush of anger, he realised it was Daizus, safely in the traditional optio's position at the rear. The century broke into a half run, and Rufinus was forced to do the same or be trampled by his own men. The Fourth Century did the same, and Nicostratus threw a frustrated look at him, which Rufinus returned in kind. He had been saving the double pace for the safer, flatter ground, once they were off the sloping smooth stone.

Sure enough men slipped and staggered, and both centuries floundered a little. Rufinus called for a return to standard pace, and the men began to find their footing better once more as they slowed. Arrows continued to come from the wall.

Finally, the road levelled out as it approached the gate in the walls, and Rufinus gestured to Nicostratus, who nodded.

'Double pace,' he bellowed, and once more both centuries broke into a jog, this time with better grip and formation. More arrows. More wounds. Men fell and had to roll aside even in their agony lest they be trampled by their mates. The walls were close now. It was time.

'Separate... and... *at the run!*'

He allowed himself to fall back a touch and out to one side now that they were in more open ground, so that he was now running alongside the men rather than in front of them. The centuries separated, Nicostratus peeling his men off to the right and heading for the stretch of wall to that side of the gate, while Rufinus and his men went left. There was a little confusion and difficulty as they broke into the run with the ladders still held overhead, but as Rufinus was about to shout commands to pull it together, they managed somehow to fall roughly into step again.

Finally the arrows slowed and then stopped. Archers atop a parapet could find it hard to angle down sufficiently to loose at figures close to the wall. Of course, Roman defenders who knew how to handle a siege would now have the archers in the towers where they could still launch arrows along the line of the wall, and would be gathering oil, pitch, hot sand, rocks and so on to drop on the enemy.

He counted off the distance to the wall in his head and cleared his throat.

'Ready...'

Almost there.

'Aaaand....'

Here goes nothing.

'Ladders!'

The men thundered to a halt close to the wall and the ladders began to rise instantly. Rufinus noted with dismay as they came upright that one of the four had come unpegged during the journey and was now only twenty feet long, the extra piece clattering uselessly to the floor. Nothing they could do about that now.

Rufinus stood twitching, watching the ladders as they angled up and up and finally clonked against the stone. Two of them had been placed too close and therefore rose well above the parapet, and the other was too far away, the top a full man's height below the battlements. Irritated, he shouted a series of orders and those three ladders were moved and adjusted to the correct angle and height, then anchored in the ground. With even more irritation, he realised a quarter of his men were still trying to raise the short ladder. Idiots! With an angry bellow, he got them to drop the useless object and concentrate on the three intact ones.

He wondered momentarily what this debacle looked like from the position of Cassius and his veteran First Century fifty paces back from the initial assault. Oddly, just as the thought occurred to him, the arrows started to fly once again, out over the top of the two struggling centuries, aiming at the Cassius' men approaching behind.

Finally, after what seemed like an eternity, the three ladders were in place and men began to climb. He scanned the scene and was gratified to note a relatively low casualty rate thus far. Given the cohort's greenness and the various hiccups they had incurred, Rufinus considered himself incredibly lucky that they seemed to be facing an enemy who were also fighting a battle for which they were insufficiently prepared. Had they been facing the men who had built these walls, there would be an awful lot more bodies on the floor by now.

Three legionaries were on the nearest ladder now, climbing with sword in hand, and Rufinus pushed his way into the press to be the fourth. A centurion should be at least *near* the front, if not at it. Vine cane tucked into his belt, he gripped his sword tight and began to climb.

As they ascended, he reaffirmed his vow to raise an altar to Fortuna. The enemy had no idea how to handle a siege. No rocks came. No hot oil or searing sand. Nothing. Not even the most common defence of the lot: a Y-shaped stick to push away ladders.

A third of the way. Ten feet was not a long climb, but it felt like it with one hand on the rungs and a sword in the other, constantly anticipating death from above. He glanced over at the other ladders, and fresh waves of irritation washed over him. On the furthest one, he could see Daizus nearing the top. The bastard was an optio. He was supposed to stay at the rear and motivate the men, not run ahead seeking glory. Rufinus was going to have to discipline him later, which would likely create dangerous ripples yet again. Damn the man.

Still, now was not the time for worrying about such things.

The first man on his ladder reached the last rung and tried to climb over but received a spear thrust to the chest that sent him howling in pain out into the air, to fall and crash to the ground amid the rest of the century. The second man reached the top and thrust with his sword. There was then a little desperate to-ing and fro-ing as the men on the ladder waited impatiently. Finally, the legionary took a horrible spear thrust to the face and fell after his mate. The third man followed in his wake, managing to cross the parapet, and Rufinus rushed up the last stretch, determined to close the gap and create a small bridgehead on the wall, protecting the other climbers.

The middle ladder was faring much worse, and men were dying repeatedly as they reached the top. Finally, one of the Sarmatians produced a scythe-like object from somewhere and used it to push that ladder away from the wall. The ladder fell and broke, men dropping from it as it collapsed. The victorious defender rushed over to the third ladder to try and repeat his success, but Daizus was climbing over the parapet now and stopped him with a well-placed sword blow.

Rufinus was only peripherally aware of the fighting at the other ladders, though. As the man who'd been ahead of him expired noisily to a brutal sword slash, Rufinus was momentarily alone atop this section of wall. Three figures were pressing him, and he ripped the vine stick free, using it to parry as best he could. He simply did not have sufficient time to take the measure of his opponents and plan as he usually did, but he was managing, through a combination of skill, determination and luck, to hold off two with parries while attempting to kill the third.

Suddenly there was a legionary next to him, and the pressure eased. He concentrated on two of the enemy now, parrying one and then driving his gladius into the neck of another. As the body fell away gurgling, and Rufinus twisted his blade and ripped it free, he turned to the other Sarmatian only to find the man now in combat with a second legionary.

His century were starting to swarm across the parapet, and even as the first of them died, another arrived.

Rufinus pressed forward and realised with a start that the figure now facing him was a woman. Not the one he'd seen at the parley, but another woman with a scale shirt and a vicious looking blade, her shield painted with strange curling designs, her teeth bared. He parried her first blow and was forced to step back slightly. She was fast, and vicious, and the second and third blow he caught and turned with stick and sword. He began to wonder why he was losing and then realised with surprise that all he was doing was parrying. He'd not made one attempt to land a blow. Despite the clear danger, his body seemed unwilling to attack a woman at some basic level.

Her savage snarl and strange, eastern words battered him and Rufinus turned another strike, though only barely, her stray sword scoring a narrow red line along his forearm. Forcing himself to think of her as any other enemy, he gritted his teeth and struck. The blow took her by surprise. Perhaps she had become complacent through his lack of attacks, but his blow took her in the side, just below the armpit, where there was a gap in her scale shirt, sinking deep into the torso in a killing blow.

The Sarmatian woman fell away and was replaced by two other defenders, one with a spear, the other a sword. Rufinus laid into them, breathing heavily with the exertion. More legionaries were arriving all the time now, and had begun to unsling their shields. They had gained the all-important foothold. Along the wall, he could see Daizus and his men in a similar situation. A brief glimpse of the interior of the place showed it to be largely empty, rather than swarming with warriors waiting to climb. There were not too many defenders after all, then. And with the hold the cohort now had on the wall, it was only a matter of time until it was over. All Rufinus had to do was survive.

His sword slashed and chopped, biting into iron and bronze and leather and flesh. His vision became blurred with sweat and dirt and a fine spray of blood. At one point he found himself facing a legionary, and they had almost struck at one another in the confusion. With the blinding mess, the men covered in blood, it was becoming difficult in the press to determine who was who without concentrating.

Finally, with a roar, he kicked a Sarmatian warrior away, his blade coming free of the wound with a sucking sound, and looked around to discover that there was no one else to fight. The wall was theirs. Mere moments later, as he wiped the gore from his face and blinked his vision clear, a familiar face appeared over the parapet as Cassius led his men into the fray.

Rufinus sagged. He felt weary, and realised that, for all his military record and the number of times he had wielded a sword since his admission to the praetorians, he had not fought in a proper military engagement since the emperor Marcus Aurelius had died, six years ago. No wonder he was fatigued. Yet, despite everything, they had won. He felt a wave of relief wash over him, and tried not to think what would happen when they found themselves facing an enemy who knew what they were doing...

VIII – A new Appius Maximus

T he total cost to the century had been surprisingly low. Twenty seven dead or beyond hope, and thirty one walking wounded who would recover to active duty in due course. Of course, all but three of the fallen came from the two centuries in the first assault, and sixteen of them were from Rufinus' Third. Along with the eight dead from the landslide and the five who had gone back south in the cart, that dropped Rufinus' first command from eighty men to fifty one. In a moment of bleak, black humour, Rufinus had suggested to Cassius that by the time they reached Apulum, unit strength would be so low they'd have to turn around and head back to recruit in Moesia again. Daizus had survived, of course, and before they moved on, Rufinus needed to bring up the issue of insubordination.

Still, they had won the day, restored Roman control over an important site, and achieved their first victory as a cohort. They hadn't bothered counting the enemy dead, which smouldered in a huge ashy pile several hundred paces from the far side of the fortress, but the Sarmatians had clearly lost many more than the cohort. The column of grey from their burning was still visible between the trees and Rufinus scowled at it, and at the second one from the Roman bodies nearby. They had not been able to bury the dead of either side – thick rock lay just beneath the surface of the hillside, and the trees did not help. Burning the dead had not been too easy either, mind, with the melting snow and damp wood, but fortunately there were supplies of logs in some of the buildings in Sarmizegetusa.

The cohort shuffled slightly in the chill. The snow was now patchy at best on the ground, but the air was damp and frosty, and the sweat of the men's exertions had dried cold on their skin. Above the sound of several hundred men waiting,

Rufinus could hear the distant screams from the hospital, and tried to block them out. He stood straight as a rod with his vine stick jammed under his arm, at the front of his men, as did the other five centurions.

There was the distant creak and slam of the gate, and finally the prisoners appeared around the curve in the road. Rufinus watched sixty one men and women trudge along the stone paving down to the once sacred temple zone, their hands bound behind them, legionaries driving them on with pila. The tribune had not yet announced their fate, though Rufinus recalled his promises from the parley and could not believe they would walk away from here intact. In a way, he was in two minds about the prisoners' fate. They were people – women, even – who had fought for a home, and warriors in war deserved a warrior's death. But that home had not been theirs to fight for, and they had beheaded Dacian locals. And somewhere, deep in the back of his mind, Rufinus could not rid himself of the memory of Tad, the Sarmatian cannibal who had tortured and tried to kill him at an imperial villa half a decade ago. Despite everything, he found the image of Tad colouring his opinion of the Sarmatians.

The prisoners were herded out into the open and lined up in five rows, with the spare prisoner added to the rear line. There was a long, unpleasant silence, over which they could all hear the gut-churning sounds of the medicus and his men at work in the hospital tent. Finally Tribune Celer stepped out from the small knot of neat-looking officers and up onto a raised stone disc at the edge of the lower terrace of the sacred area.

'You are condemned men and women. All of you. You had the audacity to invade Roman lands and to rape and murder with abandon. Now you will learn that to pit yourself against Rome carries a terrible price.'

As was Appius Maximus to the Dacians, so shall I be to you.

Rufinus shivered, and not entirely from the chill.

'Punishment details, step forward.'

Six men stepped out of Cassius' First Century, and Rufinus could see the scourges coiled in their hands, six more behind but with empty hands. He swallowed, his throat suddenly dry. He had been beaten with a centurion's stick, and it had been agonising. But that had just been a cane. The lash could cripple a man, make him bite off his tongue, leave him bleeding to death. But the scourge...

Each of the whips had fragments of bone and glass cunningly woven along the length. A scourging was not a punishment. It was a death sentence. An execution in a particularly horrible manner. Rufinus watched as the front row of a dozen prisoners were taken to the edge of the treeline, in full view of the cohort and the other prisoners, and tied to branches and trunks. Hundreds of other dark eyes watched from a distance, too. The Dacians from the valley below who had been driven out by these invaders, and who had been brought back here by soldiers over the past hour or two in order to see their enemy punished. They didn't look as happy at the proceedings as the tribune had told his men they would.

Rufinus breathed deeply as a man with a scourge lined up behind every other man. The second group of six soldiers, again veterans from Cassius' unit, crossed to the unattended prisoners. Each of them drew a knife from their belt. Rufinus felt his blood chill. The veteran legionaries were grim-faced, each and every one. Cassius, too, had a dark scowl plastered across his visage.

'I have read the stories of your people's atrocities with prisoners,' Celer snarled. 'Romans scourged to death. Romans flayed and hanged from trees for the animals to gnaw on. Thus I bring you your own horrors, visited upon yourselves. Begin.'

Rufinus watched. He didn't want to. He wanted to look away. No matter what he thought of these people, such torture was simply unnecessary, and it held rather profound and horrifying memories for Rufinus on a personal level. He would never approve of it. Not after the work of the Syrian. Cassius watched, too. They all did. No one looked away. It would be considered weakness.

The screaming would stay with Rufinus until the day he died. The piercing wails as knives sliced flesh and knotted, barbed whips tore skin and muscle away from bone. It was an appalling noise, and it took half an hour to finish off all twelve and then hang their remains from other trees before forcing the reluctant, struggling and shouting prisoners of the second line over to the trunks trees amid the gore and dark spatters and tie them in place. Then it began again.

Two hours, the Dacian former citizens of Sarmizegetusa and the men of the Thirteenth Gemina watched the enemy being tortured to death. The only relief was that despite tiring arms, the punishment details swiftly became better at their jobs and made it all happen faster. Rufinus wondered why Cassius had not rotated his men to give them a rest. The twelve weary, blood-soaked legionaries persisted until they were faced with fifty brutalised corpses, ten flayed yet still alive and wailing, all hanging from the trees.

Only when there was one remaining ashen-faced Sarmatian standing in the centre did it stop. Without seeking the tribune's permission, Cassius dismissed his punishment details, sending them off to the bath house with a chitty for a quadruple wine ration. Celer was too busy to notice or care as he cleared his throat from his ancient stone podium.

'You live. My men will give you food and coin to see you safely back to your own people, and documents of free passage with my seal. Take back news of what you witnessed here, that your fellow savages learn what it means to cross swords with Rome.'

Cassius nodded to two of his men, who crossed and took the last prisoner away, speaking to him in his native tongue, on the assumption that he had not comprehended the triune's words. Once they were gone, Celer turned to the Dacians.

'Witness the might of Rome, her mighty eagle spreading its wings over the empire, protecting her people. Never again shall raiders be allowed to reach your homes and families. Even now the legates work to strengthen and man the borders. Be safe and content within the Pax Romana.'

How magnanimous, Rufinus thought darkly.

'Men of the Thirteenth,' the tribune called, turning to the assembled legionaries, 'we shall tarry here one day as reward for your efforts. Awards will be allocated tomorrow when I have had time to go through everything. Wine rations are doubled for every man tonight, and the bath house will be made available on a rota. Centurions, dismiss your men.'

Cassius did so without delay, sending his men to the houses that had been allocated to them within Sarmizegetusa. Rufinus wondered for a moment whether the tribune had bothered to check whether those houses belonged to the refugees now returning, but decided probably not. Turning, he dismissed the Third Century and then, as the cohort dispersed, Celer and his staff moving back toward the road up to the town, Rufinus strode over to the stone circle in the floor where the tribune had been standing.

Some ten feet across, it appeared to have been an altar of some kind, mimicking a sunburst, with radiating slabs. Runnels within the structure, which emptied into a drain alongside, were clearly part of a sacrificial system, and though that could mean anything from chickens to bulls, somehow Rufinus found himself picturing children being killed there and felt sickened at the image. The last of the snow on the disc showed the tribune's boot prints where he had stood, and the image burned itself into Rufinus' brain as the perfect analogy for the empire.

Damn it, but he was beginning to think like Senova.

A presence close by made him turn and he found Cassius standing nearby, staring up at the dangling bodies in the trees.

'Your men did their duty with honour,' Rufinus said, offering what little comfort he could.

'I took volunteers only,' Cassius replied. 'Filthy, degrading work. Execution I could accept easily, but that…' He gestured to the pink and red shapes hanging in the trees at the edge of the sacred area, some still crying. 'It feels like a sick joke to do that here of all places.'

Rufinus shrugged. 'Oh I don't know. I've a notion that this place is far from innocent. Something about this altar disturbs me. I don't think I'll ever understand the Dacians. Or the Sarmatians. Or our *own* people, for that matter.'

'Our own?' Cassius snorted. 'Speak for yourself, Rufinus. I'm from Epiphania. Moesian born and bred.' He sighed. 'You've only been here a few weeks, though. Give it time.'

'I don't think I'll *have* time. Celer seems Hades-bent on racing us north to join the legion, and then I'll be shuffled off or kept busy somehow until Albinus finds a way to send me back to Cleander.'

'I don't understand how the chamberlain has the right to send praetorians away,' Cassius frowned. 'Your posting here is a mystery, Rufinus.'

The younger centurion looked around nervously. 'That's not a discussion for this place. Not one I expected to have with anyone, in fact, but perhaps we'll head to quarters and I'll talk over a cup of wine.'

Cassius nodded and then turned at the sound of thumping paws. Acheron came bounding across the wet grass and leapt up at him, planting two heavy paws on his shoulders and almost knocking him down. Senova was walking across the sanctuary behind him, her face grim.

'I told you not to come,' Rufinus said wearily.

'I had to see it.'

'No you didn't. *I* had to, otherwise I wouldn't have been here, either.'

Senova came to a halt next to them, her breath pluming in the cold, her soft shoes soaked through and cloak pulled tight about her. She looked up at the bodies hanging in the trees, some still whimpering.

'Let's go,' Rufinus urged her.

'I suppose it is only what they would do to us,' she said in an odd matter-of-fact tone.

Rufinus blinked. 'What?'

'The punishments the tribune dealt. They are Sarmatian punishments, after all.'

'You sometimes still surprise me,' Rufinus said to her.

She shrugged. 'When you have seen the threefold death once or twice and sacrificed a few animals, the squeamishness quickly fades.'

Cassius snorted. 'You could teach some of our legionaries a thing or two.'

Come on.' Rufinus grasped Senova's elbow and turned her, urging her back toward the road that led up to the fortress-town's gate. Acheron went to investigate the piles of meat near the trees and, regretfully left them alone to bound after his master. The four figures journeyed back up the slope from the grisly sanctuary in silence.

The town sulked in the cold, columns of black smoke coiling up from many of the roofs as legionaries or locals lit fires to warm their homes, whether they be temporary or permanent. Men of the Thirteenth were now in position, guarding the walls and gates, and Rufinus and his friends strode through the strangely part-Roman, part-Dacian town to the house allocated to the Third Century's commander. The building was a squat stricture of wooden boards with a stone base up to a course of around a foot from the ground. Its roof was of similar boards, giving it a drab, dour appearance, particularly in the gathering gloom of the evening.

Rufinus had not yet had time to do anything other than take a quick look in the place and drop his kit. His century were quartered in the next four houses along the line. In theory Daizus should share this place with his centurion, but the optio had chosen to stay with the men instead and Rufinus remained grateful for that.

Some helpful person had supplied the house with a tray of bread and cold cuts of meat and a jug of wine and had lit an oil lamp on a shelf near the door, closing the window shutters to keep out the cold. Rufinus shuffled wearily into his room and crossed to the cot, sagging onto it and reaching for bread and meat. Senova found a comfortable seat, Acheron curled up at her feet, and Cassius poured wine for her and closed the door before wandering over to another chair.

'Level with me, Cassius,' Rufinus said suddenly. 'You're a veteran and a good man, and I saw your face this afternoon. You're not pleased.'

The older centurion frowned reluctantly. 'It is not our place to speak ill of our superiors, Rufinus.'

'True. But there are things going unsaid around here, and such strained silence does no one any good. I think it's time we spoke our minds to one another, and I suspect your truths are less damning than mine, so I am hoping you will go first.'

Cassius, foregoing the wine, withdrew his bottle of fruit spirit and took a nip from it, sucking in air through his teeth.

'Alright. If we're opening the book of our souls, I do not particularly like the tribune. There.'

'Why?'

Another sip of spirit. 'He's a man ruled by his heart, and I think his heart is dark. He *is* good at his job, though, and that counts a lot for a senior tribune. Legions rely upon them, after all. I just worry about the directions he might take at any moment. He could become dangerous if unchecked. But he is close to the governor, and that makes him untouchable anyway, so all this is moot opinion and conjecture.'

Rufinus nodded. 'And what do you think of Albinus?'

Cassius shook his head. '*That* is not a conversation I am willing to have. Now it's your turn. Tell me why you're *really* here.'

Rufinus looked at Senova, oddly feeling it necessary to seek her approval. She nodded, and he took a drink of wine.

'Cleander sent me on detached duty.'

'That, we all know.'

'His given reason, and this has to be our secret, is to monitor Albinus and Niger, both of whom he believes have been speaking out against both him and the emperor.'

Cassius shook his head. 'They would never be so stupid as to speak out against the emperor. No one would. But against Cleander? Yes, I have heard this myself. But then half the world speaks out against Cleander when they are sure he is not listening. The man is known to be a snake. I wonder why you are working for him?'

'That's the other thing,' Rufinus replied with a sigh. 'He has me by the balls. He has my brother under his "protection", and controls the praetorian guard. And he doesn't like me – sees me as a threat, particularly since I've threatened to put a sword through his oily face more than once. I suspect the main reason I am truly here is because it is about as far away from him as he can send me.'

Cassius nodded with a strange expression.

'If we were truly safe and alone, there are things I could tell you, Rufinus. Things that would make you blanch. But not here. And not now.'

'If you could help supply me with that Cleander wants, perhaps I can go home and he might even free my brother,' Rufinus urged.

'No. Not now. Not here.'

Cassius suddenly rose to his feet, looking uncomfortable. 'I wanted to know why you were here, and I do though, gods, now I wish I did not. I am not a man for intrigues, Rufinus, like you guardsmen and your courtier friends. I am a soldier, and a good one. I lead men in battle and in garrison. And now I need to think. I will bid you good night.'

Rufinus watched Cassius leave, wearing a troubled expression, and once the door was shut again he turned to Senova. 'What do you make of that?'

'He has the face of a hen who knows the fox is on the prowl.'

Rufinus rolled his eyes. 'If we could just dispense with the weird Briton analogies for a moment?'

Senova folded her arms. 'He is nervous. He knows something that has a bearing on why you arc here, but he is reluctant to tell you of it. I think he fears the effects.'

'Repercussions,' Rufinus nodded.

'Yes. Those. Whatever he is nervous about, that is what you need to know.'

'It's going to be a bit of a task getting it out of him, though. I can't see him just dropping it into conversation.'

There was a long silence, which became uncomfortable with every passing heartbeat. Rufinus smoothed a wrinkle out of the blanket on his cot. 'I...'

'What?'

'I don't suppose you would like to stay here tonight?' he hazarded in a small, weird voice. 'Since I'm not in a barrack block or a camp tent for a change.'

Senova's eyebrow arched, and Rufinus couldn't tell whether that was good or bad. 'Like a camp follower, you mean?' she answered. 'As your woman who cannot be a wife and has to live outside the fort like a dependent whore?'

Rufinus found that his throat had gone rather dry again.

'Well, it's just that you and me... I mean, I know it's not perfect. But I'm an officer now, and...'

'You are an officer *here*. In *Rome* you are a guardsman.'

'Is that a no?' he prodded, feeling slightly crestfallen.

'No, that is not a no.'

Rufinus grinned suddenly, and Senova held up a restraining hand.

'But not while you smell like axle grease and old wet leather. Go and use the bath house and I will conjure up some real food while you are out.'

Still grinning like a child with unexpected confectionary, Rufinus dug in his pack until he found the thick blanket which doubled as a towel on campaign.

'Back shortly.'

She nodded and he almost leapt out of the door, shutting it behind him and standing there for a moment, adjusting to the chilly air. The evening had brought a strange and jarring mix of horror, tension and elation, and he was unsure how to process it all, other than to let the happiness of an night with Senova override it all and try to forget for now about torturers and traitors and centurions with secrets.

He frowned as he looked down at the street. Like most provincial towns, especially those built on a slope, Sarmizegetusa's streets collected muck and detritus at the periphery and, while the empire's great cities had slaves to sweep and clean the streets and empty the public urinals, places like this lacked such amenities. Consequently there was a thick layer of wet muck outside the house, and something about the marks in it struck him as odd.

There were footprints outside the shuttered window. Of course, there could be a hundred reasons for people to leave prints there, but two things stood out. Firstly, the prints were hobnailed, making it fairly certain they were Roman boots, and secondly they faced the house in several positions, as though someone had stood there for some time, occasionally moving to ease his leg muscles. Someone had been listening at the window, and recently, for the prints were fresh.

Feeling his heart start to pound, he crouched. There was a mark on each print. There must be a small triangular raised section on the sole of the left boot. He'd seen such things before where thrifty legionaries had patched their own boots with spare leather to save the cost of new ones. The man with this left boot had listened to Rufinus speaking with Cassius.

So the man knew why Rufinus was here.

Suddenly the veteran centurion's caution seemed all too sensible. Rufinus' gaze raked the area. Three soldiers were strolling this way at the top of the street, laughing despite the day as they passed around a flask of wine. Two dour-looking Dacian women stood outside a house's door, beating a rug and emptying the detritus that had clearly built up in their home during the Sarmatian occupation. No suspicious-looking lone figure stared back at him from the shadows.

He turned and pulled the door open, hurrying back inside and then sliding home the bolt, checking the window shutters were tightly fastened. Senova frowned at him where she was busy lighting a second oil lamp to throw back the shadows of the room.

'Trouble?'

'Bath can wait. You'll have to put up with me smelling. Someone's been loitering outside the window.'

Her face suddenly became serious. 'Cassius was right. This was neither the time nor the place.'

'Something is going on, Senova. I'm not sure what, yet, but something underhand is going on with the Thirteenth Legion and its commanders. I'm beginning to think that Cleander might actually have been right about this place and its officers. If we can survive the fighting until Apulum and meet up with the rest of the legion, I might be able to get some answers, and then we could leave and return to Rome.'

Senova nodded. 'In the meantime, you need to be careful. People here don't trust you, and some don't like you. And with people starting to take an interest in why we're here? Well, if life at court has taught me anything it's that planting a knife in someone's back is a surprisingly easy task.'

Rufinus sank into the seat again.

'And you. You're with me and they all know it. I want you and Luca to stay in your accommodation or the wagon when you're not with me, and keep Acheron close. He will protect you.'

He reached for the wine bottle, and Senova made a disapproving clucking noise.

'Remember your rule. One cup.'

Rufinus sighed. 'I think some circumstances might allow a bending of the rules, Senova.'

'And dull your senses too? I think not.'

She took the wine bottle from the table, next to his hovering hand, and replaced it with a cup of something yellowish white.

'What in Hades is that?'

'Goat's milk.'

His lip curled in distaste. 'I am neither a goat nor a barbarian.'

'Be careful what you say, Gnaeus Rufinus. I was raised on the stuff.'

'And when I want to grow healthy boobs and a hog's weight in sarcasm, I will drink it. For now, wine, water or fruit juice will suffice.'

She swept away the cup and replaced it with another, glittering clear liquid sloshing around inside. 'Water it is, then.'

With a sigh, Rufinus took a sip of water. Tonight looked like being a long night. He perked up at a thought. After all, had not Senova said she would stay? Perhaps they...

He caught her expression as she double checked the door and the window shutters, and sagged back into the cot. No. Probably not, now.

IX – True war

The high, frozen forests of Sarmizegetusa were a memory now for Rufinus, with their great walled fortress, the eerie sanctuary, the grisly hanging bodies and the funeral pyres. While the place had been fascinating in some respects, he had still been more than relieved to move on. Some things that had happened there would haunt him for many years.

The following two days brought another change in both scenery and weather. A day slogging along steep sided valleys took them out of the forested region and into open grazing lands with flocks upon the high hillsides. The chill slowly diminished and left a grey world with a suggestion of impending rain. Then, at the end of that day, the cohort rounded a bend in the valley and found themselves looking out across a wide plain, dotted with farms. They camped there and awoke in the morning to periodic bursts of light drizzle as clouds scudded across the sky at surprising speed.

With an odd mix of supressed nerves at the thought of what they might be marching to face, and gloomy acceptance of the weather through which they were marching to face it, the cohort trooped out onto the flat lands and made good time tramping south-west at a mile-eating pace. Gradually, as they passed through the land of native farms, along avenues of bare, scrubby trees and between ploughed fields, mute evidence began to appear that all was not well in the region of Ulpia Traiana.

The first sign was an empty village. Not a big place – just seven houses and a few farm buildings – but it was deserted with the fields still sown, scrawny animals left unfed in their enclosures, houses intact and containing whatever goods were not worth taking. There was no indication of a fight, but a dark patch of soil at the centre of the village was highly suggestive of blood. The tribune had his men forage and take anything they could use on their journey. It might have been practical, but the orders sat poorly with the superstitious among the men.

Not with Daizus, of course, who almost delighted in such authorised theft. Rufinus still had not dealt with the matter of the man's insubordination during the siege. The battle's aftermath, and other concerns, had delayed it, and the longer the issue stretched out, the harder it was to find a reasonable way of approaching the matter without looking like an idiot.

Cassius Proculeianus had noted at the farm then that they were less than five miles from Ulpia Traiana, and each half mile beyond that brought fresh signs of trouble. A burned out building. A deserted farm. A pile of bodies outside a shack, mouldering in the damp air. As if to add a level of bleakness to the day, the clouds continued to drop regular showers of drizzle upon them. The evidence was mounting up that this pocket of active raiders was still horse-borne and causing trouble, rather than settled and intending to remain.

Rufinus felt his nerves reach new heights as the shape of Ulpia Traiana coalesced ahead in the grey. Nestled in the foothills at the edge of the plain, with high mountains throwing distant blue grey shapes crowned with snow up behind, the city was a proper Roman town, square and heavy, on a slight rise, with four stout walls. Smoke rose from the place and it took breath-stealing moments to become apparent that it rose from chimneys and flues and not from burning houses and bodies. Rufinus felt a thrill of relief flow through him at the realisation. Then, as they came closer, something else struck him and the nerves returned. As with all cities, there was some civic overflow beyond the walls. An amphitheatre, temples, housing, a bathhouse and more lay below the town on the northern slope, and while smoke indicated occupation within the town, there was no sign of life in these outer buildings, and no smoke to indicate that the baths were operating. No local farmers tended fields, and no children played.

The rest of the cohort had clearly noted the same thing, and the atmosphere became edgy, men's eyes darting left and right nervously, picking out imagined threats. The column marched up between two buildings that stood silent and empty, past the great curve of the soundless amphitheatre, the baths and several ornate temples, toward Ulpia Traiana's north gate.

The city was more than a settlement. It was a statement. When Trajan and his armies had come and ripped troublesome Dacia from the clutches of its king eighty years ago, they had torn down his capital and garrisoned it with legionaries. They had then built a new capital here, with all the trappings of empire. *There*, Trajan was saying, *is what you were. Here is what you will become.* But times change and boundaries shift, and now the province was ruled from Apulum. This grand place was a city only, full of monuments to a controlling power that had moved.

Two men stood above the gate, which remained firmly closed, other figures in evidence along the walls. As the column came to a halt, Celer at the fore now with Cassius close by, the great timber leaves creaked open, and relief crept into Rufinus once more, though still tempered with a touch of nerves.

'Who are you?' Celer demanded of the men above the gate. 'Identify yourselves.'

'Claudius Crescens, formerly of the First Aurelia Antonina Cohort, sir. Retired. This is my colleague Julius Artemas, formerly Second Gallorum.'

Rufinus smiled. Retired soldiers were almost always stout men in a troublesome situation.

'Well, Claudius Crescens,' the tribune replied, 'perhaps you could tell me what you know of the Sarmatian raiders reportedly still operating in this area.'

Crescens nodded and disappeared for a moment. By the time the gates were fully open and the main street toward the high forum was in view, the former auxiliary soldier had appeared at ground level and strode out to meet them. He wore an old military tunic of green wool and a military belt. Though he was unarmoured, as well as a sword, a sling and pouch of stones hung at his side.

'There are maybe a hundred and fifty of them by my estimation, sir. They came months ago and tried to ravage the city. We don't have a full military presence these days, but there are quite a few of us veterans here, so we shut the gates and manned the walls and denied them Ulpia Traiana. We have two scorpion bolt throwers and a few bows and slings, so they paid in wounds any time they came too close. They disappeared for a while, and we thought they'd gone, but they reappear every now and then. We've formed a small garrison of local lads, and we keep Ulpia Traiana safe, but we're too few to take on the raiders, so there's not much we can do to protect the local settlements.'

Celer nodded his understanding. 'That is why we are here.'

'Good job, Tribune. They're somewhere nearby in the hills. They rove around the area ravaging farms and villages. We sent to the nearest auxiliary fort, asking if they would come and deal with the raiders, but they remain at Agnaviae.'

Celer waved a dismissive hand. 'The governor has issued strict orders to all military installations within fifty miles of the border to maintain their garrison in position, given the ongoing threat of further incursions. That garrison is needed in place as part of the general defensive system. What is your latest information on the raiders?'

'Two days ago they were spotted on the other side of that range of hills to the north, about five miles away. A forester and his family turned up at the gates seeking refuge, since their hovel had fallen to the raiders while they hid in the woods and watched.'

The tribune straightened. 'We shall camp here tonight, then, and in the morning, we move on the raiders.'

Rufinus felt a mixture of relief and regret. At least they would have a night's rest, but it would have been nice to be inside the walls in a bathhouse and a barrack, rather than outside under leather.

That night the cohort pitched their tents below the city walls with just pickets for defence. The Tribune spent the night in the city, a guest of the town's councillors, residing in the former procurator's house, while Rufinus spent the evening in the company of Senova and Acheron, still mindful of the fact that someone knew his true reason for being here and that prying eyes and listening ears could be anywhere around them.

'What are the Iazyges like, then?' she asked as she stitched the hem of her spare tunic.

'Those we fought at Sarmizegetusa were Iazyges, but not typical ones, I think. They're horsemen in the main. Semi-nomadic. I fought them once, back under Aurelius in my first year with the legion. They'd been part of the war for ages, and they surrendered that same year. I remember them in battle though. They charged in a mass, with lances levelled, and hit us like a runaway wagon. Only good discipline and anti-cavalry formations saved us. They were terrifying, but once you got them off their horses, they were like fish out of water and easy prey for legionaries, a bit like the ones back at Sarmizegetusa. I remember a five hundred strong unit of them serving alongside the Tenth in the last year of the war. They were considerably more dangerous, since they'd picked up Roman habits too.'

'I am baffled,' Senova said, 'why Clodius Albinus has left these groups to cause trouble for so long, when he could have used part of his own force or some local unit to deal with them.'

Rufinus sagged. 'I can see why he would keep the border garrisons in place. But I agree that the idea of leaving this half-trained cohort to deal with pockets of resistance is strange, when he must have marched the rest of the legion past these same places to get back to Apulum. Whatever was happening there, he must have considered it more important than the safety of provincial towns.'

'The gold.'

Rufinus nodded. Yes. The famous Dacian gold mines. Albinus had ignored all sorts of trouble in order to make sure his mines were secured. On a whim, he moved to the tent entrance and quickly thrust his head out, hoping to surprise anyone lurking nearby. There was no one there.

'Have you found out who was listening at Sarmizegetusa?'

He shook his head. Over the past two days he had taken every opportunity to examine boot soles when they came into view, but as yet had not spotted the tell-tale mark.

'Get some sleep,' she said comfortingly. 'You'll need to be fresh tomorrow. I'll stay here with the wagons and the town garrison, but you'll be gone early.'

'Keep Acheron with you.'

She shook her head. 'He hates it when you go without him.'

'I know. But there's no guarantee of safety for you, even with the cohort gone. I will not be able to concentrate on the fight if I'm worrying about you. Acheron stays with you this time.'

In the event, his night had been one of broken sleep and unsettling dreams, and when the cohort moved out in the morning, into constant heavy rain, he felt groggy and achy. The watery sun, visible principally as a lighter patch of cloud, had not been in the sky for long before they acquired their first information. They skirted the low hills Crescens had indicated, passing by to the east. As they rounded a spur, they passed more burned and destroyed settlements and then, three miles from the city, they found a small party of Dacians with a wagon and ox, heading south. A brief enquiry confirmed that they were heading for the city, since their village had been destroyed. Just two miles away, they said, the Iazyges had still been busy revelling in destruction a little over an hour ago.

The cohort moved on, the tension growing with each sodden step.

'Be prepared for sudden cavalry action,' the tribune called back to his men. 'Contra equitas formation is the drill of the day.'

Rufinus felt a waver of uncertainty then. It was a good formation and effective against cavalry, but were these men ready? He'd practiced it, along with several other formations, at Drobeta, and his century had managed to pull it off well enough a few times. But that was on a parade ground. When faced with charging Sarmatians, it would be a whole different matter.

He ruminated on the worry for some time, and had come no closer to contentment when word of the enemy came. The scouts returned and brought some detail. There were indeed over a hundred riders in the enemy force. They had finished looting the village that lay in the bottom of a shallow valley, but had moved a little way up the slope and were busy with what looked like a rural villa.

The tribune's face took on a stern set, and Rufinus found it distasteful to realise that Celer had been all business when the Dacians were being set upon, but now that it appeared to be a *Roman* target, the man had become incensed.

The cohort moved on, cresting a low rise until the village and its attackers came into sight. Two dozen houses flanked a narrow stream that ran along the valley bottom cutting across their path. A low wooden plank bridge crossed the stream. The villa that stood on the gentle slope beyond was no grand Roman estate, just a small rural house with a vineyard and an orchard, but it was clearly Roman. Even from here, Rufinus could identify the peristyle form, columns by the entrance, a low drum-shaped mausoleum not far away. The riders were visible too, moving in a seemingly chaotic pattern around the villa and its grounds.

The cohort was closing on the village by the time the enemy suddenly became aware of the Roman presence.

Warning cries went up, and a dragon-shaped standard was held aloft, the wind howling through it and making an eerie keening sound. The enemy began to cluster together, but made no move toward the newly-arrived Romans.

'Why aren't they coming?' asked one of the legionaries nearby.

Rufinus, his eyes still on the slope ahead, replied over his shoulder. 'They need open ground to operate. They couldn't attack us effectively down here.'

The cohort moved into the unnamed village. Signs of violent destruction were evident, though less gruesome than Rufinus had expected. Doors had been torn open and houses ransacked. Families' possessions lay strewn in the street, and a few bodies were visible among them, cut down. But some of the mess, both human and material, was clearly quite old. This village had been hit more than once by the raiders, and little had been left to loot this time. A few people had bothered reinhabiting it, and those intrepid folk had paid the price. With that knowledge, Rufinus suddenly realised that the villa had probably been looted weeks ago too. This was just an opportunistic strike by raiders who were running out of fresh targets. It struck Rufinus that, left alone for a little longer, the raiders would probably leave of their own accord. South and east the terrain became too mountainous and forested for cavalry, and north would bring them dangerously close to the legion's home fortress. Once they had run out of pickings here, and it seemed that was already the case, they would be left with little option but to return west to their own lands, or attempt to settle, as those at Sarmizegetusa had for all the good it had done them.

The tribune would not allow that, though. Quite apart from his superior's orders to take out these small pockets of Sarmatians, there was also now his personal fury at the desecration of a Roman villa. Once again there would be no quarter given. Images of flayed bodies popped into Rufinus' mind's eye.

The cohort crossed the timber bridge in the village, each man picking up the pace as he traversed the stream, horribly aware that it was at such choke-points that the worst of defeats occurred, hobnailed boots slipping and skittering on the soaked wood. Still, the Sarmatian horsemen remained atop the slope, the danger awaiting the cohort in open ground. As they passed between two long-empty houses and moved out into the field behind, where the slope began, reaching up toward the villa, Cassius called the orders for formation.

'Three columns of two centuries in five lines. Nicostratus, you have the left, Modestus the right. I have the centre. Wings, prepare for harrying cavalry, front ranks prepare for contra equitas at the first charge.'

Rufinus wondered how much of that had flown over the heads of the new recruits. Hopefully enough had stuck to make this a sensible fight. As they began to climb the lower edge of the slope, the column reformed so that three centuries marched to the front and three behind, each formed with five rows of sixteen men, giving an initial wall of forty eight shields to face the enemy. Rufinus found himself commanding the central force to the rear, with Daizus the last man in the column. The Sarmatians began to whoop and bellow now, and Tribune Celer, mounted safely at the centre of the cohort, frowned.

'There are fewer than I thought. This should not be too difficult.'

A low rumble announced the beginning of the onslaught. Rufinus had heard the thunder of hooves in a charge more than once in his time, and still found it as sphincter-loosening as the very first time. He listened as they moved slowly up the slope, feet slipping on the soaked turf and wet mud, trying to estimate distance, and suddenly Rufinus found himself far away in both place and time, above the Danuvius in Pannonia a decade ago, waiting for the first crash of the horsemen hitting his century. He'd been a new recruit, not much more experienced than these men, and had stood in the second line, listening to the thunder orf horses, dreading what was to come, in a cold sweat and with fear prickling his skin.

He blinked, his reveries swept away as Tribune Celer bellowed the order for contra equitas, echoed by the front three centurions. Those on either side of Rufinus at the rear simply gave the order to halt, knowing that five rows of men in front with a wide shield wall would take the blow from the riders' charge.

But Rufinus knew differently now. He remembered that battle in Pannonia all those years ago. Thank all the gods for the memory of that battle.

'Rear ranks turn. Form contra equitas!'

The surprise around him was palpable. The other two rear centurions said nothing, their men standing still, dithering uncertainly.

'*Do it*,' bellowed Rufinus.

Even Daizus snapped into action at the urgency and blatant power of command in Rufinus' voice, and the other two centurions were suddenly repeating his command.

Everything happened at once, then. The Iazyges' lances hit the contra equitas formation. The legionaries under Cassius' expert guidance were packed tight behind shields, second line bracing the first, all the front three ranks with pila held firm like an iron hedge above the shields. Most riders shied away before such a sight, and even if the riders continued a suicidal charge into the deadly points, their horses would generally refuse. The Sarmatians, though, were horse people, bred in the saddle and they knew both their own capability and predictable Roman tactics. Their lances were long enough that even before the horses halted just outside the range of the pila, they managed to drive home blows into the men behind the shields. The effect was impressive in its horror. Legionaries died in the press, some of the lances punching even through shields and into the men behind them, such was their strength and momentum. But with Cassius' dense formation, the line held even despite the deaths, and the Iazyges were denied the results

129

of a successful charge. Had they managed to break the shield wall, they would now be in among the soldiers, chopping and hewing with their swords. Instead, they were snarling and fighting desperately over the Roman shields, more riders dying than infantry.

Rufinus, of course, could pay precious little attention to what was going on at the front. He had his own trouble. Just as he'd expected from his memory of the battle in Pannonia a decade ago, a second wave of riders had appeared from the flank. While the cohort had been in the village, concentrating on crossing the stream, a group of riders had peeled off and skirted the open area wide, ready to fall on the unprepared rear of the Roman formation.

They charged up the gentle slope as the rear centuries were still struggling to fall into formation.

'Quickly!' bellowed Rufinus.

The second attack hit them even while the first was being hard fought at the front line. The riders charged up the gentle incline, churning the wet turf, and hit the rear centuries before they were fully braced. The only thing that saved the Romans was a simple matter of angles. The attackers were charging uphill, and consequently their lances were at shield height for the defenders and the momentum slightly less than their cousins up the slope. A few lances pierced shields and drew screams from dying and wounded legionaries behind, but many were turned and rendered ineffective.

Rufinus, in the press, caught the eye of one of his fellow centurions along the line, who nodded his thanks for the timely warning. Had Rufinus not predicted the second prong of the attack, the Sarmatians would have butchered many soldiers and now be among them, hacking the centuries to pieces. It was odd for the centurions to be at the rear of the fight because of the change in direction, and for the optios to be leading the fray, but there was little anyone could do about it now.

The initial charge spent, the Sarmatians, mostly armoured light in furs and leather, a few in chain or scale, abandoned their lances and drew straight, ring-pommelled blades, laying into the cohort in a frenzied melee, their wild hair and even wilder beards slapping around wetly in the rain. The legionaries fought back, jabbing and lunging rather inexpertly with their pila until the weapons became bent and useless, then drawing their own swords and joining the struggle.

Rufinus felt a momentary pride and confidence. He had worried unduly about his largely untested men. Yes, they had been rather slow at gathering into formation, and that had cost them a few lives. Yes, they needed a lot more training before those pila found good targets among the enemy. But they had survived a Sarmatian charge and were giving as good as they got now. And at the most brutal level of strategy, it occurred to Rufinus that there were only a hundred a fifty or so of them. Even if every death was reciprocated, they outnumbered the enemy enough to be fairly sure of victory. An unpleasant calculation to make, but a necessary one.

Disaster came in the form of a rider simply chancing his luck. Some unseen Sarmatian in the press lifted his arm, still bearing his lance, and threw it like a javelin. Given the length and weight of the thing he must have had arms like Hercules, for the great missile arced up and over the shield wall, deep into the Roman lines. Rufinus saw it coming at the last moment and experienced a moment of frozen panic that he was a dead man, but the missile dropped at the end, its momentum spent, and plunged deep into the man in front of Rufinus. The tip of the weapon punched through the legionary's torso, ripping out through his back and sending shreds of chain and leather everywhere, plunging into the turf so close to Rufinus that it rook a sliver of leather from his left boot.

The result was catastrophic and entirely chance-driven. The impaled, screaming man fell, sword lost, reaching fingers clawing for his mates. As he went down, so did the men to either side, and the man in front, legs swept out from beneath him, plunged forward too. The pressure of falling men, combined with the immense slipperiness of the wet slope played its dreadful part and a whole slew of legionaries collapsed to the turf. As the falling reached the front line, and the men facing the riders collapsed, so the horsemen, whooping, took advantage and rode over the fallen legionaries, in among the century. Their swords rose and fell and the men fought back desperately. Rufinus found himself being pushed forward as Cassius' century still fought hard up the slope, and he leapt forth, skidding and slipping on the grass, planting his feet between men struggling to stand, until he reached the first horseman. His sword ripped out with precision – this was about regaining control, not clean kills. The blade cut neither horse nor man, but leather strap, tearing through the girth. The saddle this Sarmatian used was very similar in style to the Roman 'horned' variety, and Rufinus knew just how unstable it could be unless strapped properly into place. He remembered slipping from his horse on that fatal hunt in Hispania, all because he'd not done up his girth strap properly…

The result was predictably satisfying. The Sarmatian, with a strangely high pitched squawk, tipped from the horse, gravity pulling him down to the side he was leaning with the sword. With a roar of triumph, those men still struggling to their feet began to lay into the fallen warrior. Some bright spark further forward had obviously seen what Rufinus had done and repeated the procedure on the next rider, sending him down into the mess, though taking a sword in the back as he did so. Rufinus pushed his way toward the front past confused and directionless horses, legionaries struggling back to their feet, and trampled bodies. As he reached the main bulk of the fighting, he caught a sword blow and turned it, shoulder-barging the dismounted rider and preparing to deal with him, only to see another legionary's sword slam into the man.

They were back in control and gaining the upper hand now. The gap in the line closed, men back up on their feet and two confused horses moving through the press. Rufinus found himself among the beleaguered front line, turning blades, ducking swipes and lancing out where he could at man or horse in an attempt to bring both down. At one point during the struggle, he found himself face to face with Daizus and actually suspected that the optio was going to lunge at him. Then, at the last moment, the man turned and stabbed a nearby horse. Rufinus joined in, and together they brought down horse and rider.

The blow that ended Rufinus' battle came entirely unseen. Something struck the back of his helmet in the middle of the fray and the sheer power drove his wits from him in the blink of an eye. The din of battle receded and all he could hear was a whiny ringing. His eyesight blurred, and he fell. He could see Daizus in front of him, still struggling with another rider, and in desperation he reached out to the optio, both he and Daizus falling now, collapsing to the wet turf. Rufinus' head felt as though he'd pushed it through a pin hole.

He knew he was slipping into unconsciousness. The black came to claim him, and as he and Daizus flailed on the floor, he on his way out while the optio struggled to regain his feet and rejoin the fight, something fascinating struck Rufinus. He just hoped he would remember it later. And that there would be a later for him to remember it in.

Rufinus awoke in utter confusion. For a moment he experienced a real panic that he had gone blind, but then he started to pick out muted details. He was in a room in the dark. He could discern the shutters of a window, though the very dim silvery glow suggested that it was dark outside too. The room smelled of olives and spiced food.

His head hurt. A lot. He tried to turn slightly on the bed and the movement almost made him throw up. He felt around the back of his head. His hair was matted and there was a spot that spent waves of agony through him and stars across his vision when he touched it. He slumped back and groaned.

A door opened. He couldn't see it, but he heard it well enough, now that the ringing had gone.

'Gnaeus?'

Relief. Utter relief. 'Senova. Where am I?'

'In the former procurator's house in Ulpia Traiana,' she replied softly. 'Wait.'

There were busy noises and soon two oils lamps sprang into life, illuminating the room in a warm, comfortable golden glow. The place was well-appointed and wealthy as would befit the man who used to live here, when the city was the capital and its owner was the second most powerful man in the province.

'My head.'

'Yes. The medicus said there was no permanent physical damage he could find. As long as you woke up coherent, he said you should be back on your feet tomorrow and fighting fit a day or two later. The tribune wanted to keep you in the town's hospital, where you could be constantly observed, but it was the medicus' opinion that you would be better off in comfortable seclusion. The leader of the town's ordo offered you his guest room, what with you being a hero.'

'Hero?' he managed groggily.

'Your men carried you back on a stretcher so you didn't get bumped in a cart. It seems the general consensus is that you saved the rear centuries from disaster twice. You might even have stopped them losing the battle.'

Bumped. His men. Yes. 'We won?'

'Yes. I haven't heard much about casualties and the like, but it seems you won decisively. About forty Sarmatians were brought back in ropes and sold to the slavers in town. One of your legionaries is waiting outside the door, even in the rain, to find out if you're well. I shall have to tell him to pass on the good word.'

'Where is Daizus?'

Senova frowned. 'I last saw him with Tribune Celer. The tribune was invited to a victory banquet with the town's ordo.'

Daizus and the tribune? There could be no good reason for that pairing. 'The boot was his.'

'Daizus?'

Rufinus nodded. 'I saw it in the fight. His boot has that triangular leather patch that matches the footprints outside the house at Sarmizegetusa. It was him who was listening outside. I sort of suspected that, anyway. But now I know. Daizus knows that I'm here with orders to spy on Albinus and Niger. And if he's busy with the tribune, I think we can assume that the tribune now knows. And that means that as soon as we get to Apulum, so will Clodius Albinus. My whole mission, such as it is, is teetering on the edge. A man I hate expects results. A man I was sent to investigate believes me to work for the man I hate. I would dearly love to try and bring Albinus and Niger into my confidence and try to recruit them into my side of the game, but that is starting to look increasingly unlikely, thanks to Daizus and his wagging ears.'

Senova placed a soothing hand on his forehead. 'Stop worrying about it. There's nothing you can do about it now. Soon we'll be in Apulum, and what will be, will be.'

Rufinus nodded slightly, and the activity made him feel ill again. Rest. He couldn't afford to be out for two days. He had to be fighting fit tomorrow. In this province, anything could happen.

X – Blood and gold

Micia was not beleaguered as the tribune had apparently been led to believe. The cohort had expected to arrive to find the fort and its small civil settlement under Sarmatian occupation as Sarmizegetusa had been, and none of them had relished the thought of what that meant: attacking a Roman fort with all its excellent defensive measures. Even manned by out of place Sarmatians, it would be a tough proposition, with a high cost in men. In the event, though, Micia was safe.

The cohort had travelled back east from Ulpia Traiana for a short distance, then northward along a wide basin between the mountains, ending their first day at the small spa town of Aquae. Oddly, given that the place lay firmly at the centre of the troubled region, with Sarmizegetusa a day to the east, Ulpia Traiana the same to the south-west and Micia a day north-west, the small spa town had managed to remain completely untouched and undisturbed by raiders since the initial push had been driven back by the Thirteenth. It struck Rufinus as odd to see life going on peacefully and prosperously here, while around it lay occupied fortresses, burned out villages and bands of vicious Iazyges. It was a welcome stop, particularly given that the weather had improved immeasurably and, despite a couple of bursts of drizzle during the morning, the sun had come out in due course and begun to dry and warm the land. The chance to rest in comfort and use the baths in rotation was greeted warmly by the men, and Rufinus, who had ridden in Senova's carriage all day at the insistence of the medical staff, was quite grateful for a civilised rest for the evening.

By the next morning, he was already feeling a lot better, as long as he didn't probe the back of his head too carelessly, for it was still painful to the touch. But the sickness and dizziness was gone, and he ate a hearty breakfast before the cohort moved on, waving aside medical protests and marching with his century once more. He had enjoyed the company of Senova the previous day, but leaving his men for too long solely in the company of Optio Daizus could have catastrophic effects on their outlook.

Still, he was less worried about Senova's safety now. Daizus may still be trouble, and the tribune he was unsure of, but the men of his century had become firmly his near Ulpia Traiana, and he was now sure they would never move against the lady in the carriage. In fact, he felt secure enough with her safety that Acheron now padded alongside him on the march.

The second day took them north across that flat basin and then, when they reached the wide and powerful Marisus River, they followed it downstream into a wide valley between misty blue mountains. All day as they travelled the temperature rose, the last tatters of high white cloud in the sky tearing apart and dissipating, leaving a hot cohort of sweating men and rising white dust beneath hundreds of tramping feet, the tempting cool waters of the great river running close by.

Micia was, it appeared, thriving. Rufinus greeted the sight of the place with some surprise. The way Celer and the other veterans spoke of it, it had sounded like a military frontier fort, guarding one of the main routes into Dacia from Iazyges lands along the Marisus River. But it was clearly much more than that. The fort itself was a large example, stretching from the river across the valley in a more elongated shape than usual. The civilian settlement, bordered along two sides by the fort and the river, was perhaps a quarter of a mile across, and was far from the rough stone and timber constructions of the temporary settlements usually found around frontier forts. Micia was a prosperous place in its own civil right, adorned with several large buildings, bath houses, an amphitheatre and temples, red roofs rising from walls of brick and stone, plastered and whitewashed. A port on the riverbank seemed extremely busy.

Moreover the streets were filled with locals going about their daily business, much as they had found at Aquae but, all the more surprisingly, since Micia had been one of the cohort's targets to deal with pockets of Sarmatian resistance. The column marched to the edge of the town, down by the river, and was set there making camp while the tribune took his staff and his two veteran centurions through the town and to the fort.

News of the cohort's arrival had clearly filtered through the town quickly for, as the small party of officers approached the fort's east gate, the doors were already open and a man in a senior officer's uniform stood in the archway with a centurion and a couple of his men. The wall top was dotted with soldiers in gleaming bronze scale armour, pointed helmets and bows slung over their shoulder. Rufinus and the others straightened slightly, automatically trying to make the best impression, given that they were the elite soldiers in this region, visiting an auxiliary installation. Acheron padded to a halt by Rufinus's side, drawing anxious looks from some of the soldiers.

Micia was neat and well-maintained, and its occupants seemed much the same.

'Prefect Marcus Cornelius Stratonicus, Second Flavia Commagenorum, commanding Micia,' the officer announced in strong tones.

'Senior Tribune Appius Iulius Celer, Thirteenth Gemina Legion, Prefect. Good to meet you.'

The two men shook hands, and Rufinus had to suppress a smile as he watched the pair attempting to squeeze the life out of each other, each determined to demonstrate the strongest hand shake. Finally, as if by mutual acceptance of defeat, they let go, both clasping hands behind their backs.

'I was led to believe that a group of Sarmatian raiders was at work in this area, Prefect. The governor assigned my cohort to suppress the troubles.'

Stratonicus made a *pfft* noise, which seemed to irritate Celer. 'There have been raiders in this area, but they now keep to the hills north of here. Once or twice they have ventured close to Micia, but the Second Flavia could put out a sparrow's eye with a single arrow. They soon learned not to bother the *Pagus Miciensis*. There were a little more than a hundred of them when they first came, and we killed a quarter of their number without leaving the walls.'

'So you have done nothing to bring them to heel?' asked Celer, acidly.

'Our task is to guard the Marisus valley and keep control of the Pagus Miciensis, not to hunt rag-tag bands of Iazyges in the hills, Tribune. Should we commit to such an action, we would be forced to leave the valley undefended and abandon the reason for our assignment here in the first place.'

The two men were engaged in a game of one-upping each other, and Rufinus would like nothing more than to interrupt them and move the conversation on, but could see no way to do it without stirring up further trouble.

'And you did not think it worthwhile to detach a unit to deal with them?' Celer asked.

'Archers make very good defenders, Tribune. Put my men on a tower and no barbarian will come within spear-cast. But archers are hardly suited to scouring the mountains and overcoming cavalry. That would be a job for legionaries, I would say.'

Celer bristled.

'Clearly not for a group of auxiliaries. True.'

A cloud of seething resentment boiled between the two men for a while until Cassius coughed politely. 'Perhaps, Prefect, you could give us the latest intelligence you have on the raiders?'

Without tearing his hawk-like gaze from the tribune, Stratonicus nodded. 'I believe they are operating in the valley up near Fassus, around five miles north of the river. They seem to be quite happy there, picking on the occasional gold wagon and lining their pockets.'

Celer almost exploded. 'They are harrying the gold shipments and you're doing nothing about it?'

Again, Stratonicus shrugged nonchalantly. 'Gold shipments are not our problem. The mines are all privately owned, and they pay for their own guards. I'm not about to put my men at risk to help some fat oligarch from Rome pay for an extra statue in his atrium.'

The tribune was making faintly strangled noises. Without warning, his arm shot out, his grip closing on the prefect's windpipe, nails digging into the flesh. Stratonicus' eyes bulged in shock and he gasped.

'Listen to me you provincial piece of shit,' the tribune hissed, pushing the man backward, still gripping his throat. The auxiliary centurion and his men looked startled, halfway between leaping to their prefect's defence and backing away deferentially. A senior legionary tribune was not a man to cross without good reason, after all. 'You take your little eastern archer boys and shut yourself up in that fort. I will take my men and remove the local threat, secure the gold routes, and then return tomorrow. When I do, I heartily recommend that you be absent on some trivial matter, for if I lay eyes on you again, I might just do this again and keep squeezing until my fingers meet.'

He let go of Stratonicus and the prefect fell back, gasping. Without another word, Celer turned to his two veteran centurions. 'Stop the men making camp. We can cover five miles and deal with these rats before dark, then make camp near this Fassus place. Go.'

Rufinus shared a look with Cassius, and the two centurions saluted and turned, jogging off with their half dozen legionaries back to the camp site. As he left, Rufinus glanced over his shoulder long enough to see Celer standing with his hand on his sword hilt, and wondered momentarily whether the tribune might actually draw it and maim another senior officer.

An hour later, the cohort were across the river, having commandeered sufficient boats from the dock for the purpose. The tribune had rejoined them at some point during the crossing with a look of vicious satisfaction, and again Rufinus wondered whether he'd been tempted to draw blood. The wagons and support, including Senova's carriage, had been left at Micia with a single century of men to guard them. It seemed the tribune did not trust the local garrison even to do that effectively.

Still, the cohort was moving off into the hills before long, the sun now beginning to slide from the sky. Rufinus was a little concerned that the tribune had been driven to making an impetuous decision. It seemed foolish to be marching into the unknown to face an enemy while the sun began its descent, leaving a very real possibility of camping in a dark valley filled with unseen foes. At least Senova was safe in Micia. He recalled suddenly the words of Cassius back in Sarmizegetusa, when the centurion had voiced the worry that Celer might make rash decisions and cause trouble if unchecked. Rufinus was beginning to see Cassius' point.

The valley to which the tribune directed them followed a small, winding river north, passing repeatedly through gaps between spurs of hills and each time opening out into wide flat basins. The going was easy, and there were signs that this valley was used to regular traffic. The rough road they followed showed traces of wheel ruts from many wagons, and horse manure, old and dry, lay here and there. The small river became gradually narrower until it was little more than a stream. They passed half a dozen small hamlets, each engaged in arable farming, and enquired of news of the raiders at each place. It seemed the prefect had been quite right. The locals confirmed that the Sarmatians were operating near this Fassus place, and were far more concerned with the gold trail than bothering with poor Dacian villages, which suited the locals fine.

The sun had just vanished behind the western ridges when the cohort came to Fassus, the light beginning to acquire that indigo tone of early evening. Just as the farmers in the last village had said, Fassus was little more than a junction and a market place with a few houses. It sat upon the eastern slope of the valley, where a small side vale branched off. The main road along the valley there met another smaller track coming from the east, both roads converging and bringing gold shipments through Fassus to continue south to Micia and the Marisus River.

Mute evidence of the regular raids was visible on the cohort's approach. Half a dozen wagons sat idle at the edge of the village, their gleaming burdens gone, their beasts detached and drivers and guards also gone, presumably dead. There was no sign of natives. No sign of life at all, in fact.

As the cohort moved into the tiny village, Celer dispatched north and east his scouts, who had been kept close throughout much of the journey. There was no doubt that this place had played host to the Iazyges raiders for some time. Of the natives or the wagon crews there was no sign, but the houses were being lived in by men who treated them as little more than temporary hovels, littering, ravaging, and urinating in the corner, judging by the ammonia smell emerging from each doorway.

The two places that *had* been well-maintained were a large corral and a single shed with a huge, impressive lock. As the centuries were moved into position in the village, Rufinus and Cassius smashed the lock and threw open the shed. Its contents made Rufinus' breath catch in his throat. Inside were twelve small chests, one open and displaying its innards. There was enough gold in this one shed to pay the cohort until retirement day.

Rufinus and Cassius examined the ingots. They each bore two stamps – one the mark of the mine and its owner, one Nymphidius Barus, and the other the stamp of the Dacian procurator, signifying that this gold was now owned by the state and bound for the imperial coffers.

'How does this gold mining system work?' Rufinus mused, turning over one of the ingots, feeling a thrill of excitement.

'The mine owners are concessions,' Cassius replied. 'They come from Rome or from the greater cities and buy the right to mine off the state. The gold and the land belong to Rome, but the mine belongs to the individual. The state acquires the mined gold, but the owners take a share, making their fortune in the process. The mines here are small and generally poor. This must represent half a year's work, I suspect. Wait until you see Alburnus Maior. That's the centre of mining, and the hub for two major transport routes.'

'This is a *small* amount?' Rufinus whispered.

Cassius laughed. 'You think Rome came to Dacia for the weather?'

Further conversation was impossible, for suddenly the cadence of the cornu honked outside, calling the cohort to arms. Rufinus and Cassius dropped the gold, jammed on their helmets and hurried back outside, pausing only to shut the door. As they hurried into the square, where Celer and his musician stood with two clerks, Rufinus could see the distant figures of horsemen along the valley, racing toward them.

'It appears we have taken their base from them while they were out raiding,' the tribune said with a great deal of satisfaction. 'We have their gold?'

Rufinus and Cassius nodded. 'Plenty of it, all in the shed.'

'Good. They will have to come against us, else they lose all their loot. And we have the advantage of a good defensive position. There are three main approaches to the village. Each will be garrisoned by one century of men, while you two, First and Third centuries, will guard the gold store. Do not let the Sarmatians in. If they re-acquire their gold and manage to get it out, then they can run and we may never catch them.'

Saluting, Rufinus and Cassius dashed off toward their men, conferring as they went, Acheron pounding along at the younger man's heel. As they reached the two centuries, Cassius, being the senior, addressed them hurriedly.

'Our task is to protect the shed containing the imperial gold shipments. The First will take the northern side and the Third the southern, meeting at the front and rear of the shed. Three lines deep. No throwing of pila. You will need them against horsemen. Now, move.'

Cassius' men hurtled off to the north side of the great shed and he carefully placed his men so that they covered half of the building in a triple-lined arc. Rufinus did the same at the southern side, the two centuries meeting seamlessly and forming a solid cordon around the important shed at the edge of the settlement.

Rufinus settled his musician and standard bearer safely at the rear of the ranks, by the door of the shed. Losing the standard was unthinkable dishonour, but if the enemy reached those doors it would mean the century were all dead anyway. He positioned himself at the shed's southern side, in the front line, Daizus around the corner at the shed's rear.

They had been in place mere moments before it began. The sounds of battle echoed across the village and round the valley, bouncing off the slopes and sounding ever more impressive. Horses burst into sight, racing not for the legionaries in a frontal charge, but in a great circle around the entire village, shed included. Their reason became clear very quickly. At least half the riders had discarded their lances before reaching the village, drawing their bows.

'Shields up. Watch for arrows,' Rufinus shouted, just as the mounted archers began to release.

The Iazyges may have been barbarians, but Rufinus had to admire their skill. He was a reasonable horseman himself, despite his life now being spent in the infantry. He had ridden the family's estate in Hispania and hunted and even practiced fighting from horseback before joining the Tenth. But these men were true instinctive horsemen. Born in the saddle, it seemed. They steered the beasts with knees alone, despite having to maintain the arc of their path and their place among the force, both of their arms being employed with the bows, which they held steady and leaned, turning to loose their arrows rearwards in the famed manner of the Parthians. They kept their mounts moving well, yet managed to release arrows swiftly and with a good eye. Despite the large body shields the Romans held and their defensive position, arrows bit into flesh here and there and men shrieked. Rufinus watched his shieldwall fall apart in three places, quickly repaired with men from rear rows, but they were taking casualties fast, while unable to touch the enemy as they raced past.

They had to make some kind of move, or they would all fall to the arrows without bloodying a sword. With a start, he heard Daizus' voice close behind. Damn the man, he was supposed to be in position at the shed's end.

'We've got to do something, Rufinus.'

The young centurion's nerves prickled at the optio's lack of respect for his rank, simply calling him by name. But the man was right. If they didn't do something, they were going to lose to a force just a quarter of their size.

'Front rank, ready pila. Mark your men and those your neighbours are marking. Make every pilum count. If you can, mark an archer.'

'You'll leave us defenceless against a charge,' Daizus yelled, echoing Cassius' initial instructions.

'Corpses can't make good use of a pilum,' Rufinus snarled in reply. 'Ready... mark... throw.'

They weren't good. Despite two engagements and several weeks' practice at Drobeta, it was clear the men were still novices. The pila did not arc up gracefully and fall in a deadly rain as Rufinus had seen happen against the Marcomanni. Here they flew in a dozen different angles, some knocking into each other, one or two spinning in the air so that they fell harmlessly, sideways.

But some hit. Eight of the attackers fell, two of the riders pierced by the missiles, six others striking the horses. It was neither pleasant, not elegant, but it *was* effective.

'Pass pila forward.'

The second rank handed their missiles to the men in front, and Rufinus gave the order to throw once again, half a dozen more riders falling to the shafts. He could hear the same commands being given by Cassius on the far side of the shed now. They must have taken out a third of the riders, and the circling force had definitely thinned out. It was tempting to launch a third volley, but they did need to keep enough pila for the front row, and they were now passed forward at his command, held forth defensively.

A distant roar from numerous voices in Latin suggested that something important was happening across the village. A moment later there was a break in the racing horsemen. Those who had just passed were wheeling their mounts and preparing to ride either back the way they came, or directly at the Roman defenders. The men in the village must have fully engaged the enemy, then. Time to do the same.

'Prepare to charge in open formation.'

The men around him set their shields, front rank with pila held out, the others now with drawn swords.

'Charge!'

The horsemen were racing toward the Romans now, though their whooping became more frantic and high pitched as they realised that the Romans were also charging them.

The legionaries and the Sarmatians met with a crash, a few of Rufinus' men falling beneath churning hooves, but most stepping out of the way thanks to the open formation and meeting the swords and spears of the riders with shields and weapons of their own. What happened then was much more satisfactory than the badly-thrown pila. The swords of the soldiers lanced out again and again, never bothering to try and pick off the riders, each going to work on the horses, bringing the beasts down as swiftly as possible. There were, by Rufinus' estimate, only a dozen riders facing his fifty or so men, his century having been regularly depleted during their skirmishes. Rufinus watched with grim satisfaction as each and every horse was brought down, its rider hacked to pieces on the ground, wailing in agony. The men were remorseless, and Rufinus saw one legionary with a Sarmatian arrow jutting from his thigh, cursing the barbarians as he delivered his revenge blow by blow against a pulped rider who was clearly already dead.

They had won. And they had won swiftly and decisively, with few losses. That was it. Their mission to deal with the surviving pockets of raiders was complete.

Rufinus let out a sudden strangled gasp as he felt something smash into his back, the blow sending him staggering forward. He reeled, struggling, turning, a numbing pain racing down his left arm. Whatever it was had sent shattered chain links falling to the floor and had seriously bruised him on the left shoulder blade. He gasped again as he turned.

Daizus was standing there was a look of sheer malice. His sword was unbloodied, but the blade unsheathed and gripped tight.

The bastard.

Before Rufinus could do anything, Acheron was there, his jaws closing on Daizus' left leg. The optio howled in agony and tried to pull the limb free. He made to use his sword against the beast savaging his leg, and Rufinus leapt, his own blade knocking his deputy's aside.

'Back down,' he barked, then, without taking his eyes off the optio, 'Acheron, heel!'

For a moment, it looked like Daizus might actually strike again, and that Acheron intended to bite right through the leg – the latter would not surprise him at all – but at the last moment the dog released his grip and trotted behind Rufinus, who stood shaking with rage. Daizus staggered, his leg slick with blood, a great rent in his shin and calf that would require stitching.

'Your bastard dog,' snarled the optio.

'He was protecting me from you, you treacherous piece of shit,' Rufinus snapped in reply.

The two men stood glowering at one another, swords still in hand, both gripping the hilt tight and huffing.

'What the fuck is this?' Cassius shouted, appearing from nowhere. Rufinus took a deep breath, preparing to accuse his enemy of the worst sort of betrayal, but another voice stopped him, cutting through the tense silence.

'Sheathe those blades,' roared Tribune Celer.

Rufinus did so immediately, Daizus a heartbeat later. Their gazes remained loaded with daggers.

'What is the *meaning* of this?' Celer bellowed.

'His dog mauled me, sir,' Daizus said, making sure all present heard him quite clearly.

'I knew that savage thing should have been put down,' snapped the tribune.

'Respectfully, sir,' Rufinus objected, 'Acheron was protecting me, since Daizus here tried to plant his blade in my back during the fight.'

The optio suddenly acquired an expression of injured innocence. 'That is the most slanderous lie, Tribune. I am an officer in the Roman army, not some gutter assassin.'

Rufinus turned, using his right hand to indicate the shredded chain and scored leather on his shoulder. 'This is your evidence, sir.'

'A Sarmatian sword,' snorted Daizus. 'Tribune, the centurion has never liked me, and repeatedly attempts to belittle and offend me. Now he sinks to trying to accuse me of seditious offences.'

Rufinus felt cold fury settling in him. 'Listen, Daizus, I have just about had enough of...'

'Silence,' bellowed the tribune. 'Did anyone see this blow of which the centurion speaks?'

No voices rose in Rufinus' defence. He looked around the gathered faces of his men. They had finally become truly his men at the villa fight near Ulpia Traiana, yet not one opened his mouth now. Most appeared entirely open and innocently silent. After all, it had been in the midst of a furious fight, and all attention would have been focused on the falling horsemen, not on the deputy officer at the rear. The others who were not in the fight – the musician and standard bearer – had been around the corner at the door of the shed out of sight. From a few downcast faces, though, Rufinus realised what was happening. A few of the men perhaps *had* seen, but the tribune's expression suggested he had already condemned Rufinus, and the man hated Acheron and all dogs. None of Rufinus' men, no matter how much respect he had earned, was going to speak up in his defence now.

'I see I am to be betrayed not only by my optio, but by my men too,' he said, loudly and in an accusatory tone that made more gazes drop to the ground. There was a long silence.

'Tribune,' Daizus said, 'I need to see the capsarius, but I would request my centurion be arrested, detained and tried for this obscenity.'

Celer was regarding the pair of them with a cold expression. Rufinus saw in the blink of an eye something pass between the two men – a nod of assent and agreement made only with the eyes. Damn it, but he should have known, when Senova said she'd seen Daizus with the tribune. The optio had told Celer everything he knew, and now Celer believed Rufinus – legitimately so, unfortunately – to be a spy for the imperial chamberlain. There was no way Rufinus was coming out of this well.

'The evidence seems to support your optio's words,' Celer said flatly. 'Your animal savaged him for an offence you claim but which has left at best circumstantial evidence and no witnesses. Given the nature of your master in Rome and your detached duty here, Rufinus, I do not have the authority to deal fully with you. However, an incident like this cannot simply be washed over. You are hereby removed from command and all duties within the Thirteenth. You will hand over your crest and vitus. You will remain with the column until we reach Apulum, where the matter will be decided by Governor Albinus, who *does* have appropriate authority to pass judgement. Now get out of my sight.'

Rufinus, shaking with barely-suppressed rage, glare still locked on the feigned innocence of Daizus, swept off his helmet, unfastened the crest and removed it, pulling his vine stick from his belt and handing them both to the clerk who stood close to Celer's side.

That had to be the shortest recorded centurionate.

Damn it, but Daizus had won in the end.

XI – Revelation in seclusion

Rufinus travelled now in the carriage with Senova and Acheron.

Following the dreadful incident at Fassus no one had spoken to him. He had been assigned one of the urine-soaked, stinking huts for the night and had made his miserable bed in it. He'd looked outside the door but there had been no guards, and that was hardly a surprise. It would make life easier for all of them if he wasn't there. The troublesome spy from the capital. The next morning the cohort had packed up and marched back to Micia before breaking their fast, doing so before the walls of the auxiliary fort. The argumentative prefect of the place was conspicuous in his absence, which came as no surprise, given Tribune Celer's threat. Rufinus had absolutely no doubt the man would carry it through, too. They had finished their morning repast and then collected the wagons and the carriage and spare horses, then moved on, back upstream to the east, on the main road to Apulum.

As they travelled, Rufinus felt keenly the absence of Cassius, to whom he had turned throughout his time in Dacia not only for sensible opinions, but also for knowledge. No man seemed to have the local knowledge of the province that the centurion had displayed. Rufinus had wondered why this road was such a major highway, when its westward terminus had to be the border and Iazygean territory, and had lamented being unable to quiz Cassius. It had been Senova who had clarified that in the end.

'Gold.'

'What?'

'Gold. The Marisus is one of the largest rivers in Dacia and a good, navigable one. Small gold mining communities, like the one you went to, ship their gold down to places like Micia

151

and it is taken upriver to the capital. And the real bulk of gold comes down from the heart of the mountains over two routes, down the Ampelum valley and to Blandiana on this river. The road is here because of the river. It's the river that's more important.'

Rufinus frowned. 'How do *you* know these things?'

Senova rolled her eyes. 'You were gone chasing brigands for half a day, Gnaeus. What do you think I do when you're not around? Moon about reading poetry and coiling my hair like a Roman matron?'

No, thought Rufinus. *Not at all, You consort with hairy locals in dangerous stinking drinking pits, don't you?* But he wouldn't voice his opinion on that matter for fear of earning frosty silence. Senova the quiet, careful slave girl… gone but not forgotten…

'I spent the evening talking to the locals at Micia.'

'You should not go in to town on your own.'

'I am not a wet girl, Gnaeus.'

'Well, no. But still.'

'And I had Luca.'

'Well that's fine, then. A seven year old with a wobbly lip and a runny nose will scare a dozen violent Dacians into line, I'm sure.'

There was a dangerous silence.

'How will you make this right?' she asked suddenly, changing the direction of the conversation at a hair-raising tangent as she was wont to do. Rufinus adjusted his brain to the new conversational angle as quickly as he could. Senova gave him headaches in a way poppy juice or wine never could.

'I don't know,' he admitted. 'The tribune cannot do anything to me, even with Daizus snapping at his heels for a death sentence. And I suspect that Clodius Albinus will be even more circumspect in his approach. He may not like me or the reason I'm here, and he might hate Cleander – probably does, but even then he will not wish to draw the chamberlain's attention and anger, especially if he *is* up to something. I think

I will walk away from it safely, but I also think completing any level of my mission here for Cleander is going to be just about impossible now, with enemies and suspicion surrounding me.'

'Cassius is your friend.'

Was he?

'Cassius has not been to see me since the incident. Not even exchanged words. I think – I hope – that he is not angry or disappointed, but that he is protecting himself. If I am to be labelled Cleander's man and reviled among the Thirteenth, then he cannot afford to be associated with me as he has thus far.'

They fell silent again, listening to the world going by outside the carriage. In addition to the endless rumbles, squeaks and groans of the carriage and the gentle snoring of Acheron in his cushions where, from the drool, he was probably dreaming of eating Daizus' leg entire, there was a vast symphony of sound from outside. The sun had become even warmer today, like the hotter days back in Hispania, sizzling the land brown and dry and making men sweat uncontrollably. Birds chirruped and bees buzzed, crickets rasped and animals rustled in the undergrowth. And above all half a thousand booted feet crunched on stone, men sang and horses nickered.

And Luca, up on the wagon's bench, whistled. Endlessly.

Rufinus had to smile. The boy had been a dour, downcast slave assigned to Senova by the legion, and in less than a month of Senovas's control he had become a bright and cheerful companion. As often as not Rufinus forgot he was a slave at all. Senova let him sleep in the tent or carriage, gave him plenty of blankets, made sure he was given the same food as her, and even spared the boy a few coppers for the markets when they were in towns for fun at the markets.

The day wore on and Rufinus and Senova relaxed somewhat. He passed the time by giving her a potted history of Rome from the days of Aeneas right down to the emperors, both good and bad. Often, she surprised him with her knowledge of the emperor upon which he expounded, only to be reminded that she had spent years in service to the heiress of the imperial line. Still, it was good to give her more of a grounding in what it meant to be Roman, and help ease those last strains of provincial roughness from her. Not that he'd tell her that, of course.

The cohort made good time, thanks to the flat, easy terrain, the good metalled road in an excellent state of repair and the dry, hot weather. Such good time, in fact, that they reached their next stopping point early, at the height of the afternoon rather than dusk as had been anticipated.

Germisara was more of the frontier post that Rufinus had been expecting of Micia. The fort itself, a strangely stretched complex on a ridge above the river, looked well-maintained, but distinctly more militaristic than the gleaming walls of Micia. Below the ridge lay a small civil settlement with a bath house and mansio, and a small dock on the river. Rufinus felt strangely at a loss as the cohort moved into position to encamp for the night on the wide grassy plain by the river, not concerned with fortifications given the presence of the garrison on the hill. The men were occupied, led by 'acting centurion' Daizus, setting up the camp. The tribune once more went to see the local commander, but this time took only Cassius with him, ignoring the fact that Rufinus was even there.

Overlooked and in virtual solitude, Rufinus and Senova took the carriage and made their way to the mansio, delivering the vehicle and both beasts to the stable slave there, while the four of them made for the main door of the building. Given that Celer had no authority over Senova, only dubious seniority over Rufinus given the disparity in their units, and seemed to have forgotten that he'd assigned Luca to them at all, they assumed they were free to do as they pleased, and Rufinus decided to dig into his purse for a good room for the night.

Reaching the mansio, he politely stepped forward and pulled open the door, gesturing for Senova to enter. The sound of conversation and a gentle reek of burning lamps, spicy food and body odour washed outwards. Senova opened her mouth, presumably to object to being the first to enter, but then a broad smile washed over her and she nodded and entered. Rufinus, frowning in confusion, followed her, letting Luca hold the door behind them for Acheron.

He stopped in the entrance, his brow folding even further as Senova threw her arms wide and announced something in a weird, guttural tongue he didn't recognise. There was a moment's silence, and then the man behind the bar and the two men in Roman auxiliary uniforms having a drink at the counter turned and grinned back at her, replying in the same language.

'What in Hades' name?'

Senova turned, her face beaming. 'These men are Brigantes, Gnaeus. *My* people!'

Excellent. Just great, thought Rufinus, sourly. Ostracised by his own people, forced to turn solely to Senova for conversation and instead she finds someone else to talk to that Rufinus could not understand.

'Can we speak Latin?' she said, as if reading his mind. 'My... man here is from Hispania and doesn't know civilised talk.'

The barman laughed. 'I hear the Hispanics speak some weird language that sounds like an ox farting.'

Rufinus could feel his face reddening. '*I. Am. Not. Hispanic.* I am Roman. I mean, I was *born* in Hispania, but...'

'Come, Master Hispanic but not Hispanic,' laughed one of the soldiers. 'Sit. Have wine.'

Rufinus contemplated saying no, but explaining his history with alcohol was hardly likely to endear him to these rough northern lunatics. He plastered his warmest smile across his face and followed Senova to the bar.

Acheron padded along behind him, with Luca at the dog's side, and Rufinus was impressed to note no reaction other than a raised eyebrow at the animal's presence. People were so often scared of Acheron that it seemed peculiar to Rufinus when they reacted calmly.

'Are dogs allowed in?' he asked, rather late.

The barman nodded. 'It'd be a pain if we didn't. The fort have a dozen like him for hunting bears.'

Rufinus blinked. They used dogs to hunt bears? What on earth went on in these people's heads. But then, he supposed, if you were going to set a dog on a bear, Rufinus couldn't picture a better breed to choose than Acheron's.

'What brings cultured men of Brigantia to this end of the world?' Senova asked, and Rufinus noted sourly how, after a year of listening to her Latin accent improve in good circles, it immediately dropped back into a thick, northern taint now that she was with these people. He tried not to dislike them. He failed a little.

'We serve here,' one of the soldiers said expansively, waving his arms. Germisara is home to the Numerus Singulariorum of Britannic Infantry. Bit of a mouthful.'

'As my wife keeps saying,' snorted the other infantryman.

'There are hundreds of Brigantes here?' Senova exclaimed with delight. Rufinus winced.

'Not quite,' admitted one of them. 'Most of them are local recruits these days. Marcus here, and me, we've been here fifteen years now. There are maybe forty lads from the island here, nine of them Brigantes.'

'Not me,' snorted the barman. 'I'm Parisi, from near Eboracum. We used to throw stones across the river at you lot when I was a kid. But I'm same unit, retired and now running this place.'

'So what's a good looking Brigante woman like you doing down here, and in the company of a beat up Hispanic soldier then?'

Please don't mention the praetorians, wished Rufinus fervently, not wanting to get on the wrong side of a fort full of hairy Britons.

'Detached duty, my man,' said Senova loftily. 'On his way to Apulum. We have a *carriage*,' she added somewhat unnecessarily in Rufinus' opinion.

'Ooh, get miss lah-de-dah in her carriage,' laughed one of them. Must be important your other half, is he?'

'Not really,' she said rather blandly. Rufinus had been silently urging her to downplay his position and now that she had, he felt oddly hurt that he had been so easily dismissed.

'Long way from your home,' Rufinus noted, cursing himself for his total lack of ability with small talk.

'Good posting, though,' the one called Marcus said. 'Better than Apulum or Micia.'

'Why's that?'

'Got every amenity, this place.'

Rufinus was about to ask what those amenities might possibly be when they door opened behind them, and a voice called his name.

'Rufinus? You here?'

He turned to see Cassius standing in the doorway. 'I'd not thought to speak to you again.'

'I had trouble finding you, but someone saw your dog.'

'Lucky it was Acheron, then. I gather he's far from the only one of his breed at Germisara. We thought it best to stay out of the way.'

'A long way out of the way,' Cassius nodded. 'Get your horse and meet me at the far side of the fort in a quarter of an hour.'

And with that he was gone. Rufinus stared at the door, which quickly rattled closed.

'Friends in high places, eh?' murmured one of the men. 'Legionary centurions, eh?'

'A friend,' replied Rufinus, and to Senova: 'you'd best come on.'

She turned with a frown. 'He never mentioned me. Just you and a horse.'

'I can't leave you alone.'

The men at the bar laughed. 'We'll look after her.'

That's half what I'm afraid of, thought Rufinus, but Senova was nodding. 'I've not heard my home tongue in years,

Gnaeus, and I'm going to be here chatting for a while. You toddle off and play with your centurion friend. Luca will look after me.'

Rufinus bit down on a reply that held scathing comments about the ability of slave boys to save headstrong women from a gang of hairy soldiers. Somehow, he knew that this was one of those arguments he simply was not going to win.

'Alright. I'll be back... I don't know. I'll be back when I'm back.'

'If I'm asleep, don't wake me.'

And with that he was dismissed. He stood for a moment feeling horribly out of place – a Hispanic-born Roman, listening to Britons in Dacia. However did he get into these messes? He bade a weak farewell to the three men, then to Senova and finally to Luca, feeling rather foolish showing such regard for a slave he didn't even own, then he strode from the room. He held the door for a long moment, looking meaningfully at Acheron, who dithered, undecided, but then followed him out into the late afternoon.

Around the back of the mansio he found the stables and retrieved Atalanta from a slave who was busily feeding her. He thanked the slave, then cursed himself for doing so, thanks to Senova's ongoing influence, mounted and rode her out and through the small settlement in the opposite direction to the legionary camp. It was still very pleasantly warm, and with the wide valley the sun was still well in evidence. Warily, watching for anyone who might be observing him suspiciously, he rode around the village and up the slope, around the corner of the fort. He finally spotted Cassius waiting for him by a small stand of trees and, urging Atalanta on and with Acheron close by, he trotted over to the centurion.

'What's all this about?'

'Hush. Ride with me.'

The centurion put his heels to the horse's flank, and started off down a narrow road heading off north along a smaller side valley. A good road led this way, well-trodden, so wherever they were bound, it was somewhere oft-visited. Rufinus followed, fascinated and worried in equal measure. Slowly the fort receded into the distance.

'Where are we going?' he asked finally, breaking the silence.

'I've a pass from the tribune to use the thermal complex nearby. It's about four miles away. Three now,' he corrected, looking back at the fort. 'I wanted to talk to you. Without prying ears around.'

Rufinus looked around in the late afternoon light. The sun was now sinking into the western hills, but it would be light for more than an hour yet. Maybe even two. Still, it would be dark when they returned, he presumed, so it must be important. At least out here, a mile from Germisara and in a wide, open, apparently uninhabited valley with not a soul to be seen, there was no chance of such 'prying ears'.

'What is it, Cassius?'

The centurion, riding alongside him, looked suddenly extremely doubtful. 'You were in the legions?' he said quietly.

'Yes. Tenth Gemina. You know that.'

'So you know all about oaths and loyalty. The *sacramentum* we all take. I am extremely uncomfortably spreading dangerous words about my commander.'

Albinus. Rufinus felt his nerves tighten. He urged the man to go on.

'This is not gossiping in the forum, Cassius. This is you and me. *Just* you and me.'

'And Cleander. I've never met the man, but everything they say about him is terrible. I don't like potentially selling out my commander to a man such as he, even if there is good reason.'

Good reason. Rufinus felt achievement thrilling through him at last. But he had to keep this going...

'Cassius, I was sent here by Cleander, but I'm a praetorian. I serve the interests of the emperor, and the emperor alone. It is because of potential threats to the divine Commodus I am here. And the only information I am interested in is just that. I don't *care* what Clodius Albinus thinks of Cleander. Frankly, he can't have a much lower opinion of him than I do. Cleander is a bag of shit. This is all about the emperor, and it is to him you took your oath. To him, Rome and the eagle, not to the governor.'

Cassius nodded slowly. He still looked unconvinced, but as Rufinus opened his mouth to speak again, the centurion held up a hand to stop him.

'I think it's about the gold, Rufinus.'

The gold. He felt his heart flutter again. He *would* have something. Something good to take back, which he might be able to barter for Publius' freedom. He waited. Pushing Cassius might just make him clam up.

'There were discrepancies,' the centurion said finally. 'In gold production at Alburnus Maior. I mean *big* ones. It's normal for a governor to rake off a little of the profits for his own gain, and I know that the administration overlooks it. That's one of the perks of being the governor. It's pretty much the only reason why nobles from Rome come out to Dacia in the first place. It's one of the most lucrative positions in the empire. But the discrepancies at Alburnus Maior went far beyond a little rake off.'

Rufinus felt his pulse quicken. Clodius Albinus was stealing from the treasury? In large quantities? That might just be enough, if he had some evidence.

'How do you know?' he asked. 'I mean, you're not in the administration, after all.'

Cassius looked a little embarrassed suddenly. 'I have a friend on the procurator's staff. He's ex-Thirteenth. One of my men who took a leg wound. Couldn't go on in active service, but he makes a damn good clerk, so he moved into the procurator's office but he's still on the legion payroll. The procurator had become aware of the mine discrepancies, you see, and word filtered down to me. Put me in a bit of an awkward position. The two most powerful men in Apulum. And I knew something I wasn't supposed to.'

'So how would I get access to the records?' asked Rufinus eagerly, earning a glance of warning from the centurion.

'You don't. That's the thing. The procurator set things in motion to open an investigation into the matter. He was all ready to move in, but then suddenly he fell very, very ill. Died the next morning. There's supposedly another procurator on his way to Dacia to take up the post, but I'd wager that any record of the proposed investigation has long gone from the office. And suddenly the governor was very interested in the soldiers working in the procurator's office. I've spent months now watching my back, waiting for the accusation. Somehow it seems my friend has been overlooked, maybe because he's still on legion lists and not the administrative staff, and my name has not come up, but I'm expecting it any time. And if you go and stir the pot up, not only will you probably wake up dead the next morning, but you might land me in the shit too.'

Rufinus shook his head. 'I can keep you out of it. Especially if you tell me who it is in the procurator's office that connects you. Then I can't even cause trouble accidentally.'

'No. The procurator's office is out of bounds for you, Rufinus. You'll have to find another way, but I'm not having you accidentally unearth something that gets me killed or dishonourably discharged. This time next year Albinus will be gone to another posting and I'll probably have a good, honourable commander again. I just have to bide my time and stay safe. However, if you can find a way that doesn't involve the procurator's office, and stay well out if it but still get evidence for your master, then that is a victory for everyone, I would say.'

A thought occurred to Rufinus. 'Tribune Celer is in on it, isn't he?'

Cassius shrugged, but his face answered the question in the positive regardless.

'I thought so,' Rufinus said. 'He was all very polite with me and listening to my advice and so on until Sarmizegetusa. Then Daizus overheard us talking.'

Cassius went pale instantly.

'Not you,' Rufinus added quickly. 'You didn't say anything. Nothing incriminating, anyway. And as far as I can see you're still trusted, so you're fine. But Daizus knows about me and why I'm here. About Cleander and Albinus and Niger. He ran straight to the tribune. They were together at Ulpia Traiana – Senova saw them. And then suddenly Daizus steps up his campaign against me from just pissing in my bed to knifing me in the back, and though there's plenty of doubt over the whole thing, the tribune demotes me and promises me hard justice from Albinus. It all fits. *Shit!*'

'What?'

'Something else just occurred to me as well. Back in Viminacium, I met the governor of Upper Moesia. What was his name? Something-or-other Capella...'

'Quintus Naevius Capella,' Cassius offered.

'That's the one. Like a walking cadaver. Face like a half-starved vulture. I wondered at why he would let the governor of another province recruit his manpower and take them away. Capella told me that he and Albinus had an *arrangement*. Could he be paying the Moesian governor for manpower?'

Cassius shook his head. 'I don't see why. To be honest, I thought that the ban on recruitment among Dacians following the troubles was a bit much. Most of them are perfectly loyal, as you've seen. That might be *part* of this, but I suspect something bigger.'

Rufinus nodded. It did sound a little small for a man stealing large amounts of gold from the imperial treasury. Another thought occurred to him.

'Where did you say the discrepancies were found?'

'Alburnus Maior. It's the biggest site for mines in the province. Churns out gold like horses churn out shit. I've been there a few times. It's unbelievable, the work there.'

Rufinus nodded. 'Is it easy to get to?'

Cassius' brow rose. 'Easy enough. Follow the valley west from Apulum up through Ampelum where the gold route splits and there's a small garrison. Then keep going as the route turns north and into the mountains. It's about fifty miles in total, I reckon. And the roads are good, since they're well-maintained for the gold shipments. But you can't go there at the moment.'

'Why not?'

Cassius tapped his temple with his forefinger. Think back to what you heard when you first arrived in Dacia, Rufinus. We were left behind in Drobeta to mop up the remnants because the governor had had word of a local rising near the gold mines. I don't know what's happened since then, but either the mines are in lands swarming with rebels or the Thirteenth has moved in and dealt with them. Either way, they're going to be surrounded by either angry Dacians or men loyal to the governor. I wouldn't give a coin for your chances.'

Rufinus fretted. 'But that's something else that fits into this mess too. Suspicious that with all this you say about the mines and the governor, suddenly there's an extra rebellion near the mines and Albinus rushes to deal with it. I think I need to get into Alburnus Maior, unless you're willing to change your mind about the procurator's office.'

Cassius shook his head. 'That's far too dangerous for us all.'

There was a long, uncomfortable silence, and finally Rufinus sighed. 'Thank you, Cassius. Thank you for telling me. You're a good man, and I'll make sure that whatever happens does not reflect on you.'

Cassius nodded. 'There are times when duty becomes a burden hard to bear, young Rufinus. Pray you don't reach that point.'

Rufinus gestured to Cassius with his left hand, displaying the marked and scarred fingers, missing all five nails. 'I discovered that long ago, my friend.'

They rode on for some time in silence, though a more pleasant one as the sun finally dipped behind the hills, and as they reached a marker pointing the way to a place called *Thermae Dodonae* Rufinus cleared his throat 'Isn't it going to be a little late for bathing? They shut the baths in Rome at dusk.'

'This place is a little different,' Cassius smiled as they climbed the side road toward the collection of buildings on the hill. Rufinus noted three things in quick succession as his friend fell silent: that the smoke from chimneys and flues was thick and billowing above the complex, suggesting many, many heated rooms, that the whole place was aglow like a giant oil lamp, meaning that everywhere was occupied and open, and that the sound of a dozen harmonious melodies played on a dozen different instruments wafted out across the valley.

'What is this place?' Rufinus murmured in wonder.

'One of the best secrets of Dacia, and why Germisara is such a popular posting,' grinned Cassius.

Rufinus opened the door to the room in the mansio at Germisara and staggered slightly, falling against the door frame and giggling like an idiot.

'Where in Hurod have you been,' whispered an angry, concerned voice from the darkness.

What was a *Hurod*? He had to stop Senova talking to barbarians if he ever hoped to understand her.

'Spa. Baths. North. Place called... Therm... Therm... Threm something.'

'You're drunk.'

'Atalanta noticed that when I rode her into a tree.'

'Stupid. And dangerous, given your history. I need you to take a few days off now.'

'I pissy ee. Dunno. Not problem.' He chuckled as he tried to remove his sock and fell onto the other bed. For a moment, he contemplated trying to climb into hers, but then decided against it. He was almost certainly going to be sick shortly, and women, he was led to believe, did not like being vomited on a lot.

'So Cassius took you out to get drunk?'

'S'bit more than that. But Thermae... Thermae-whatever is a really good place. Best baths 've been to out. Side Rome,' he added, then hiccupped. 'Bet... even than Aquae Calidae back home.

'Good wine, clearly.'

'Liss... listen,' he said, swallowing noisily as he sat on the edge of the bed. 'Cassius told me...' he made a noise that sounded like *bluerk* and swallowed again. 'Told me everything. S'about gold.'

'Gold?'

'Mines at Alburn... at some place north.'

'Alburnus Maior,' Senova said quietly. 'Gnaeus, I think there might be trouble brewing.'

Fnarf, was all he could say, then made a lip-flapping deflating noise as he lay face down on his bed.

'Gnaeus, I heard things from the locals. They say the troubles up around the mines aren't rebellious Dacians. They reckon they're Sarmatians.'

'Know... know how to kick Sarmatian bastards now. Easy.' He giggled. Finally, he began to remove his tunic. 'Liss.... Listen. I know we not married. An s'odd. I know. But...' He made a hopeful noise.

From the other side of him a young voice said 'Mistress said no rumpy if you were drunk, sir.'

Rufinus' heart nearly punched through his chest. He'd forgotten Luca was there.

With a deflated sigh, he passed out.

XII – The white general

It was hot and blue with not a cloud in the sky as the cohort arrived at Apulum. Rufinus would have appreciated the place a lot more had he not been astoundingly hungover at the time. Senova had been neither kind, nor understanding. How the hangover had quite happened was beyond Rufinus. He had intended to have only one cup of wine in the remarkable bath complex of Thermae Dodonae, and Cassius had pressed him as to the reason. Still somewhat embarrassed to reveal such personal weakness, Rufinus had been reticent, with the result that the veteran had plied him with more wine and pressed further. Much of the following evening was a blur, though the place would most certainly go down in Rufinus' books as the best spa he had ever visited. He was not entirely sure whether he had, in the end, opened up and told Cassius about his past and the addictions to which he'd been prey, and he was now in the odd situation of not being able to ask without opening up further anyway. Fortunately he was saved such weird conversations as Cassius returned to duty on the march and Rufinus returned to his exile in Senova's carriage.

Twenty miles northeast they rumbled in the searing sun, along the Marisus valley to the capital of the province.

Apulum stood on a low rise that dominated a wide plain, the fortress of the Thirteenth Gemina as powerful as any legionary fortress Rufinus had seen – and these days that included quite a number. But Apulum was different from the others. It shone. The walls were of a stone white enough that they flashed in the sun's rays. The civilian town clustered around the base of the place was pretty impressive, too, well-appointed and thriving. Oddly for a Roman town's organisation, the great river Marisus ran past a mile distant from the centre, a small port there connected with the town by a busy road.

The cohort crunched and rumbled into the town, along the main street and toward the impressive white gate of the fortress on the hill. Rufinus frowned as he squinted from the carriage window in the bright sunshine. Those walls were blinding. Either the builders here had found the whitest stone he had ever seen, or they were regularly whitewashed to increase the effect. One thing was certain, Apulum stood out.

He could hear the soldiers in the town calling out to their fellow legionaries arriving from their long journey, and Senova suddenly nudged him.

'What happens now?'

'I guess we see Clodius Albinus. I can't say I'm looking forward to the meeting, though.'

They rattled on along the street and came to a halt in a square at the centurions' whistles. Orders were given and the men marched on to the fortress, while a small knot of riders including Tribune Celer trotted back along the column to the wagons, reining in outside the carriage.

'You will come with me,' the tribune said, pointing at Rufinus. 'Clodius Albinus does not favour the luxury of the governor's palace in the town. He will be in the fortress. The lady will be shown to the mansio where she may rest overnight at the expense of the administration.'

'I will come too,' Senova said defiantly.

Rufinus put up a warning hand. 'Take the gear, Luca and Acheron and secure a room. Depending on the outcome of this meeting I will find you soon.'

She gave him a narrow-eyed, disapproving look, and her nod might as well have carried a threat, but with all the other threats facing him today, she would have to stand in the queue. He alighted from the carriage and made to unhitch Atalanta and mount up, but Celer shook his head. 'You will not need a horse.'

Feeling oddly like a captive slave at a triumph, Rufinus followed the tribune and his cronies through the fortress gate, while the carriage was led from the square along a wide street. The horsemen passed into the Thirteenth's base with Rufinus padding along behind and looking rather out of place. All that was missing was a rope from Celer's hand to Rufinus' neck. He did not like the feeling, nor the sense of foreboding it brought about. He noted in passing that the stone *was* whitewashed, though the nooks and crannies where they had missed were still pretty white anyway.

Through the fortress they passed, coming to a halt at the principia. Rufinus' wandering gaze happened to catch the familiar shape of Cassius Proculeianus striding back toward the gate having dismissed his troops, though the centurion did not meet his eye. Celer sent his men off to various duties and then dismounted, handing his reins to one of the legionaries by the impressive headquarters gateway with its four grand pillars, its intricate architrave of gods and soldiers, its white stone and red-tiled roof. Once the tribune was on foot, he beckoned to Rufinus and strode inside, the men saluting as he passed.

The great courtyard of the headquarters was much the same as any other, and they passed into the long basilica hall, making for the office of the legatus. Two men stood guard there, too, and they saluted as the two travel-worn men approached. Celer asked whether the commander was in and free and, on receiving an affirmative, rapped sharply on the door.

A gruff voice bade them enter and Rufinus followed Celer into the office of the most powerful man in Dacia, possibly in this whole corner of the empire. Rufinus was not sure what to expect from Clodius Albinus. He was sometimes referred to as an 'African', hailing from the city of Hadrumetum, though his heritage had to be anything *but* African, to Rufinus' mind. He had never seen so pale a figure. Albinus was almost alabaster white, though otherwise very robust in appearance. His hair and beard were dark and naturally curly, his pale skin weathered and marked by years of service. He was clearly a very military man, completely aside from the scars he bore that attested to campaigns and war, for there would be a sumptuous palace for him in the city, yet here he sat in the fortress of his legion, wearing military uniform rather than a rich toga.

Rufinus felt an odd pull. There was something about the governor that demanded respect, and the young praetorian had to force himself to remember that this man was up to no good for some unknown, nefarious reason.

'Celer,' the cultured voice greeted the tribune. 'Welcome back. You have a cohort of good men now?'

The tribune made a noncommittal shrug. 'They're getting there, sir. A little more training to sharpen them up, but they acquitted themselves well in three separate engagements.'

'You've cleared out the pockets of raiders, then?'

'Dacia Malvensis and Dacia Apulensis are free of incursions and entirely under Roman control, governor. The province is restored.'

Albinus nodded. 'Good. I have had word from Niger, who is in Porolissum now. It seems he has secured the north and begun work to strengthen the borders against future troubles. It would seem that all is returning to normal. I shall prepare a missive for the emperor to ensure him that Dacia is his entire.'

Rufinus stood silent and immobile, though he felt a flutter in his stomach as the two men turned to him.

'And this is?'

Rufinus opened his mouth to answer, but Celer held up his hand. 'This is Rustius Rufinus, a praetorian guardsman that Cleander has seen fit to send here to spy on you. Initially I gave the man the benefit of the doubt as I needed any veteran I could get for the journey, but he has proved to be divisive, untrustworthy and dangerous, just as any follower of that imperial serpent would be.'

Rufinus bridled, and had to fight down his denials. Arguing would not help, he suspected.

'Tell me,' Albinus said quietly, motioning to Celer.

'He has been attempting to suborn men to his cause. He has been found more than once in collusion with Cassius Proculeianus. I have faith in the centurion, and now that we are in Apulum, he can be removed from this rodent's unhealthy influence.'

Rufinus was starting to feel truly angry now. Misrepresented and maligned, how was he supposed to defend himself?

'Moreover, he accused one of my veterans of mutiny – a case for which I might note there was no evidence and no witness – and set his Sarmatian hound on the man, savaging his leg. There were, however, *plenty* of witnesses to that. The victim, Optio Daizus, is requesting the full weight of military law be brought down on Rufinus for the offence but, given his origins, I thought it best to leave the matter to you, sir.'

Albinus nodded and drummed his fingers rhythmically on the table. 'A thorny problem. I have no intention of playing host to Cleander's spies. The chamberlain is a poison at the heart of the empire, and I will not have his black rot at work in my province.'

Oddly, Rufinus felt a strange warming to the man at his clear hatred of Cleander, though it would be of no use to him right now.

'What have you to say for yourself, soldier?'

There was a tense silence. Rufinus took a breath. To deny his mission was pointless. It was now clearly open knowledge. He could play on his own hatred of Cleander and hope to come to better terms with Albinus but, even if that were possible, he wasn't sure it was a good idea. Whether the man hated Cleander or not, there was still the accusation that he also spoke against the emperor, and then there was the knowledge imparted by Cassius that Albinus was stealing gold in large quantities for some unknown reason. Attempting to ally with the governor might just lead to even deeper trouble. All he could do, then, was tell the truth and hope that Fortuna was still watching over him.

'Governor, in certain aspects, the tribune has the right of it. I *was* assigned to Dacia and to your forces by Cleander, who commands me to seek out subversion and sedition. I am not saying that I have found such a thing, or even that I believe there is such a thing to find,' he added carefully, keeping his voice neutral. 'But that is my mission. To pursue enemies of the state and report such activity. As to the matter with Optio Daizus, I recognise that the evidence of his attempt to butcher me in the midst of battle is scant and, though I believe there were witnesses, unit-loyalty will side with the optio over a recently-appointed praetorian. I maintain my innocence in the matter and that my dog merely leapt to my defence. I request only that I be allocated a position in the Dacian military until I feel that I have something worth reporting back to the chamberlain or until I become convinced that there is nothing to report.'

Albinus' eyes narrowed to a squint as he regarded the newcomer. Tribune Celer cleared his throat. 'I am personally dissatisfied with the presence of this man. I do not like him, I do not trust him and, given your authority, I would stripe the man's back with the lash and send him back to Rome in disgrace. Better still, stripe him with the lash until he expires.'

Rufinus blinked. Death? His heart thundered for a moment, but began to settle as the white-faced general opposite shook his head. 'No. This is a delicate situation, Celer. Given our current position, I do not think executing or even flogging one of Cleander's men would be a wise or popular decision. No matter how much I hate the chamberlain, he is powerful above all men in the capital now. He not only has the ear of the emperor but, if I am to believe what I am told, then he controls the administration himself, wielding Commodus' authority. That is not a man to cross openly.'

Rufinus nodded. An astute appraisal of the situation, and one that might just save his own skin.

'What will you do, then, Governor?' Celer asked in a hiss. 'We cannot have this man at liberty to work his poison in Apulum. He must be removed or constrained.'

Albinus was nodding now. 'I will not have the snake's men in my city or my legion. Send him to Porolissum. He can be Niger's problem. Perhaps my esteemed colleague can lose him over the Iazyges' border there.'

Celer looked unhappy at the notion. 'Respectfully, sir, that's just brushing the problem under the rug.'

'Brushing the problem under *someone else's* rug,' corrected the governor. 'Niger can deal with it. Part of the garrison of nearby Bucium are in Apulum for a night. They can take this man back with them and deliver him to Niger. See to it, Celer.'

The tribune, still looking decidedly unhappy at the decision, nodded and saluted, turning and motioning for Rufinus to leave. As they departed the office the tribune, lip curled, addressed Rufinus as though speaking down to a slave.

'Consider yourself most fortunate. And behave yourself now. Dacia is a small world and Porolissum is but a few days' ride. If I hear one word of you causing trouble, I will be there in the blink of an eye and I will deliver so many stripes to your back you will look like a zebra as you die. Do not doubt me on this.'

Rufinus clenched his teeth. There was no point in snarling threats, denials or curses at the tribune. The decision had been made by a man more powerful than either of them. And if the time came when Celer sought him out, he would be damn well ready for the man.

'Come with me,' the tribune snapped, and marched from the headquarters through the extensive fortress. As they moved among the endless barracks, Rufinus tried to put things in place in his head. He was alive and had escaped punishment. That was his immediate concern and had to be considered a victory, in the circumstances. In the process he appeared to have turned Celer from a disapproving commander into a direct enemy, but at the moment a restrained and impotent one. Though that could change in time, for now the man could do nothing to him. Clodius Albinus was not going to be the ally in the great game that Rufinus had hoped and was very clearly up to something dubious. In addition to everything Rufinus already knew or suspected, he had taken careful note of the fact that Albinus had been lenient with him *'given their current position'*. He was to be sent to Pescennius Niger, which was clearly also a win. Cestius had liked Niger, and that was a good recommendation. Perhaps Niger might be the ally that Albinus could not? Perhaps he might even be the man to go to with anything Rufinus found out here. He was to travel north with a new unit, presumably an auxiliary one. Really, despite everything, he had entered Apulum smelling of shit, and would leave smelling of roses. His smile at the thought of small victories was tempered a little by the realisation that he would be saying farewell to Cassius. The centurion was home now and, given what the tribune had said, it seemed unlikely the man would be permitted to associate further with Rufinus.

'There,' Celer said, gesturing at a barrack block identical to the others. As they approached the door of the centurion's room at the end, Rufinus noted the sign on the wall. '*Locum Peregrinum.*' The foreigners' barrack, where visiting troops would be quartered. It brought a wry smile to Rufinus' face to realise that it neatly echoed the *Castra Peregrina* in Rome – the home of the frumentarii.

The tribune gave a single hard knock at the door and a rough, deep voice snapped at him to wait. Rufinus almost smiled at the twitch that appeared beneath Celer's eye at being spoken to thus. There was a long pause, accompanied by the sounds of a man fastening a belt and belching within. Rufinus couldn't help himself. The smile emerged. It faltered a little as the door was ripped open and what appeared to be a bear in a centurion's tunic glared out below brows that looked like small woodland animals.

'What?' His voice was oddly-accented and rough. Certainly not local.

'You are bound for Bucium in the morning, I am informed.'

'S'right, Tribune. Me and the lads are going home. We've delivered the fat pillock from Optatiana as ordered, drunk a small lake of your best wine, impregnated a few of your girlfriends, crapped in your sock drawer, and now we're leaving.'

Rufinus snorted, earning a black look from the tribune, who was awash in a sea of distaste right now.

'I have extra orders for you, Centurion. This soldier is to be delivered to Porolissum into the hands of Pescennius Niger. I will have the orders written up for you before you depart in the morning, as well as a letter to pass to the legate there. Do you understand?'

'Dropped off a fat pillock, picked up a thin one,' confirmed the hulking, hirsute centurion with a grin missing only five visible teeth. Celer rolled his eyes. 'I shall leave you to get acquainted. I'm sure you're perfectly suited. Make sure Rufinus here is out of the fortress by sundown. He is staying in the mansio in town.'

Without another word, the tribune turned and marched away. Rufinus felt his spirits lift slightly. He might be saying goodbye to Cassius, but at least he was also saying farewell to Daizus and Celer. Every cloud had a silver lining.

'What are you?' the hairy man asked in his gruff tone, 'legionary officer?'

Rufinus shook his head. He wasn't sure whether the truth might damage their relationship from the outset, given how popular the praetorians were with the regular army, but he could hardly lie and claim to be with the Thirteenth now.

'Praetorian,' he replied with a sigh. 'On detached duty.'

The big man looked him up and down. 'Not a painted pretty boy, though, like some of them.' He gestured to the hand with no fingernails, his eyes tracing a route through the visible scars in Rufinus' flesh. 'Battle-hardened, are ye not?'

Rufinus nodded. 'Formerly of the Tenth Gemina up in Pannonia.'

The big centurion nodded. 'I remember the Tenth. Fought like lions. We were scouting out the field before the battle, and we saw the whole thing.'

Rufinus frowned. 'You're scouts?'

'S'right. Numerus exploratorum Germanicianorum, currently based at Bucium in the north. We ride the frontier day in, day out, and make sure no more hairy barbarians get in. There's only room for one hairy barbarian in my fort.'

He laughed, and the sound was like a small animal fighting against being sucked down a drain.

'I am Gnaeus Marcius Rustius Rufinus. I'm travelling with a lady called Senova, formerly of Britannia, a big black dog, and a young slave lad called Luca,' though he wondered at that moment if the tribune would remember that and take Luca off them again. 'I hope you can accommodate all of us on the journey? We have a carriage and I have a horse.'

The big man chuckled. 'We're scouts. We can adapt to anything, Rufinus. I am Pontius Narcissus, centurion of the reprobates currently quartered in this place. Frankly, I cannot wait to get back on the road. This place is too civic and too rigid for my liking. Men like the tribune there who think in straight lines and wouldn't know a joke if it punched them in the testicles.'

Rufinus grinned. It seemed he had fallen on his feet. Narcissus appeared friendly and genuine. He checked himself at that thought. So had Celer at the beginning. From compliments to death threats in mere weeks.

'How long does it take to get to Porolissum?' Rufinus asked.

Narcissus tapped a hairy lip. 'Three or four days by horse. Twice that with a carriage. Why. You in a hurry?'

Rufinus shook his head, his mind whirring with possibilities, recalling Senova's map. 'Can we step inside?'

Huge furry brow furrowed, the centurion stepped back into his room and gestured for Rufinus to join him. The room smelled of fart and sour wine and Rufinus' eyes began to water as soon as the door shut. He took a deep breath, preparing himself to take a risk.

'How long would the journey take if we were to go via the Ampelum valley and Alburnus Maior?'

The big man's frown deepened. 'You proposing to hack out some gold on the way? A ring for your woman, perhaps? Think again. Them miners have to move a ton of rock just to find a speck of gold. They have to demolish a mountain to produce an ingot.'

Rufinus sucked on his teeth. 'Is it feasible, though? The detour, I mean.'

Narcissus shrugged. 'Anything is possible. It's probably only about twenty or thirty miles further that way, but the terrain beyond Alburnus is hilly and forested. Going will be slower with a vehicle. Eight days to Porolissum by carriage on the main road. Fifteen or sixteen by way of Alburnus. Unless your woman will ride a horse and get rid of the carriage?'

Rufinus pictured Senova's face if he took away the vehicle and handed her reins. He couldn't imagine it making him popular. That being said, the carriage had been assigned by Celer, and it was possible the tribune would take it back off them now anyway.

'No. Fifteen or sixteen days is acceptable for me. Is it to you?'

The centurion's frown was back. 'Why do you want to go that way? It's longer, worse terrain, and they say there are bandits and rebels near the mine regions. Sounds like you're looking for trouble to me.'

Rufinus shook his head. 'Look… it's complicated. And a bit secretive. I want to get to Alburnus Maior to comply with my orders from Rome, but the Dacian governor has sent me to Porolissum. I'm hoping to find a way to do both, but it relies upon your willingness to escort us via a strange and

~~Th~~ornaby Central Library
Tel: 01642 528117
Email:
~~th~~naby.central.library@stockton.gov.uk

Borrowed Items 14/11/2019 10:49
XXXXXX8429

Item Title	Due Date
* Eagles of Dacia	05/12/2019

* Indicates items borrowed today

Opening hours:
8:30 - 5:00 Mon, Wed, Fri
8:30 - 7:00 Tues and Thurs
9:30 - 4:00 Saturday
All library cards are due to be updated.
Please see a member of staff who will
check we have your current details
and renew your membership on our
system.

troublesome route. All I can do is ask you to trust me.' He tried to plaster a trustworthy expression on his face, though was fairly sure such an expression just made him look constipated.

Narcissus stretched, and Rufinus was once more reminded of the man's similarity to a rearing bear.

'Did you hear about the miser's will?'

Rufinus frowned, nonplussed. 'Er... no?'

'He made himself his heir.'

Narcissus roared with laughter and Rufinus could not help but chuckle, partially at the fairly poor joke, but mostly because the centurion's attitude was infectious. The big man rumbled to a halt, took a deep breath and patted Rufinus on the shoulder. 'I will make you a deal. We will travel the Ampelum valley and attempt that route across the mountains, but if we encounter real danger, such as I hear is evident there at the moment, then we might have to reconsider. There are only twenty of us, and we are lightly equipped, not prepared for a proper fight.'

Rufinus nodded. 'That's more than fair, Centurion. I cannot imagine there is trouble there now. Albinus brought the Thirteenth back north in order to secure that very issue and ensure gold production goes on. Since he is resting comfortably in Apulum, then I can only assume that Alburnus Maior is business as usual.'

In fact, he was less than sure on that fact. Something was amiss with Dacia and the governor's gold interests, but there was only one place he was going to learn more, and that was in Alburnus Maior.

'I will wait for the letters and authorisation from the governor in the morning,' Narcissus said in rumbling tones, 'then I shall bring my men and collect your party at the mansio. Do me a favour and have your carriage ready to go by sunup. Your route's a long way, and I want to get a jump on the day.'

Rufinus nodded his thanks. 'Can I ask you one last thing?'

'Go on.'

'Could you not mention the change of route to anyone until we're out of Apulum and on the road?'

Narcissus' brow furrowed again. 'You're not one of the frumentarii are you? This smacks of their sort of intrigue.'

Rufinus laughed. 'No. I'm not nearly devious enough for that.'

'Not that you'd admit it if you were, of course.'

'There is that,' Rufinus grinned.

He bade the friendly centurion farewell until the morning, and strolled out of the building and back toward Apulum's south gate. The mansio was easy enough to find. He'd seen down which street the carriage had gone when they departed and, following that direction, he found the mansio about half way to the river, on the edge of town. The lamps had already been lit, despite there being over an hour of sunlight left, and a friendly glow emerged as Rufinus walked through the main door. The large common area was busy and noisy and he scanned the room for Senova, Luca and Acheron, but found none of them. Perhaps the noise and smell and heat was too much for them. He strolled over to the counter and enquired after his room. He was informed that his wife was already there and where to find it, and he felt a moment's relief. He hadn't realised how much he'd suddenly worried about her until the worry lifted. Moments later, he had crossed to the stairs, climbed them and moved around the left wing of the building, hunting room XV. When he finally found it, he was about to open the door and then paused, knocking politely.

'Come in,' came Senova's voice, and he relaxed further. This sojourn in Dacia was putting him very on edge. He opened the door and was greeted by the sight of not two people, but three. Senova was busy mending a hole in a cloak, with Acheron curled up at her feet. Luca was busy mixing wine and water. And Cassius sat on the couch, upright and tense-looking.

'Rufinus. You're alright?'

Rufinus nodded. 'Too many potential repercussions in Rome to cause me any real harm. But Albinus wants rid of me. They're sending me to Porolissum to be a bother to Niger there.'

Cassius closed his eyes. 'Good. I think there might be trouble and you're best off staying out of it. Trouble might be targeting me, now.'

Rufinus frowned and dropped into a seat opposite the centurion, waving away the drink that Luca offered him. 'What's the problem?'

Cassius looked about as though ears might sprout from the very walls. Leaning forward, he spoke in low tones.

'My friend in the procurator's office – the one I told you about? – he's gone missing. And the governor's had his people going through the place like a wildfire. If there's anything incriminating there, he will have found it. I'm concerned, Rufinus. Everything in Apulum seems to be drifting along as normal, but there are undercurrents.'

Rufinus nodded. 'Do what you have to do to keep yourself safe, Cassius. I'll be out of your hair and heading north in the morning.' He paused and looked around equally furtively. 'I've persuaded my escort to go via Alburnus Maior. If there is any evidence to find, I will find it.'

Cassius nodded, still wearing a worried look. 'It seems that the main revolt there is over. Or that's the talk among the officers here. Officially all is well at Alburnus. But there's something not quite right here. I can feel it in the air. Watch yourself on your journey. With luck you can complete your mission with Pescennius Niger and return safely to Rome. If so, drop by here on the way and let me know how things went. On the assumption I'm still here, that is.'

'Keep yourself safe,' Rufinus said again. 'And start by getting back to the fortress and not being seen with me. I will try and get word to you if I find anything out.'

Cassius nodded, rose and crossed to the door. He stopped there and turned. 'Despite everything, it's been good to know you, Rufinus. Go with luck and may Mercury give you wings.'

Rufinus took the proffered hand and shook it firmly. 'Good luck to you, too. Stay out of trouble and steer well clear of Celer for a while, though I think he's more interested in me.'

Cassius smiled wearily. 'Someday soon it will all be over and we'll just be proper soldiers again without all this mucking about.'

Rufinus chuckled. 'I wouldn't be too sure. One thing I've learned this past few years is that once you start to play the game, you don't get out easily. The players change, but the great game goes on.'

'Not for me,' Cassius sighed. 'Retirement beckons and right now it cannot come soon enough.' He turned to the others in the room. 'Goodbye Senova. Keep him safe. Luca.'

Acheron rose and padded over long enough for Cassius to give him a good scratch behind the ears, and then the centurion saluted them in a friendly manner, stepped out of the door and was gone, the wooden portal closing with a click.

'We won't see him again, will we,' Senova said quietly.

'I doubt it. He's a good man. I hope he stays safe and that his friend has not come to grief.'

Senova stretched. 'We are going to your gold mine tomorrow?'

Rufinus nodded. 'In the company of a score of Germanic scouts and their centurion. Big hairy, ugly fellow with bad wind and worse jokes. It'll probably feel like being back home to you.'

Senova gave him a black look. 'The soldier who escorted us to the mansio said that someone would be round late in the morning to take the carriage back to the fortress. I told him not to be overly concerned if it wasn't here.'

Rufinus' eyes widened. 'You can't just *take* a legion's vehicle.'

'I'm not taking it. They gave it to me. I'm just keeping it.'

Rufinus stared, and finally let out a breathy laugh. 'On the bright side, we'll be miles from Apulum before they know it's gone.'

'Good. Because if you think I'm riding a horse into bandit-infested mountains, you've another thing coming, Gnaeus.'

XIII – Mountains of gold

They left Apulum at dawn. It irked Rufinus that the slave boy Luca actually grumbled at having to rise so early to secure the horses and carriage, as though he had the same rights as the rest of them. Had it been Rufinus in control, he would have given the slave a swift backhand and told him that cheek like that got slaves beaten. But Luca was Senova's slave and had been given unhealthy realms of freedom.

In the end, the carriage was made ready and their gear stowed as the cockerels began to greet the morning and the blast of a horn announced the change of watch up in the fortress. The three of them had eaten a hearty repast in the mansio, which catered well for early morning travellers, and the entire party were waiting outside with Acheron urinating against the front wall when the German scout unit appeared.

Narcissus may have joked that there was only room for one hairy barbarian in his fort, but evidence suggested otherwise. The last time Rufinus had seen such hairy individuals was at Sarmizegetusa, and they had been Sarmatians. He had to admit, though, that the men of the Numerus from Bucium were at least neater. Apart from Narcissus, their beards were trimmed and their hair plaited to keep it out of the way. Two of them wore helmets with the silvered facemasks of Roman cavalry parades and sports, and were armoured in cuirass and greaves, with laminated shoulders. The rest were armed in mail shirts and without helmets, just their oval shields and spears, with a spatha hanging at their side and their scarred faces framed with long, thick hair. They were an imposing bunch, but the way they joked with one another and their plain appearance somehow made them seem genuine and trustworthy, like their centurion.

The party rattled off out of Apulum with the rising sun, passing beneath the eastern walls of the great fortress of the Thirteenth, which made Rufinus slightly nervous since they were taking an unauthorised route and a stolen carriage with them. To the north of the fortress, which brooded but apparently failed to consider a stolen vehicle noteworthy, they left the northern road, marked with Potaissa, Napoca and Porolissum, and took a different route, heading for the hills to the north-west. A marker here mentioned only Ampelum, though Rufinus knew from both maps and conversation with friends that Alburnus Maior lay beyond the Ampelum valley.

The valley was not wide, but relatively shallow at first, with farmsteads dotted around the slopes, hay standing in stooks in the fields, silent sentinels of the gold route of Dacia. The road was, again, well-maintained, and throughout the morning of travel they passed numerous inns and small markets, which had clearly sprouted over the decades to serve the gold route and its caravans.

The first day, Narcissus informed them, he intended to travel twenty five miles to the town of Ampelum, where they would stay at a well-appointed mansio. It would be probably the last good and safe night until they reached Bucium. Between the terrain and the potential of local rebels, they would be moving slower after Ampelum, and the mansios and inns en route would be cruder and smaller, if they were still there and operating at all.

The journey was an interesting one for the company alone. Rufinus had, of course, encountered such *speculatores* and *exploratores* units before, particularly during the wars against the Marcomanni under the divine Marcus Aurelius, and he may even have come across this very unit, but he had never spent any time with them. They were always this peripheral and very insular bunch with more native tendencies and habits than Roman, and they were only in the presence of the legions when reporting on the terrain ahead.

It was fascinating, therefore, to spend time with the German scouts, only four of whom, he discovered, were actually German. Also, they took offence at being labelled that, two of them proudly proclaiming themselves Suebi, one Alemanni and one even Batavi. To Rufinus' mind, given the revolutionary track record of the Batavians, he'd have kept that quiet rather than shouting it from the rooftops, but still the man was defiant and full of tribal hubris.

The men of the numerus were about as undisciplined a bunch on the ride as Rufinus had ever met. None of the men addressed Centurion Narcissus by rank or name, calling him *Hailagaz*, which it turned out was a tribal honorific for a native priest. Narcissus, it seemed, was more important as a priest of their gods than as a centurion of Rome. Rufinus spoke with interest to some of the men, many of whom were Dacian born recruits, and was fascinated to learn that Narcissus led all religious rites for the unit, incorporating the Dacian gods and several of the more important Roman ones in his devotions.

They swore like no men Rufinus had ever met, using eye-watering language and some words that Rufinus had to ask the meaning of, and often regretted doing so. They belched and farted and snorted and spat and picked their noses and scratched their arses with disturbing regularity. Yet every time anyone did anything that might be considered uncouth in Roman circles, they automatically apologised to Senova, who found the whole thing highly amusing, which in turn concerned Rufinus somewhat. She already had far too many worrying habits, to his mind, without starting swearing like a German and scratching her arse at dinner.

Yet they were also a friendly bunch. None of them seemed to be overly concerned that they were going wildly out of their way and through notably dangerous territory on the whim of their guests. They asked about the history of the three of them, shared their own, and all patted Acheron and fed him from their own meals. They joked and laughed. The jokes were often nonsensical and usually off-colour when they did make any sense, but they were in constant good humour, and when Rufinus or Senova chipped in with a jest of their own, it generally earned them uproarious laughter and a slap on the back.

Moreover, despite the unruly nature of the men, Rufinus' shrewd military eye cut through the mess and recognised them as men who were clearly very good at their job. Of the twenty one riders, there were only ever fourteen in the column, the other seven constantly roaming ahead and to either side, often an entire valley or two away. They warned of any natural terrain trouble, of settlements or signs in plenty of time, and they cycled their men through the outriding so that their horses were always well-rested. Best still, with most of them being Dacian born, and the Germans having learned the ways of the locals, they were received well by the natives and often came back to the column with fresh bread or fruit, or pots of honey and other treats.

It was an entirely different experience to journeying with the legions, and not for the worse. Rufinus had travelled and quartered with the Tenth Legion, the praetorians and the Thirteenth Gemina, but there was something relaxed and freeing about travelling with Narcissus and his men. They reached Ampelum in the late afternoon of the first day and stayed in, as promised, one of the best mansios Rufinus had ever visited. The fort there, a small affair in place to monitor the gold route, stood silent and empty, its cavalry garrison moved to the border during the recent troubles. Still, the place did not seem to have suffered depredations in their absence though there was no evidence of gold caravans passing through recently. The next day, also as foretold, the terrain changed.

From Ampelum, the valley began to narrow and the forest closed in. The hills began to rise to ever greater heights, and Rufinus was reminded of the first time they had moved into the valleys of the Carpates, what seemed like months ago now. The farms gradually became fewer and fewer, until all they could see to either side of the road and the small but fast river it followed were the tall, narrow trunks of pine trees. It became much easier to imagine Dacian rebels and Sarmatian raiders hiding behind every hill and, though the road remained well looked after, the settlements they passed became gradually more reticent and close-mouthed. The inns they saw no longer bore Latin signs but were marked out in some local script he could not read. Rufinus was, consequently, ever more grateful for Narcissus and his men, who seemed to be more or less treated as locals by the people they passed.

The second night they stayed in a rough inn that smelled of smoked meat and sweat, and Rufinus tried his best to avoid joining the scouts for a drinking session, especially given that what they were consuming was either a beer that smelled like wet socks and had things floating in it, or that throat-flaying liquor to which Cassius had introduced him. Fortunately, Senova managed to convince the riders that she had imposed limits on Rufinus. This, of course, earned him good-natured derision and the nickname *Biosmaz*, the meaning of which no one would tell him, but over the past two days the riders had become respectful enough of Senova not to question her decisions, and it *had* saved Rufinus from trying to explain. Besides which, after Argentulum and Locusta, he was fairly hardened to nicknames. The food when it arrived took some getting used to, since everything he picked up seemed to have either a hoof or knuckles, but he managed, and if he forgot its shape it was actually pretty tasty.

That night brought one of the strangest moments in Rufinus' life. Rufinus had been sitting in the corner of the room with a cup of water, examining Senova's map and making notes on his tablet, while the riders had been drinking enough foul ale and burning spirit to drown a small village. Then, suddenly, one of them who had been by the window gestured outside and shouted something. There was a cheer, and the whole place erupted. Narcissus went to speak to the innkeeper, and then grabbed Rufinus' wrist.

'What is it?'

'A good moon. The gods are listening. Time to please them. Leave your maps, Biosmaz, and come with us, lest you want your gods to overlook you in these dangerous hills.'

Rufinus had been about to object and point out that he'd promised an altar to Fortuna and that she'd been quite obliging so far, but Narcissus, with his bear-like strength, simply hauled Rufinus from his seat and dragged him from the building. Outside, he was surprised to see they had also roused Senova from her room and she was grinning and cheering along with the rest of them. Luca looked nonplussed, but had been brought to join them as well, and was cheering dutifully.

Acheron, who had been lying next to Rufinus' feet, merely stretched and followed them out, rather than rushing to his master's rescue as he was manhandled from the building, which is what Rufinus would have preferred from a loyal hound.

There, he was released in the dusty street. He noted that over the past day it had remained sunny and blue, but the temperature had begun to drop as they climbed into the hills and now, emerging from the warm inn with its log fire into the dark, he shivered and wished they would allow him to collect his cloak. But no, they were moving again instantly. Two of the riders seemed to have procured a piglet from somewhere and the thing was struggling in a panic as the two men carried it. Narcissus disappeared for a few moments but, as the scouts moved off into the trees behind the inn, he quickly rejoined them, wearing a grey robe and wielding a long staff decorated with bones and feathers and beads. Incongruously, with this strange, native getup, he had folded part of the robe over his head in the manner of a Roman priest.

They moved through the trees, following directions Rufinus could not fathom, and suddenly arrived in what could only be some sort of sacred space. The trees had been kept clear in a circle wide enough for a village to stand in and, indeed, there were locals there, silent and respectful, waiting. A series of tall wooden posts stood around the circle, each carved in that same local tongue that Rufinus did not know, and each bearing a rather stylised image of a bearded face. At the centre of the circle was a wide stone disc with a runnel, which left Rufinus in no doubt as to its purpose.

Within moments, the place was crowded. The German scouts, the inhabitants and guests of the inn, the local villagers and the visiting Romans were all gathered in a circle around that disc.

Narcissus began by raising both hands imploringly toward the moon, stick rattling in his grip. He started to spout off praise and benediction in a tongue that Rufinus recognised from his time in the wars as a Germanic dialect. This was then repeated, every few sentences, in what he now knew to be Dacian for the benefit of his local visitors, and then Latin for his few Roman guests. Eventually, he turned and locked Rufinus in a blue-eyed, ursine gaze.

'Great Mercury and Hercules, Mars and Minerva, Derzelas and Zalmoxis, and...?'

He paused, and Rufinus realised the whole glade was watching him expectantly. At his shoulder, Senova shouted 'Sacred Brigantia, mother of battle and protector of the people!'

There were nods of approval around the circle.

'Er... Fortuna, lady of... er... fortune,' he announced rather weakly. There was another pause, while everyone looked at him as though something were growing out of his head, and then Narcissus shrugged and threw his hands higher. 'Brigantia and Fortuna! On this most auspicious night of hunting moon and stars aligned like killers,' Rufinus looked up, and wondered what shape killers were supposed to take, since it all looked rather random to him. 'Hear our plea,' finished the centurion-priest. 'Favour your people, protect this village and the honourable travellers passing through. Bestow bounty upon these folk of your lands and keep the harm of rebels and raiders and wicked overlords from their door.'

Rufinus wondered idly if he represented the category of wicked overlords in this gathering, but no one seemed to be bothered by his presence. The piglet was brought forward by the two scouts and Rufinus watched as it was ritually sacrificed on the circular stone disc, Narcissus up to his elbows in blood. One by one, the people in the crowd stepped forward and the centurion bestowed some kind of benediction upon them by marking their forehead with the pig's blood. There was a sense of immense satisfaction at the successful conclusion of the rite, and each marked man or woman walked away with a contented smile. Senova hurried forward as soon as there was a gap, urging Luca to come along with her. Rufinus hung back. He wasn't sure whether Fortuna would approve of his celebrating her with barbarian rituals alongside Dacian gods. He rolled his eyes as Senova returned, marked, and took Acheron forward, and he almost exclaimed his disbelief when Narcissus marked the dog using the same words as he had for the people. It was all made slightly surreal and humorous thereafter, as other folk rushed forward to be marked while Acheron tried to hustle them aside and lick the blood from both the priest's limbs and the stone disc. Soon, though, everyone but Rufinus was marked, and the centurion looked at him expectantly.

'You would do the gods dishonour and miss out on their favour?' he asked in Latin.

Wearily, and nervously, Rufinus stepped forward. He would never be able to explain what he felt afterwards, but as the centurion marked him on the forehead with some arcane barbarian symbol, the young Roman felt an odd frisson of electric energy run through him, his hair crackling and standing proud. He stepped back in a mix of wonder and alarm, and Narcissus pronounced the rite at an end, heaving the remnants of the carcass from the disc onto the grass in front of Acheron, who went to work devouring the remains.

Rufinus tried not to watch, still wondering and slightly alarmed at the result of the ritual. They returned to the inn, the locals all thanking the priest for his work, many of them giving him small gifts, which he took with a solemn nod. Rufinus fell in with Senova and Luca as they walked, trying not to pay too much attention to the great black dog that was triumphantly carrying half a disembowelled piglet at his side.

'That was strange.'

'To you,' Senova said. 'It was different from home, but not by too much.'

'I don't mean the ritual. I could see reflections of Rome in that. But when he put the blood on me, I felt... I don't know. I don't know what I felt. But I felt something.'

'You felt the gods,' Senova said with disturbing confidence.

'You felt it too?'

'Of course. You feel the presence of the gods at such a time. Otherwise what would be the point in such a ritual or priests?'

Rufinus could not answer that, and the fact disturbed him. He realised with a start that he had attended appropriate rites his whole life, including the ones held on a legion's parade ground, and yet he'd never once felt the strange energy he'd experienced tonight. When they arrived at the inn and Narcissus was there, back in his customary uniform, Rufinus looked at the centurion with a whole new level of awe. He had been right in Apulum: he really *had* fallen on his feet, and Fortuna was with him, more so now than ever before. Back in the inn's common room, the owner distributed his throat-searing liquor freely and with wild abandon. Rufinus prepared himself for the embarrassment of refusing and was surprised when Senova took his cup and filled it for him.

'Special occasion. Don't get used to it.'

There was precious little chance of that. Two cups of the stuff and his throat and chest felt like Crassus must have when the Parthians poured molten gold into his mouth. He longed for wine, but realised that there was none on offer. Probably a good thing. He awoke the next morning with a strange, positive feeling and, incredibly, no hangover.

The third day was much the same as the day before, though Rufinus noted a slight change in the attitude of the scouts. Though the jokes still flew and they maintained their laughter, there was a constant sense of awareness and concern about them that confirmed Rufinus' opinion of their professionalism. The hills became higher again, and Rufinus could see odd, red-gold rock formations poking from the tops of the trees. The third night was spent in the barns of some kindly farmer, who Narcissus praised and paid with good copper coins. Ironic, since the ground beneath them probably contained gold.

The fourth day was even colder, a chill wind running along the valley beneath incongruous blue skies and amid blossoming trees. Only an hour after they set off, they took a side valley, and now more scouts than ever were sent out to keep an eye on the land around them.

'We are close?' Rufinus asked Narcissus, bringing Atalanta alongside the centurion.

'We shall be in Alburnus Maior by nightfall,' the big man replied, though his eyes were straying constantly around the valley.

'You expect trouble?'

'Always. It's the job of a scout, to expect trouble. But yes, there is something in the air. Keep your hand on your sword, my praetorian friend. You will need it before the sun is high. Did you hear about the young man whose father bought him one of a pair of mules?'

Rufinus shook his head.

'He ran down to the market and bought the second, because he would never do anything half-assed.'

Neither of them laughed. Rufinus dropped back and fell in alongside the carriage. 'Narcissus expects trouble.'

Senova nodded. 'I can feel it in the air. It's like the hour before a thunder storm.'

What was it with these Celtic people? All Rufinus could feel was cold and an itch somewhere he couldn't scratch in front of a lady. 'Anyway, you have my spare sword and the silver spear in the gear. I suggest you get the former out. Just in case.' He left her arming herself, passed up his dagger to Luca, and rode forward once more. Acheron had moved into a hunter's lope alongside. Even the dog sensed danger.

Finally one of the riders – Julius Rathold, Rufinus remembered – came hurtling back from the valley ahead. 'Warriors lie in wait, Hailagaz. By some rocks ahead.'

'Details.'

'A dozen. Well armed and armoured but on foot. Dismounted Roxolani, I'd say.'

The centurion nodded and turned to Rufinus. 'A difficult decision. If they are lurking, and Rathold knows an ambush when he sees one, then they mean to fight. We are twenty two to their twelve, but they are well armoured warriors. We will win, but there will be casualties, and these men are all my brothers. I do not throw them away for good reason. Talk to me.'

Rufinus fretted. 'Is there another way around?'

'Two days extra. And probably similarly watched over.'

'Why would the Roxolani be here?' Rufinus asked, remembering the map, which placed their people some hundred and fifty miles east of here, all the way across Dacia.

'They move where the fighting is,' the centurion replied. 'Mercenaries for hire as often as not. If they are setting an ambush for us, then either someone is paying them to do so, or their pay has run dry and they have turned to banditry. Such a thing is not uncommon.'

Rufinus nodded, remembering the ex-legionaries who attacked them in the marshes. 'I *need* to get to Alburnus Maior, Narcissus.'

'If it has a cost in the blood of my riders, I need to know why.'

'I asked you to trust me,' Rufinus said, plaintively.

'Trust works both ways, praetorian. We have gone out of our way for you and taken you into the brotherhood, yet you will not trust us with your reasons?'

Rufinus felt a hole opening up beneath him. He was so close. He would never get another chance to come here, and could imagine no other way to secure the proof he needed. He swallowed.

'I believe that the governor in Apulum is up to no good.'

'That is in the very nature of governors,' Narcissus said.

'I have good information that Clodius Albinus has been siphoning off large quantities of gold from Alburnus Maior that was meant for the imperial coffers. He has already killed a procurator, if my information is to be believed, and has covered his tracks in Apulum. The only place left that there might be evidence is at the source, in Alburnus Maior, so you see why I have to go there. I am here for the emperor himself,' a white lie, since Cleander had signed the orders but then, as Albinus had said, Cleander now wielded the emperor's power. 'I am here to investigate Clodius Albinus for the imperial administration.'

Narcissus' eyes narrowed, bringing those great hairy brows low.

'This is for the emperor.'

'Of course. I am a praetorian. It is in my very duty. Everything I do is for the emperor.'

The centurion nodded. 'You will remember, when it matters, how the Numerus exploratorum Germanicianorum helped you?'

'Of course.'

'Then we ride and we kill Roxolani. Come, my praetorian brother.'

With a shouted command, the unit burst into lively activity. Two men dropped back to protect the carriage and its occupant while the others adjusted their equipment and several more riders emerged from the trees to either side of the road in answer to the call. Moments later there were sixteen of them, moving at pace and in unison along the valley, Rufinus amid the scouts.

'What will the Roxolani be like?'

Narcissus coughed. 'They are horsemen in the main, like other Sarmatians, but if they are setting an ambush it will not be on horses. Prepare for spears and traps.'

They rode on and after a short while, curving round the valley, Julius Rathold pointed to a small collection of amber rocks at the valley side. 'There. Behind those rocks. A game trail runs parallel, above in the woods, from which I saw them.'

Narcissus nodded. 'Rathold, take seven men and ride for the lower edge of the rocks making plenty of noise. Watch for ropes. Dismount at the approach and go in carefully on foot. Keep them occupied.'

The deputy saluted and gestured to a group of riders, who trotted off down the valley toward the rocks. Narcissus gestured to the rest of them and then up to the trees at their right. It took Rufinus a moment to spot the trail, an arch of darkness amid the tree boles, but with Narcissus in the lead, they rode into the treeline and out of the open valley. Rufinus thanked a number of gods for his experience on horseback in the forests of northern Hispania. Most infantry plonked into a saddle would have been out of it within ten heartbeats trying to ride such a narrow trail. Thin branches whipped at them and they were repeatedly forced to duck or lean-to avoid thicker limbs. Finally, they passed a more open glade and caught sight of the rocks below. Rufinus could hear the sound of fighting already in the open air.

'They are in trouble.'

Narcissus shook his head. 'They are holding the enemy, not risking themselves. Rathold knows what he's doing.'

They emerged from the game trail at the top of a grassy incline with the rocks below them. The Roxolani were already engaged with the other scouts, who had rounded the rocks on foot.

'For Woden!' bellowed Narcissus, and the cry was taken up by the other riders with him as they kicked their steeds into speed, racing down the hill at the enemy. Rufinus found to his embarrassment that he had automatically invoked the

Germanic god without thinking, but raced down the hill alongside the others. Once more he was grateful for his years of experience in the saddle. Riding straight down a steep slope without coming to grief was every bit as much of a skill as riding through a wood at speed.

The scouts levelled their spears and closed. The Roxolani suddenly turned at the realisation of a new threat emerging on the hillside, and half of them broke away from the fight, bringing their spears around. It was then that Rathold finally released the killers at his command, who had been simply keeping the enemy busy. As the Roxolani turned, Rathold's scouts began to attack like demons, swords biting, spears impaling. Rufinus wondered whether he would even get his sword wet before the dismounted scouts killed everyone. Acheron raced alongside, snarling, seeking a kill.

The riders from the hillside hit the pitiful, confused remnant of the Roxolani like Vulcan's hammer. Rufinus managed one slash with his sword in passing, drawing blood, but as he turned Atalanta and went in for the kill, the wounded man had already been dispatched by one of Narcissus' riders. Only one of the enemy remained alive, and he was on the way out, Acheron's powerful jaws around his throat. In heartbeats it was over. Twelve Roxolani lay dead.

The cost was light in Rufinus' opinion, though the centurion seemed less pleased. One of the men Rathold had commanded lay on the ground, a spear through his gut so far that he could not roll over. Another man had taken a terrible arm wound, white bone visible amid the blood and gristle.

'Corbus, set the bone and bind the wound,' Narcissus commanded, then dismounted and went over to the man with the spear through his gut. He crouched by him, whispered a few things in his ears that brought a weak smile from the doomed rider, then swiftly dispatched him with a blow through the heart The centurion rose and crossed to Rufinus as he dismounted.

'One dead, one badly wounded. For the emperor,' he reminded Rufinus.

'For the emperor.'

As the wounded man was tended and a shallow grave dug for the remains of the dead rider then piled above with stones in a cairn, the others went through the possessions of the Roxolani. Rufinus stood to one side, watching the carriage and its escort arrive and two more scouts returning from their circuits. Narcissus finally walked over to him, carrying two things.

'Mercenaries. Who paid them, I do not know. They had this,' he said, passing over a large gold nugget. 'Whether that was pay or loot, I cannot say, but they were not looking for us, else their response would have been more effective. We were a target of opportunity only.'

Rufinus took the other thing from the centurion. It was a legionary gladius of good manufacture. Near the hilt, the blade bore four names, the sword's various owners, probably having come to Dacia in Trajan's wars.

L PYLADVS
L A GAMBVRIO
M I FIDVS
P MODESTVS

'This is a Roman blade.'

'Quite.'

'Were they in the pay of Romans?'

Narcissus shrugged. 'This could just have been loot, taken from the dead some time in the past. Or, yes, they could have been paid by Romans, but what would be the purpose? The mine owners would lose out, for they cannot ship their gold. The miners themselves are little more than slaves, and often *precisely* slaves, and cannot afford to hire men. Why a soldier or officer would want to employ mercenaries to disrupt mining I cannot understand, and if the governor is, as you say, taking an unhealthy cut from the top, to do this would ruin him as much as anyone else.'

Rufinus nodded. 'Yet these men remain in the area and Albinus does nothing about them, sitting in his fortress at Apulum while gold supplies fail to flow. And the *Dacian rebels* turn out to be Roxolani mercenaries. I don't understand why, but I feel that Albinus is behind this somehow.'

'Perhaps you will gain your answers today, then. We ride for Alburnus and shall be there before nightfall.'

XIV – Secrets uncovered

Alburnus Maior was cold. That was Rufinus' initial impression of the place. The sky was a wide arc of cloudless blue, but the air was chilled to shivering point. Rufinus had expected the gold mining centre of Dacia to be some mountain fastness of grey stone and bleak scree amid high white peaks and driving snow. While it was certainly as *cold* as snow, in fact Alburnus Maior sat in the midst of a wide, green valley, spotted with copses and woods, farms and wide open fields.

The town itself was small and utilitarian, mostly given over to housing or workshops and storage sheds. There were no walls and no grand temples, just something that might pass for a forum to those who had never been to a city, and a small bath house. The people of Alburnus looked dour and grey, while the peaks around them, surrounding the valley, did not. They were high and brown-yellow.

The small group of riders with their carriage, Acheron loping alongside, entered the town from the higher slope up the valley, and Rufinus' eyes, having scoured the place and taken everything in, moved to the periphery. It took some squinting and attention, but with closer examination he could see the workings. All around the peaks were small black apertures, each the entrance to a mining shaft or adit. There were so *many* of them. Like an ant's nest.

Dozens of wary eyes watched the riders move into town, and the feeling emanating from Alburnus was uncomfortable, to say the least. Rufinus frowned as they moved into the centre. This was the first place they had passed through on their journey where the scout riders had not been immediately treated as locals. Why so wary, unfriendly?

The answer came as they entered the main square: what had clearly been the grandest building in Alburnus Maior – the council house of the town's leaders – had been destroyed. All that remained was a shell of brown stone, streaked with soot and mud and filled with charred beams and rubble. One might have mistaken it for an accidental fire but for the marks on the ground outside. There was no paving here, just russet-coloured grit, and the weather had been dry enough that the stains of blood had simply sunk in and remained in-situ rather than washing away. And the four marks were in a perfect line, evidence of deliberate executions rather than a random struggle.

'The Roxolani again?'

Narcissus nodded. 'They or other friends of theirs. There must have been many such groups at work in the area for it to be considered a rising by the governor's men.'

'But it was no rising,' Rufinus said once again. 'Mercenaries doing a specific job. And that job seemingly included removing the council at Alburnus and burning down their chambers.'

'There will undoubtedly be more to find,' the centurion replied. 'For gold caravans are not travelling the usual routes. We shall see what we shall see.'

An old woman with a wicker basket full of blankets looked up at the riders with suspicion as Narcissus reined in alongside her.

'Where can I find someone in authority?'

The woman's face turned sour. 'There is no one. All dead.'

'Who looks after the interests of the mine owners, then?'

'What mine owners?' spat the woman, and hurried on.

The centurion, flicking a concerned look at Rufinus, collared a young man. The fellow was perhaps eighteen or nineteen years of age. His complexion was pale and clear, his hands smooth and unmarked. Not a manual worker, then.

'Where are the mine owners? Where do they live?'

The young man frowned. 'They live in their compounds, when they are here. Often they stay in the city, though, or down in the lowlands and let overseers work for them. One even stays in Rome and never comes here.'

Rufinus nodded. Now they were getting somewhere. 'Which is the most important mine? The richest one? Who among the owners is the leader?'

Narcissus shook his head. 'They are all private businessmen. There is no strata among them.'

Rufinus snorted. 'These men are Romans. There will always be a pecking order and, believe me, there will always be a leader.'

The young man thought for only a moment. 'The biggest concern is that of Aurelius Adiutor. Down the valley half a mile. You cannot miss his compound. Look for the red columns.'

Rufinus smiled and the centurion nodded. 'That's our man, then.'

To the young man: 'Thank you.'

He hurried off, and the riders, carriage in tow, rattled and clopped down the gritty road, out of the western edge of Alburnus and alongside a curiously red-gold looking stream. The young man had been quite correct: it was hard to miss Adiutor's compound. A huge fenced area with a gate surrounded a sizeable villa with a red-painted colonnade and a whole complex of other structures. Rufinus' breath caught in his throat at the sight, for the gate lay wide open and there was no sign of life within. The centurion motioned to his riders and, as they passed inside, two men had Luca draw the carriage up by the gate, staying with it on guard, one of them the man with the blood-soaked, bandaged arm from the fight earlier.

The other riders spread out, moving around the complex as Narcissus and Rufinus headed straight for the villa. The door there was open, too. Sharing a tense look with the centurion, Rufinus slid from the saddle and tied Atalanta to the hitching rail alongside Narcissus' horse. They drew their swords and moved carefully into the building.

It was clear from the entranceway that the danger was long gone. The small altar to the household gods way lying on its side on the floor, the small statues and offerings smashed and scattered. The impluvium's fountain in the atrium directly ahead was not flowing, and the small, square pool was filled with the remains of the villa's occupants. Though it was almost impossible to tell male from female amid the bloated, two-week old corpses, grey and rotting, it was clear that they were rich and poor alike, left in a pile. Expensive tunics and stolas among the grey slave clothes – Adiutor and his wife, presumably, as well as their family and staff. The Roxolani had been thorough. Trying not to breathe in the fetid, stinking air, Rufinus and Narcissus checked out the other rooms.

The place had been ransacked. Anything of value had gone, the occupants butchered and stripped of jewellery. Rufinus was standing in the tablinum – the owner's office – when Narcissus joined him, sheathing his sword. 'This all happened weeks ago,' the centurion said. 'The mercenaries raided. Killed everyone. Took everything.'

The young praetorian nodded, addressing the centurion without taking his eyes from the ransacked office. 'What is odd here, Narcissus?'

The centurion frowned and scanned the room. 'Nothing. Looks like all the other rooms. They broke into all the cupboards and drawers and took what they found.'

'Including documentation?'

Narcissus' brow folded even deeper. 'What?'

Rufinus turned, eyes sparkling. 'What sort of Sarmatian raider takes wax tablets of notes and records, scrolls and books of letters and documents? Everywhere else they have stripped bodies and stolen the valuables, yes, and that is consistent with thieves and opportunists. But documents? And I'm willing to bet that Roxolani mercenaries are not going to be well versed in Latin script. This is more than a raid. This is deliberately covering up something altogether more devious and important.'

Narcissus nodded. 'P'raps the rest of the compound will provide clarity?'

The two men passed the stinking pile of bodies and emerged from the building to find the scouts gathered out front.

'All looted. All staff dead,' one of the scouts announced.

'One building burned,' added another.

Rufinus' ear pricked up, the hairs on his neck standing proud. 'Oh? How specific. Just like the council house in town. Come on.'

With Narcissus in tow, he strode around the compound, which was filled with human remains and discarded tools, to the blackened shell of a building. It lay separate from the work sheds and bunk houses, with only one other building nearby. It was a small structure of timber, now mainly charred beams and ash. Rufinus walked past the other building. 'What was this?'

'Guardhouse, we think,' Rathold replied. Eight men dead in there, all with chain shirts and swords.'

Rufinus nodded. 'Guards in place to protect the house from any trouble with the workers. There are marks here – a dividing fence that's been torn down in the action. But I think… I think the guards were not positioned precisely there *just* to protect the house.'

He hurried over to the burned out building, picked up a long broken handle from some unidentified tool and began using it to sift through the ash and carbonised deposits. With a hiss of satisfaction, he lifted a piece of something blackened and charred from the ash and displayed it to the others.

'Scroll rack. This was the mine's office, where the records were kept.'

Narcissus reached out and touched the ruined furnishing, which crumbled and collapsed under his fingers. 'You were right. This is covering something up. All the records in the complex burned. And the council chamber in town? The same there. We need to check the other mines.'

As they turned, Senova leaned from the carriage. 'What is happening?'

Narcissus glanced only briefly at Rufinus, then gestured to the two riders at the vehicle's side. 'Take the lady into the town and find somewhere defensible for us to stay the night. Protect her at all costs.'

'Now listen here...' began Senova irritably.

'And keep Acheron with you,' Rufinus added. 'The mercenaries at work in these hills are brutal and have no qualms about killing women and children.'

The Briton began to argue, but Rufinus waved the riders on and at their centurion's nod, they escorted the vehicle back toward the town with Senova still cursing inside.

Over the next two hours, as the sun descended, Rufinus and the riders located and examined three more compounds, finding the same situation in each. All the occupants had been butchered, whether they be owners, guards or even workers. Everything of value had been taken. Every record office burned, all documents gone. As they moved through the mine complexes of Alburnus Maior, Rufinus became more and more convinced that this was all part of the grander conspiracy, and more and more disheartened that any evidence had clearly gone.

Finally, in one of the higher compounds, overlooking the town from a hillside, Rufinus and Narcissus stood by a charred building, the scouts scouring the wreckage in the very last indigo light of evening.

'That has to be it for the day,' Narcissus announced. 'The light is going and we need to get back to town and make sure your woman is safe. We will have to move on for Bucium tomorrow, though I will not press for departure immediately. I'll give you an hour in the morning with fresh light to try and find what you seek before we leave.'

Rufinus nodded dejectedly. 'This is the governor's doing. Of that I have no doubt.'

'That is a dangerous thing to announce in public without evidence.'

'Listen. Hear me out. Clodius Albinus takes a hefty cut of all gold production here – gold that is earmarked for imperial coffers. What he uses such a large fortune for, I don't know, but I think some of it might have ended up in the vault of the governor of Moesia Superior. The procurator gets wind of it and plans an investigation. Then the procurator suddenly dies. I find it hard to picture that as anything but the work of Albinus. The procurator's office is picked clean by the governor before the replacement sent from Rome can arrive. There is therefore no record of his wrongdoing, or even of the potential investigation into it.'

Rufinus was starting to slap his fist into his palm now. 'But there was still a loose end. Here in Alburnus Maior there were mine owners who had to have been a party to the crime. And there must have been many administrators and clerks who were privy to it. Likely at least someone in the town's council knew about it too. And now they are all dead, and all records destroyed by some native rising that has apparently been faked using Roxolani mercenaries. Albinus has covered his tracks *very* thoroughly.'

'But then why has he not sent in the Thirteenth to clear out the raiders and reinstall order?' the centurion mused. 'Now he's simply losing out on gold production and running risk that someone might learn what happened here, as we did.'

Rufinus nodded. 'I think it's a further level of security. He does not want to put down this rebellion until the new procurator has arrived. That way he can blame all the troubles, any deficiency in gold quantities and the whole mess, on the rebels and appear to be a hero of Rome in putting them to the sword and instilling order at Alburnus, right under the procurator's nose. He is in the clear, exceedingly rich, with no evidence against him and in addition he gets mentioned in the new procurator's dispatches to Rome as the hero who resolved it all. Very neat.'

Narcissus sighed. 'Albinus was already a rich man by comparison with most. I will never understand why rich men must always try to be richer.'

Rufinus tapped his lip in thought, but a shout from one of the scouts drew their attention. The two men turned, along with the rest of the riders, to see one of the unit pointing with his spear. A figure had emerged from a copse near the compound's entrance, wearing a grey tunic and a woollen cloak against the cold, hands held high to indicate peaceful intentions.

Rufinus and the centurion, leaving their horses tied to the rail near the vehicle shed, walked over to the gate, which stood open and abandoned, as did everything in this deserted place. The man was approaching the gate with a serious expression. Though bearded, he was clearly not Roxolani. In fact, he was rather swarthy skinned, suggesting an origin somewhere far to the south and east of Dacia.

The young praetorian's shrewd eye scanned the man and picked out a number of salient points straight away. His hair and beard showed a few weeks' growth, perhaps a month, but had previously been neat and short. His skin was scarred with old wounds. His tunic may be civilian, but the belt he wore was a military one with the plates removed. He moved with a lurching gait, his left leg dragging slightly. Rufinus felt a tiny chill run through him.

Surely Fortuna could not favour him *this* much? But it all fitted.

'You are.. not from the governor's office.' the man said. A statement, not a question.

Rufinus shook his head. Interesting. First concern not *are you with the Roxolani*, but *with the governor*. 'No. We are not. Nor are we from the Thirteenth Gemina or the procurator's office.'

'I've been watching you. You've been investigating.'

Rufinus cast a glance at Narcissus, who had the grace to look faintly embarrassed that his eagle-eyed scouts had failed to pick up on a lone observer.

'I am, as you say, investigating.' He chewed his lip. Time to leap into the pool with both feet. 'I am a friend of Cassius Proculeianus,' he said clearly.

The man's eyes widened for a moment, then sank into slits. 'Explain yourself.'

'Yes,' Narcissus said meaningfully. 'I'd appreciate that, too.'

Rufinus grinned. 'This man was a soldier from the Thirteenth until his leg wound saw him pensioned out. Then he started working in the procurator's office. It was him who first brought this gold conspiracy to light, Cassius told me about him.' He turned to the man in the grey tunic. 'Your former centurion is concerned. You disappeared from Apulum without a trace. He thinks the governor is on to you and that he will be next.'

'Cassius will be safe. I left no record that could lead to him, and I am gone. I shall not return to Apulum, or very likely I will disappear for good.'

Rufinus nodded. 'So when you disappeared, you came here?'

The man coughed. 'It became clear that Albinus was covering his tracks. I wanted to make sure he failed in the end. It was a dangerous journey. The mercenaries were already at work on the gold trains when I came.'

'What *happened* to the gold. We never saw a hint of the caravans on our journey, and there was no evidence of them being butchered by Roxolani either.'

The soldier clapped his hands together. 'Oh they took the gold alright, but not for themselves, well not *all* of it at least. Most of the gold went back by another route, deep in the mountains back to Apulum. I would wager it's in Albinus' coffers now along with the rest. What's left of it, anyway.'

'What do you mean, "what's left of it",' Rufinus frowned.

'Come with me.'

The soldier walked back toward the trees and reappeared with a mangy-looking horse. Rufinus and Narcissus mounted once more, and the scout party followed him down the hill toward Alburnus, the man leading the way in silence, the two investigators sharing intrigued glances. They passed through the town swiftly, and no one even glanced at the man, Rufinus realised. He was clever. He had somehow managed to insinuate himself into life at Alburnus to the extent that he was more or less invisible, even when travelling with the scouts. For just a moment, Rufinus wondered whether the man was one of the frumentarii. If not, he damn well should be. He would work well with Vibius Cestius.

Finally they reached the compound of Aurelius Adiutor, the very first site they had investigated on their arrival.

'What are we doing back here?' Rufinus asked quietly, peering into the ever-increasing evening gloom and trying to make out any detail they might have missed on their first visit. 'And what do I call you, anyway?'

'I think a lack of names might be prudent,' the man replied. 'And I don't particularly want to know yours. But if you're truly bent on investigating the governor, and it's proof you seek, then proof I have. Come with me.'

The ex-soldier dismounted, hissing as his crippled leg touched the floor, and then, after tying up his horse, lurched off toward one of the entrances into the hill, a mine shaft like the many others in the township.

Rufinus and Narcissus looked at one another and shrugged.

'Stay here and keep watch,' the centurion told his second, and Rathold saluted, waving the other riders into the best positions to observe the surrounding countryside. Leaving them to it, Rufinus and Narcissus made for the mine entrance. As they moved through the darkness, Rufinus heard rather than saw the centurion draw his blade. He turned a questioning glance on the man.

Narcissus shrugged. '*You* might know him. *I* don't know him from Vesta herself. Better armed than dead.' Despite his strident belief in the crippled soldier, Rufinus found himself drawing his own blade too. The actions did not seem to concern the ex-soldier, who was now in the entrance of the mine, lighting three oil lamps. Each was a sizeable lantern and, though the glow did little to penetrate the gloom of the compound, in the confined space of the adit it created a warm, golden glow that caressed the walls and ceiling and lit the way ahead.

Taking the lamp that was offered, Rufinus fell in behind the man, with the centurion and his own lamp at the rear. They need fear no attack from there, Rufinus felt certain, with Rathold and his men watching the entrance. After only a few feet, the shaft began to descend, and around and over the head of the man in front, Rufinus could see only an endless straight passageway sinking down into the rock. The sudden oppressive weight of a mountain on top of them insisted itself upon him and he broke into a cold sweat, though, despite the fear building, Rufinus' natural curiosity won out and he cleared his throat.

'Why is the tunnel this shape?' he asked, his voice echoing eerily along the passage. Rather than a simple straight tunnel, the miners had carved the passageway into a strange shape – almost a stretched hexagon.

'The shape best takes the weight of the rock. It distributes the pressure without the need for wooden props. Makes the whole thing a lot safer and a lot more efficient. There have only been two collapses in all the Alburnus mines during my time in the procurator's office. Compare that to lead mines where they rely on timbers and you'll understand. See these?' he asked, pausing and gesturing at the wall. There was a distinct line all around the passage, as though they were passing through an invisible portal – a slight lip in the rock, and beside it a small hollow carved from the side.

'What is it?'

'Each of these lines marks a day's mining. The niche is for lamps. Each team of miners dig as long as the lamp light lasts, then they return to the surface and another team begins.'

Rufinus felt the presence of decades of work as they descended and he saw line after line, niche after niche. How many men had died in this tunnel, quarrying rock and rarely experiencing anything approaching freedom. He was suddenly glad Senova was not here, or he would be experiencing an acidic lecture on the evils of slave-miners by now.

They spent a quarter of an hour moving through the tunnel, though it levelled out after a while, and they passed numerous side-passages. Occasionally they turned a corner, and he could only assume the man they followed knew precisely where he was going. Rufinus vowed not to lose sight of the man. Without him, the chances of them getting out of this warren of tunnels were extremely thin.

Finally, their guide turned into one of the many small chambers they had passed, which usually coincided with junctions of numerous passages. This one, however, seemed a dead-end. All it contained was a cart full of tools and a pile of broken oil lamps.

'If I give you the proof you seek, what do you intend to do with it?'

Rufinus frowned. 'You've brought us this far, surely you trust us?'

'Tell me. Or I will not lead you back out. Some things are bigger than one man's life.'

'Spoken like a soldier,' Rufinus said quietly. He had thought on the issue a little, though not through to a full conclusion yet. But still, he had an idea. 'I am bound for Porolissum. There I am to present myself to Pescennius Niger. I am a member of the praetorian guard on detached duty, sent here by the emperor's chamberlain to investigate this very matter. Niger has been recommended to me by someone I trust. I will present him with the evidence and see that Albinus is prosecuted for it.'

The ex-legionary frowned for some time, apparently trying to decide whether Rufinus' plan was satisfactory.

'I'm not keen on such a vague reliance, but better going north to Niger than anywhere near Albinus or even most of the provinces to the south and west.'

'Why?'

'You'll see.'

The man crossed to the small mine cart and moved the tools and a rough sack, fishing something out from beneath them. It was clearly heavy, and the man lifted it with a grunt, favouring his good leg, then held it forth in shaky hands. It was a wooden box roughly a foot and a half long and a foot in each other dimension. It was strapped tight with leather ties that were sealed with a wax seal. The letters P S F had been scored into the wooden top, followed by ROMA.

Rufinus frowned, taking the box, his arms dipping with the sudden weight.

'How do you know what it is if you've not opened it?' Rufinus asked quietly.

'It's not the first one of these I've seen. Not even the tenth. Not even the fiftieth. I know what it is. But all the others have gone. This is the only one that remains and I kept it safe, hidden down in this mine.'

'I'll need to open it.'

The man shrugged. 'That might make it inadmissible as evidence, but then Niger would want it opened when you produce it anyway. Your oath as a praetorian on an altar of Apollo should be enough to satisfy most people. Open it, then.'

Rufinus placed the casket on the floor. 'This is Albinus' seal?'

The man nodded, and Rufinus took his eating knife from his belt and, careful not to destroy the seal, sawed through the leather straps it covered. Finally, he had cut enough and he pulled the box from the leather straps with a grunt. There was a keyhole to the box, and he sucked on his lip for only a moment before ignoring the lock and using his knife to lever out the pins holding the hinges at the far side. The ex-soldier smiled.

'With a mind like yours, you should work in the procurator's office too.'

Rufinus snorted and lifted the lid. Though he had been expecting it, the sight of the gleaming precious metal still made his heart skip a beat. Three bars of gold sat in the box, each unmarked and unstamped, officially owned by no one. Secret gold. With them was a scroll case, also sealed. Taking a deep breath, Rufinus used his knife to slice open the end of the leather tube without disturbing the seal. A sheet of vellum slid out.

The young praetorian lifted it to the light and read, his breath locked behind his teeth and his eyes widening as he moved down the brief missive. In a neat hand, the author put forth a request that one Durmius Pavo be assigned as a praetor in the city of Rome. The letter was marked from D C S A.

Rufinus looked up. 'D C S A?'

'Decimus Clodius Septimius Albinus,' the man confirmed.

A praetor. Rufinus had no idea who this Durmius Pavo might be, but if he were made a praetor in Rome, and he owed it to Albinus? Rufinus shivered. One task of the praetors was to preside over cases of corrupt governors. Albinus truly *was* covering himself.

'So who is he asking to secure this position for Pavo?'

The ex-soldier tapped the lid, where the three letters were marked.

'But who is P S F?'

'In Rome, I can think of only one name that fits and might have the influence to secure that position,' the man replied. 'Publius Seius Fuscianus.'

Rufinus felt his blood chill. The urban prefect. The man almost ran the city of Rome, though he did so only with Cleander's say-so these days. Fuscianus controlled the urban cohorts who kept the streets of the city safe, he oversaw the city's guilds and colleges, the mint, the grain supply and much, much more. Yes, if any man in Rome could simply appoint a praetor, other than Cleander or the emperor that was, it was Fuscianus.'

'This is… this is… is it treason? I don't know. It's certainly very dubious and illegal. And this is not the only one, you say?'

The ex-soldier nodded. 'Dozens of them over the past year. I saw it go to a dozen provinces or more and more than half to Rome itself though not through official channels. The gold is slipped out before it becomes marked officially, side-lined into boxes like this and sent all over the empire.'

Rufinus felt the hairs rise on his neck again. How big was this conspiracy? He suddenly pictured the cadaverous Quintus Naevius Capella, governor of Moesia Superior, opening a box like this and grinning at the gold within, accompanying a letter asking for levies of men in the province. *We have an arrangement*, Capella had said. How many other arrangements like this were there? All over the empire, and right into Rome. Something suddenly occurred to him.

'This Durmius Pavo… he's one of the mine owners, isn't he?'

The ex-soldier smiled. 'You're quick. Yes. In exchange for gold from his mine, Albinus secures him a good post in Rome. And to secure that post, he sends the gold to the urban prefect. All very neat.'

Behind them, Narcissus gave a confused rumble. 'But Albinus gets nothing from it? The mine owners and other people, no doubt, get positions of power and influence, and those people who secure the positions get the gold. All Clodius Albinus gets is the job of moving it all back and forth.'

Rufinus shook his head.

'What Albinus gets is debts. Everyone owes him. The mine owners *and* the powerful men, and I'd be willing to bet the only mine owners who died here are ones who have not been part of this grand plan. Those involved all know Albinus has done them a favour. And while every last one of them is party to Albinus' crime and could bring him down, none of them would dare, for they are all as deeply in it as him. The man's a twisted genius. He's built a web of rich and powerful men with himself at the centre. All he has to do is pull on a thread and he could change the whole empire.'

The enormity of that suddenly struck him.

'Albinus is preparing for a *coup*. He has his eyes set on the throne. He is manoeuvring his pieces into position on the board. Gods, but the man's clever. Pompeianus would have trouble with this one.'

'You think he would really try to overthrow the emperor?'

Rufinus shrugged. 'Why not. It's been done before. Look at the end of Nero. Vespasian had his pieces in place. One son in charge of one of the largest armies of veterans in the empire, popular and with a string of victories. The other in Rome, influencing everything in preparation for their father's triumphant arrival in the city and claiming the purple. A brother commanding the praetorians. Jove, but this is *huge*. It doesn't matter that I've opened this box. If this gets back to Cleander, Albinus's head will be on a spike in days, along with everyone else in that web. I have to get this to Niger, as soon as possible.'

And this is just big enough that it might buy me Publius' freedom, he added silently.

Narcissus nodded. 'We ride for Porolissum at first light and move as fast as we can.' He looked over at the ex-soldier. 'You should come with us. You'll be safe there.'

The man shook his head. 'I'm going to disappear. No one will look for the lost man of the procurator's office and I've been officially discharged from the military, so I'm not a deserter. A life of comfortable obscurity awaits me.'

Rufinus frowned. 'I imagine you have a box with a few of these in somewhere private, eh?'

He man shrugged. 'I shall not be poor,' he replied with a sly smile.

'Probably a good thing I don't know your name after all. Thank you, though. You've done me a great favour and the empire a huge service.'

The man straightened. 'Let's get back out of the mine. I'm sick of the sight of Alburnus Maior.'

For the first time in months, Rufinus felt hope course through him.

XV – Into the borderlands

The journey became arduous immediately upon leaving Alburnus, and Rufinus swiftly realised why the scout centurion had given him such a length journey estimate. Ever since they had left the Danuvius what felt like a lifetime ago and travelled into Dacia they had, Rufinus now realised, travelled on actual roads, whether they be modern Roman ones, routes of the Dacian people from the time of their kings, or humble native trade routes.

But nothing travelled north of Alburnus Maior. Apart from a few sheep trails and local village tracks, there was no way through these hills. People simply did not travel through them unless it was perhaps to the next village to barter for chickens. It was bad enough terrain for the horses, let alone for Senova's carriage, and Rufinus really had to appreciate how, despite everything, Narcissus constantly found ways wide enough for the vehicle, even if only at a scrape.

Bare, blasted moors. Forests with little more than widened game trails. Rocky outcroppings. Deep valleys with grey cliffs and azure waters. And all just wide enough to manage the carriage, though the vaunted suspension could no longer do anything to counteract the bone-shaking awfulness of the journey. Rufinus had tried one afternoon in the vehicle and has quickly given up in disgust and returned to Atalanta, who provided boundless comfort by comparison. He couldn't understand why Senova didn't just abandon the carriage and ride a horse. No one was going to care about improprieties, *especially* in this company. It had to be British pig-headedness, or perhaps feminine bloody-mindedness. Either way, she lived with every teeth-jarring bump. Even Acheron now shunned his blankets and cushions for a brisk walk.

The same scene repeatedly characterised their journey.

'Ah, good,' the centurion would say, satisfied. 'The Padas market road. We should make better time for a while.'

Rufinus would look at the thing at which Narcissus was pointing. 'That,' he would say, 'is not a road. That is simply some dirt that is a different colour to the dirt on either side.'

Or.

'Excellent. We have joined the Metlad logging road.'

'One wonders how even a log manages to travel this road, let alone a wagon.'

Or.

'Thank the gods. The Aureus crossing.'

'Narcissus, for a river to have a crossing, it needs to be shallower than the rest of the river.'

Yet slowly, painstakingly, they moved on north. And despite the troubles they encountered on an hourly basis, Rufinus found he was taking it all in the most incredibly good-natured manner. The astounding and unexpected success of their visit to Alburnus Maior had infected him with a positivity he had not felt in a very long time.

Senova seemed to feel it too, from the shaking confines of her carriage. She had not told him off in days, and seemed not to find his very presence a cause for irritation and wry commentary. Six days they spent, travelling in the highlands, through valleys and woods and over moors, and finally they began to encounter more level and comfortable terrain. There Rufinus began to see something new. Earthen embankments across narrow valleys, half-finished towers, areas of mass deforestation. The centurion explained it to him.

'The *Limes*. This is the edge of the empire, Rufinus, my friend. You pass that tree you can see on the horizon and take a shit on the other side and you're defiling Iazyges lands.'

'So close?'

Narcissus shrugged. 'Nah, not really. It's a bit further than that in truth, but we *are* close now. In fact only one fort lies between us and the Sarmatians: place called Resculum. Weird place. Hispanic auxilia and Greek settlers relocated there to try and make it feel less like the arse end of the empire. But that's just part of the whole defensive system. What you're seeing here and there are marks of the *Limes Porolensis*. Used to be there was just a few signal stations and fortlets right at the outer edge of Roman influence but, since the incursions, Pescennius Niger's been strengthening the border all the way along with levels of defence. Ramparts across the most open areas, actual customs posts and towers. There's a full system gradually coming into place, all the way from the Danuvius to the northern wilds. It's a work in progress, but it's coming along.'

Rufinus nodded. He'd been outside the empire, of course, during Aurelius' Marcomannic Wars, but somehow seeing such a delineation marked in turf and timber and stone was different. In a world where he had been brought up to believe that Rome was boundless and all non-Roman territories were simply lands yet to be included in the Pax Romana, he was suddenly aware that Rome – Hadrian specifically – had drawn a line on a map and said 'beyond here will never be part of the empire.' Strange to consider.

On the seventh day, the weather changed yet again. The Dacian gods had thrown their weather die and the cube had come down showing 'showers'. Showers it was, then. The skies remained a deceptive blue, the weather warmer than it had been high up in Alburnus, and yet repeatedly delivered lead-grey clouds out of nowhere that raced across the sky so quickly that by the time you realised you needed shelter, you were soaked and the cloud was gone again, leaving clear blue once more. Every now and then Narcissus would pause and point off into the distance at some invisible target naming a fort that he knew but that they would be going nowhere near, very helpfully.

The jokes continued, too. Every day a plethora of pointless gems.

'Did you hear about the Aegyptian merchant? He had to ask how much a five-cup flask held.'

'There was a Cumean who went swimming, and when it started to rain he went into the deep end so as not to get wet.'

'Did you hear about the gladiator with such bad breath that when he put on a helmet it was counted as suicide.'

'There was this Athenian travelling by ship when a storm hit. Everyone tied themselves to something just in case, so he tied himself to the anchor.'

Rufinus was in such a good mood that he actually laughed dutifully at more than half the jokes.

On the eighth day, late in the morning, they crossed a small river and Narcissus let out a bellow of relief. Rufinus, startled from a daydream, looked around sharply. 'What?'

'At last, a Roman road.'

Rufinus stared. If that was a road, Roman or otherwise, then he was a suckling pig wearing a bladder for a hat.

'Narcissus, that will break the carriage,' he replied, peering in dismay at the winding, climbing line of jagged stones, potholes and gravelled bumps.

'You have such little faith, my praetorian friend.'

They pressed on, and it took Rufinus a full half hour to become accustomed to the sound of the carriage being systematically shaken to pieces behind him. Acheron paced alongside the road on the green verge and after only a short while Rufinus realised how sensible the animal was and followed suit. Finally, a little after noon, the big centurion smiled and gestured ahead expansively.

'Behold fabled Bucium.'

Rufinus frowned at the squat, brown shape on the hill ahead. 'We're supposed to be going to Porolissum?'

'Porolissum is further on. Two more days. Bucium is on the way, so we will change horses and resupply, and I will report to the acting prefect there.'

Bucium was as 'frontier' a fort as Rufinus had ever seen. It stood on a bluff with steep slopes to two sides and a gentle descent from the others, a good field of vision, its walls of turf and seasoned timber. A small vicus had built up next to it, but it would never be anything more than a settlement of hopefuls and illegal wives. This, Rufinus decided, was not a fort with a future as a colonia or city. At best it was a latrine masquerading as a military installation. He tried to hide his feelings about the place, given Narcissus' clear sense of pride in his home. As if to deliberately add to his discomfort, it began to rain.

As they moved through a small hamlet by the stream and up to the fort, the civil settlement proper lying on the far side to the north-east, the people seemed friendly enough. Moreover, the fort's walls and towers as they crested the rise and approached were immaculate. A certain type of commander ruled here, he realised. A fussy one, but one who kept things right.

They were admitted with a certain level of formality, despite the best efforts of Narcissus to lower the tone of the exchange, and the centurion took Rufinus and Se   nova, with Acheron beside them, his tongue lolling, to see the commander, while Luca saw to the beasts.

'Narcissus?' Rufinus said, looking around at the sturdy timber buildings in ordered rows.

'Yes?'

'This is a sizeable fort for a small cavalry scout unit. I mean there can't be more than a few score of your riders, and this fort was built for a thousand men, I reckon.'

The centurion nodded. 'Yes. We shared it with a unit of Hispanic cavalry until the troubles, when legatus Niger took them away to join his punitive army. I daresay they'll be back, but we've made sure to take all the good quarters while they're away.'

The headquarters was pristine and well-kept. As he'd done in a dozen forts across the empire, Rufinus saluted the guards, crossed the square past the store rooms and the well, into the basilica with its colonnade containing statues of very stoic looking men in armour. Across the basilica and into one of the rooms.

A man in a senior officer's uniform was busy making notes and looked up in surprise. He looked faintly fishy to Rufinus. Big, rubbery lips, bulging eyes and a waxy complexion. The young praetorian half expected to see gills open when the man sighed.

'Narcissus,' he susurrated, 'it is customary to knock. Even in the civilian world, let alone in the office of a superior.'

Rufinus was shocked as the centurion laughed and dropped unceremoniously into the seat opposite the man. 'You're not my commander, Evagrius. Just the poor bastard the cavalry left behind to look after the place.'

The officer's eye began to twitch uncontrollably, and Rufinus was fascinated watching the interplay between them.

'I've new orders from Apulum. Taking these folk to the legatus at Porolissum. I'd appreciate chitties for a complete resupply?'

Evagrius' eyes shrank to mere white pearls. Rufinus' own eyes were watering just watching them. This was probably the closest that piscine face could come to a frown.

'Narcissus, you were expected *days* ago,' the man said with rigid disapproval.

The centurion lifted one buttock and let out a huge, reverberating fart, then chuckled. 'New orders, as I said.'

'Even so you are days overdue. I am not pleased.'

'Good for you.'

'And I am calling your unit to stand to.'

The centurion sat upright. 'What?'

'One of the work parties at the frontier has been attacked. I want you to track them, find out who was responsible and bring them in. The legatus will appreciate our efforts.'

'Piss off, Evagrius.'

The prefect, for that was what he appeared to be, rose angrily to his feet, wagging a fishy finger.

'I outrank you, Narcissus, and I am the de facto commander of Bucium. Believe me, if the First Hispanorum were here I would entrust the duty to them rather than you dirty, disorganised slackers, but life is what we make it and all I have to work with are your men. You will take all your riders out before dusk and ride for the frontier, where you will find me the men responsible. You may not like me, and gods know I don't like you, but you *serve* here, and I *command*, and unless you want to find yourself whipped for insubordination, you will do AS YOU ARE FUCKING TOLD!'

The officer stood, white faced and panting, and Rufinus had witnessed enough anger in his time to see the ire boiling up in the scout centurion. This was doing no one any good. He opened his mouth to say something. He wasn't sure what yet, but he had to calm the situation. To his surprise, it was Senova's voice that cut through the tension.

'Don't trouble yourself, Narcissus.'

They all turned to look at her. All three of them had more or less forgotten she was there, she had been so unusually quiet.

'Miss?'

'You said it was two days to Porolissum? Gnaeus and I travelled a month together with no escort, all the way from Rome to Dacia. I would be a poor daughter of Brigantia if I could not manage two more days inside good Roman territory. And Gnaeus might look like a wet rag with a bad haircut, but I assure you he is a good, strong warrior.'

The prefect looked faintly embarrassed as he turned to Senova. 'There is another matter, miss, I'm afraid. There are reports of a carriage gone missing from Apulum the same time you departed. You will have to leave it here, for I have orders to send it back to the capital if and when it shows up.'

Senova shrugged. 'I can ride a horse.'

Rufinus stared at her, exasperated. Where was this easy-going malleability when he'd needed it half a month ago while contemplating a long journey in the mountains?

'Sir,' Narcissus said, wrapping his tongue with distaste around the word, 'this land is still not fully secured. You cannot intend to send a Roman matron into the countryside without an appropriate escort?'

Senova was there again, instantly. 'Gnaeus has money. We will hire men in the village. And a guide. Do not fear for us.'

The big centurion cast an apologetic look at Rufinus, who smiled reassuringly, trying not to think of the seriously dwindling pile of coins in his purse. He had taken three months' wages in advance from the praetorian coffers before he set off from Rome, but they were now largely gone, and no governor or provincial legate was likely to want to pay him without direct orders from Rome. Hopefully Niger would be sympathetic and help. 'We'll be fine Narcissus,' he said, pushing the worry from his mind. 'Say goodbye to the men for us and catch the Iazyges bastards who did for the work party. I will commend you to Pescennius Niger when I see him. You've been a good friend and a great help.'

Narcissus bowed his head and held out a hand. As Rufinus shook it, the centurion said, 'Go to Maska's stable. He will know good men. Men you can trust. Use my name.'

Rufinus smiled, and then more so as Narcissus bowed so low to Senova he almost overbalanced.

'It was a delight to know you, lady Senova.'

'And you, you big, hairy bear. Look after yourself and your men.'

Rufinus saluted and left, all-but dragging her from the building.

'What is it?' she asked as they emerged into the open courtyard.

'I don't like that. The prefect knew about the carriage and that we were travelling with Narcissus. Word of our movements has reached Bucium before us. The faster we get this evidence to Niger, the better.'

Rufinus found Maska's easily enough. The man spoke what Rufinus could only describe as 'rudimentary Latin', but he seemed to be friendly and genuine, especially when Narcissus recommendation came up, and his prices were so reasonable that the young praetorian offered as much over the odds as he dare spare to secure extra loyalty. By late afternoon, they had four horses between the three of them – Rufinus, Senova and Luca, who mysteriously seemed to be far less important to the legion than a carriage – and plenty of supplies. They had also acquired four local guards with unpronounceable names, only a dozen teeth between them and less command of Latin than your average pomegranate. Still, again, they seemed genuine, and all were well armed if not well armoured.

They made good time out of Bucium and by the time night fell they had reached a place some eight miles away called Largiana, where the guide in his thick accent had explained they could overnight. Largiana turned out to be another fort, though this one had been wrecked and damaged recently, presumably by Sarmatian invaders during the troubles. Men had died here in brutal action, judging by the state of the place, though the bodies had been disposed of and things were slowly being put to rights.

They found soldiers staying in the fort. Two tent parties of legionaries from the Fifth Macedonica – Niger's legion – were at Largiana with orders to make the place liveable and defensible. After a brief moment of uncertainty and suspicion, they were given access to the legionaries' camp fire, and things became much easier.

'So you're engineers?' Senova asked with a smile as she unpacked the food they had purchased and began to slap the pork onto the skillet from the luggage, while one of their escort hung the cradle over the fire. As the pan lowered over the flames and the meat began to sizzle, the legionaries laughed. 'Hardly. *Cato* over there's an engineer. The rest of us are here to lift and carry.'

The man chuckled, a friendly sound, but there was something in his eyes that set Rufinus on edge, and he found his hand straying to the pommel of the gladius lying on the ground next to him. He noted two of the escort they had hired at Bucium starting to hover at the edge of the firelight, expectantly, weapons sheathed but fingers twitching.

'You say you're bound for Porolissum? For the legatus?' one of the men asked.

'I'll get more firewood,' muttered another, rising and moving out into the night.

Rufinus, eyes tracking the disappearing legionary, nodded. 'Assigned to Porolissum by Governor Albinus.' Perhaps the dropping of names might divert any unpleasantness.

'And the woman?' another asked, leering slightly. Senova's face rose across the flames, and Rufinus was relieved to realise he could see in her expression that she had caught wind of the way things were going, but there was always that worry with Senova that she might do something unexpected and untoward.

'Senova is a friend of General Pompeianus in Rome, and my travelling companion.'

She threw him a look that suggested he might regret not claiming her openly as his.

'*Companion*,' nodded one of the soldiers with a smile. 'Been a long time since I had a *companion*. Cold and lonely out here, it is, eh?' he murmured, his gaze, hungry and wicked, playing across the other men. Rufinus could feel the situation slipping out of his control. Would direct confrontation help prevent it, or might it simply advance the problem?

'I'm his woman,' Senova said starkly, throwing a meaningful glance at Rufinus, who was busy weighing up odds. Fourteen legionaries. They looked tired and cold, but they were well armed and a man fighting for something always found unexpected reserves of strength. There were nine of the travelling party: four guards, one guide, Rufinus, Senova, a slave boy and Acheron. The big dog was standing near the fire, salivating at the smell of the frying pork. Rufinus gave a barely audible whistle, and Acheron turned to look at him. Rufinus flicked his eyes at the biggest legionary, a brute of a man who had not yet said anything, but was sitting and taking everything in, eyes alert.

One of the guards had marked the man who'd gone for firewood, so that was good. Acheron on the big man. The dog had returned to watching the pork, but periodically his head turned to the brute, so Rufinus was confident Acheron knew what was needed. Beyond that he would use his initiative as always. The guide may only be a local villager, but he carried a small hunting bow and there was a large curved knife at his belt. The other three guards had now picked up on the atmosphere, watching the legionaries carefully. He realised that before they'd reached Alburnus he had leant Luca his pugio for defence and had completely forgotten to take it back. Thank the gods for his memory lapse, for the lad had the blade tucked naked in the side of his belt. Only Senova was unarmed, though she was far from the most pacific and defenceless of the group.

The legionaries were of a mind. He could see that. None of them would hold back. He had to make sure his own people were prepared, especially since they were outnumbered and outmuscled.

'Listen,' he said clearly, 'let's avoid any nastiness or trouble. We're expected at Porolissum, getting there is important, and there are enough of us that a fight will be ugly and costly. We're not worth it just to warm your bed. Hug a blanket and keep your skin for another night.'

The man who'd done most of the talking, a weaselly fellow with grey hair and a black moustache, narrowed his eyes, his fingers drumming on his knees.

'I don't know who you think you are, fella,' he replied in an edgy voice, 'but your men are local shit-diggers and farmers. We're the glorious Fifth.'

'Rape and murder is hardly glorious,' Rufinus said in leaden tones. 'We'll finish our meal and move on. Find somewhere else to camp.'

'I don't think so. Bet you've got loads of stuff with you, too. Good stuff. Man who can afford to hire guards and guides and horses?'

Damn it. There was clearly going to be no getting away from this. Rufinus glanced around again. The guard who'd been at the edge of the circle, watching the wood-gatherer, had vanished after him into the darkness. The others were drawing blades, and even the guide had slipped an arrow from his quiver and put it to the bow, ready to draw. Acheron was looking at him expectantly, and Luca had his hand on the pugio.

'Let's not do anything we regret,' Rufinus tried once more.

'Go right,' barked Senova suddenly, and Rufinus turned a frown on her just as she flicked up the skillet, sending sizzling meat, searing fat and a whole collection of glowing orange embers into the gathered crowd of leering legionaries. Rufinus' shock was nothing compared to her victims, half a dozen men shrieking and clawing at eyes and faces, arms and legs, where sizzling burning matter ate into their flesh.

Oh well done,' Rufinus grinned. In a heartbeat, Senova had evened the odds. 'Acheron, kill!'

As Rufinus rose, sword leaping to hand, the black shape of furious violence incarnate hurtled across in front of him and hit the big legionary like an angry bull. The big man went back over the rock on which he was sitting with a cry of shock and agony as razor teeth snapped and tore at him, his sword forgotten as he tried desperately to heave the ball of brutality off himself, barehanded.

An arrow thrummed across the golden glow of what was left of the fire and struck another legionary full in the chest, sending him flying back into the darkness, gurgling. The guards joined the fight with the remaining legionaries, and Rufinus found himself a moment later facing the talkative rodent-like one with the moustache.

'Seems like your night just went to shit,' Rufinus smiled.

'Fuck you.'

The man lunged. Rufinus let the sword whisper past him as he twisted and brought the pommel of his gladius round into the back of the man's neck. Only the legionary's momentum saved his life, for the weapon could easily have broken his neck, had he not been moving and robbed the blow of some force.

The man was a veteran, though, and no fool. Having underestimated his foe and taken a thump for his trouble, he turned and began to advance again, sword whirling and slicing, fast and deadly. Rufinus watched his eyes rather than the sword. The man was confident, thinking he had Rufinus on the defensive. Let him keep thinking that. The young praetorian risked a quick glance behind him to be sure of any obstacles, but he was in a relatively clear space. He began to give ground, thrusting out his own gladius periodically to turn the advancing blade, making it appear that he had nothing to give and was fighting to survive. The man came on, leering, his sword play becoming more intricate, yet less dangerous as he showed off subconsciously. Rufinus clanged the blade away again twice, and noted when the man was briefly vulnerable during his repetitive flurry of blows.

He struck suddenly. Coming to a firm halt, no longer stepping backward, his sword came up, clattering heavily against the legionary's blade and sending it out wide. His left hook that had been building ready for three heartbeats struck the legionary full in the centre of the face and there was more than one crack of bone amid the pulverising of flesh and the spray of blood.

He was not good with his left, or at least not as good as his right, but with adequate planning and build-up for momentum...

The sword fell from the man's hand as he staggered back, blind and in shock, face ruined, nose little more than a smudge across his cheek. As he tottered, blearily, making gagging noises and pouring blood, Rufinus took a step forward and brought his right hand up, sword held horizontally, using only the fist wrapped around the hilt. The uppercut shattered the man's jaw and sent him flying backward to land with a thud on the cold earth.

He looked around. It was almost over. Two of his guards lay among the fallen, and two legionaries were still struggling to defend themselves. One was pinned in place with a pugio, a snarling, howling slave boy still twisting it in the foot while a guard fenced with the shrieking soldier. There were other men who had survived, though. Some of those hit by the embers and the fat had fled into the night. Even as Rufinus tried to work out the numbers, Acheron, having finished savaging the big man, suddenly hit one of the two still standing in the back, sending him to the ground. The great jaws closed on the man's neck with a crunch and Rufinus shivered

Senova was stretching. 'Eleven,' she said, gesturing to where their guard was returning from the darkness, dragging the body of the wood-gatherer.

'Yes. Three got away. We'll have to be careful. They might think twice about coming back, but they're legionaries and all their kit is here. They can't go back to their units without their gear, or they'll be deep in the shit. But I think we scared them properly. They'll wait until we're gone, then come for their stuff.'

'Will you be in trouble in Porolissum?' she asked in a concerned tone.

Rufinus shook his head. 'There's no way any survivor will own up to this. Rape and murder's bad enough, but being resoundingly beaten by a bunch of villagers, a woman, a boy and a dog? They'd never live it down. This'll get blamed on rebels or Sarmatians.'

He gestured to the two remaining guards and their guide. 'We need a constant watch tonight, though. We sleep in the bath house. It's the only fully stone building, so it can't just be fired by unseen hands in the night. Two men on watch at any given time, and I'll join the rota.'

'What of not-killed?' the guide murmured, pointing at the man whose face Rufinus had ruined, who was lying on the floor, whimpering. There were three or four men who would live, though they might regret doing so.

'The survivors? I'm not killing legionaries in cold blood, even if they are lowlifes like this. We tie them thoroughly to the horse rail outside the bath house. Let them spend the night bound and uncomfortable. Their friends can release them when we've gone in the morning.'

As the men began their work, and Luca cleaned the pugio while Senova fished out more food and began to rebuild the fire, Rufinus sighed and looked around the scene of carnage. A great start. They were one day now from the camp of the Fifth Macedonica and they'd already killed or maimed a dozen of them. He just hoped this wasn't a sign of things to come.

XVI – Fortress at the edge of the world

Porolissum was not what Rufinus had expected. It was no legionary fortress, just a standard auxiliary fort on the frontier of the empire, as far from civilisation as it was possible to reach and still call Roman. And yes, there was a procurator based here and one of the 'three Dacias' was named Porolensis, yet still Rufinus had been all over the north and had formed certain expectations of frontier auxiliary forts, and Porolissum did not match them.

The fort itself was an imposing stone edifice on the highest point for miles, sitting like the will of gods, glaring down on the world around it, the land sloping away in every direction, sometimes quite vertiginously. And unlike Bucium's rather small and ramshackle vicus, the town that had grown up around this bastion of Rome was a thriving metropolis. In fact, the place had grown so large and so busy that it had spread to cover the land on the slopes to the east, south and west, the north left clear, facing the barbarians. Rufinus could see as they approached just how much of a lively city Porolissum had become. Smoke from several bath houses rose into the blue grey sky, tempting further rain, though playing with sunlight for now. A sizeable amphitheatre of stone and tile and plaster rose amid the buildings, and there were seemingly games on at that very moment from the sheer noise and the cheering that rose and fell like waves in the sea, crashing into tense silence only to rise again into a deafening roar.

It was the *nundinum*, he realised, peering up the slope at the town, the ninth day of the weekly cycle in which markets were held across the empire, festivals cropped up, towns filled with people and many workers downed tools for the day.

'Busy,' he noted.

The three men still travelling with them nodded.

230

'Is there a less hectic way in?'

'This,' replied one of them, pointing off to the left, where a rougher road skirted the edge of the town, passing close to the great curved wall of the amphitheatre where, apparently, some poor bastard had just been bloodied for the edification of the crowd, judging by the noise. The track followed a contour, and as they moved around the periphery of the busy place to the west, Rufinus was treated to a view of the other aspect of Porolissum.

This place truly was the edge of the empire in a way Rufinus had never before contemplated. The good metalled road they had followed from Bucium entered the town from the south, and they had seen another such highway marching off slightly north of east, along the very edge of the province. But to the north and west there lay something wholly different. Rufinus could see defensive systems climbing the hills and filling the valleys. To the north and west, where the Roman world ended, there were great turf embankments and timber palisades, watch towers and fortlets in staggering quantity, cutting the landscape into manageable pieces where any incursion could be easily dealt with. Clearly some of it was already old, dating back to the early days of the province, but much of it was new, Pescennius Niger's response to the Sarmatian attacks.

Rufinus whistled through his teeth as he took in the complex systems crossing grey-green hills and skirting dark, looming forests, all under the watchful eye of that great square stone sentinel on the hill. Porolissum was more than a town or a fort. It was a last outpost of imperial power on the threshold of the barbarians. Moreover, Rufinus could see Niger's army now, for the fort was not large enough to accommodate the Fifth Macedonica, let alone the numerous other units the legate had drafted in from his part of the province to secure the borders. The legion and at least a score of other auxiliary units were encamped on the slopes to the north and to the east and west, beyond the town and in the lower ground.

They skirted the corner of the fort, where a road ran down to some sort of border control or customs house in the nearest line of defences, the paved way dotted with temples and shops. The walls of the fort towered above them now, as they passed the last of the civilian settlement. Even from this, the shallowest surrounding slope, the plateau on which the great fort was constructed added to the massive walls to create an image of unassailable power. Gleaming shapes of men moved along the top, ever-watchful, ever-alert. The huge gatehouse with solid, drum-like towers stood facing the Sarmatian world, ready to spew soldiers at a moment's notice, the gate open with men on guard beside, within and above. A centurion stood with his men, addressing them on some matter, but the conversation halted as the small party approached the fort. The centurion stepped to the centre of the gate, vine stick grasped behind his back as his men stood straight and tall.

Rufinus realised what they must look like after so many days of travel with few chances to bathe and even then not in a proper establishment. He was wearing the red military tunic that he'd been given in Drobeta to replace his praetorian white, but his armour was bagged up on the pack horse, and he looked dirty and drab. He had also begun to look quite fashionable, with flopping wavy hair and a burgeoning beard that was already curling naturally. The first opportunity he got to visit the baths, this lot was coming off. Beards were always too itchy, no matter how fashionable. With a travel-worn woman, a young slave, a giant black dog and three armed natives, they would make an interesting party. Rufinus decided to grasp the situation by the curlies from the outset.

'Good afternoon, Centurion. I am Gnaeus Marcius Rustius Rufinus of the praetorian guard, on detached duty to Dacia's military. The governor in Apulum assigned me to the forces of the legate Pescennius Niger here. I have here a travelling companion from Rome and her slave who will also require admittance, though our local escort will now be on their way.'

Excellent. Sounded very official. He turned and passed over the last of the payment to the guide who, with the two remaining guards, nodded their thanks and then wandered off to amuse themselves in the thriving town, leading their horses.

Rufinus turned back to the centurion, who was studying him as though he were something a cat had brought in and left on the rug.

'Centurion Rugio, Second Dalmatian, part-mounted. Documents?'

Rufinus fished in his bag and retrieved the two sets of papers, one from Cleander assigning him to Dacia and the other from Clodius Albinus, sending him to Porolissum. The centurion took them, examined them carefully, and then handed them back with a nod.

'Welcome to Porolissum. Lucky for you the legatus is still here and currently in the headquarters dealing with administration. I will take you to him now.' With that, he beckoned and turned, marching through the gate and on up the slope of the fort within. Rufinus corrected himself as he passed through the gate, leading Atalanta, and took in the mass of internal buildings. This was bigger than most auxiliary forts he'd been in. It might just have fitted a legion at a push. It was well-appointed and well-kept, clean and strong. He nodded his approval as they passed a building that had the look of a granary but was being cleared out and repaired by industrious legionaries.

'Given the level of destruction and ravaging I've seen throughout Dacia, I'm impressed at the level of control here. Your military zone is quite something.'

The centurion drummed his fingers on his vine cane. 'The war is over. I don't know what the Thirteenth were doing buggering about for so long with rebels and pockets of resistance and so on. The legatus *here* responded quickly, gathering a huge force and securing the north, driving out the Iazyges and the Costoboci. This place has been back under proper control for months. The whole of the north, in fact.

While the south have been faffing under the governor's control, we've been busy rebuilding, strengthening, fortifying. We've put up new walls and gates across the salt road into Sarmatian lands. The big trouble has been food and harvests. Years of troubles have left the locals in dire straits and half the job of the army has been to bring in grain shipments from other parts of Dacia out east and keep the populace fed, and to help them rebuild their settlements and sort their planting and harvests. I expect the praetorians know little about that sort of thing, but a legion based out in the provinces have to turn their hands to many things to keep peace and control.'

Rufinus felt irritated at the slight, though it contained less bile than was commonly aimed at the guard by the rest of the military.

'I was formerly of the Tenth Gemina,' he replied defensively. 'I know the situation.'

The centurion's eyebrow rose for just a moment, but he simply walked on.

'I see the whole army seems to still be camped here?' Rufinus murmured conversationally. 'Quite a few thousand eh?'

'Hardly,' the officer replied. 'Half the army has already been sent back to their garrisons, and half what's left are busy working on the walls and the damaged forts. But we're nearly fully repaired now. In fact, you were lucky to catch the legate. In a day or so the Fifth will be returning to Potaissa, and the rest of the units will depart, leaving just us faithful Dalmatians in control again.'

Rufinus felt relief flood him. The last thing he'd want was a repeat of his first few days in the east, chasing legates who had always just left to go somewhere else. They reached the heart of the fort a moment later and the arch of the headquarters stood before them, a soldier to each side. Another fort, another headquarters, another commander. Rufinus was busy listing them mentally as the centurion explained that Senova, Luca and Acheron would have to wait there with the horses.

'On the assumption we are staying the night here,' Rufinus said to Senova as he rummaged in the kit on Atalanta and found the all-important package, 'you might want to enquire about stabling and the location of the mansio or the cheapest inn you can find.'

Senova nodded, though Rufinus had no confidence in her sparing his purse in that regard. Still, he had more important things to think about, right now. Turning, he followed the centurion into the building, striding across the courtyard with its statues of Jupiter and of the emperor, and into the long basilica hall. The shrine of the standards was full and gleaming, a soldier on guard beside it, and he watched Rufinus suspiciously as the two men approached the other guarded door: the commander's office. A brief exchange between the centurion and a man inside whose voice was smooth and urbane, and Rugio stepped aside and gestured for Rufinus to enter.

The office was occupied by three men. A clerk stood to one side with an armful of tablets, looking harassed, a senior officer – an auxiliary prefect, Rufinus thought – sat in a chair in the corner with a cup of wine, and the man who could only be Pescennius Niger behind the desk in the centre of the office.

Rufinus came to a halt, straightened and saluted.

'Gnaeus Marcius Rustius Rufinus, assigned to Dacia by the imperial chamberlain and directed to your command by the governor at Apulum,' Rufinus announced, fixing his gaze on a point just above Niger's shoulder where he could take in everything yet remain at attention.

Niger was tall, perhaps more than six feet. His skin was the smooth olive of a native of southern Italia, and his hair was a dark blond, wavy and short, while his long beard had been curled elegantly. He wore a well-tailored uniform that was neat and clean, almost diametrically opposite to Rufinus' shabby, travel-worn tunic. The reason for the man's unusual cognomen – Niger, 'the black' – became clear at first sight. Rufinus had known men with birthmarks before, usually the colour of old plums, which appeared as splotches on the skin like a piebald horse, but Niger's was different. A patch of dark brown, like a giant liver spot covered the left side of his neck – so dark it was almost black. The legate had an unusually large white scarf, and between that and the beard the birthmark would be well hidden under normal circumstances, but at that particular moment, the legate had loosened the scarf with the warmth of the building and had turned toward the prefect, revealing the left side of his neck. The legate turned languidly back and regarded the visitor.

'Rufinus. Praetorian guard. Man who saved the emperor,' he said in those same, calm, urbane tones.

'Yessir.' Impressive. Rufinus had met few people who had retained that information in the years since his great moment of glory.

'Gaius Pescennius Niger, legate of the Fifth Macedonica. Well met. I was at those games that day in Rome. A great achievement for a young guardsman and, if what I heard was correct, an impressive pilum throw.'

Rufinus nodded, flushing slightly.

'And now you are out here in the provinces, dirty, tired and largely unrecognised I would wager. How fickle is Rome, eh, Rufinus? Glory in one moment and obscurity the next. Take it from me, though, sometimes obscurity is to be treasured, and even sought.'

There was something oddly wistful in the way he said it that made Rufinus frown.

'So Albinus has sent you to me. No, no, no,' he waved away the documents Rufinus was busy digging out. 'The centurion has seen them. That will do. Let me see if I can get this right. Cleander, may the hydra rise from his latrine and stick thirteen heads up his ignoble behind, assigns you to Dacia because he doesn't trust us. We have too much military might and too much gold and are a long way from his grasp. You arrive to take up your post with Albinus, but the old man won't have you. Doesn't trust you, so he sends you to me, thinking I might be able to lose you on the frontier. Am I close?'

Rufinus blinked. 'On the nail, in fact, Legatus. *Entirely* on the nail.'

'And somehow you intend to earn my trust in a way that you could not with Albinus?'

Gods, but this man was sharp.

'All I can say, Legatus, is that trust engenders trust. I am in a distant land, previously unknown to me, far from my unit and any friend, sent to men that the chamberlain feels might be untrustworthy. Yet one man vouched for you. A man told me to look for you and to commend him to you. A frumentarius by the name of Vibius Cestius, who I count as a close friend.'

Niger broke into a wide grin.

'Vibius Cestius. Now there's a name I haven't heard in a year or two. How is the devious goat?'

'As irascible as ever, Legatus.'

Niger laughed aloud. 'Very well. A friend of Vibius Cestius already comes highly recommended to me, and as I now realise he is also the man who saved Commodus, I cannot but lay a mantle of trust on you. Would that you could so easily do that with me.'

Again, there was that odd wistfulness in his tone. Rufinus became acutely aware of the fascinated stares of the other two men in the office and that there were sounds of other soldiers and officers out in the basilica hall.

'Can we speak privately, Legatus? It is a matter of some importance.'

Niger pursed his lips for a moment, as though holding an inner dialogue, and then nodded, gesturing for the prefect and the clerk to leave. The latter closed the door as he exited, leaving the two men alone in the office.

'Go on,' Niger prompted.

'This might be rather hard to believe immediately, Legatus, but bear with me. I was sent by Cleander to search for signs of treachery and disloyalty to the throne in Dacia. I did not truly expect to find any. Simple hatred and defamation of Cleander is hardly a sign of treachery, for it would be hard to find a man more hated, so that could hardly be worth noting.'

Niger smiled, and Rufinus breathed slowly, preparing himself.

'However, through chance information, a little investigation and some judicious searching, I have uncovered a plot, the scale of which I find staggering.'

Niger leaned forward now. 'Go on?'

'The governor, Clodius Albinus, is misappropriating huge quantities of gold from the mines at Alburnus Maior before they are logged and stamped by the procurator's office. The unmarked gold he thereby acquires is being sent to Rome and to various men in power in the provinces, lining their vaults in return for favours for Albinus and for men who represent his clientele. He is using state gold to build a web of people in positions of power and influence. I can only conclude that he is preparing a coup against the emperor.'

Niger's brow folded and he steepled his hands. 'That is a very serious accusation against any man, young Rufinus, let alone a powerful provincial governor who has been close to the emperor at times. Talk like that gets men into a great deal of trouble.'

Rufinus paused. The legate looked troubled, and well he might. Bringing him in on the matter would put him in every bit as much danger as Rufinus.

'Albinus is not a good man,' Niger said quietly. 'In fact, he is a scheming felon who I would trust no further than I could spit a cow. I had *assumed* he was up to no good, and probably that his intrigues involved the gold mines, but even then this is something of a grand and dangerous accusation. Is there any way you could be mistaken about this? If you are to accuse a man of such a thing you need to be sure and certain, and aware of the danger in which it will put you. So I ask again, are you sure, or could you be mistaken?'

Once again there was an odd edge to his voice. Discussing treason seemingly did not sit well with Pescennius Niger.

'No, Legate. I am certain. Moreover, I have evidence. The only evidence left to be found in Dacia, since Albinus has been across the land like a forest fire, destroying all record of his affairs.'

He fished out the box from under his arm and placed it on the table.

'There.'

Niger, a frown of concern etched in the lines of his face, leaned forward. He examined Albinus' seal on the cut leather straps, the scratched letters on the lid. He lifted the top and peered inside at the gold, opened the scroll case and read the vellum contents.

'A really good lawyer could probably destroy you in court over this. It's very strong evidence, though not fully conclusive. And having opened it, you've removed half its veracity anyway.'

'It's strong enough,' Rufinus said firmly.

Niger sighed. 'Yes, I suspect it is. No lawyer, no matter how good, is going to be able to deny it for long in the face of Cleander and the court. And once the Palatine torturers get their hands on Publius Seius Fuscianus, he will inevitably reveal all, including the whole web of conspirators. A neat package.'

The legate straightened. 'I presume you heard enough?' he asked loudly.

Rufinus felt a great chasm yawn suddenly beneath him as the door opened with a click and a familiar voice replied '*More than enough.*' The young praetorian turned to see Tribune Celer standing in the doorway, a sneer of disgust on his face. Behind him, Rufinus could see the awful shape of optio – now apparently *Centurion* – Daizus, and a number of dismounted legionary cavalrymen from the Thirteenth.

Shit.

Shit, shit, shit.

239

He'd not anticipated this. How could a man so careful as Vibius Cestius have been so wrong about Niger?

Celer walked around the edge of the office and picked up the evidence, tucking it beneath his arm. He eyed Rufinus, whose fingers were snaking down his side slowly. 'If you touch that sword I will see you broken in the most dreadful manner. Hands up where we can see them.'

Blood chilling, stomach churning, Rufinus raised his hands. The soldiers were in the room now, blades out, surrounding him in an arc. 'Was he alone?' Celer asked, in a tone implying that he rather doubted it.

'He came with a woman, a boy and a dog.'

'Have your men round them up and bring them to me,' Celer said officiously, as though Niger did not, in fact, outrank him.

'I will do no such thing. You wanted the praetorian and any evidence he carried. I complied, against my better judgement, but I will not deliver women and children to your twisted ministrations, *Tribune* Celer. I've heard of your love for the lash.'

The senior man of the Thirteenth turned a snarl on Niger. 'You will do as you are told. Rufinus is dangerous. He needs to be disposed of before he can do further harm. His woman is of no consequence and the boy is just a slave. The dog? The dog should be skinned and burned. In fact, all of them should.'

Niger rose behind his desk and thrust a finger at the tribune.

'Watch your tongue around me, Celer. Your master might think of himself as emperor already, but *I* am in command here. This is *my* fort and *my* legion and *my* land. While you were busy leaving everything to go wrong down south so you could hide your mischief, we have put everything right in the north and done our duty as Romans and as officers and men of the legions. Do not think to command me in my own fort. Even *Albinus* would think twice about that, and you are not half the wolf he is.'

'I warn you, Niger,' hissed the tribune, 'kill them all. Dispose of the evidence. You'll regret it if you don't, I promise you.'

The legate's lip twitched. 'Take your box and your men and go back to your quarters. If I hear of you causing any trouble in my fort I might be tempted to send you back to Albinus minus a head.'

The two men glared at each other, the rest of the soldiers watching in tense silence, and Rufinus, for one mad moment, wondered whether he might actually be able to slip from the room while they were busy. The silence ended suddenly, as Pescennius Niger turned to Rufinus and the men behind him and beckoned through the door.

'Take our young friend here to appropriate accommodation and make sure that he is very secure. Remove all weapons and items of import and value from him, leaving him with just his clothes and boots and cloak. Then find his woman, the boy and the dog and bring them to me.'

'Kill them,' snapped Celer.

'No. I am not so short-sighted and foolish as to kill a praetorian sent here personally by the chamberlain. A man who works for Cleander and who was personally decorated by the emperor? He is no threat to you or Albinus now, with no evidence. And I do not kill innocent women, children or dogs.'

Celer continued to glare at him. Two more legionaries entered the room, though these were men of the Fifth, accompanied by the centurion who had first admitted them to the fort. The men swiftly disarmed Rufinus and then took the place of the dismounted cavalry, swords drawn. Tribune Celer gestured for his men to leave. For a moment Rufinus thought Daizus was going to spit on him, and then they left, Celer exiting last. The tribune paused in the doorway. 'You have no idea how big a mistake it is letting this man live. I will not be going back to Albinus just yet. I want to watch Rufinus cause you trouble.'

'Get out of my office,' roared Pescennius Niger.

The men of the Thirteenth departed, and Rufinus sagged. 'I trusted you. Vibius Cestius trusted you. And you are in *league* with them?'

'Gods, Rufinus, but the world is so much more a tangled web than you perceive. I had no wish to do this, and had there been any other way I would have avoided it. I tried to turn you aside. Even with Celer listening at the door, I tried. Now I am bound and there is little I can do. But what little I can, I will. Celer will not have his executions. You will be imprisoned for now, and I promise you I will see your companions safely accommodated and well-looked after. It is all I can do.'

He nodded to the centurion, and Rufinus was urged from the office at sword point. As he was marched out into the basilica, he realised what the legate had meant by trying to 'turn him aside'. Niger had been trying to stop him presenting his evidence. Subtly. Carefully.

I trust you. Would that you could so easily do that with me.

Sometimes obscurity is to be treasured, and even sought.

Talk like that gets men into a great deal of trouble.

You need to be certain and aware of the danger. So are you sure, or could you be mistaken?

Damnit, he'd known from the outset that Niger was sharp. Why had he not been listening more carefully? The man had repeatedly thrown him clues that something was not right and had even offered him a way out with the option of retracting his accusation. But no. He had blundered on in his usual good-natured, honest way. How long must he play the great game before he started to think like Pompeianus, or even Niger?

Why, though? Why had Niger done this to him? Everything Rufinus had heard during the exchange had suggested that Niger was not part of the plot, or at best peripherally so. He had tried to save Rufinus, had even *managed* to save him from execution, and had promised to look after the others. Something deep inside Rufinus insisted that Niger *was* the good man of whom Cestius had spoken. But somehow he was subservient to Albinus. He owed the governor perhaps? Was *frightened* of him? Did Albinus hold something over his fellow legate? His mind furnished him with an image of his brother Publius back in the court with Cleander. Wasn't Rufinus exactly the same? Here he was doing the dirty work of a man he hated because Cleander had his brother.

Yes. That was *it*. The way Tribune Celer had spoken to the legate, was like an man of authority talking to a plaintiff, rather than a soldier to a superior officer. Somehow Albinus *owned* Niger the way Cleander believed he owned Rufinus. The question was: how long could Niger keep Rufinus had his friends safe if that was the case. The legate might argue against Celer, but Rufinus could not picture the same happening with Albinus. If Albinus were to hear of his capture and the evidence, his death warrant would be sealed within the day, and Niger would have no choice but to comply.

As he was marched across the courtyard, a splat of rain suddenly battered his forehead. Great. To top it all off, the rain was back. Moments later, the deluge was bouncing high from the floor and a crash of thunder echoed across the hills.

'Don't worry, lad,' the centurion said, not unkindly. 'We'll bring you towels and a fresh tunic. But for now, I'm afraid you're going in the old granary.'

With all the other rats, thought Rufinus bitterly as the rain soaked him, saturating his clothes and stinging his skin. Well he had done it. He had unpicked a plot that reached across the empire, had found evidence to support it, and had promptly handed both it and himself straight over to the enemy.

Where was Fortuna now, the fickle bitch?

XVII – Captivity

Rufinus leaned back in the cart and quickly decided that was not the best decision he could have made, for he now realised just how effective Senova's carriage's suspension had actually been. This thing was shaking his bones apart. At least he was free to move. His wrists were bound, tight enough that there was no hope of twisting out of them, but his legs were free and he had not been too tightly confined.

There had been another argument about that in the fresh blue morning the day after the storm had passed. Celer, backed by his little coven of legionary cavalry and Centurion Daizus, had demanded Rufinus be placed in a cage for the journey, tied to the interior and guarded by Celer's men. Pescennius Niger had acidly refused. He had ordered that Rufinus' hands be bound to prevent any attempts to free himself and that he be placed under guard in one of the wagons at the rear of the column, but beyond that he had seen that Rufinus had acceptable comfort for a prisoner. Moreover, Celer had eyed Senova sourly and glared at Acheron, demanding that the dog be placed in a cage for the safety of all concerned. Given the way Acheron's lip curled back when he saw the tribune and Daizus, and the low threatening growl that issued in their presence, that might not be a stupid move, Rufinus admitted. Senova was pretty good at keeping the animal out of mischief, but Acheron might just take it upon himself to savage one man or the other, and that would certainly see the dog put down and Rufinus in ever deeper trouble. Still the three of them remained free despite Celer's constant demands.

Senova and Luca, with Acheron pacing alongside, travelled in an expensive carriage along with Niger's family, just behind the Fifth's officers where she was safe and, coincidentally also unable to converse with the prisoner. Celer and his men rode slightly apart from the column, which consisted almost entirely of the Fifth Macedonica, periodically coming close enough to sneer at Rufinus. They could come no closer than that, though, thank the gods, because of the legionaries of the Fifth who guarded Rufinus' wagon as it bounced along the road.

Two full contubernia of men kept watch over him, and Rufinus had to take it as a sort of complement that the officers felt he needed sixteen men to keep him secured. Rufinus had tentatively tried to strike up a conversation early in the journey, half expecting to be slapped and manhandled roughly down into the cart. In a pleasantly surprising turn of events it seemed that the legion's legate had given no orders to prevent interaction and, indeed, had told the men to make sure Rufinus was comfortable and safe. Whether this was from genuine personal concern or fear that Cleander would hear of any mistreatment Rufinus couldn't tell though, given what he'd seen of Niger, he suspected the former.

In any event, the soldiers exchanged some history with Rufinus and when it turned out that a vexillation of the Fifth had been part of that great push against the Marcomanni across the Danuvius under the old emperor and that Rufinus, as part of the Tenth Gemina, had fought in the same battle, an instant camaraderie arose, albeit a little strained in the circumstances.

'The Marcomanni were *real* barbarians,' a legionary called Iustus sighed. 'Proper baby-eating, skull-wearing, "dance naked and drunk in the woods and worship a stick" sort of barbarians.'

Rufinus chuckled at the description.

'Not like the Iazyges and the Costoboci. Or the Roxolani. They've been around Romans and Dacians for so long they're almost civilised. They know cavalry tactics and can use a spoon.'

Again, Rufinus laughed. 'In fairness, I'm not sure the Marcomannia actually eat babies. I never saw it happen.'

'Well no. We were at war. You like a roll in the hay with a farm girl, I'll bet, but you probably wouldn't do it on the battlefield.'

Another laugh. There was something oddly impenetrable about the man's logic.

'Gargilius did,' snorted another. 'Remember her? Rosy-cheeked Chatti girl. There we were moving through the forest, swords out, waiting to be jumped at any moment and we find Gargillius up against a tree with her as if he's got not a care in the world.'

Raucous laughter broke out among the guards and one red-faced soldier told them all to do something biologically improbable to themselves.

And so it went on, an odd mix of good-natured banter and strained prisoner-guard relations.

Throughout the day, especially when Celer and his men swung by to be offended by his continued survival, the men of the Fifth would apologise that they could not keep the tribune further away, and would note how unhappy they were keeping prisoner a veteran whose crime was so spurious that none of the officers seemed to know, or at least wouldn't talk about. When the legionaries had quietly tried to pry that information from their charge, Rufinus had simply sighed and stated that he'd got on the wrong side of Celer and the man had stitched him up. It was *part* of the truth, so he didn't feel too guilty about the rest being omitted. The suggestion that somehow an honest soldier had been sold down the river by an unscrupulous officer only increased the respect the men gave him and made them hate the visitors from the Thirteenth all the more. Good, Rufinus thought. he could not yet see a way out, but building bridges with his captors and opening rifts between them and Celer was a good start, whatever he decided was possible in the end.

The journey from Porolissum on the frontier to the legion's base at Potaissa would take three days, moving at the peace-time speed of a full legionary column, and Rufinus disembarked that first evening feeling like a shirt of rusty chain that had been put in a barrel of sand and rolled around for cleaning. He had felt every rock and even pebble beneath the cart's wheels, and it took some time for him to be able to stand straight upon alighting.

They camped that first night on the edge of a small town called, rather worryingly, Draco. The officers, including Celer and Daizus, found lodging in a mansio that served the regular traffic between Porolissum and Potaissa, while the legion encamped close by, near a stream. On passing, Rufinus noted a small temple on the edge of the town and wondered what deity was most revered in this area. Always best to know which god was most present to pray to. When he discovered that the shrine was to the strange witch goddess Hekate, its threshold host to the rotting corpses of three sacrificed dogs, it did nothing to improve his opinion of the place. Named for a monster and worshipping a witch goddess. Wonderful.

Rufinus was shown to a tent where the basic amenities were made available. In fairness, it was actually somewhat *more* comfortable than he'd been used to when on campaign with the Tenth, and he had no complaints, especially as he had it to himself with no snoring, farting tent mates. When he needed to use the latrines, one eight-man contubernium accompanied him while the other guarded his tent and then, as the evening set in, they instituted a watch system with always five men guarding the prisoner. He was going nowhere. Even if he could slip past the five men, he was in the middle of a legionary camp, and could neither find nor free Senova and the others anyway.

Rufinus was leaning back on his blankets and starting to settle in when there was a cough at the door of the tent.

'Yes?'

'Visitor,' announced a legionary, and Rufinus sat up, blinking away the tiredness of the journey. The tense worry that it would be Celer faded as the tent flap shifted aside and Senova appeared in her warm cloak, wrapped tight against the night's chill. Summer was almost upon them now, but the evening still held something of a bite.

'I'm surprised they let you come,' he said. 'They *did* let you come, didn't they?'

Senova smiled. 'I'm breaking no rules, and I have not brought you a small siege engine and a panoply of armour with which to escape. Celer did not want us to see one another, but Pescennius Niger is according me every civilised comfort. He asked me to check on you and make sure you were being well treated.'

Rufinus nodded. 'Better than prisoners could normal hope for. I'm actually being well looked after. The lads guarding me are all good men. We're sort of friendly already.'

Senova shook her head with a smile. 'It's you, Gnaeus. You make friends easily. Shame you make enemies even easier, but still, we can't have everything.' Her nose wrinkled in distaste. 'You smell a little like Acheron.'

'I'm not getting to bathe. And they won't let me have a knife, so I can't even shave. Sounds ridiculous, but in the cart today I started to pull the beard out hair by hair. Then I decided it was taking too long and I did a clump in one go. Never again. I'll have a bald spot on my chin forever now.'

'The guards aren't letting Celer near you are they?'

'No. Luckily. I think if he came too close I might kill him with my bare hands. I could, too.'

'I know. Don't. You're in enough trouble already. Niger is keeping a close eye on the tribune and Daizus. Doesn't let them out of his sight. Celer repeatedly demands your death and both he and Daizus have threatened to kill you personally.'

'Be careful around him, Senova. He might just go for you to annoy me.'

'Legate Niger has assigned me a pair of his personal guard. No harm will come to me or Luca, or Acheron. I've been staying with the legate's wife last night and tonight, too. So I'm quite safe. Paccia Nigri is a lovely woman. Quiet and pleasant. From somewhere called Capua.'

'That's where Spartacus started his gladiator war,' Rufinus said, absently.

'Who?'

Rufinus smiled. 'I'll have to get you a good history to read sometime.'

'Anyway,' Senova went on, Paccia is travelling with her husband and she has her niece with her, too. A girl called Septimia Apera. Nice lass. Reminds me of me when I was free, back in Britannia.'

'Gods help the world, then,' said Rufinus, rolling his eyes.

Senova gave him a hard glare, then sighed. 'I think Niger is beholden to Clodius Albinus in some way.'

'I felt that might be the case,' Rufinus agreed.

'I tried to wheedle it out of the girls, but they become very tight lipped on the subject of Clodius Albinus. Neither of them seem to like him. And Septimia's father apparently *despises* him. You've met her father, I think. I have. I remember him at a party at Pompeianus' house. I was serving the drinks at the time, but Septimius Severus was there. He was a governor, I think?'

Rufinus' eyes bulged. 'Severus? He was a questor for Sardinia at the time, but yes he's a governor now. Last I heard he was in charge of Gallia Lugdunensis. He hated Cleander, I remember, so he certainly can't be all bad.'

He frowned for a moment in silence. 'You mean Severus is Niger's *brother*?'

'In the loosest possible sense,' Senova replied. 'It was complicated. I'll see if I can remember. Severa is Severus' daughter by his old wife who died last year. That wife was Paccia's sister. So Severa is Niger's niece-in-law, which I suppose would make Severus his brother-in-law-in-law?'

'That's not a real thing,' Rufinus flicked his eyes skywards. 'But there *is* a connection between Niger and Severus. Severus liked me, too, I think. If only we could get word to Lugdunum, he might be willing to help.' He sighed. 'Dreams. That's all. Lugdunum is a month away even by courier. By then Albinus and Celer will have found a way to dispose of me.' His frown returned. 'What is Severus' daughter doing here anyway?'

'Apparently, after her mother died, her father sent his daughters to distant relations while he hunts a new wife. Severa is here with her aunt. Her sister is with a cousin in Hispania.'

Rufinus sagged back. 'All fascinating, but nothing that can help me right now.'

'I will continue to do what I can,' Senova said. 'Niger may be indebted to Albinus in some way, but his wife has his ear, and she is sympathetic. We will continue to work on it, and I will keep going with my attempts to unpick what it is that Albinus holds over him.'

Rufinus smiled. 'If you *really* want to help, ask Niger if someone can give me a shave.'

'And a bath. You smell like you've been rolling in a fuller's trough.'

She left shortly thereafter. The night passed peacefully and with blissful quiet, and even though only two blankets lay between Rufinus and the turf, it was still more comfortable than the cart and so lulled him to sleep with ease. He awoke early, dawn still glimmering on the horizon, to the sound of the Fifth Macedonica striking camp.

The second day was much the same in terms of travel, though the weather had warmed and the sky remained clear blue. The wagon continued to bounce across the stones and flags and pits in the road, adding bruise after bruise to Rufinus' growing collection. The terrain changed, the high hills and deep valleys of the borderlands falling behind to leave low, rolling green hills and shallow vales with farmland everywhere, from terraced hillsides full of crops to roaming herds of sheep, goats and cows.

There was no visit from Celer or his men that day, which suited Rufinus fine. It seemed that Senova's influence, via the lady Paccia, was having an effect. At the noon meal break, that supposition was confirmed when one of the legion's expert barbers came round and shaved Rufinus, trimming his hair back once more. He felt a hundred times better that afternoon, climbing into his cart. He might not be so fashionable now, but at least he didn't itch, and he'd started to worry that something had been living in the tangles, too. The only thing that marred his fresh appearance was the patch of raw skin on his chin where he'd torn out a piece of beard. It was still sore to the touch.

The column moved on south, staying the night at a place called Colonia Aurelia Napoca, a sizeable town with a very traditional Roman feel, all the great buildings one might expect of such a place and very little sign of native Dacian influence. Once again, the legion camped on the green slope across the river from the town, while Pescennius Niger, his family and all the senior men were wined and dined by the senior councillors of the town. Rufinus noted another temple on the periphery as they passed and half expected to find more dead animals and witch goddess statues. His relief at not finding them was brief, however, as his eyes lit on the statue of Charon, the boatman of the final river the dead crossed. What was going on with this place. Witches and death and dog's corpses and dragon towns. Weird.

That night Senova did not visit and Rufinus worried that something untoward had happened to her. A troubled night beset by dreams of witches riding dragons left him feeling groggy and tired, and he climbed into the cart the next day somewhat dispirited. He assumed in the end that, with so many of the Fifth feeling sympathy toward him, he would have been told if something had happened to his companions. But it still irked him that Senova had not visited. He had missed her last night in his solitude, and found that he was missing Acheron achingly too. Even Luca popped into his thoughts every now and then, though that only served to annoy him all the more. As they set off and rumbled and lurched along the road on the last leg of the journey, he fell into a deep grump, irritated that Senova was living the high life with the officers and their ladies, probably drinking good wine and lounging by fires and had not given thought to visiting Rufinus in his lonely prison.

He was thoroughly disgruntled by the time they reached Potaissa toward the end of the third day. His bad mood had only worsened, and the way he had snapped at the men guarding him had driven them away, severing their friendly interaction, which only served to make him all the more irritable.

Potaissa was huge; as large as Apulum had been, and rather reminiscent in many ways. The fortress of the Fifth Macedonica sat huge and powerful atop a spur of land that fell away on three sides, the civilian town clustered around the northern and eastern slopes, hugging the contours between the fortress and the river. At first glance, it looked more run down and basic than Apulum had, though Rufinus changed his mind as the column passed by its northern edge and to the great fortress. The place was actually no dirtier or less organised or maintained than Apulum. The difference was that Apulum seemed to give weight to appearance, the fortress whitewashed, the town neatly painted and adorned. Potaissa was different. More care had clearly been paid to its usage and organisation than to its appearance. If the differing aspects were any indication of the men now controlling the two great fortresses, it made Niger look good.

All this, of course, only sank into Rufinus' mind unnoticed and ignored, filed away for later, for his foul mood was still upon him. The cart clattered through the west gate and into the huge fortress, between rows and rows of barrack blocks. He felt his temper fraying further as the cart was pulled up in front of a solid-looking building that lay between the headquarters and what appeared to be cavalry barracks. Similar structures seemed to be workshops, though this one had clearly been fitted out as a prison, with no windows and a solid lock only on the outside of the door. To add to the misery of the situation, Rufinus was unimpressed at the sight of Celer, Daizus and their cavalrymen loitering close by with no sight of Niger or his officers to restrain them.

The door to Rufinus' new home was unlocked and he was helped down from the cart by the men of the Fifth, allowed to pace around for a moment and let the life return to his legs, and was then ushered through the door. The interior was extremely gloomy, and for a moment Rufinus was worried that there was no light source at all. In fact, there were small apertures below the roof tiles that let in just enough light to make out basic details once the eyes adjusted from the open daylight. As Rufinus was marched in and the bonds removed from his wrists, his rapidly adjusting eyes picked out half a dozen shapes in the room, three at each end. Other prisoners of the Fifth, and all legionaries, clearly.

'Orders from the Legate,' announced the man who'd removed the ropes, addressing the prisoners. 'This man is not to be harmed. Any man who damages him in any way can look forward to the kiss of the scourge.'

Rufinus felt a slight touch of relief. This was unknown territory for him, and he could do with any advantage offered. The soldiers retreated outside once more, and suddenly the shapes of Daizus and Celer blocked out the light as they moved into the room. Rufinus turned just in time to catch a gobbet of phlegm full in the face. Snarling and wiping it away with the back of his hand, he flexed his knuckles. Daizus, whose spit it had been, drummed his fingers on the pommel of his gladius.

'Please do, Rufinus. It's all the excuse I need, especially with all these witnesses.'

Rufinus deliberately and slowly unfolded his fists and held them by his sides. The former optio laughed and then pushed his head back and hawked up more phlegm.

Celer, standing beside him, suddenly barked out 'Centurion!'

Daizus snapped to attention.

'There is no need for such demeaning behaviour,' the tribune hissed. 'Spitting at him just makes you look uncouth.

That is not how a centurion behaves. Daizus, sneering, retreated through the door, making throat-cutting motions at Rufinus behind the tribune's back. Rufinus, helpless, stood still and careful as Celer came so close he could smell the man's breath.

'Your loyalty is to be commended, Rufinus. You're wrong, and because of it you are dangerous. But despite everything, I do respect your loyalty. You took an oath with the guard and you are living by it, even in the face of a horrible death. But what you have to remember is that an oath to a weak and corrupt man is not worth the breath it takes to repeat.'

'Corrupt like your master?' Rufinus spat, nastily.

'He is *strong*,' Celer said flatly. 'He is strong, he is clever and he has the good of the empire at heart. What an emperor he would make. But you are wrong on so many levels, you fool. You favour a weak ruler and his corrupt chamberlain, and you think you serve *them* by trying to undermine *us*. But you are wrong, even there. You think Albinus plots against the emperor, and you are wrong. We are not traitors. Just prudent men. The time of the Antonines is coming to an end, young fool. Their glory has faded and now only a self-interested, deluded boy sits on the throne. None of us are disloyal. None of us will lift a sword against the emperor. But his time is marked. He will fall. He is a Nero. A Domitian. And when he falls, with no heir, the empire will be plunged into chaos as it was after Nero took his own life. Only a fool does not prepare against such a thing. Albinus is a loyal subject, but with no heir in place, he prepares, and he *will* be the next emperor. Do not doubt it.'

Rufinus stepped back, this revelation knocking him somewhat. Was it possible? Of course it was. And Albinus was exactly the sort of man to do such a thing. Did that make Albinus' crimes less, though? Did it stop him being labelled a traitor?

He shook his head. 'You almost moved me there, Celer. But he still stole gold from the emperor. He still killed a procurator. He still started a small war that butchered and burned innocents to hide his crimes. It matters not whether he raises a blade, he is already condemned. I will see him fall.'

'This, Rufinus, is why you cannot be left alive. Why I hate you so much. You are too rigid in your thinking and you would ruin the world to uphold your misplaced loyalties. But this is Dacia, and Dacia is in the hands of the great Clodius Albinus. He let you live once rather than risk upturning the apple cart in the capital. But he is strong and well-protected enough that Cleander cannot damage him, and after your recent escapades I have little doubt that he will order your death with a clear conscience. And before you argue, Niger cannot stop such a thing. He might fight *me*, but he will bow to Albinus.'

He took a step back. 'Enjoy your quarters, Rufinus. Other than the lash and the blade, they will be the last thing you see.'

'Fuck off, traitor,' snapped Rufinus, his mood as low as he'd ever experienced.

The tribune, stony faced, turned to glance out through the door. The legionaries outside were deep in conversation with Daizus. Taking the opportunity of their distraction, Celer gestured to the other shadowy shapes in the room. 'I am Governor Albinus' second. Niger might be your legate, but ponder on my power. I might be tempted to find a complete pardon for the man who makes Rufinus' life most miserable tonight.'

With that he ducked out of the room and was gone. Two heartbeats later, the door was shut, plunging the prison into semi-darkness. Rufinus stood where he was, breathing heavily. There was a shuffling noise in the darkness.

'Forget what he said. I'm no easy mark.'

Another shuffle at the other side. Rufinus regulated his breathing carefully. He could make out the shapes in front of him. Three men at the far end, though one of them had pushed himself to his feet and begun to pace slowly forward. The young praetorian's ears twitched. Two men were moving in on him from behind. One was advancing with cat-like steps, nimble and quiet. The other was a solid man but with a short stride. Small and stocky, then, his friend wiry and light-footed. The man in front was a very average size and shape with a big head. Their eyes were probably better adjusted to this place, but they might have been here for some time. They were probably all poorly-nourished and weaker than they should be.

'Last chance. I'm in a pisser of a mood, and I've a good mind to take it out on someone.'

The heavier footsteps faltered and then stopped. The stocky one had taken note and changed his mind. Good. That made things easier. He heard that man returning to his seat at the edge. The cat-like one behind him was now moving almost silently on the balls of his feet. The one in front came on confidently with plodding steps, trying to mask the sound of the one behind Rufinus. They were working together like hunters.

Rufinus tried to picture the men he'd seen in that single moment when they'd entered. Three men off to the right. Yes, a stocky one, and close by a reedy, tall one. Couldn't be him from the size of the strides he could just about still hear. The third man, then. Not memorable, which suggested that he was indeed average size. Wiry and light, but of average stature. That would put him about Rufinus' height. Height was important in placing blows unseen...

The young praetorian stood perfectly still, flexing his fingers silently in the gloom. The one in front was moving deliberately slowly, allowing a sneak attack from behind first. Clever enough, if you weren't a man weaned on the inter-unit boxing circuit.

The man behind him was close now. He felt the unseen assailant tensing, ready to leap. At the tell-tale whisper of a foot finding purchase, Rufinus ducked and thrust out a grasping hand behind him. The man had gone to throw his arms around Rufinus' neck from behind, only to find that Rufinus was already ducking. Simultaneously, the praetorian's fingers closed on his assailant's crotch and he gripped the testicles hard, squeezed and pulled, all in one fluid motion.

The scream that issued from behind him cut through his nerves like serrated steel, and went on and on and on. For a moment, Rufinus wondered if he'd actually torn the attacker's manhood clear from the body, but his fingers released and the man fell away, landing on the board floor with a thud and continuing to shriek and wail like nothing Rufinus had ever heard.

The man in front of Rufinus had stopped, his hands raised, and now he was backing away.

Good. Lesson learned.

The door was ripped open a moment later and two of the legionaries on guard were silhouetted in the doorway, swords drawn.

'What was that?' one of them demanded, somewhat redundantly as the meagre light that burst in illuminated a figure lying on the ground, tunic up around his middle, coddling his privates as though they were an egg that might break. One of the guards hurried over to the injured man and crouched.

'Move out of the way, Titus,' he called to his friend at the door, who stepped aside to let in more light. Rufinus almost laughed. In the extra daylight he could see the man's crotch. His scrotum was the size of a cabbage and already going a deep purple colour.

'What in Hades happened to him?' the man beside the whimpering prisoner breathed.

'Fell over and hit his balls on something,' Rufinus said in an emotionless, dark tone, casting his eyes round the other prisoners in the gloom.

'On a spiked club or something?' snorted the legionary, then, to the injured man: 'you'll live. Go sit down and stop wailing like a girl.'

As he passed back toward the door, he threw a knowing look at Rufinus. 'Try not to kill any of them.'

Rufinus just nodded and the door was shut again a moment later, the sound of the lock being fastened muffled by the timber. He could hear scraping sounds as the ruined prisoner dragged himself back across the floor to his accustomed place.

'Plenty more where that came from,' Rufinus grunted to the room at large. 'Leave me be and I'll extend you the same courtesy.'

He crossed to the most unoccupied area and sat on the low bench at the edge. Finally, the activity over, the stench of the slop bucket in the corner insisted itself upon him. He wondered wearily whether Senova would visit him tonight, but decided probably not. Niger would not want her coming here and, to be honest, with that smell and Mister Purple Scrotum whimpering endlessly, he did not think it would be a good idea anyway.

Oddly, the incident had done something to lighten his mood a little, or at least to focus his thoughts past it. Now to sit in the darkness and try to think of a way out of this mess.

XVIII – Legionary hospitality

Rufinus awoke at the first noise. He had slept incredibly lightly, which was hardly surprising, since so did the other occupants of the building. Some hated him, he knew – especially one. Some were ambivalent about him. *All* feared him, though, and fear made people do stupid things, so Rufinus had slept with one eye open, metaphorically. Four times during the night he had launched upright, ready to fight at a noise. Three times it had proved only to be men who were stirring in their sleep. The fourth time the disturber had almost soiled himself on the way to the slop bucket when Rufinus appeared like an avenging spirit in the darkness before him.

'Gods, can you not even let a man *shit* in peace?'

The light was still little more than a faint glow when he heard footsteps approaching the building. It seemed hopelessly optimistic to think a visitor might be destined for any of these other reprobates, including mister purple scrotum, who still lay on the floor coddling his giant, tender loins.

There were the sounds of a lock clicking and a bolt being thrown back, and the door scraped open. Five sullen voices inside cursed, snapping that even this low light was too much, the other muttering something plaintive about his balls.

Rufinus was already standing, hands behind his back, commanding the situation, when the early indigo light hit him. He blinked for a while and, when his eyes had settled and adjusted, felt a chill as he realised that there was no sign of the usual guards outside. Instead, the men silhouetted in the daylight bore the elongated shields of cavalry troopers. As two of them entered and pushed Rufinus roughly outside it came as no surprise to see Celer and Daizus there and no sign of the men of the Fifth.

'Bring him.'

Rufinus muttered a curse to Nemesis as the troopers hauled him forward. For a moment he reeled, ready to struggle, then three spear points grazed the flesh of his neck in warning. The horsemen had him and there was little he could do.

The fortress was still coming slowly to life, and the first watch had not yet been sounded. It was not officially dawn, just that odd purple pre-dawn, and most of the legionaries were still abed. A few men were emerging from their barracks, yawning, stretching, farting, throwing cold water over their faces from the plain fountains. Others were coming off shift, tired and stumbling. Not so the cavalry of the Thirteenth. The troopers marched him west and toward the gate through which they'd entered yesterday.

At the great heavy portal the legionaries on duty refused to open the gate, giving Rufinus heart, momentarily. Whatever Celer intended, since it was clearly to be carried out beyond the walls, it would not be good. The tribune let forth every morsel of a senior legionary officer's fury, leaving the guards trembling and panicked. One of the bravest, risking the fury of a superior, reasoned that opening the gates before first watch without authorisation purely on the say-so of a man from a different legion was impossible without a centurion to agree it. Celer had almost exploded, and had told the man to find his precious damned centurion then, but in the meantime the gate would be opened.

It was. The left hand of the great heavy wood and iron doors was unbarred and hauled open and the small unauthorised party exited the fortress as the sun put in its first appearance behind them, a faint yellow glow on the horizon. Rufinus was a little disappointed in how easily the guards had agreed without written authorisation, but he had no time to brood on it as he was dragged from the gate toward the great flat parade ground nearby. It was dispiriting, if not entirely unexpected, to see three other cavalrymen fixing a seven foot, T-shaped stake arrangement in the ground.

'This is a turning point, Celer,' Rufinus said quietly.

'Oh?'

'Until this point all you have done is your master's bidding. You could still claim innocence and walk free. But this changes things. Once you do this it, becomes personal.'

Celer gave a cold laugh. 'I'm sure your mouldering corpse will cause me *endless* trouble.'

'I'm not that easy to kill. And you're breaking your orders now.'

'Clodius Albinus will sanction this. He would sign the document here and now if he were in Potaissa. You are a stupid and dangerous man, Rufinus, and I am concerned with every moment you draw breath that you will do something heroic and stupid and try to stop the inevitable progress of empire.'

'If that *progress* is from the legitimate emperor to a provincial gold thief, then yes. I will.'

'And that is why this must happen. If it is any consolation, I will strike as hard as I can and make it quick, though by quick I mean it will last less than half an hour. If you were a smaller, weaker man it would be faster, of course.'

Rufinus tried to say something pithy and cutting, but a rag was stuffed into his mouth rather unceremoniously. He fought not to gag, partially from the sheer discomfort and partially from the last moment realisation that the rag was, in fact, someone's underwear.

He was grasped and held. He had to give some credit to the men, for they knew their job. Not once did they give him enough freedom to fight back or slip free. His tunic was yanked back over his head and torn from him. Strong hands shoved him to the post and began to lash his wrists to the horizontal. He braced himself, standing facing the post.

Nothing happened.

After a full count of fifty he turned his head and his eyes widened. Sweat began to break out on his brow. Celer held a lash, but he had cast it aside as Rufinus watched, and accepted from one of his men a scourge. He held the weapon in a tight grip, admiring the shards of sharp pottery, metal fragments and shattered glass cunningly woven into the strands.

Gods, no.

Rufinus' bladder began to leak involuntarily. He had seen men die by the scourge twice in his time, once so recent the memories were still fresh. It was, without doubt, the most brutal punishment the army could inflict. Beheading was horrible but was over in one or two blows, unless you were unlucky and the executioner had not sharpened his blade. Pushed from a bridge, stoning, fustuarius beatings and so many more things were dreadful but all at least quick. A scourging by an expert could last an hour and leave a man looking like a half-prepared meat dinner. And Rufinus was pretty sure that Celer would be an expert. This was the man who had had men flayed and hung from the trees like grisly ornaments back in Sarmizegetusa, after all. At a nod from the tribune, the gag was removed and Rufinus sucked in grateful, desperate lungfuls of air.

'This, praetorian, gives me no pleasure.'

Rufinus was about to comment acidly, but Celer let out a humourless laugh.

'I jest, of course. This will give me the *greatest* pleasure. Would that you were a cat so that I could put you through it nine times.'

Rufinus spat. 'And would that my dog was here to eat your head, you bastard.'

'Turn around, praetorian. I'd hate to catch your face and finish this too soon.'

In the distance a horn sounded.

'First watch,' Rufinus said. 'I'm assuming this execution is not authorised and that Niger will be pissed off with you. Best hurry, or they'll realise what's going on.'

It was probably the most unwise goading of all time, for Celer nodded. 'Quite right.'

The rag was stuffed back in his mouth and the soldier retreated out of the way. The tribune's arm came back. The scourge coiled and whirled, then leapt into the air at a jerk of the tribune's arm.

Rufinus had never experienced such pain. No, that was not true. What was done to him at the imperial villa by the Syrian torturer matched it. But nothing in the past five years, and it had taken much of that time to kill off the nightmares that episode had rooted in his brain. The sharpened fragments tore the flesh from his back right down to the ribs, leaving not just a new red line among those already there, but a gaping, horrible wound, dripping gore and sending rivulets of crimson running down to his breeches.

He gasped and slumped against the post.

One blow and it had almost unmanned him.

His beleaguered mind dredged up a memory from his early days as a legionary. Gallus, the stupid bastard in the Tenth who'd stolen from the senior tribune's wife. He had taken eight of these. He'd survived, miraculously, though he'd been ejected from the legion as unfit for service and had never quite worked as a human body afterwards.

Gallus had been an arsehole. Rufinus was damn well better than him. He would certainly last more than eight.

There was a drawn breath.

'How are you feeling, Rufinus? I see from your back you've had a beating before, possibly *more* than once. Shame I shall likely never shake the hand of the man who landed those blows. But they are minor wounds compared to some you've clearly survived. I'd wager I'll top your list by the end, though. Bite down on your mouthful, praetorian.'

The second blow was agony. Absolutely indescribable. His bladder gave way. His bowels held, miraculously. His back was on fire and he felt pain through every nerve from his hair to his finger- and toe-nails. It was too much. This was no way to die. Fortunate was he that his scream and subsequent whimpering were largely silenced by the gag.

He consoled himself with the knowledge that at least Senova was not watching.

'You could have been an *asset*, Rufinus, but you had to keep pushing. For a time, from Drobeta to Sarmizegetusa, I had my eye on you. Thought you might be useful, yet you have proved determined to ruin everything. And now I shall ruin you in return.'

There was a heavy silence as the tribune pulled his arm back and prepared for a third blow. Rufinus could feel blood – or urine, or likely both – pouring down his pelvis and legs. He clenched.

'What is the meaning of this monstrosity, Tribune?'

Rufinus almost wept at the sound of Pescennius Niger's voice. Bracing himself, he turned his head. The legate of the Fifth was in just tunic, boots and cloak, his hair wild. Straight out of bed. Bless that man at the gate. He'd run off to his centurion and clearly word had passed upwards until this man, the most powerful in the city, had come at a run before even combing his hair.

'I am interrogating the prisoner, Legatus,' Celer said in a bored voice.

'I heard no questions, Tribune. What questions do you mean to ask this man?'

Celer snarled. 'Stay out of this, Niger.'

'That is *Legatus* to you, *Tribune*,' roared Niger, snatching the scourge from the man's hand. 'You are engaged in petty revenge, directly countermanding my orders in my own damned fortress.'

'You seem to think you rule in Dacia, Niger.'

The legate fixed Celer with glittering eyes. 'You seem to think that *Albinus* does, Tribune. In fact, the *emperor* rules here, and in Commodus' empire the law still applies, let alone military hierarchy. Slink back to quarters this moment, Celer, or I will have you strapped to that same post and use this atrocity myself.

There was a dangerous, loaded silence again, and finally the tribune and his men departed. Moments later legionaries were there, cutting the bonds and helping him stand away from the post. Someone removed the gag and turned him gently. Men in the uniforms of the Fifth Macedonica. Despite everything that had happened, Rufinus' heart went out to Pescennius Niger. The man's face was so conflicted. Whatever Albinus held over him must be dreadful.

'I will have you moved, Rufinus. One of the tribune's houses where the other prisoners cannot cause you trouble. Once you are discharged from the hospital, that is, of course.'

Rufinus felt like pointing out that it was not the other *prisoners* who had done him any damage, but he was so grateful and in such pain that he did not trust himself to speak without crying out. Tribune Celer and his men marched off across the parade ground, back toward the fortress, and Rufinus watched them go, Daizus turning his head as he went to cast a glare of hatred as a parting shot.

'I command here, Rufinus,' Niger said with a sign, smoothing down his hair, 'but the influence of the governor is so strong that on occasion some of my men forget that and bow to Albinus' wishes. I will have the guards changed and the men that abandoned their posts and allowed this to happen will be disciplined appropriately.'

Rufinus simply whimpered. Two legionaries helped him carefully and gently across the turf toward the fortress gate once more. Rufinus looked back as he went and was unsurprised to see a trail of dark droplets on the grass in his wake. Thank the gods Celer had been stopped at two lashes. Thank *Pescennius Niger*, in fact. As the soldiers helped him through the gate, he caught sight of Senova running toward him, her face ashen, Acheron and Luca loping along beside her.

'I just heard,' she breathed as she stopped in front of him. Rufinus opened his mouth, but struggled for speech. She walked round behind him and made a horrified, squeaky gagging noise. 'Oh, Gnaeus!'

'S'alright,' he managed, gritting his teeth. 'Had worse.'

Only once. And it had damaged him for life. But it was true.

'I will find a way to report the tribune for this,' she said firmly.

Rufinus swallowed. His strength was returning and, with it, the power of speech. 'To who? Niger knows but is powerless to do anything about it. Albinus could discipline him, but the governor is more likely to thank him. Unless you can get a message to the praetorian fortress in Rome, we're on our own. And even if you could do that, Cleander might just send Celer a reward instead. No. We're on our own, Senova.'

'Then we must get you free,' Senova said.

Rufinus jerked his eyes meaningfully at the legionaries helping him along the street, and she nodded and fell silent. Still full of concern, Senova scurried alongside the guards as they half-escorted, half-lifted Rufinus through the fortress, the spattered trail gradually dissipating as the blood crusted on his back. Luca was at Senova's heel like a dog, while Acheron was pacing ahead like a vanguard, ready to push aside anyone who might get in the way. No one did. A few men looked on in shock at the sight. No one seemed ready to gloat.

A few moments later they rounded a corner and arrived at the *valetudinarium*, the fortress hospital. A white colonnade shaded the front wall and Rufinus was lifted between the columns and in through a doorway into an entrance hall. Even at this time of the day, the hospital was working – a fortress of five thousand men meant a constant stream of work for the medical section. Six men sat around the walls of the entrance hall on the painted wooden benches. Arms in slings, feet bound in linen, crutches leaning against the wall, a man clutching his stomach and groaning in pain. An orderly opened the door ahead and paused in the room.

'Next?'

The man with the bound foot threw up his hand, but one of the legionaries at Rufinus' side overrode him. 'This man, on the orders of the legate.'

The orderly nodded and, while foot-injury glared at Rufinus in irritation, the wounded, bleeding prisoner was escorted to that door in the wake of the orderly. The man stopped in the doorway, though. 'No dogs. Not in the hospital. He'll have to wait outside.'

Rufinus looked over at Senova who, face grave, gestured in turn to Luca. 'Take him back to the room. I'll be back soon.'

As the young slave boy left with Acheron, who looked rather disgruntled and kept glancing over his shoulder on the way out, Senova gestured onward and they passed through the door. The orderly pointed along the wide corridor to the left. 'Examination room seven. The medicus will be with you momentarily.'

The soldiers helped him down the hallway, though Rufinus was starting to feel stronger and less prone to whimpering collapse now. The pain had become a constant wail in his nerves rather that that blinding, terrifying white scream it had initially been. His feet were no longer staggering and tripping.

They found the number seven and Senova pushed open the door, the legionaries helping Rufinus through. Beyond was a vestibule that was barely big enough to contain the three men, let alone Senova as well. There were three other doors leading off, the ones to either side labelled 'VII A' and 'VII B'. The door ahead was marked 'INSP.' This door was opened and the room beyond was a little larger. A hard-looking but spotlessly-clean bed lay to one side with a white sheet on it. A desk contained several books and a wax tablet, and there were two chairs. The men helped Rufinus onto the bed, face down, sharing looks of distaste at the damage to his back.

The four of them waited in an uncomfortable silence and the door opened eventually, a man in a long white robe entering. He glanced once at Rufinus, then at Senova and the two legionaries.

'Out of my hospital, you two' he snapped.

'Legate said...'

'The legate runs the camp but this is *my* hospital, soldier, and your boots are covered in mud and shit, which you've traipsed in from gods' know where. Go back to the entrance hall, get a bucket and cloth, remove your boots, then clean away the trail you've left and then, only then, can you come back and wait outside this door in your socks.'

The two men, chastened and looking down, embarrassed, at their boots, hurried out. The door clicked shut and the medicus eyed Senova. 'Wife? Concubine? Slave?'

Rufinus started to say 'friend' in a weak voice but was drowned out as Senova said 'wife' firmly,

'Very well. You can stay, but sit there and do not interfere.'

Rufinus felt the man removing his boots and taking them with a sour sound of disapproval. 'You are filthy, young man.'

'I've been...'

'I don't care what or where you've been. I will treat your back. You will then be escorted to the hospital's balnea, where you will clean yourself thoroughly with the aid of an orderly, making sure not to get my work wet. Your wife can wait for you in your room, which will be seven-a, next door. A woman might cause something of a stir in a bath house full of naked men.'

Senova smiled for the first time that day.

'Now,' the medicus said, leaning over him, 'let me see. You've suffered some horrendous damage in the past. Given the wounds I can identify, you're hardy and a good, quick healer. As such, this should not cause you trouble long-term. In fact, in days it will have knit enough that you will be able to function relatively normally. Within the month you should be back to full fitness.'

'Really?' Senova frowned. 'It looks so bad.'

'It looks worse than it is because of all the blood, young lady. I asked you not to interfere.'

Senova sat back in a huff and folded her arms, and the medicus went on, gently prodding and eliciting hisses and groans from Rufinus. 'In fact, the damage is actually minimal for such a weapon. It seems to have been wielded rather inexpertly for pain rather than damage.'

Rufinus ground his teeth. In his opinion that *was* expert, rather than inexpert. Celer had been trying not to kill him too quickly. He'd wanted it to last a long time.

'Luckily both blows were with the same arm. A good punishment detail will change arms with each stroke so that the blows cross and do more harm. These blows are parallel and therefore much less trouble and much easier in the treating and healing.'

Rufinus lay still and grasped the sides of the bed with his hands, trying not to whimper or yelp as the man poked and prodded. Shortly the medicus called for an orderly to fetch everything he needed. Rufinus' back was washed carefully, though not as comfortably as he had expected.

'You are tensing and hissing, young man. If you are experiencing real pain, I am willing to dose you with poppy juice and hensbane?'

Rufinus did not have the chance to reply before Senova's voice cut through the room. 'No drugs. He will be fine.'

The medicus frowned at her in disapproval, and then looked to Rufinus.

'She's right. No drugs.'

'Very well. But try not to tense or shiver. It makes my work more difficult.'

The washing seemed to take forever and Rufinus felt some distress at the amount of blood that seemed to be removed, spattering the floor in droplets and turning the water in the washing bowl dark red.

'You are clean,' the man announced. 'I am about to stitch and bind. Are you sure you do not want poppy juice?'

'Quite sure,' Rufinus and Senova said simultaneously.

'Very well.'

The medicus went to work. Senova kept leaning this way and that, admiring the skill of the man. Rufinus half expected her to criticise the medicus or make 'helpful' suggestions, and he was quite grateful that she kept silent throughout. The pain was intense, though not as bad as the scourging had been, by any length. The whole task took half an hour. Once the wounds were stitched, he was washed again with a fresh bowl of water, dried gently, and then a salve of honey and herbs was applied across all the damage, followed by strips of cooled linen that clung to his back, held there with sticky honey. A large pad was applied atop that. Senova was then co-opted to help Rufinus to his feet and support him while the medicus washed the rest of his torso and dried it, then bound his whole middle with thick bandages, surprisingly tight. As Rufinus slowly got used to breathing shallowly within the confines of his bindings, he realised that the pain was quite manageable. The medicus had done an excellent job.

'Go to the balneum and wash yourself. An orderly there will help you to do so without wetting the dressings. You stink and you will engender disease and illness if you are not thoroughly clean. I insist on all my patients being cleaned at least twice a day as long as they are in my care.'

'And how long will he be in your care?' Senova asked.

'I estimate three days. If he is showing significant progress, I may release him after two. If there are complications, then longer. But I anticipate only three days.'

Three days, Rufinus sighed. Three days of peace and relative luxury, and then Niger had promised to move him somewhere safer and more comfortable. None of it helped him find a way out of this mess, of course, but it was still a vast improvement on the dark shed of shit buckets and villains to which Celer had easy access.

Senova then waited in room VII A on the medicus' say-so while the examination room was cleaned up, the medicus moved on to the next case, and Rufinus toddled off in his underwear looking for the hospital's private bath house.

The balneum was a small affair, fitted into a corner of the complex where the drains carried all the unpleasantness of a hospital out of the fortress and down beneath the town to the river. A changing room large enough for three people and three small rooms containing hot and cold baths, with a steamy warm room in between.

An orderly helped him out of his underwear and found the cleaning materials. Rufinus was escorted to the warm room, where he stood feeling rather self-conscious as the orderly washed his lower half roughly, then set about the skin with strigil and oil. Once that was done, he was made to lie across a stool on his front and his shoulders, arms and head were cleaned. Next, a bucket was placed beneath him and his hair was thoroughly washed. Finally, since he could not fully submerge in water, the orderly washed off the oil with warm water again. Despite the man's best attempts there was a little dampness about the dressings, but Rufinus said nothing, grateful simply to be clean again. He visited the hot bath and was only allowed to sit on the top step, the water barely covering his groin. A big legionary with a bandage around his scalp sitting in the bath at the far side looked at Rufinus as he slipped in but said nothing. One of his eyes kept wandering sideways and it both fascinated and distracted Rufinus watching it. A similar light dip in the cold bath, and finally the orderly pronounced him done and handed him a plain white linen tunic, telling him to return to his room.

Rufinus stepped out into the corridor that ran around the entire building in a square, rooms leading off every few paces. The smooth marble flooring felt cold, yet comfortable beneath his bare feet. He was starting to feel a whole lot better already.

The attack took him entirely by surprise, and was over as fast as it began.

He was calmly wandering along the corridor when a figure stepped out of a side door and delivered an unexpected and incredibly painful punch to his ribs. Rufinus fell against the opposite wall, crying out in pain and alarm. The blow had been to his kidney and hurt like the fires of Tartarus, but that was nothing to the pain all across his back as stitches pulled within the sticky bindings.

He staggered and righted himself, pulling himself upright and raising his fists as though in the boxing ring. Who was he kidding? His right arm wouldn't come up because of the pain in the ribs beneath it, and he was lacking in strength and movement. The figure in front of him laughed, and Rufinus felt bile and ire rising up in him.

Daizus gave him a leering grin as the centurion stepped back. In his other hand he held his muddy boots, his footsteps almost inaudible in just socks.

'Just a reminder from the Thirteenth that nowhere is safe, Rufinus. Make the most of your time in here. The tribune's sent word to Apulum. Two, maybe three, days and I can pretty much guarantee a death warrant will arrive in return, signed and sealed by the governor. When you leave this hospital it will be to go to the execution post and then the graveyard. And you're not part of the burial club in any unit round here, so you won't even get a tombstone. Unknown and forgotten. Just as you should be.'

Daizus turned and walked off, swiftly. Rufinus stood, breathing hard, recovering from the blow for long moments. The balneum orderly appeared from the baths, gesturing to him.

'Heard you shout, soldier. You alright?' He hurried toward Rufinus.

'Just slipped. Fell against the wall.'

'Be damned careful,' admonished the orderly, lifting the white tunic and examining the bindings. 'No fresh blood. You've not torn a stitch I don't think, but it's easy enough to do, so go slowly and with more care.'

Rufinus nodded and returned to his room, where Senova waited with what might pass as sympathy in her eyes. He didn't mention Daizus as she helped him slip into the bed. Better not to add to her concerns. But...

Two days. Two days and then death. And Daizus was right. The governor would sign it.

Two days.

XIX – Hope springs anew

Rufinus couldn't say how he knew things had changed. He just knew.

For two days now he had languished in the hospital, in that small room with only a bed. Senova had been allowed to visit him only once each day, though with no sign of Acheron, who was not allowed across the threshold and remained in quarters with Luca. Other than that, he had had no visitors. In a way it was a good thing, as other visitors might well have meant Celer or Daizus.

The day consisted of a languid and repetitive routine for patients.

Up at the blowing of first watch at the nearby east gate, then to the balneum for a wash and shave, if necessary. Head-wound-and-wandering-eye always seemed to be there, too. Morning food – porridge that was apparently nourishing but tasted like old bread mashed with pond water. Morning appraisal by the medicus. A telling off for moving wrong or having the wrong sort of legs or something like that. Unbinding and checking of damage. Nicely healing each time. Probably still three days. Re-binding along with some unguent that smelled suspiciously like Cassius' fiery liquor. And, wait.

Wait.

Wait.

Wait.

Noon meal. Either cheese so mild it was hardly there, or meat boiled for so long that it might well have been cheese, all with bread and butter and just water to drink. Then the afternoon:

Wait.

Wait.

273

Wait.

Evening meal. Some kind of stodgy stew manufactured in a cauldron the size of a small province and cooked for so long it was impossible to tell the ingredients apart, even the meat or fish from the vegetables. More bread. More water. More waiting.

Back to the balneum for another cleansing.

Evening check by the medicus, more telling off, more unguent and another binding.

And all of this had been under guard for Rufinus. The medicus may have been the master of his hospital, but Celer had insisted that a guard be maintained and Niger had agreed, putting three men on Rufinus' room at all times. Two stood outside the door in that small cramped vestibule in the dark, grumbling about having pulled the worst duty, and another standing outside the window, just in case. There was no escape, even if Rufinus had considered fleeing the room into the heart of a sealed legionary fortress to be any kind of escape anyway. The guards went with him at all times, watching him eat, guarding the balneum while he was cleaned, even listening to him crap from just outside the door.

Two days. Sadly, what might have been a relaxing – if mind-numbingly slow – routine was ruined by the constant tense knowledge that Celer was waiting in his quarters for a courier bearing a death warrant. Once that arrived, all this care over Rufinus' wellbeing was immaterial.

He had gone to bed last night when the orderlies blew out the oil lamps, and had lain awake for two hours or more, nervously waiting for that fatal knock at the door, announcing that his death warrant had arrived and that Celer had collected up his scourge once more in preparation. Finally, he had fallen into a fitful sleep, listening to the guards outside the door discussing the relative merits of two of the girls in one of the town's lower-class establishments. He had dreamed, then, of being on a boat out in the ocean, with Senova and Luca and

Acheron and no one else. Totally free and unfettered. It was fairly easy to work out what had triggered *that* dream.

But yes, something had now changed.

Rufinus' eyes flicked open suddenly, his heart pounding, even on waking. He'd *known*. Even asleep he had somehow become, or been made, aware of a change. The silence outside the door was different to that he'd noted the past two days. He couldn't say why, but it was different silence, and that difference had woken him.

He hauled himself up to the edge of the bed. His back had become little more than a dull ache now, unless he moved sharply or twisted wrong. If he was careful and slow it was quite bearable, so long as he remained tightly bound.

With a hiss of breath, he pushed himself to his feet. He teetered for a moment, and reached out to the wall to steady himself, shaking and cold and unused to this. On silent bare feet, he padded to the window and peered between the slats of the shutter, which were angled down to prevent easy observation inside and too much intrusion of light from without.

He could see no feet and legs. Of course, it was perfectly feasible that the guard out there had gone for a surreptitious piss, or was simply leaning against the wall to either side, out of sight. But Rufinus didn't think so. Heart beating out a staccato rhythm in his chest, he moved across to the door. The room had been kept locked for the last two days except when access was needed. All the hospital's rooms were lockable only from the outside, in case of violent or deranged patients. Same was true of the shutters on the windows.

He tentatively tested the handle.

It turned.

He pushed.

It swung silently open into the dark vestibule. He squinted into the gloom.

Empty.

His heart picked up the pace once more, thundering away like that wagon on the hill down to the villa all those years ago.

Why empty? What was happening?

He almost tripped over the pile outside the door. With some difficulty, thanks to his tight chest bindings, he knelt and felt around in the darkness. Breeches, tunic, belt and boots. A cloak, too. There was an odd thought knocking around in his head that this could be some sort of trap. Perhaps Celer's request for a death sentence had been refused and the tribune was engineering an attempted escape in order to catch him and execute him legitimately?

It was plausible. *Highly* plausible. Apart from the fact that Rufinus could not imagine Clodius Albinus doing anything other than sign and seal the warrant.

Whatever the case, he was out of time. He'd had a stay of execution tonight, quite literally, but tomorrow would almost certainly see that document arrive and Rufinus executed. Beggars, as they said, could hardly be choosy. He had been offered a line and he had to grasp it, no matter how dangerous or dubious it might seem.

He grabbed the pile and shuffled back into the room. As quickly and quietly as he could, he slipped into the clothes, hissing with pain as he shrugged the tunic over his shoulders. It was a red wool one, standard for most legions and new, from the feel and smell, too. Fastening the belt took some doing. It was a civilian version with no metal plates, and tucking the end down inside the belt prevented the buckle moving about. The boots were his. They had been cleaned off and oiled, but they were definitely his boots. Throwing the cloak about his shoulders he tied the ends, since there was no brooch in the pile. Carefully, he lifted the boots and carried them in his left hand, slipping back out of his room and into the dark vestibule once more. There, he paused. This could all still be some great horrible trick.

He had no other option.

Reaching out, he tried that handle too. It opened.

The huge corridor that circled the hospital was dimly-lit with oil lamps in niches every twenty paces, and Rufinus looked this way and that. No movement or noise, apart from the background snoring and groaning of other patients in their rooms, muffled by the doors. He slipped along the corridor toward the entrance, grateful that the medicus had done such a good job, both on the wound and on the bandaging. He felt little more than achy and rather constricted.

The door to the entrance hall clicked open with an alarmingly loud noise, and Rufinus paused for a moment, worried, heart still thundering. No one reacted. No one came. The door opened fully and the hall was empty. Hair bristling on his neck, Rufinus hurried through the large open space and stopped at the last door.

There was a chance now that he might have to run at any time. Crouching with difficulty and a little pain, he slipped his boots over bare feet and tied the laces. Rising, he tried the door, amazed that his pulse had not woken the whole fortress.

The street outside was empty. It was the middle of the night. Men would be on guard at the walls and gates, by the principia, and might well be wandering up and down one of the main roads in the camp, but this was a small side street and rather out of the way. A rising panic over what he might do next disappeared in an instant as his gaze slid sideways to where he knew his room to be, where a soldier should be standing guard on the window. Instead of a tired and bored legionary, two horses were tethered to a ring in the wall two windows further along. His heart almost leapt as he recognised Atalanta. Both animals seemed to be loaded with packs.

What in Hades' name was going on?

He let the door shut quietly and hurried over to the horses, worrying about his boots crunching on the stone and gravel of the road. He reached Atalanta and checked her over. She had been well cared for, fed and groomed, and the packs on her back were mostly his own travelling packs with two new bags added. The other horse was less loaded down, but had several packs of its own. He was a bay gelding, beautiful and strong. A soldier's horse. A cavalryman's horse.

One of the new packs was not fastened and he reached up to tie it shut then paused. Instead, he fished inside. It was full of packages that felt suspiciously like food, but on the top, just inside the flap, were a small scroll case and a jar. He opened the leather case and slid out the contents. All it contained was a scrap of parchment with two words:

PASSWORD: FORTUNA

He stared at it. Could it be?

'Rufinus?'

He almost jumped from his skin at the word and rose, looking over the horse, heart thundering along. Senova was hurrying toward him, cloak wrapped around her. Luca was at her heel as always, and Acheron following on, tongue lolling.

Rufinus tucked the scroll case back into the bag and examined the jar. Unstopping the lid, he examined the contents and sniffed. He almost sneezed at the acrid content, but recognised the smell as that same unguent the medicus had been slapping on his wounds since dawn yesterday.

A ready-made escape.

Senova and the others rounded the animals and she stared at him.

'Where did you get the horses?'

Rufinus countered with 'how come you're here?'

'I had a note pushed under my door that just said "Rufinus". I thought you might be in danger, so I came running and brought Acheron just in case. The horses?'

'Provided by a mysterious benefactor.'

'Pescennius Niger,' Senova said, with conviction.

Rufinus nodded. 'I cannot think who else. This is dangerous ground. He could land himself in terrible trouble if this *is* him.'

'I suspect his involvement might be rather hard to prove.'

Rufinus looked over the packs. 'It's all here. My armour. Shield. Helmet. All my kit. Yours too. I…'

He frowned, and started to look urgently round the horse, feeling the packs and even looking underneath the beast's belly, which took some twisting and effort and made him gasp in pain.

'What is it?' breathed Senova. Rufinus continued, searching the other beast.

'It's not here.'

'What?'

'Everything *else* is here, but not that.'

'What?' repeated Senova impatiently.

'My *hasta pura*. The silver spear. I mean, it's kind of hard to miss. Even packaged up it's quite long and obvious.'

'Oh, that,' Senova said in an offhand manner, waving a dismissive hand.

'Yes, that,' Rufinus said, eyes narrowing suspiciously.

'I sold that,' she said, shrugging, and then started looking at the bags on the other horse.

Rufinus' eyes bulged. He gasped. 'You did *what*?'

'I sold it.'

'Why?'

'When you were captured in Porolissum all your things were given to me and Luca. I looked through it all, and there was no money left. You'd emptied the purse we brought.'

He gasped again. '*I? I* emptied it? All those expensive rooms and so on, when we could have made do with a tent? And *we* brought? How about *I* brought?'

She glared at him. 'I was a freshly freed slave, Gnaeus. Just how much cold solid coin did you expect me to magic up for the journey?'

'But the silver spear…' It sounded rather wailing and plaintive even to Rufinus' ears. Like a child bemoaning the loss of a favourite toy.

'We needed cash and you were carrying something pointless and worth a lot of money. Either we would escape

279

and need the money to travel, or you would die and I would need the money to bury you and survive afterwards. It was practical.'

'But my silver spear...' moaned Rufinus. *A gift from the emperor himself. A prize for valour above all others...*

She produced a bag of coin that chinked as she shook it with difficulty. Rufinus stared. She passed it to him and he took it, the weight almost pulling it out of his hand so that he struggled to keep it up.

'That's a lot of money.'

'See? Silver. Worth a lot. Soldiers all wanted it so much I had to auction it.'

'My spear,' he said again, in a petulant, hollow voice.

'And now you might live long enough to spend it. More use than a bloody spear any day.'

'Senova...'

'Do you perhaps think this argument can wait until we're safe?' she interrupted. 'Tribune Celer is going to find out about this sooner or later, and I think it might do us good to be a lot of miles from him when he does.'

Rufinus, suddenly acutely aware of the fact that they were standing in an empty fortress street in the middle of the night and arguing in subdued hisses, nodded. 'Yes. Come on.'

He grasped Atalanta's reins.

'Shall we mount up?' she asked. He shook his head. 'Might be a bit too obvious clopping around on horseback – draw too much attention. We'll walk the horses for now, and mount up outside the fortress. On the assumption the password I've been given is correct, that is.'

Swiftly, he untied Atalanta from the ring and then did the same for the bay, handing the reins to Senova. With Luca and Acheron at heel, they moved quietly down the narrow back street. At the end Rufinus paused for a moment, checking this way and that. He saw a legionary walking away down one side, scratching his behind, and then the man turned a corner and was gone. Rufinus nodded to Senova and they stepped out into the cross street. A thought occurred to him and he pulled close to Senova.

'We ought to leave the boy,' Rufinus whispered.

Senova blinked, then frowned and looked round at Luca.

'No. And why?'

'Because we can travel faster without him if we need to be on foot, since he has little legs. Because of the expense, since he's another mouth to feed and bed to find every day and night. Because we have two horses and three people, which doesn't divide well. Because he still belongs to the Thirteenth Legion and if he runs with us he becomes an official fugitive. He can be killed then for running. Also because we don't know what we might face out there – cannibal Sarmatians, Roman patrols, forest fires and angry bears – and he will be safer here. Because of these things and many more besides.'

Senova shook her head. 'You're right on most counts, but not on two. He is a slave, and a slave can be killed just for serving the wrong wine, let alone running away, so he's no better off where he is. And he is certainly not safer here than with us. If Celer finds we have gone and Luca stays, they will torture him to death to learn what he knows. I am *not* leaving him.'

Rufinus sighed. He'd not really expected to win that one, but he'd had to try.

'Alright, but he's your responsibility. He shares your horse until we can get him one of his own, too.'

'Acceptable,' she agreed.

They moved through a few more streets, heading east toward where Rufinus knew the nearest gate to be, which would also lead them nowhere near the headquarters or the officers' houses.

'Say nothing at the gate,' Rufinus cautioned her. 'You too, Luca. Let me do any talking or answering.'

'With pleasure,' Senova answered, Luca nodding his agreement. Acheron yawned, and Rufinus was treated to a view of a huge collection of serrated white teeth and a tongue the colour of old blood. 'And you try not to do that at the guards,' he told the dog. 'I don't want them to suddenly think you're a threat.'

With that they emerged from the side road onto the main via praetoria, mere paces from the heavy, closed gatehouse. Taking a deep breath, he strolled over to the gate, leading Atalanta, the others in tow. Two pila were crossed in front of him.

'No exit, friend,' one of the legionaries said firmly.

'Even with the password?' Rufinus said, questioning, his brow wrinkling. 'A password like *Fortuna*?'

The two men shared a look.

'No man of the Fifth leaves the fortress without signed orders from an officer,' the other guard said, though he didn't look particularly happy. 'Standard orders.'

'I'm not of the Fifth,' Rufinus said hesitantly. He was approaching dangerous ground now.

'Must be one of the visitors from the Thirteenth,' one said.

'No,' replied the other. 'He's the one they captured up at Porolissum. The praetorian what got fitted up by that poncy tribune. I saw him being brought back in after they tried to kill him the other day.'

'Great.'

'Look,' the one who'd recognised him said, 'it's not that I'm not sympathetic – I heard that tribune from the Thirteenth well and truly screwed you up – but we've got orders. We can't just open the gates.'

Rufinus shook his head. 'But I think you can. You've no orders denying egress to men from visiting units, and I have the correct password. There's no reason to stop us.'

'Well, no,' admitted one of the guards, 'not as such…'

'But we'll end up in the shit, Aulus,' said the other. 'I know it.'

'Ask yourself,' Rufinus tried, 'how I know tonight's password if I'm not supposed to be leaving?'

'You probably beat it out of some poor sod,' replied Aulus, doubtfully, his pilum wavering.

The other guard snorted. 'After what they did to him on the parade ground? He couldn't beat up a daisy now!'

The two men shared a look.

'Listen,' Rufinus began again, seeking a new tack to the argument, but suddenly Senova was next to him, fishing in his saddle bag. He made an odd strangled sound as he turned to her, but she simply fished out what she was looking for and wandered over to the men.

'You look hungry and thirsty, Aulus,' she said with a motherly, sympathetic smile. 'I don't think you're looking after yourself. Much more of this and you'll end up in the infirmary. Take this and when you're off duty you can get some of the good stuff.' She dropped two gold coins into the man's hand and Rufinus boggled. No wonder they were broke. That represented a month's wages for a legionary. He made that strangled noise again and watched in shock as she repeated the process with the other gate guard. 'And you I think need some relaxation too,' she murmured comfortingly.

The two men shared that look again. 'I suppose...' one hazarded, 'we can't be disciplined if they've not actually broken any rules?'

'And the poor bastard's in the sights of that shit of a tribune.'

'So really it would be the good and decent thing to do, I suppose.'

The men nodded. 'Open the gate,' one called. A voice from the shadows called back, 'Why?'

'Shut up and open the gate, they've got the password.'

There was some muttering in the gloom of the gate's interior, and then there was the sound of a bar being lifted and the left hand of the two wooden doors swung inwards with a deep groan.

'Thank you. Fortuna be with you,' Rufinus said to the two men.

'And with you, mate. Now go before we change our minds.'

Rufinus felt as though every care that the world had heaped upon his weary shoulders was lifted as they passed out from under the gate and crossed the small open space, down the slope and into the civilian town. They turned the first left-hand corner they could find and as soon as the fort gate was out of sight, Rufinus let loose an explosive breath.

'Right. Mount up. And Senova? If you're going to try and bribe someone, I'd like you to run it by me first. Just *one* of those four coins would probably have bought every man at the gate.'

'So I got us out while you floundered around and all you can do is complain about it?'

Rufinus fell silent, grinding his teeth as he reached up to the saddle and realised that with his back and the bindings there was precious little chance of this happening.

'Bet you need help again, don't you?' Senova said with a smug smile. Rufinus judiciously ignored her, struggling and panting, whimpering and wincing as he tried to pull himself up into the saddle. He was about to admit defeat and beg Senova when suddenly Luca was there, helping. The lad crouched down and made his back into a mounting block. Rufinus, feeling horribly guilty about it, used the boy and climbed up into the saddle, collapsing therein with a sigh of relief. Damn it, but why *should* he feel guilty about accepting help from a slave? Wasn't that what they were for?

He turned to find Senova giving him a look that would wither plants. He gave her a weak smile and thanked Luca, then cursed himself in turn for thanking a slave.

'What now?' Senova said, as she settled into the saddle and held down an arm to help Luca up.

'Now we stick to the back streets and get through Potaissa, out toward the east, away from the main road, so the town's between us and the fort.'

They rounded the corner of the street, passing a building that displayed good copper and ironware in its windows, then along the front wall of an inn that probably sold dangerous alcohol and things with knuckles on steaming platters. Rufinus jinked left and then right to avoid a main street where a beggar and a drunk were having one of the strangest fights he had ever seen, flailing and staggering in a disordered, careless way, occasionally falling into a wall. They disappeared into a street that was mostly residential, though with a bar that was closed at this time, and the entrance to a livery where a young lad was silently sweeping up by torchlight. There was a strange, oppressive silence suddenly, and Rufinus realised that the sounds of nature had disappeared. The world had gone completely quiet apart from the *shuff, shuff, shuff* of the boy's broom in the stable yard.

Then he realised why. The first raindrops pattered on his scalp and, as he looked up, more dotted his face. It was not that heavy, deep thunder rain that battered and blatted like the stuff from up at Porolissum, but more a gentle drizzle that insisted itself upon the world, soaking clothes faster than a person expects.

Somewhere a dog barked and Rufinus started at the sound. Damn it, but he was getting nervous. They passed from that street down an alley and across a small wooden plank bridge over a stream, and then up past a brewery and a fuller's workshop that stank beyond belief even in the rain. Past some more housing, and finally they emerged from the last building into green grass. The small road they had been following petered out and became a farm track between an open green field and a small orchard of neatly spaced trees in rows, winding across the valley and up the slope ahead.

At Rufinus' gesture they turned off the track and disappeared beneath the branches. They sat there for a moment, listening to the rain clattering off the leaves and hissing out in the open, the moonlight coming in brief, scudding grey glimpses between the clouds.

'So what now?' Senova said, finally.

Rufinus had been pondering that very question all the way down from the gate and had come to a conclusion about which he was not very happy, but could find no feasible alternative.

'Remember the map? I'm hoping it's still among your things, packed away, though we can't afford to waste time looking for it now. Anyway, the fact is: we can't go west for sure. That's all land controlled by Niger and while he's been sympathetic and probably even the one who let us go, he can't afford to do so twice and Albinus will have our descriptions circulated around the entire region over the next two days. And we can't go south, because Apulum is less than forty miles south of us. That would be like us flying directly into the spider's web and carrying a sign that says EAT ME. If I remember rightly there's just a border road and a fort or two north of us, beyond which are the Costoboci, who are unlikely to extend us much courtesy, given that they recently invaded and were pushed back out by the legions. Beyond that it's just Germanic and Gothic barbarians for a thousand miles until you get to the frozen seas in the north where the amber comes from.'

'You're painting a bleak picture,' Senova noted.

Rufinus nodded. 'It's a bleak situation. Pretty much everyone in the province of Dacia is going to be looking for us shortly with a view to cutting out important parts of me and throwing them to the birds. And those who don't want to kill us will be told to do so by those who do. And it's not like we can easily hide in Albinus and Niger's territory. A couple travelling with a great black dog will attract attention if our descriptions have gone round.'

'So?'

'So we cannot go north, west or south.'

'What's east, then?'

'I'm glad you asked,' Rufinus said with a sigh that suggested the words were said with some degree of sarcasm. 'Eventually, the Euxine Sea. That has to be our destination. We can't travel through Albinus' province, so we need to go east and get to the coast. There are many ports along there both large and small, and we'll be able to get a ship from there going back east, maybe even as far as Rome. I think getting out to sea will be easy from there, and once we're on the waves we'll be safe from everything but opportunistic pirates, gold-hungry untrustworthy sailors, sea monsters and love-starved porpoises. But getting *to* the Euxine Sea might prove difficult.'

'Because of what lies between?'

'Quite. If I remember the maps rightly, for about a hundred miles just south of east from here there's little more than farmland and native settlements. The odd tiny provincial Roman town, but not much. It's a peaceful, settled area, and there won't be people there actively seeking us. Then we reach the edge of Roman territory again, but in the east. In the mountains, again, too, like when we came over Vulcan's Pass. The Transalutanus border, they call it. There are forts there and a few towns, a bit like Bucium and Porolissum, but it's far from Albinus' centre of power and right at the edge of all Roman influence. We get past there and we are free of Albinus for good.

'And what is past that, then?'

Rufinus took a deep breath. This was the bit he wasn't looking forward to. 'Then it's the Roxolani lands, where Cassius lost his dog in endless fighting. About another hundred miles of Roxolani territory, then we'll have to cross the Danuvius back into the Roman world in Lower Moesia.'

He paused, waiting for an explosion of refusal and was surprised to see Senova nodding.

'You seem very calm?'

'These Roxolani,' she replied thoughtfully, 'they are Sarmatian? They are horse people. Proud. They might be no friends of Albinus, but then neither are we. I would rather crawl a thousand miles through their lands than ride a hundred through those of Albinus. We will be much safer among the Roxolani.'

Rufinus blinked. Safe? Was she mad?

'It will not be easy.'

'Nothing worthwhile ever is,' she replied with a smile. 'But beyond their lands is Moesia. I thought Moesia was dangerous too? The governor had taken money from Albinus, yes?'

'Moesia *Superior* we were in, where that cadaver was on Albinus' payroll,' Rufinus corrected her. 'Near the coast is Moesia *Inferior*. Different province. Different governor. Of course, he might still be in Albinus' pay, but then he might not, and so it's the safest option. Still, if we get there…'

'*When we get there.*'

'*If* we get there, we will have to be careful just in case. Move quietly and subtly and find a small provincial port, not some great metropolis. Look for a private ship, no questions asked, even if we have to pay over the odds. You should be good at that,' he added, with a wry grin at her.

'Well,' Senova said, leaning back in the saddle and looking up, 'we have food and we have horses and we have money. We can travel for many days like this without worry. More use than a spear,' she reminded him with an acidic jibe that he wearily ignored. 'And best of all, the rain is stopping.'

Rufinus looked up. Between the clouds he could see the shape of the moon glowing. The pattering droplets around him were simply those hoarded by the trees and then dropped in stages over the next hour.

Somewhere behind them, up on the hill, a horn sounded loud and long. Desperate and urgent. Bells clanged and more horns and whistles rose to shatter the night. Lights began to bob this way and that as men ran along the fortress walls.

'I think our absence has been noted,' Rufinus said.

'What now?'

'Now, we ride.'

XX – Flight

They rode for that first day with few pauses to rest, all three of them knowing full well how imperative it was to put as huge a distance as possible between them and Tribune Celer, who would have been rampaging around Potaissa blaming Rufinus, the Fifth Macedonica and very specifically Pescennius Niger. The countryside to the east and south of the great legionary fortress consisted mostly of rolling green hills and shallow vales with trickling small rivers, occasional stands of leafy trees and periodic Dacian farms and villages. They saw no sign of a Roman town or fort all day and, when Rufinus paused once and rummaged in the pack until he found the map, he had been able to confirm their route.

They crossed country, shunning the arterial roads and making directly for their next destination. They no longer had a vehicle with them, and their mounts could easily handle this gentle terrain. This had numerous benefits as a plan. Avoiding the roads, they would find only native settlements, as they indeed had, they would be harder to track, for word would not circulate so easily. Plus a direct line made the travel that little bit faster.

Their destination: Castrum Sex. It was marked on the map some two days' hard ride from Potaissa, where the foothills of the Carpates began once more. Senova had queried the sense of making for a Roman position important enough to be marked on the map, but Rufinus had been adamant. The best part of a hundred miles from Celer and his men there shouldn't be too much trouble. Castrum Sex was close to the frontier and therefore probably more concerned with the mountains and what lay beyond them than with the administrative affairs of the governor. And Castrum Sex had a symbol on the map which, investigating similar in places through which they'd already been, suggested it had a mansio. They would be able to clean up and get a good night's sleep before tackling the mountains and the passes toward Roxolani lands. And at a mansio, Rufinus would likely be able to get wind of any news or rumour concerning them floating around the cursus publicus. It might be a little risky, but the potential benefits outweighed the dangers, in his opinion.

The day was marked with difficulties for Rufinus. Extended periods in the saddle were extremely uncomfortable for his back with the tight bindings, though he could do nothing about that but suffer. At least is was more ache and discomfort than actual pain. Whenever they needed to mount up, he still needed Luca's help to get into the saddle. And when he dismounted, he lifted a leg over the saddle horns with some difficulty and slid to the ground, every time suffering a pulling of all those stitches as he landed, though they felt tighter and better knitted with every passing day now.

Acheron loped alongside Senova's horse on the journey and Rufinus felt oddly betrayed that the great black hound now often favoured her over him. He suspected it was all those journeys lying in cushions in her carriage. The beast had gone soft. Senova had wanted to change Rufinus' dressings at noon, but he had refused. He would wait until they reached Castrum Sex and he could clean down properly. *Then* they could apply fresh unguent and re-bind him.

As they travelled those calm, easy valleys, the day warmed and the shreds of cloud that had brought the shower during the night vanished, leaving only a wide blue sky and a glowing sun once more. Had the constant threat behind them not soured the experience it would have been a most pleasant journey, even at this pace.

They stopped whenever Rufinus felt the horses were starting to tire, trying to coincide such halts with local settlements. There, they supplemented the supplies they'd been given at the fortress with fresh produce. They bought a few extra things too: a roll of wool that they could use as new bandages in an emergency, a pot of some goo that a local woman seemed to be claiming was good for wounds although, from the strange leery hand motions she made, it might just as easily have been an aphrodisiac. Extra food, some wine that smelled like feet, and finally two new weapons. It was time, Rufinus decided, considering the circumstances, to make sure they were all adequately armed.

A blacksmith in one of the larger villages had a small selection of blades up to a foot long or so for sale on a table. Rufinus had told Luca to choose one, which would mean he could have his good military pugio back at last. He'd expected Luca to choose one of the daggers, but the boy had instead picked up the large wood-axe standing by the table. Rufinus had shaken his head and told the lad to choose something more sensible. Luca had spoken then, and Rufinus realised with a start it was the first time he'd actually ever heard the boy talk.

'I am more comfortable with the axe.' He had a Greek accent.

Rufinus frowned. 'But it's too big.'

At that, Luca had stepped back and begun to swing the heavy axe like an expert. Rufinus watched in surprise and as the lad finally swung the weapon down and rested the chisel head on the gravel, the praetorian whistled. 'Where did you learn that?'

'Chopping wood. I am a slave,' reminded the lad, and Rufinus was irritated to feel himself colouring again.

'Very well. The axe for the boy,' he said, and then repeated himself with appropriate hand motions to explain to the smith. He then turned and rolled his eyes. Senova had rounded the table, ignoring the sensible blades and was examining something hanging on a wall.

'What is this?' she said, tapping the weapon.

Rufinus shuddered at the sight of it. 'It's a falx. A sort of scythe meant to harvest humans. Brutal bloody thing.'

'I like it. Can I try it?'

'No,' Rufinus said flatly. 'It's too big and too dangerous. In Trajan's time thousands of legionaries died because of them. They're the whole damn reason we have a reinforced cross on the top of our helmets these days, 'cause those things went through the old helmets like a knife through a boiled egg.'

'I like it. If it kills legionaries, it might be handy.'

Rufinus shuddered again. 'Anyway, it's not for sale. This table is the shop.'

Senova blithely ignored him, unhooked the falx from the wall and carried it over to the man, who shook his head and blathered away in his native tongue.

'I think it's his,' Rufinus said. 'Or possibly his father's. That thing is probably a hundred years old. It probably killed Romans in Trajan's wars.'

Senova wandered across to Atalanta and started to rummage in a bag. Rufinus hurried over to stop her, but her glare of warning pulled him up short and he watched unhappily as she produced five silver coins, which was probably enough to buy everything on the table, and held them out to the smith, gesturing to the falx. He nodded, greedily. Of *course* he did for five denarii. Damn the woman, but they'd be broke again in a week at this rate. She was a Briton and a former slave and consequently had seemingly no clue about the relative values of goods and of Roman coinage. But then, he remembered hearing that the Briton tribes used to mint their own coins, so maybe she was just generous and bloody-minded. Either way, Rufinus decided to divide the bag of coins and hide a sizeable portion of it among his clothes to make sure they could still afford a ship when they reached the coast.

They rode on through the lush green hills and valleys, Rufinus repeatedly rolling his eyes at the sight of the other horse, bearing a woman and a slave boy, with two huge and brutal, very masculine weapons strapped behind the saddle. He was fairly convinced they were more likely to hurt themselves or each other – or possibly him – than the enemy, should they be attacked. But woe betide a man who tried to stand between Senova and something she wanted.

Finally, with the sun setting behind them over the rolling hills, they passed through another native village and Senova suggested they stay there for the night. A local inn with a warm inviting glow was definitely an attractive proposition, and Rufinus only turned it down with difficulty. 'We keep going for another mile or two and camp in the wild.'

'Why? Are you trying to save money?'

'Someone has to make up for the small fortunes you keep doling out,' he said, then held up mollifying hands at her dangerously narrowing eyes. 'No, Senova. I just don't want to spend any time somewhere where too many people can overhear and repeat. And I want to be somewhere defensible with a good view, just in case.'

This logic overcame Senova's irritation, and they rode on out of the village along the valley, angling more south than east, currently. Some two miles further on, they reached the end of the shallow valley where it met another, wider one stretching east to west. Rufinus reined in and pointed up to his left. A hill dominated the place where the valleys met, a small copse of beech and oak trees sprouting from the crest. While the valley through which they travelled was already in shadow, the sun was still lighting the top of the hill.

They worked their way up the side of the slope to the higher reaches. Reining in near the trees, Rufinus tethered the beasts in an area of good lush grass, sliding with the same grunt of pain from the saddle, removing the packs and locating the tent. He was starting to remove it when Senova called to him and pointed out a cave that had been hollowed out hundreds, possibly even thousands, of years ago. It had clearly been used more recently as a den by some wild creature, and Rufinus considered the distinct possibility of an angry bear arriving in the middle of the night to find them asleep in his home, but they were armed and he and Luca would take turns on guard so they would have warning. He tucked the tent away again and removed the bedrolls, handing them to Senova.

'You two start making up the camp for the night. I'm going to gather firewood.'

As they busied themselves, Rufinus wandered over to the copse and began to search for fallen dead wood. There was plenty of it, and despite the one light shower the place had seemingly suffered early in the day, the fuel was dry enough to light a good fire, and quickly. The only problem he had was getting down to the wood to collect it with his back bound as it was. The pain was still little more than an ache, but the bandaging was rather restrictive. He had to resort to an odd swivelling motion to drop to a crouch and pick up the wood, and then the reverse to rise again. It was a slow job. Every now and then as he shuffled about beneath the boughs, gathering up thin branches and sticks, he would hear scuttling noises or odd snuffling grunts and stop, straightening bolt upright and hissing at the discomfort that would cause in his back. In the event, each time it proved to be some small woodland-dwelling rodent or bird among the bushes and, after almost half an hour of gathering, he emerged from the woodland with an armful of wood and a sore back. He would have to sleep carefully tonight.

He strode across the greenery toward the low cave where the other two had begun to set up everything they needed, and where Acheron lay gnawing on salted beef. The sun had finally begun to set properly, and only a delicate arc of light stood proud of the western hills now. His eyes dropped from the dying glow and slid down the hillsides to the valley below.

His blood chilled and his heart started to pound. Less than a mile away, along the valley, a small party of men on horseback had reined in and were gathered in a group. A score of them, Rufinus reckoned, and the dying light glinted on each figure, confirming that they were armoured. Armoured and in dark clothing. Legionary cavalry. They *had* to be.

Dropping the pile of sticks, he stooped as best he could, which wasn't much, and hurried across to the cave.

'You took your time,' Senova said in a tone half-mocking, and Rufinus waved his hands. 'Shhh.'

'What?' she asked in a quieter voice.

'Riders. Has to be Celer.'

He gestured for her to follow and skirted the hillside, staying close to undergrowth to minimise the risk of being seen. Finally, he reached an adequate viewpoint and looked down. The horsemen had moved off the road and dismounted. They were setting up camp for the night by the narrow river and near a similar copse for adequate firewood and water supplies. Two men remained on the road as the camp was being set.

'You were right not to stop in the village,' Senova breathed.

'Definitely.' Had they done so, these men would have been on them an hour ago. 'Can you see the two riders in the road?' he asked. 'See what they look like? I can't make it out.'

'I don't know. Maybe some sort of brown cloak. Spears, too.'

'No armour or helmets, though,' Rufinus pointed out. 'Nothing shiny apart from the spear heads. And I can't see shields unless they're strapped to the horses. I reckon they're scouts. Native ones. Dacians hired at Potaissa. Might even be the ones attached to the Fifth there. That explains how they've managed to follow us so swiftly, considering the route we took and the pace we set. But I suppose once they were on the trail they only had to ask at any house and everyone would remember us, for Acheron if nothing else.'

'It's definitely Celer, then?'

Rufinus shrugged and hissed in pain, regretting the movement. 'Who else would it be? We're a long way from any military installation or official Roman settlement or road. It's Celer and Daizus and the cavalrymen from the Thirteenth. And there'll be no quarter given by them now. There's no

Pescennius Niger here to help us. It's just us and them, and we can hardly hope to face twenty of them, even with your falx and that axe-wielding lad back there.'

'What do we do, then?'

Rufinus sighed. 'We just have to stay ahead of them. We can't fight them, and we'd have to be really wily to lose them with their native trackers on hand. We just need to get somewhere safe before they can catch us. At least they don't know we're up here, or they wouldn't bother camping down there so close.'

Senova rose and began to move back to the cave, Rufinus in tow. 'So what do we do?' she asked again. 'Ride through the night? Get ahead by a few more miles?'

Rufinus shook his head. 'Got to be careful with the horses. Can't afford to break them. We might not be able to replace them easily and we can't fit all three of us and the packs on one animal. The horses need a night's rest or we'll hardly get anything out of them for the next day. What we do is move camp to the other side of the hill so that there's no chance of movement catching their eye. But one of us needs to be here watching at all times. Luca and I will take shifts.'

Senova shook her head. 'We will *all* take shifts. I have better eyes than either of you, and I'm probably better rested than you, too.'

Rufinus nodded. 'Alright, then. Two hours each. That should mean we're ready to move an hour or so before sunup. That way the horses will be rested, and we'll still get the jump on the morning, getting out well ahead of them. I want to be halfway to Castrum Sex while they're still yawning and scratching their privates.'

They returned to the camp and relayed it all to Luca. Over the next few moments they took everything to the far side of the hill, using one sheet of the tent with two trees to make a lean-to rather than putting up a full tent that would take too long to pull down in the morning. With no fire and only cold salted meat, it was a miserable and tense evening meal and the shifts were quickly decided. Rufinus would go first. To aid his healing, he could not afford to have his sleep broken in the middle of the night. Senova would take the middle shift and Luca who, as a slave, was used to being up early in the morning, would take the final one waking them an hour before dawn.

Rufinus left them to it and found a good sheltered position where he could watch Celer's camp. They had a warm, blazing cheerful fire, which irritated him immensely. For two hours, shivering in the cold and listening to the eerie sounds of nature at night and the very distant noises of the cavalry camp, he sat on a rock, feeling tense and miserable. Every now and then he would rise and wander round in circles out of sight among the undergrowth, bringing life back to his freezing feet and exercising his back. It was definitely improved and getting better all the time. Thank the gods the sadistic bastard down there had been scourging for pain rather than damage. Finally, when he was starting to worry about dozing off on his rock, he jumped as Senova appeared suddenly.

'Get some sleep,' she whispered.

'Why are you awake already? I was going to wake you when I came back.'

'Had trouble sleeping. Nerves, I suppose.'

Rufinus noted with a twitch that she carried the antique falx with her. 'If you have to use that, we're already done for.'

'What about wolves?' she replied, hefting the horrible weapon. 'Or bears? Celer is not the only danger out here.'

That was a comforting reminder, as Rufinus returned to their camp and slid into the warm blankets. *Great*, he thought, *now she's implanted worries about wild animals too there's precious little chance of me sleeping*. It was the last thing he thought before he fell into a deep and dreamless slumber.

He awoke with a start, knowing that something was wrong, though not precisely what. He blinked in the cover of the lean-to and rose with difficulty, looking around. Senova lay next to him, making gentle snoring noises, like the whisper of wind through leaves. Luca was away on guard. But something was wrong. It took him a moment to realise. There was light.

Light.

Only the very faintest earliest light of day, the glow that heralded the approach of the sun behind the hills. But that was wrong. They should have been on the road for an hour by now.

'Shit.'

He crouched again with difficulty and a hiss of pain and shook Senova.

'Whampff?' she asked blearily.

'Something's wrong. It's morning.'

She was alert and on her feet a moment later. 'Come on.'

They scurried out of the lean-to and across the hilltop, keeping to the edge of the undergrowth and around to the viewpoint they were using. Rufinus felt his anger rise. The sun was almost ready to put in an appearance, and Luca was leaning against a rock, fast asleep. The young praetorian hurried over, bent down with a hiss of discomfort, and shook the boy. Luca made to yelp and Rufinus' hand went across his mouth to stifle it immediately.

'You stupid little shit.'

Senova hissed. 'Don't blame him.'

Rufinus turned his angry eyes on her. 'Falling asleep on watch is a beating offence at *least* in the legion.'

'He's not a legionary. He's a frightened boy. Leave him alone.'

Rufinus glared at her. Sometime soon they were going to have to have a frank discussion about the nature or slaves and what was, and what was not, acceptable. She was too bloody soft for her own good, except with Rufinus, of course. Luca was shaking with terror. Rufinus removed his hand.

'Quiet,' he warned, then rose and squinted down the valley.

'Shitting shit. They've broken camp.'

There was no sign of the encampment or its occupants down the valley between the trees and the small river. His desperate eyes scoured the countryside and a moment later he dropped to a crouch, ignoring the pain it caused and pulling at Senova to do the same. The riders were at the bottom of this very hill, close enough to spit at.

'Move,' he hissed at the others, and the three of them, trying to keep close to cover, hurried back across the hilltop. Rufinus paused for a moment near the cave where they'd almost stayed and peered back. The riders had stopped. Damn it. Moments ago they had been riding past into the east-west valley ahead. Now they had stopped. Even as one of the scouts turned in his saddle and looked up at the hilltop, Rufinus dropped out of sight and ran.

At the other side of the hill, Luca and Senova were busy packing things on the horses.

'Forget the gear. Loose the reins and ride.'

'What?' Senova whispered as Rufinus hurried past her and untethered the horses.

'They're coming. They'll be here in moments.'

'Up the hill?'

'Yes, up the bloody hill. Move.'

Senova mounted and Luca dropped to form a mounting block once again. Rufinus, trying not too seethe with anger at the lad, used him to mount with some difficulty. As the boy took Senova's hand and clambered up behind her on the other horse, the woman frowned. 'If we leave all this…'

'They'll know we've been here anyway. Their scouts know. It's all about speed, now.'

He kicked the horse into a run and began to descend the far side of the hill.

'What now?' Senova asked breathlessly as her horse fell in alongside his.

'Forest. There's forest down there which goes for miles. If we go out into the open valley we're done for. If we get into the woods, we might just be able to lose them. There'll be streams and animal tracks and all sorts. I'm good at riding in woodland, and I'm not a bad tracker. My brother and I used to hunt in the forests of Tarraconensis. I reckon I can move faster in there than your average cavalryman. Come on.'

They raced down the slope and toward the dark, brooding treeline.

'There,' hissed Rufinus, pointing to a darker aperture in the gloom. A trail through the forest. A good place to start.

Taking the lead, he headed for that opening and hunched down as best he could with the tight bindings on his torso. Even so, as he passed into the eaves of the forest, twigs and leaves and other flora whipped and battered him, and Atalanta made her displeasure at the terrain known in a dozen subtle ways. He reined in a few dozen paces into the trees and motioned for Senova to do the same. Carefully, he wheeled his horse and walked her toward the edge of the woods once more. His eyes rose to the hilltop where they had been only moments earlier.

A dozen or more mounted figures hoved into view up there just a heartbeat later and Rufinus' heart raced. Damn, but that had been close. The riders moved around the hill, pointing out bits of their camp. Some dismounted to examine things closer. Likely the blankets were still warm, suggesting that they had only just left. His heart skipped a beat as one of the riders pointed directly at him, but the man then also pointed slightly to the right and then at the wide east-west valley.

Rufinus backed his horse deeper into the trees.

'I have no doubt they'll follow us, but we should be able to gain a little distance over them. This is my sort of terrain.'

With that, they pressed on into the woods. It was eerie in the pre-dawn gloom, mist rising from the ground, especially since they moved without speaking, staying as quiet as they could. Rufinus used every trick he could think of, finding streams and riding along them for a way before taking an odd tangent the way they had come, doubling back and then zig-zagging to another stream to move down and gain more distance again.

At one particular fork in a game trail, Rufinus sent Senova off down the main one, while he moved off along the side branch, making sure to walk across the mud and leave the most visible hoof prints he could. He then shifted onto less malleable ground and sought a more open area of woodland. There he put on his helmet and lowered his face to prevent being hit by whipping branches and moved through the heart of the forest until he converged with Senova on the main path once more. It would not fool a pursuer for long, especially a trained scout, but it might just throw them off long enough to buy extra time.

Gradually the light came up and it became easier to see where they were going. Finally, at a clearing somewhere in the deep forest, they paused. 'We need to eat,' Rufinus said, and dismounted with a thud and a wince at the pain it caused. Senova and Luca slid from their horse and, as Rufinus began rummaging in the bags, Senova wandered off to the edge of the small glade and started to examine the trees one by one.

'What in Hades are you doing?' Rufinus asked as he unwrapped the bread they had bought yesterday.

'Do you know what direction we're travelling in?'

Rufinus nodded. 'East-ish.'

'I don't think so. I think we've gone off course and started to turn. I think if we're not careful we'll be going back on ourselves.'

'Rubbish.'

Senova put her hands on her hips. 'Really? And how do *you* know where we're going then, Mister I've-hunted-in-woods-like-these?'

'I've been keeping my eye on the tree moss. Like you are now. See how the moss grows on the south side of the tree? That's how I know where we're going.'

'You poor urban fool,' Senova sighed.

'What?'

'Moss doesn't grow on the south side. Moss grows on whichever side gets the most moisture. And the rains we've been having have generally been carried from the north or west. I reckon all this moss you've been thinking of as south is actually west, and that means we're currently going north.'

Rufinus snorted. 'What is that, some native Briton magic thing?'

'Just common sense, Gnaeus. Moss grows in the wet, as anyone can see. So wherever moss grows is going to be the wettest part. We're going north.'

They ate a small, quick and cold lunch in an irritable silence. Rufinus glared at Senova for calling him a fool and at Luca for causing this mess. Senova glared at him for not believing her and at Luca for not backing her up. Luca kept his head down. Acheron ate meat.

Finally, they saddled up and began to move again. A quarter of an hour later, they reached an open hill with a wide grassy valley running beneath it. Rufinus rode out into the open and looked up.

The sun was in the wrong place.

He felt a shiver of embarrassment and turned to find Senova glaring at him with one raised brow.

'Alright, I concede that one. You're in charge of directions, then.'

As the afternoon set in, they moved into another forest, repeating the same tricks and ruses, moving with speed despite the difficulty of the terrain. The afternoon slid toward evening, though the sun was still considerably proud of the horizon when they emerged from the woodland into another wide valley.

Ahead, they could see hills rising with more forests atop them, higher than the ones they had been travelling through for the past two days.

'If your map's anywhere near accurate, and it should be given that it came from the legion, then Castrum Sex will be just beyond those hills. Maybe an hour's ride. Less than two, certainly.'

'Do you think we've lost the cavalry?'

Rufinus sighed. 'I hope so. I've done everything I can think of. If they followed our trail we should have bought several hours. We can be some distance ahead while they're still floundering around in the woods at dusk.'

Fortuna don't desert me, he begged silently. I know I promised an altar and haven't delivered it yet, but I will. I will. I really will. Just see us through Castrum Sex and into the borderlands.

XXI – A night of tension

Castrum Sex had, to Rufinus, something of the same frontier feel as Porolissum had, though without the latter's added feeling of civilisation that came with being the seat of an imperial procurator and the heart of a grand defensive system.

As the weary trio and their canine companion closed on the place, Rufinus took in everything he could in the late afternoon sunlight. Constructed within a loop in a good-sized river and lying at the meeting place of four valleys, the place was built upon a spur of land on three distinct levels. On the flat ground, by to the water and in a 'U' shape, were industrial buildings, a small dock, and what were clearly the less reputable locations in the town. They surrounded a higher middle plateau that dominated the flat land, with a small Roman township constructed upon it. That town in itself lay at the base of a steep slope, atop which lay a domed hilltop containing the humps and bumps of a long-abandoned timber-and-turf fort, probably dating back to the conquest.

All of it had a slightly disaffected and neglected feel to it. The lower town appeared somewhat dingy and glum. The middle town Rufinus thought looked as though it was struggling to be something more worthwhile that a frontier settlement. The fortlet was a ruin of grassy lumps, nothing more.

The small party rode in from the northwest, weary and achy after their days of traversing forests in unpredictable patterns. Already, late in the afternoon, torches and lamps were being lit against the coming darkness or – Rufinus' wary eyes strayed to the woodlands in which they'd spent their day – possibly bears? He'd forgotten during their mad dash through the forests that the hilly forests in Dacia were home to wolves and bears.

After all, Acheron's breed were kept here to hunt the damn things. He and Senova may well have been lucky to get to Castrum Sex without an angry bear attack.

They entered the town quietly, passing between a large factory of some sort and a waterfront dive where busty women made lewd suggestions at Rufinus and, rather dishearteningly, more often at Senova. Even Luca took his share of suggestive offers. Ignoring the cat calls and the lascivious jokes, they trotted along the main street, past hovels and cheap businesses, and then began to climb the slope toward the higher town.

Rufinus decided as they passed into that tier that perhaps he had been unkind with his initial judgement. There was a certain rugged charm about the place and, while it may not be adorned with the great structures of a Roman city, it was actually far more civilised than a number of towns he had visited in Pannonia, Noricum and Northern Italia.

They moved into the heart of the settlement, a square surrounded by houses of stone and timber. Though Rufinus was constantly wary, the hair standing proud on his neck, all they came across was locals, shouting and laughing, calling one another names, and all in the Dacian tongue. No Latin at all. A few women shouted at them. Men glared in distrust but swallowed their beer and went about their business. Rufinus risked approaching one of the quieter men.

'Mansio?' he hazarded.

The man threw up on Atalanta's hoof.

He tried someone else.

'Mansio?'

The man shrugged and walked off.

The third attempt was more successful and the man pointed off down one of the more major streets. Consequently Rufinus and his companions walked their horses slowly down that street, eyes constantly roving across their surroundings, testing, searching, Acheron trotting along at their side with his tongue lolling.

'That'll be it,' Rufinus announced, pointing ahead. Amid the squat buildings stood a larger structure of two stories with a sign hanging outside by the door showing a legion's eagle standing on a bunch of grapes.

'Looks like an ordinary tavern,' Senova replied doubtfully.

'A lot of the more rural ones do, but the eagle's a give-away. I'm sure that'll be it. Let's go check.'

The walked on down the street and, as they closed on the building with suspicious native eyes tracking their every step, Rufinus' eyes narrowed suspiciously.

'Wait,' he hissed suddenly and hauled on his reins, bringing Atalanta to a halt.

Frowning similarly, Senova stopped. A horse had been brought out of a side-alley and was being led across the front of the probable-mansio by a groom, taking it into the building's stable.

'What?'

'That's a Roman horse. A cavalry horse.'

Senova sucked on her lip. 'How can you tell? Looks like any other horse to me.'

'Trust me. Those fittings are cavalry fittings and that's a Roman saddle.'

As if to lend weight to his words, another groom led two more from the alley into the stables.

'Get off the street,' Rufinus hissed, pointing to a small yard full of barrels. Swiftly they ducked into the side-yard in the gloom. Rufinus walked Atalanta carefully back to the street corner and peered around it at the mansio. The grooms had gone back and were leading two more horses each. All were fitted legionary-cavalry-style and, if Rufinus had needed any more proof, one of the cavalry troopers from the Thirteenth chose that moment to step out of the front door and check on the progress of stabling the horses. Rufinus drew back from the corner and hurried over to Senova.

'It's them. Absolutely no doubt.'

'What are they doing here? You were sure you could lose them in the forest.'

Rufinus gave an exasperated hiss. 'Senova, they got here before us so they weren't following us at all. I just *assumed* they would pursue us into the forest. Their scouts had to be good enough to know that's where we went, after all. Celer is a gambler, it seems. He must have decided that we were making for Castrum Sex – it *is* the nearest sizeable settlement in line with where we were travelling – and simply bypassed the woods and came here to wait for us.'

'Clever.'

Rufinus nodded. 'In a way we've been incredibly lucky, though.'

'Oh?' Senova replied. 'How?'

'They're probably hoping to surprise and trap us, letting us walk into their arms. Instead, we've discovered they're here while they are settling in. *We* know *they're* here, but *they* don't know *we* are. That has to be a win, I'd say.'

'What if they ask around. A lot of the locals will remember us.'

Rufinus smiled. 'Celer and Daizus will have made their enquiries on the way in before us, before they got to the mansio. They'll have wanted to make sure we didn't beat them here. Now they'll be comfortable that's not the case.'

Senova nodded, breathing steadily. 'So we keep going and get ahead of them?'

Rufinus shook his head. 'We have the same problem we had last night. The horses are tired from the day. More so today, because of that stupid woodland trek. And there will be nowhere open at this time to buy horses, even if there's anywhere at all in this place – it would attract a lot of unwanted attention. No, the animals need a good rest or we'll be in trouble tomorrow.'

'You're not suggesting we stay in town?' she replied, incredulously.

Rufinus smiled oddly. 'There was nothing wrong with the plan last night. It would have worked had sleepy here not dozed off on watch.'

Luca gave him a look of dreadful embarrassment and abject misery, and Rufinus sighed as he regretted his words. He was going to have to stop considering the feelings of slaves. He was slowly turning into a mushy bundle of soppiness.

'You *are* suggesting we stay?'

'We can't keep going, Senova. The horses need to rest, and so do we. But we've got the advantage, so we'll stay clever. We'll lay a false trail and then stay somewhere just right.' His eyes drifted up the steep hill. 'Come on.'

Moments later, using two back alleys so that they did not step out into the street near the mansio, the small group returned to the main square, where they made a great show of speaking to one another in Latin. Rufinus consulted their map very visibly, pointing off to the south and loudly speaking the name of Romula, a city back down near the Danuvius. Senova nodded her head, also pointing off south and replied with the name Arutela, also a fort off in the same direction. Fake decision made, they rode out of the town around the edge of the hill, heading south-west, talking loudly as they went.

Once they passed beyond the last few homes and a farm and into the countryside, Rufinus gestured and they moved off the road and began to climb the slope of the hill. Here, away from the town, it was a relatively gentle incline and in half an hour they had reached the crest of the hill, an impressive view to both sides. Now silent and careful, they moved along the ridge, climbing steadily all the time until they reached their goal.

The fort after which Castrum Sex was named was long gone. Likely it had only existed briefly after the conquest, before the more permanent borders were decided. The fort's defences had been timber and earth, and all the internal buildings also wooden. With more than half a century of neglect, all that timber was gone, reused in local construction or burned in fires on cold winter nights, but the shape of the fort was clear, and the reason for its name came clear with it. Given the terrain on the hilltop, the earth banks had followed available lines, resulting in a fort of a roughly hexagonal shape, with two dips to north-east and south-west where the gates had been.

The four of them walked across the interior of the small camp to the far side and looked down. The town they had left less than an hour ago lay twinkling perhaps a hundred and fifty feet below them. The sun had dipped below the horizon as they climbed the hill and now the evening was turning a darker shade of purple with every heartbeat, those glowing golden lights in the town making it seem so attractive and welcoming to tired travellers stuck on a bare hilltop. Well, not bare as such. As well as the earth banks, there were quite a few trees and a lot of undergrowth, particularly around the periphery and on the slopes.

'We make camp here, but with no fire. Set up the tent and we'll have a quick cold dinner and get an early night, setting off straight away in the morning, long before sunup. The horses will be rested enough and we can get away, hopefully without pursuit, given the false trail we've laid.'

Senova nodded, then paused thoughtfully. 'We don't have all the tent.'

'What?'

'We left one piece of it on the hill beyond the woods.'

Rufinus sighed. 'Use my spare cloak as the front. It'll do for tonight.' He turned to Luca. 'Three shifts on watch. Tonight, you get the first shift. You fall asleep and I will tie your arms and legs together and throw you down the hill for a distraction while we ride off. Got it?'

Luca nodded miserably and Rufinus had to fight down the urge to apologise for shouting. 'I'll take the middle shift,' he went on. 'Senova, you have the morning one. Two hours each. We'll be off and moving while it's still night-time, that way.'

The evening was miserable. The food was good enough, but they were all hungry for something warm and filling, and sitting in the dark to eat it was hardly a heart-warming experience. Moreover, though the day had been warm and clear, the top of a hill at the meeting of four valleys turned out to be a surprisingly windy and chilly place and, even wrapped up, the small party of travellers shivered.

Luca was sent out once they had finished their meal with strict orders to sit at the old ramparts and keep an eye on the town. Every quarter hour or so he was to make a circuit of the old fort defences, keeping a particular watch on the town and on the route they had taken up the hill. And he was *not* to fall asleep.

As the slave boy went out, miserable but determined to redeem himself, Rufinus and Senova huddled down under their blankets in the part-makeshift tent and stayed close for warmth. Despite sore eyes and tiredness from their very trying day, Rufinus found sleep difficult and interrupted. The knowledge that they might be relying on Luca for their very lives and that the boy could very well be snoring on a rock made him uneasy and he woke periodically in a semi-panic. Thus he was still weary yet half-awake when Luca pushed aside the hanging cloak and gestured for Rufinus roughly two hours later.

The praetorian nodded with a profound sense of relief and left the boy to climb into his blankets while he stepped out into the chilly night air. The stars above painted a thousand pictures in the night sky, and the landscape took on an eerie, other-wordly feel in the dark. Rufinus trotted off toward the southwest gate from whence they had approached. A careful scanning of the hillside revealed nothing but a lone owl swooping over the grassland and hunting for food.

He stopped by that gate and urinated with a sigh of relief into the undergrowth. A quick circuit of the rampart to both north and south followed, and then he moved to the top of the slope above the town, where he found a piece of broken log that from the footprints Luca had been using for a seat. He sank to it, grunting at the difficulty of the wrappings on his torso. He'd been meaning to change them tonight. They were supposed to be in a comfortable mansio with baths and every amenity. Instead they were on another bare hilltop and he was still wearing the same bandages he'd been bound with for several days. He had to admit he was starting to smell a little pungent. Oddly, though, there was no real pain. It had been four days now and the wounds had become little more than a constant ache, so ever-present that he only really noticed it when he actively thought about it. He decided that when it was time to change shifts, he would ask Senova to help him unwrap and check the wounds. If it was already well on the way to healing, as the medicus had suggested it might be, then he could just re-bind the wounds in a looser, more giving manner. If not, then at least the dressings would be fresh.

He sat on the log, watching the winking lights of the town.

How had he got into this mess, and what in Tartarus was he doing about it? His father was busy selling up the last of the family's property in Hispania in some crazed attempt to inveigle himself back into imperial circles in Rome. His younger brother was a prisoner – albeit a comfortable one – of the most hated and dangerous man in Rome, and consequently Rufinus was forced to play henchman to Cleander. The emperor seemed to have forgotten about ruling his world and was said to be playing games while his chancellor and praetorian prefects ran everything for him. Provincial governors were cheating the imperial administration while lining up ready for a possible civil war of succession. And, through it all, here he was sitting in a hilltop near the edge of the civilised world, hiding from his own people with a slave and an ex-slave, planning to ride out brazenly into Sarmatian lands.

The situation seemed hopeless, and their current plan insane, but there was truly no alternative. He was sure – *absolutely* sure – that no matter how rabid and angry Celer and his pet centurion became they would not leave the empire just to follow them. Once they passed that line of forts at Commodava and left Dacia, Rufinus was certain that Celer would give up the chase. They would be free of the threat from the lunatic tribune and his men. Of course, they would be in Roxolani lands for more than a hundred miles with no ability to communicate with probably-hostile natives. That in itself was probably a stupid part of the plan, but again a necessary one because at the end of all this there was a ship which could take them to Rome, and Rufinus would present what he had learned to Cleander and hope it was enough to buy him Publius' freedom. He would even debase himself if he had to. He *would* get his brother released.

And then he would find a way to kill the serpent Cleander.

Of course, there was a lot to get through before all that. Tonight, for one thing.

He returned his gaze to the town and then finally, with a sigh, rose and set off around the defences again on a circuit. He had just passed a small, willowy tree when he heard the sound of wood snapping. His heart suddenly racing, he leapt behind that thin bole and peered down the hill. He was close to the south gate again, where they had entered the camp.

The noise could have been anything. Some nocturnal animal on the hunt. Possibly even a bear, his imagination reminded him. But he had spent enough time in the forests of Pannonia listening out for Marcomanni warriors that the sound of a stick breaking underfoot had become unmistakeable.

From this particular vantage point, he could see nothing. Hazarding a guess at the slope of the hill and the height of the remaining ramparts, he ducked low and scurried out from the tree, careful to tread only on the grass. He reached the turf bank swiftly and rose just enough to look over it.

A man was climbing the hill, moving slowly and carefully. Rufinus peered down, pulse thundering, sweat breaking out cold on his brow. Even by just the meagre light of the stars and the narrow moon, he could see that the man was not Roman cavalry. That should have been a relief, especially when more detail made it clear that the fellow was a native, dressed in standard Dacian clothes.

There were probably a thousand reasons for a local to climb the hill in the middle of the night. Of course, he couldn't think of any particular one right now, but he was sure there were. The man stopped suddenly and Rufinus peered down, watching him turn and put his hands to his mouth. There was a very convincing cry of an owl, followed by a similar hooted reply from lower down the slope, and then a second figure emerged from the undergrowth further down. Two men creeping about in the dark, signalling each other carefully.

They might well be poachers or criminals or other townsfolk of Castrum Sex, but if so it was a damned strange coincidence that they climb the hill on which the fugitives were camped. Whatever the men's intentions, they were clearly coming up to the top and would encounter Rufinus and the tent. Whether they were Celer's scouts on a mission or just nefarious locals, they almost certainly represented trouble and, if they caused *enough* of a disturbance, the town below might become aware, and therefore so would anyone suspicious staying in the mansio.

In a moment of irritated realisation, Rufinus stupidly remembered that his sword was lying in the tent, alongside Luca's axe and Senova's falx. He'd not even considered bringing a sword on watch. Idiot. He deserved to be slapped every bit as much as Luca for that oversight. Swiftly, he hurried back over to that small tree. The tent was too far away. He'd be there when the men crested the hill. He'd not seen weapons, but there was every chance that one of them had a bow. If Rufinus was over at the tent fetching his sword when the man arrived, he would have the time to get off one, maybe two, arrows before Rufinus could be on him again, and that would be enough to end it all.

He couldn't risk running back to the tent, then. But he was unarmed and needed to put these men down before there was enough commotion to reach back to the town. Scanning the ground, he spotted a rock the size of his fist protruding from the grass and prised it free with his cold fingers. Clutching it behind his back, he rose once more. He could hear the man closing on the old gate-gap in the turf rampart now. Time was up.

It turned out his instincts were spot on, and he'd been right not to run back to the tent. The man who lurched into view had a bow over one shoulder and a quiver of arrows at his side. A good archer, given the open hilltop, could have put Rufinus down remarkably quickly if he'd been far enough away. Instead, the man stepped into the camp, eyes searching the interior and alighting upon the shabby tent in the middle. He turned and made an odd wildlife-sounding noise back to his friend.

Moments only. Just moments to react.

Rufinus stepped out from behind the tree. Perhaps they were locals hunting nocturnal life, after all.

'Good evening.'

The man's reaction put paid to that notion instantly. His eyes widened in surprise and, even as he began to rip his sword from its sheath, he turned and shouted something down to his companion in his native tongue.

At least now there was no doubt or ambiguity. Whether they were Celer's scouts or not, they were definitely enemies. Rufinus threw his stone. The rock smacked into the man's forehead as his sword cleared his scabbard and the effect was impressive. The blow sent the man flying back to the grass, arms flailing. His bow string somehow snapped or came loose and the bow fell away. The sword, only half gripped, flew out across the ground and disappeared into a bush. The quiver became entangled with the man's leg and arrows clattered out to the grass as he landed on his back, winded and with a cry of shock.

The second man, somewhere down the slope, shouted and Rufinus heard him start to run, struggling up the incline. The young praetorian started to think. Two men, one now down temporarily, though the blow had been far from enough to put him out of the fight for good. Rufinus was unarmed. He…

The need for planning evaporated as Acheron, snarling like every malevolent spirit every released, hurtled past like a giant black, hairy ball of death and vanished over the turf rampart. There was a squawk of horror from the slope. Rufinus smiled as he threw himself on the first man, who was beginning to recover and attempt to rise. The man's breath was knocked from him as the solid-bodied praetorian landed on him, but the move had a very similar effect on the attacker. Even as the Dacian groaned and struggled beneath him, Rufinus was momentarily blinded by the pain in his back. He'd lived with the ache long enough now to forget that it was still a relatively raw wound. He felt two or three of the stitches pop and fiery pain rushed through him. Thank the gods he still wore the original tight bindings, or that stupidity might have opened up the whole lot again.

Rufinus lurched up, staggering, wincing and moaning at the now-fresh soreness on his back.

Through the tears, he saw the other man rise, blinking away blood, the wound to his forehead growing into a lump as blood poured down his face. Despite the blow, the man was sneering at him. His bow and sword both gone, the Dacian raised his fists.

Rufinus grinned. Despite the discomfort left as the pain dissipated a little, this was now good, familiar territory. The man flexed his knuckles.

'Celer,' Rufinus said quietly. The man's reaction, narrowed eyes and a slight tensing of all muscles, pretty much answered the praetorian's unspoken question. There could be no doubt now that these were the tribune's scouts. Celer and his men had probably settled into the mansio but his scouts, either following orders or on their own initiative, had somehow tracked them to the hill, presumably from sightings in the town and then an exploration of the road they had taken out of the place.

Damn it, but why had he not been more careful with their tracks? Still, these men were professional scouts and hunters. Likely any measure Rufinus had taken would not be enough. An odd realisation thrilled through him at that thought. These were Celer's professionals. Without them, the tribune would find it much more difficult to track Rufinus and his friends. Here was an opportunity, then.

The man took a step forward and swung. Rufinus ducked easily aside, but the counter-swing he'd intended never happened. The pain that rippled across his back with the sharp movement was too intense. Damn it, but he'd grown so confident he was almost healed even after only four days. Thanks to the excellent wrappings of the medicus, the fact that the most difficult thing he had done was slide off a horse, and Luca's repeated use as footstool, Rufinus had been lulled into a false sense of recovery. But now he was required to fight, the truth of it came back rather bluntly: he was not well enough to fight. But he had to put this man down.

He straightened, tears blurring his vision, and the man opposite him paused to wipe the blood from his head wound out of his eyes. It might have been comical under other circumstances, two men blinded and floundering. Rufinus took advantage of the pause and threw out a jab. The blow connected but was misplaced and weak, partially through his blurred vision and partially because of the intense pain that had surged through him like a wave as he threw out his arm.

The man staggered back a step, but his vision was clear with a last few blinks and his return punch glanced off Rufinus' shoulder as he tried to back out of the way. Both men winced and gasped and staggered back.

This was no good. It had to end, and if it went on like this, it could go either way. At least from the savage, feral sounds down the slope, the second man was unlikely to be joining them any time soon. Rufinus contemplated his problem. Throwing out right and left arm caused equal pain in his back, and neither was going to land an adequate blow. His head was still good. His legs... well, he didn't know how much using them might hurt.

The scout stepped forward, wiping away the blood once more, hands coming up ready, menacing. Rufinus settled on his decision. A twin attack that would take the man by surprise. The first might just be too painful to resort to the second, but he'd try anyway.

His own hands came up and he clenched his fists and danced them left and right before him like some exotic Aegyptian dancer. The scout frowned, and Rufinus pulled back one as though making to throw a punch, but then lowered it and pulled back the other. The man's eyes flicked back and forth between the two hands, attempting to ascertain where the true danger lay.

He failed, as Rufinus' foot connected with his crotch with a horrible crunching noise. The scout's face drained of blood in an instant. Rufinus suspected his had done much the same, though. He'd felt another stitch snap with the move and the searing pain was there again. Still, he'd endured worse and so he fought through it, moving to the second blow. Even as the scout gasped and gagged, his ashen face dropping to look in horror at his nethers, Rufinus' forehead smashed into the man's scalp.

His head-butt caught a glancing blow on the bloody lump the rock had left, and the man gave a brief gurgle and collapsed back onto the grass again.

Rufinus staggered. He felt sick as though he had drunk a thousand jars of wine on a diet of naught but fish sauce. He lurched back and forth, stepping this way and that, and then spewed forth an impressive fountain of vomit onto the grass.

Hands were there a moment later. Senova's hand, he knew from the soft skin, and Luca's smaller, rougher palm. One on each arm, keeping him steady, holding him upright. Gradually the nausea faded and he was left with an ache that felt as though a carriage had ridden over him a number of times. He stood still, gulping down air as his vision settled.

The scout on the ground was groaning and shuddering. Rufinus stared, bulge-eyed, as Senova let go of his arm and stepped forward, slowing raising that dreadful falx with the curved, razor-sharp blade. He shook his head – *bad idea* – and made negative sounds, trying to stop her. Killing a man like that in cold blood was a life-changing thing. Even he, a veteran and a soldier, hated it. It corroded a little of a person's soul, and he would save Senova that life-long memory. His arm shot out and stopped her. He couldn't do much about it himself in this state, mind, and Luca's axe? Well, the lad should not have to do such a thing at his age.

They were saved the decision a moment later as Acheron, like some ancient spirit from Tartarus, padded back through the gate, his head and paws coated, hair matted and glistening, blood running from his jaws. Even Rufinus shuddered at the sight, and even more so as Acheron calmly sauntered over to the shaking man and, as though nudging the food in his bowl in thought, ripped out the side of the man's neck with one clamp of his terrible jaws. The man gurgled, too oblivious and half-dead already to scream, as blood sheeted from his neck onto the grass.

'Were they Celer's men?' Senova asked quietly, eyes wide.

Rufinus nodded – *bad idea* – and breathed deeply the metallic-tainted air of the hilltop. 'His scouts. Both of them. Acheron's dealt with the other down there. I think... I think I've opened a wound again.'

'I will re-bind it,' Senova said firmly.

'Not now. Now we go.'

'What?'

'The horses have had three hours' rest. It will have to be enough. Celer might be expecting these men to report in at any time. All it needs is for him to take an interest and look for them and we're in real trouble. We'll have to hope the false trail we left in the minds of the townsfolk works and Celer thinks we're making for the river down south. Either way, we have to go. Senova, saddle the horses and gather the things, and quickly. Luca, come with me.'

Senova hurried off to deal with their camp and with Luca's help Rufinus, grunting and hissing, stripped the fallen man of his tunic, trousers and cloak and threw the bloodied corpse down the slope into some bushes. They repeated the action with the second body when they found it, though Rufinus decided to leave the clothes, considering all the tears, teeth marks in the cloth and the huge swathes of blood soaking them. That body joined the first and, carrying his drab haul of clothes, Rufinus returned to the horse. Tucking the items into a bag, he noted Senova frowning at him.

'Native clothes might come in handy.'

With that, still tired and somewhat dispirited, the three of them mounted once more and set off from Castrum Sex, making for the borderland forts and the edge of the Roman world.

XXII – Frontiers

If Atalanta had ever been close to ridden to death, it was over the next day. The three of them, with Acheron running alongside, had raced away from Castrum Sex in order to put as much distance as possible between them and the tribune's men. They had travelled fast and far through broad valleys between ever higher hills as the mountains began to rise once more, and the blue sky, buzzing bees and steaming sun could do nothing to break the tension among them.

Rufinus' solid belief that safety lay beyond the borders of Rome had become the goal and the conviction of all of them, and everyone looked to Commodava as the gateway to freedom. In order to add a little weight to the false trail they had laid the previous day, and to circumvent the town as widely as possible and avoid too much risk of bumping into watchful enemies, they had left along that same road to the south-west but had soon – as soon as they found ground which would not easily mark with tell-tale hoof prints, anyway – veered from that road and cut across a hillside to the next valley, where the other main southerly road marched off in the direction they truly sought.

The journey to Commodava and the frontier forts was somewhere in the region of seventy miles, mostly along good flat valleys and easy terrain, with a short climb over a low pass toward the end. Rufinus had hoped to make it in one day and be free of pursuit with the following sunrise, but it swiftly became evident that his hopes were highly over-optimistic. On a good day, with a fresh, strong horse, a man might hope to cover seventy miles with adequate rest stops. Racing at speed to put distance between them and Castrum Sex before even dawn, with only a short rest and after a previous exhausting day was too much even for resilient Atalanta and the cavalry horse from Potaissa.

In the event, they managed a little over thirty miles that day and even then they had come close to breaking the horses altogether. They stopped for the night nervous, tense, watchful and exhausted. Given the previous two nights' failures, this time they chose a small area of clearing in woodland in the loop of a small river. The field of vision was not good, but they were far from the recognised road and, Rufinus figured, if they could not see much, they would be equally difficult to spot for other travellers. They slept in blankets under the stars, cold and uncomfortable, taking two and a half hour watches each, allowing more time to rest than the previous two stops. Despite the discomfort, they passed the night in peace with no attacks or searching natives. Rufinus began to feel that perhaps he had been right and killing the two scouts had seriously hampered Celer's ability to track them. Either way, they awoke the next morning having had more sleep than they'd managed since the night before the escape in Potaissa, and were back on the small country road before dawn with horses that were far from content and strong, but were at least better rested than they had been thus far.

The second day out of Castrum Sex they moved with a little more ease and confidence. Far from *relaxed*, of course, but less tense than the previous two days. Rufinus found himself thinking ahead and wondering what to expect of the Transalutanus frontier. It would be different, he reasoned, to the borders he had witnessed thus far. Along the journey to this place, the Danuvius had provided much of the border and beyond it had lain an endless flat plain – the lands of the Iazyges. Then, on the journey to, and around, Porolissum, the terrain had been a rolling landscape of high hills and broad valleys, green and dotted with woodland. But the map they had relied upon throughout showed this new frontier as lying amid true mountainous terrain – the Carpates, the same range they had crossed when first moving into the province from Drobeta.

And *there*, they had been close to long-term Roman lands, such as Moesia and Pannonia. *Here*, on the other hand, they were on a *real* border, with only Sarmatian tribes beyond it. He doubted it would have even half the civilised feel of the west.

He was right.

They came down from that last climb into a wide valley perhaps three or four miles across, and on the far side of it lay the Carpates. This was no steady climb into the mountains over days as they'd experienced while making for Vulcan's pass. This was a flat valley and then sudden lofty hills, behind which towered great grey peaks streaked with white snow and half-obscured by cloud that clung to them like a sobbing lover.

Commodava was not hard to find. The valley was partially cultivated by native farmers, and small settlements and villages could be seen dotting the landscape, but the only place of any real substance visible was a Roman fort and its civil settlement sitting defiant in the centre of that valley, silent guardian of the Roman world.

Despite the past day of relative ease, Rufinus cautioned them to care and the small party approached the town. They left the main road as they descended and travelled along narrow farm tracks between fields and small stands of trees, moving through tiny villages and around small farmsteads to the far, south-eastern side of Commodava. Finally they stopped by a farm's cattle shed, no sign of human life manifest, and Rufinus nodded to the others.

'I'm going into the town, but for safety I should go alone. One man might escape notice, but the three of us and Acheron are too memorable together.'

Luca nodded his understanding. Senova huffed. 'Why go at all? It is dangerous, and there is no reason to risk it.'

Rufinus gestured at the group. 'We need more supplies. If we're crossing the mountains we need to be prepared for hardship, and we don't know what to expect in Roxolani lands beyond the passes. Fodder for the animals might be very hard to come by too, though I guess we can buy that at one of the farms. Most importantly, all we have to go on is a rather grand-scale map, which doesn't give us much detail as to where we're headed. The locals will know the passes, hills and valleys. I've got to speak to people here and find out more. So you two wait here with Acheron. I will be as quick as I can.'

With that, he divested himself of the sword he'd been wearing and slipped from his cloak and tunic, donning the Dacian ones he'd taken from the body on the hillside. The change would have been slightly more convincing had he also changed into the native trousers but the difficulty and potential pain of dismounting, changing trousers and mounting again was too much to contemplate after hours in the saddle.

Suitably attired and non-threatening, he bade the others farewell and rode out from the farm buildings along the narrow track. After half a mile it joined a local road, which was really just another farm track, though a wider, better-used one.

Rufinus entered Commodava settlement trying to look unobtrusive and forgettable. Commodava was perhaps the most *frontier* place Rufinus had ever seen. The whole town was constructed of timber and clods of daub, the roads through it little more than dust and gravel and horse shit. Animals were tied to hitching rails outside buildings, and they were not all horses, either. A few large cows and, notably, two goats were tied up in the main street. The people looked to be generally natives with little visitor blood evident. That being said, the main tongue he heard was Latin, albeit spoken in a thick eastern Dacian accent.

The fort itself was clearly old, dating back to the conquest, probably. Consisting of an earth bank with timber ramparts and gates and wooden structures within, it looked as rough and makeshift as the civilian town outside it. To Rufinus' trained eye there were signs that the fort had spent some time abandoned and empty and had only been reoccupied for a matter of months. The re-creation of the border was clearly at work here.

Even sitting on Atalanta at the heart of this town, Rufinus was assailed by the feeling that he was on the very edge of civilisation. The white-topped serrated mountains lay brooding at the edge of the valley, guarding the ways into Roxolani lands. Rufinus tried to shake off the feeling and dismounted, grunting with the pain, but the feeling was still there, like those same mountains, no matter where he looked.

Rufinus produced a sack from the saddle bags and hitched his horse outside a shop that was only any different from the other buildings because of a trestle table outside advertising some of the wares to be found within. Inside, a woman with a face like the sole of a military boot and a man who might well have been old enough to remember Trajan's armies coming into Dacia, shuffled out to sell him their goods. In fact, their wares proved to be rough and basic but of good quality and hearty, and Rufinus bought a few things he thought might be useful on the trip as well as a selection of hardy preserved foodstuffs.

Bagging up the supplies and handing over a few extra coins for their excellent service, Rufinus prepared himself with a steadying breath.

'Do you get much business from the Roxolani?' he asked as casually as he could manage while organising the bag's contents.

'Roxolani?'

'Yes,' Rufinus said, still trying to sound casual. 'From across the border. I presume there are passes around, what with a fort being built here? Surely the Roxolani come across and trade?'

Boot-face and her ancient husband shared a frown and Rufinus wondered if he'd made some kind of blunder with his question. The woman turned back to him, though. 'Some Roxolani. Few. Border ones. Live in hill. In mountain. Come buy food. Not common. Only bad winter or troubles. Roxolani not come. Worried. Romans not friend to Roxolani.'

Excellent. While that boded some ill for Rufinus and his group travelling in their lands, it also meant there was little chance of Celer wanting to interfere with them. It added weight to his opinion that the tribune would not pursue them.

'There's a valley just to the east,' he said, still maintaining that casualness in his tone. 'I guess that leads to a pass?'

'Many passes.'

Oh good.

'You want go pass? Roxolani?'

Shit. 'Not especially. Just interested.'

'You want know mountains, speak Scoris. In. Inn. In inn.' She sniffed and Rufinus smiled.

'Have a good day,' he nodded to them and slipped out of the building, almost walking straight into two auxiliary soldiers wearing uniforms of an alpine regiment. They lurched out away from the building to go round him, but otherwise paid him little heed – another dirty man dressed in native clothing. Rufinus was about to unhitch Atalanta and hurry away when he heard one of the men say the word 'legion.'

It was too much of a coincidence. There were only two legions in Dacia and they were both based hundreds of miles from here. Hefting the sack over his shoulder to help cover his features he gasped at the pain that caused in his back. Biting down on it and managing not to cry out and draw too much attention, and hunching over to add a little age to his appearance, he shuffled along the side of the street in the wake of the two soldiers, trying to look downtrodden and inconspicuous, yet stay within earshot. His back burned like acid from the pain and he had to concentrate not to groan.

'Who the fuck does he think he is anyway?' grumbled a bearded auxiliary. 'Tribune from some high and mighty pissy legion off in the west giving orders out as though he was anything to do with us.'

Rufinus felt a chasm opening up beneath him. Celer had been here? Possibly still was? How was that possible? His mind quickly ran down the map he'd been using. There was no quicker route from Castrum Sex to Commodava than the one they'd used. But then Rufinus and his friends had veered off the route to camp in the woods last night, limited to slow movement due to their exhausted horses. Celer and his men would not have been troubled by such things. They had all the authority in the world and nothing to fear. Celer probably just commandeered extra horses in the town and rode here in a day. How he knew to come here was a different matter, though. Had he found their tracks? Did he have new scouts now, hired at Castrum Sex? Or had he just reasoned out Rufinus' plan? Whatever the case, he had clearly reached Commodava before them.

'Prefect says the posh bastard is second to the governor,' the beardless soldier replied. 'No one's going to deny Albinus' pet, are they?'

'But so many of them. Bang goes the dice game tonight. And I'm on a winning streak, too. I was going to make a pauper out of Blaesus tonight. Now I'm stuck doing double duties here, while that poor bastard is sat up in some pass shivering his arse off.'

Pass? Rufinus' flesh prickled.

'At least he picked the *low* pass. Imagine the poor sods who were sent to the high ones near the snowline.'

The two soldiers suddenly stopped at a fish stall, laughing about the smell, and Rufinus, trying hard to look like a local going about his business, veered around them and walked on one building further, then turned down an alley. He risked a very brief look back, then, but saw that the soldiers were involved in some foul conversation about the fish, snorting and laughing, so he hurried along the alley with his sack.

As he'd left the shop, he had intended to head straight back to Senova and the others, purchase hay from some farm and head off down the main pass through the mountains. That notion had been blown away like dry leaves in a gale by the conversation he'd just overheard. His heart thundered as he hurried along the alley. Not only were Celer and his men here, but they were so completely ahead of the game that they were closing the passes to him. The tribune must have realised that there was only one route open to Rufinus and was determined to seal him in and trap him. Damn the man. And if he had enlisted the garrison of Commodava for the job, they would be thorough, for they knew the region well, obviously.

Damn it, damn it, damn it.

He'd wanted to spend as little time here as possible, given the dangers, but now he had a new task first. He would have to go to the tavern and look up this man who knew the mountains and the passes. Scopius? Scortius? *Scoris.* That was his name.

Judging when he'd gone far enough along the alley, he turned into a stinking back-street lined with shoddy timber houses and scurried back along it further than the distance he'd followed the soldiers, then turned and rushed back toward the main street. He emerged close to the store where he'd almost run into the auxiliaries in the first place, and glanced left to make sure. The two men had moved on and were approaching the fort gate now. Rufinus turned and went the other way, remembering seeing on his way in a tavern sign displaying a fat looking pig. Some ten buildings further down, he found it.

The Jolly Pork. The badly-painted pig appeared to be dancing and playing some sort of pipes. These people were weird.

Rufinus pushed open the door and was hit by a smell that was most certainly porcine, though far from jolly. The smell of overcooked meat was laced with a stench of sweat and the odour of burning lamps, and the combination was eye-watering and thick. The room was busy, though. More than a dozen locals drinking, chatting, eating, gambling. *No soldiers.* Rufinus relaxed just a little. He couldn't imagine Celer dropping in here, mind. Not when the prefect up at the fort would likely have far better wine.

The disguised praetorian ambled over to the bar, eying the locals as he went. He needed to be as inconspicuous as possible. Given that not one man in that bar was drinking wine or water, Rufinus knew his ill luck was still holding. More than half of them were drinking beer that had things floating in it and looked like it should probably house a frog. The rest were on that perfectly clear Dacian spirit that Rufinus suspected would strip rust off a blade in heartbeats.

The barman nodded a greeting and Rufinus gestured at the back of the counter where all the drinks were kept and decided to gamble. 'One of them,' he said vaguely. The barman frowned as though Rufinus was playing a trick on him, but turned with a shrug and opened up the tapped keg, filling a large clay beaker. Rufinus shuddered at the glugging noise. The beer looked revolting, but it was probably still a safer bet than the spirit. He took the mug, paid the two copper coins with a thank you and tapped another on the counter. 'Don't suppose Scoris is in?'

The barman's frown deepened, but his gaze dipped to the coin. He pointed at a wide fireplace. 'Over there.'

Rufinus turned to look. Two men were deep in conversation. Both had that perpetual outdoor complexion that made their skin look like badly-worn saddle leather. Both had beards the colour of yesterday's fire ash and long enough to hide a ferret. Both wore the traditional Dacian hat and the tunics and furs of hill men like those he'd first met months ago in the Vulcan pass. He decided not to bother pursuing the question as to which one was his target. Instead, he slid the coin to the barman with another nod of thanks and then slowly wandered across the room to the two men. As he neared them, he cleared his throat. 'Scoris?'

One of the pair looked around suspiciously.

'What?'

'Might I have a word in private?'

Scoris shrugged and said goodbye to his friend, gesturing to a door. Rufinus followed him through it into a back room with a long table set up for some large-scale meal. The room was empty of life apart from a mangy-looking beige dog lying on a thick rug, who opened one eye in curiosity and then closed it

again and went back to sleep. There were two other doors –
one to the kitchen and one out to the back, Rufinus surmised –
but both were firmly shut. Scoris closed the one behind them
and leaned on the wall.

'What?'

Rufinus breathed slowly. This was a dangerous moment.
'I'm looking for a way over the mountains into Roxolani land.'

Scoris nodded slowly. 'One not full of legionary sentries, I
guess?'

Rufinus nodded. 'Something like that.'

'Why are they after you, then?'

Rufinus felt his heartbeat jump. This was descending into
the level of dangerous discussion rather quickly. 'I can't say.'

'Then I can't help.'

The young praetorian fumed, sucking on his teeth while
Scoris simply leaned on the wall and watched him calmly. 'I
escaped punishment at Apulum fortress. I'm on the run from
the Thirteenth.'

It was the truth, after a fashion. He hoped the man wouldn't
be curious as to why such a large detail and a senior tribune
had been sent after him. Fortunately, Scoris simply gave an odd
grin.

'Fell asleep on duty? Pissed on a centurion? Shagged the
tribune's wife?'

Rufinus shivered. *Much worse. Much, much worse.*

'I had a bit of a problem with my optio. We ended up
coming to blows. I mangled his leg.'

Again: all the truth, after a fashion.

Scoris nodded. 'So you ran from a beating? And now if
they catch you it'll be a lot worse.'

'*Fatally* worse,' Rufinus nodded.

'Ah, that tribune's a tossbag,' Scoris snorted. 'And his pet
centurion's a thug, too. I've a mind to help you, runaway
soldier.'

Thank you, Fortuna. Thank you.

'I'm so grateful. I…'

'Cost you, though.'

Rufinus nodded. Of course. And whatever his price, it would be worth it.

'Three gold aurei.'

Rufinus' eyes widened. His memory slammed figures into his conscious mind. That was something like seventy five denarii! Near half a year's pay for any of those men in the fort. A month's pay even for a centurion. His shock must have shown on his face, for Scoris' expression hardened. 'That's my price to go behind the back of the Roman army and put my life on the line.'

Rufinus hurriedly nodded a lot. 'No, that's fine. Three aurei. It's a lot, but for the risk…'

'More, then,' the man said. 'And I bet if you're willing to pay three without argument, then six is likely too.'

Rufinus' eyes narrowed. 'I'm not rich.'

'Me neither, but I'm a free man. Would you rather be poor or dead?'

Rufinus ground his teeth. 'Six, then, but no more. And your help better be worth it.'

Scoris nodded and held out his hand. Rufinus dropped his bag and rifled in his purse. To make it clear how little he could afford, he did it quite openly, and had to find silver to make up the cost when he discovered he had only five aurei. Luckily, of course, much of their coin was hidden in his kit on Atalanta outside the shop. He handed over the coins.

'You sure you want to go into Roxolani lands?' the man asked. 'Might be easier handing yourself over to the legion.'

Rufinus shook his head. 'Roxolani. Nearest direct route that won't be guarded.'

Scoris shrugged. 'All the passes and crossings will be guarded. Nowhere where there's a straight crossing. The way will be difficult.'

Rufinus nodded quickly. 'Fine. Tell me.'

'You'll need good horses. There's a logging road near here but it's steep, long and narrow. You'll see two valleys off to the east opposite Commodava. They fork, you see. The right hand one runs over the mountains and is quite wide. An old trade road. That'll have a garrison. The left only runs into the hills and turns northward. But you'll find the logging road about two miles along it, off to your right. Can't miss it. There's an old stone there carved with local markings. Follow that road. There are lots of crossings and side tracks, but you need to make sure you keep heading straight east for a while. You know how to do that? Check the moss on the trees.'

Rufinus nodded. 'Wettest side,' he said, cursing and blessing Senova simultaneously under his breath.

'Yes. In those hills the moss will generally grow on the south side. Keep heading east. Once you get to the highest point, you'll pass some big rocks and an escarpment. You'll be able to see a great big cliff. Aim for that. Behind that, which will take some getting to, you'll find an old abandoned mining settlement. The track that leads down from there will take you about six miles further on. You'll come to a tiny village called Coido. Follow the stream from there down the valley and you'll eventually meet the main pass I first described, but by then you'll be outside Roman territory and in Roxolani lands. The men watching for you will be up in the high pass and you'll have gone round them at some distance.'

Rufinus nodded, trying to commit it all to memory. 'I don't suppose I can persuade you to guide us?'

'Unless you robbed the gold mines in Alburnus, you ain't got enough money for that.'

Rufinus snorted. *How close to the truth...*

'Alright then. Sounds straightforward enough. But I warn you, if you've lied...'

'No lie. No point. You'll not last a day among the Roxolani. They don't like Romans much, and legionaries not at all.'

'Thank you.'

Scoris simply shrugged and opened the door, slipping back out into the bar. Rufinus made to follow him and his blood froze at the sight of two legionary cavalrymen sitting at a table near the door with their feet up. They gave a toast to some fellow called Tullus, clacked wine cups together and threw down the contents in a single gulp, laughing. Damn it. Scoris gave him a crafty grin and then wandered back to the fireplace to talk with his friend. Rufinus let the door close and then hurried over to the other exits. Both the kitchen door and the exterior one were locked tight. He hurried back to the bar one and pushed it open a tiny bit. The innkeeper was pouring out two cups of wine, but ran out and had to go for another jar. They had to be for the soldiers again – no one else in the place was drinking wine. Rufinus needed to get past them unobserved. He needed a distraction, for they were facing the door and would most definitely see him. If there were a way he could also perhaps put them out of action, even for just a while?'

His gaze dropped to the fireplace in the dining room, where yesterday's ash remained uncleared as yet, and he grinned. Old trick from training days with the Tenth: when you wanted to get out of some awful duty, you mixed ash into your drink and sucked it down. It made you so sick as a dog you actually went green and threw up copiously for an hour or so. Just long enough to convince a centurion or even a medicus you were actually ill. Then you recovered quickly and the rest of the day was yours.

He emptied the coins from his purse into his other pouch, then crouched and quickly swept up ash into it. Taking a deep breath he opened the door and walked out into the bar and over to the counter.

'Can I have one of those breads?' he said, pointing at a pile of small loaves at the far end of the bar. The barman looked irritated as he had just been making to pick up the wine cups to take to the soldiers. Rufinus slid him a coin and he grunted and hurried away along the bar to get the bread. Rufinus quickly upended the purse into first one cup then the other, stirring them with his fingers. He'd just dropped the purse back down below counter level when the barman returned with the bread.

'Here.'

Rufinus took it with a word of thanks, then wandered over to stand by the wall, waiting. He watched as the barman delivered the drinks, placing them on the table in front of the soldiers. The innkeeper then turned and walked back to the bar. The soldiers made a toast to some woman called Apinna and then lifted the cups and threw back the contents. There was a single heartbeat of silence and then both men cried out angrily, coughing and gagging, rising from their seats and turning to the bar. Rufinus left the wall and slipped out through the door during the commotion.

As he hurried off down the street, he could hear the shouting and anger in the "Jolly Pork" behind him. Both men had drunk it all, and would be sick beyond limits for the next hour or so. Good. Rufinus reached Atalanta and tied the sack to the saddle, mounting with some difficulty, even with the aid of the ready-make block there. Finally in the saddle, he moved off. He would not risk staying on the main street, and turned into that side alley again, then along the filthy back road all the way to the edge of town, where he walked the horse out through the fields until he felt safe and then began to trot and then canter back to the farm.

He had a plan. Celer might be clever, but Rufinus was more so. He would slip through the tribune's net and make it to freedom in the next day or two. It was tantalisingly close now. As he rode, he ran over Scoris' instructions again and again, hammering them up on the wall of his memory to stay there for immediate recall later. And at the farm he would tell them to Senova and Luca. Then they would be as prepared as they could.

Roxolani lands awaited.

XXIII – The end of the world

S coris had been perfectly accurate with his instructions. The left-hand fork of the twin valleys curved around to the north, rapidly narrowing into a deep cleft with high sides covered with thick forests of pine, brown and green against the grey of the hills and the blue of the sky.

They moved at speed, knowing that Celer was somewhere in the area and his men with him, as well as the Raetian auxiliaries from Commodava who occupied the passes and crossings, watching for them. The only human life they saw in that mile from the town and the two up the valley, though, was a local hunter with a bow over his shoulder and a dog that looked like a brown reflection of Acheron. The man nodded a greeting and wandered on about his own business.

They found the marker just as Scoris had said they would. A stone standing by the side of the valley on a low plinth with indecipherable markings scratched across the lichen-coated surface. Beside it, a narrow track climbed the hillside, just wide enough to move with a horse, branches cleared out of the way to allow a beast of burden to descend dragging timber. Rufinus took Atalanta up it first, Acheron padding out ahead, with Senova and Luca on the other still-unnamed horse behind. There were marks of regular usage by men and beasts along the track, though not in recent days as far as Rufinus could see, which gave him a little confidence.

The track climbed back along the side of the valley and then, as it neared the top, turned and marched off at a tangent, heading east into the mountains. Rufinus remembered what Scoris had told him, and had passed it all on to Senova and Luca too. They crested the hill but were not treated to any stupendous view due to the ever-present forest that covered every hill. Continuing on east, occasionally checking the moss

334

of the trees, but equally using the sun whenever the arboreal canopy allowed, they followed the trail, ignoring the various side tracks that joined it, leading off presumably to logging sites.

They had travelled perhaps a mile across the hills when disaster struck. Rufinus did not see it happen, riding ahead and keeping his eyes fixed on the track they followed. All he heard was the shouts of surprise from Luca and Senova and he turned just in time to see them tumble from the horse. Senova fell some distance and thudded against the bole of a tree, winded. Luca, unimpeded by the pines, rolled off some way down the hill, yelping, before he scraped to a halt in the bed of mud and needles.

The horse was down, but struggling to rise.

Rufinus slid – painfully as always – from Atalanta and tied her to the nearest branch, then hurried back along the track. Senova was already rising, dazed, but waving her hands at him, protesting that she was fine. Luca was some distance down the slope, but had stood and was staggering slowly back up. Rufinus went over to the horse, content that both his companions were unharmed. The animal had risen finally, and he thought for a moment all would be well. Then he grasped the beast's reins and tried to lead it forward. The horse hesitated and, when it placed its fore near hoof to the ground and moved, it almost collapsed in a heap, that leg trembling and skittering beneath it.

Lameness. Not just a strain or something either, but a more major injury. He let the horse stand still and gently, calmly ran his hands down the leg from shoulder to hoof. He found the break at the hock and shook his head sadly. Even a cavalry fort's equine surgeon would be able to do nothing about that. The beast was done for. Not a step more. It must have trodden in one of the many rabbit holes that abounded on the hillside and broken its leg.

Senova was stepping toward the horse, making soothing noises, and her eyes widened in shock as Rufinus drew his pugio.

'What are you doing?' she hissed. Rufinus ignored her, making soothing noises to the horse as he moved close. Stroking the animal gently, he ran his hand down its neck, then up again, looking for the correct point beneath the jaw.

Senova's mouth opened to an O of shock.

'No!'

But it was done. The beast shuddered and tried to buck, collapsing on its broken leg as blood jetted from the sharp wound, almost catching Rufinus has he leapt back out of the way. It fell in a shuddering heap and quickly fell still as blood continued to pump from the wound.

'What did you *do*?' Luca whispered, climbing over the edge onto the track with ashen face and wide eyes, all the deference of the slave forgotten in this awful scene.

'What I had to,' Rufinus said bleakly. 'He was lame. *Badly* lame. He'd not manage another step.'

Senova nodded slowly. She still looked unhappy, but she understood. Luca clearly didn't.

'But...'

'One cut. Quick, and as painless as I could make it.'

'But...'

'The alternative was to leave him to die of exhaustion and exposure, in pain, possibly prey to bears or wolves. This was a kindness, Luca.'

The boy was crying now, and Senova embraced him in a crouch as though he were her child. Rufinus busied himself removing the packs from the already-still horse. Dragging them over to Atalanta, he began to throw out anything he considered unnecessary, combining the packs and consolidating everything.

'We're going to be slower now,' he said with a tinge of irritation. 'Atalanta will have to carry the packs and we'll have to walk.'

'Luca needs to ride,' Senova said.

Rufinus turned to her, preparing his arguments against such idiocy, but one look at her face told him that this was a debate he was destined to lose. He nodded. It took a short time to prepare everything, but soon they were moving again. Acheron still padded ahead, Rufinus leading Atalanta by the reins, Luca and the packs weighing her down, and Senova following on at the rear.

They rounded a bend at the next crest and Rufinus paused for a moment, peering ahead through the trees. He could see blue sky. There was a steep descent coming, then. His scouring gaze managed to penetrate the deep forest and he could just see the brown expanse of a cliff in the distance through the trees. He thought back to his instructions at Commodava.

Once you get to the highest point, you'll pass some big rocks and an escarpment. You'll be able to see a great big cliff. Aim for that.

That brown expanse had to be the cliff of which Scoris had spoken, and that meant that the steep slope he had noted coming up must be the escarpment. Scanning the area he spotted the rocks among the trees. He moved on slowly once more, careful and watchful for a change in the gradient.

'Gnaeus!'

His head snapped round to see Senova at the back, pointing. She had stopped walking. Rufinus hooked the reins over the back of the horse's neck, passing them to Luca, and then hurried past. Stopping beside Senova, his eyes searched the forest in the direction she was pointing. It took him a moment. Movement in the trees not far back.

'It could be locals?' she hazarded. 'Loggers or hunters maybe?'

Rufinus shook his head. The figures glinted occasionally as the sun penetrated the high, narrow trees and reflected off their armour.

'No. It's them.'

'Are you sure? They could be other men from Commodava.'

Rufinus was still shaking his head. 'No. They're cavalry – *legionary* cavalry – not auxiliary infantry. It's Celer and his men. Damn it, but the man is like a bad rash: all over us and never seems to go away.'

'How could he have found us? His scouts are gone and surely he didn't even know we were at Commodava yet anyway?'

'Scoris. The filthy bastard took our money in return for directions, then probably took a hefty reward from the fort for selling us out.'

'Or maybe Celer beat it out of him.'

'Possibly. Either way, whether he did it willingly or not, Scoris sold us out. And this time we're in trouble. It's the end. Nowhere to run.'

Senova shivered. 'We could scatter into the woods on foot. They wouldn't be able to follow us on their horses.'

'True, but there are a lot more of them than us. And if we move off this trail and get lost we lose any chance of ever leaving here. And Luca can't outrun them anyway with his little legs. And we know there are bears and wolves and probably boars in this region. No. We're out of options. I've got to face them.'

'Gnaeus, there are too many. You won't stand a chance.'

Rufinus was nodding. 'But possibly, just possibly, Celer will be arrogant enough to face me himself. He's that kind of man. And if I can kill Celer...'

'If you can kill Celer, then Daizus will be next.'

Rufinus gave her a nasty, feral smile. 'Daizus doesn't worry me. I can kill him.'

'Then the rest of the riders come at you. It's stupid, Gnaeus. Fatal.'

'It's also the only choice,' Rufinus sighed. 'You will take Atalanta and Luca and Acheron...'

Senova was shaking her head. 'I'm going nowhere without you.'

She jerked with shock as he spun and gripped her by the upper arms, holding her tight and staring into her eyes. 'You are, Senova. There is no argument to be had here. This is not a democratic decision. I have to face Celer now and there's no alternative. But by doing it, I can buy you and the boy time. You need Atalanta for the gear, and Acheron is as loyal to you now as he is to me. You need him for protection. Get through Roxolani land to Moesia and the coast. Take a ship back to Rome – there's more money hidden in my socks. Find Vibius Cestus and tell him everything. Somehow he might be able to use it to save Publius.'

Still she was shaking her head. 'I can't do it on my own.'

'Then you and Luca will die here too, Senova. And Acheron. And Atalanta will be theirs and no one will ever know what we found out, and Publius will languish in Cleander's care for the rest of his life. Nothing will change and we'll have lost. Is that what you want?'

There were tears in her eyes now. 'I can't leave you.'

'You *have* to. I have to do this, and I can only do it if I know you're getting away.'

Luca was waving at them now, beckoning Senova.

Behind them a number of cries issued from the slope below as the cavalrymen spotted the small party. 'They'll be on us in moments. Go.'

He pushed her toward the horse and then followed up behind.

'We'll get to the crest. You can see the valley falling away. You and the boy can get down the slope and I'll be able to hold them there for a while.'

Senova was sobbing now as they hurried toward the escarpment, the blue sky between the trees becoming gradually more visible with each step, the shouts of their hunters becoming louder, closer, clearer.

They almost fell. The track veered left suddenly at the escarpment and in their misery and desperation they had almost walked straight over the edge. Rufinus looked down. It was not a cliff, but a steep, rocky, scree-covered slope, far too sheer for a horse to manage, and probably too much for a man, too. The track ran along the upper lip for a few hundred paces and then descended at the side, a little close to the escarpment for Rufinus' liking, then descended to the valley below and disappeared off east toward the world of the Sarmatians.

'Go,' he said, pointing along the track.

'Gnaeus…'

'Go.'

He kissed her once, quickly, then pointed off down the slope and drew his sword. Luca inexpertly began to walk Atalanta forward along the edge, toward the descent, and Senova paused, tears streaming down her face, staring in agony at Rufinus. After what felt like a lifetime, she muttered some prayer to her beloved Brigantia and scurried away.

It took Rufinus precious moments to realise that Acheron was standing nearby.

'Go,' he ordered. The dog did not move.

'For the love of Jove, dog, go. Protect them.' He gestured off after the disappearing party with his sword, and Acheron turned his head, looking at the sobbing woman and the terrified boy beginning the descent. Still, he didn't move. Rufinus took a deep breath, then stamped a foot close to Acheron, menacingly, pointing again with his sword and commanding the animal to go.

There was a long and painful moment, and then Acheron turned and trotted off along the slope in the wake of the others. Rufinus watched them for a moment until he was sure they were safely descending and then turned toward the approaching babble of their pursuers. He drew his pugio dagger and held it in his other hand. He took a couple of experimental swings with each, every movement tracing pains across his back and bringing a stinging tear to his eye. Who was he kidding? He couldn't even beat Daizus in this state, let alone Celer.

Still, he had to try. Every heartbeat he held them back was a few paces extra toward freedom for the others. He stood still, weapons unsheathed by his side, waiting.

Was this how it felt to face death? He'd never really done so consciously. He'd always been too busy fighting for his life to think philosophically about it, or on one notable occasion had been in such agony that simple thought had been far beyond him. But this was probably it. He was alone to face death. *Everyone's* alone in the end, he thought. *Right* at the end. And the only worthwhile death was one that saved someone else. He hardened himself. He would save Senova and Luca.

There was a crack of branches and the thudding of hooves and figures emerged up the slope.

Rufinus turned and glanced back down the escarpment over his shoulder. Senova was already perhaps a quarter, even a third, of the way down.

Celer looked smug and self-important. Rufinus realised in that moment that he hated the tribune almost as much as he hated Cleander. Both were cheating, devious bastards. Both were traitors in their own way, he knew. The worst thing about Celer, though, was that he truly believed that what he was doing was right. In Rufinus' experience if you had to hide what you were doing and kill to keep it secret, then it probably wasn't right. Albinus was a thief and an abuser of position at best, at worst a traitor and conspirator. And Celer was his attack dog.

Daizus, who crested the rise next, leered like a cat cornering a mouse. Daizus wasn't worthy of hate. He was just an arsehole.

More cavalrymen, then. Several of them. A dozen or so. The riders fanned out in an arc near the top of the escarpment and Rufinus was struck by how between them and the edge of the drop they had formed a makeshift arena. Still, that was hardly a surprise. He knew what was coming next.

Daizus slid from his saddle and drew his sword with a feral grin, but Celer waved the man back. 'This is my fight, Centurion.'

The tribune vaulted easily from his steed and landed with catlike grace, handing his reins to the nearest trooper. He stretched and rolled his shoulders, shaking out his arms and stamping his feet, then drew his sword. He turned to Rufinus, his face an immobile mask of confidence.

'You brought this on yourself, Rufinus. You could have joined us, but instead you kept digging away for your weasel of a master in Rome and defying us. Yet I have a certain grudging respect for you in a way, for your tenacity and invention, if nothing else.'

'You're all heart,' spat Rufinus.

'I would offer you a soldier's death,' Celer sighed. 'Quick and neat. As painless as I could make it. You probably deserve it, despite everything.'

'All heart,' repeated Rufinus.

'But the sad fact is that you've caused me no end of trouble. Upset everything at Alburnus Maior Caused trouble between the two legates with your impressive subversion of Niger. The dog will bow his head to Albinus in the end, but they will never quite see eye to eye again and you're a large part of that. And above all else you dragged me and my men across the province at endless expense and discomfort, right to the edge of the empire. I had important things to do without chasing halfway across the world to snick off a loose end.'

'Are you trying to bore me to death?' Rufinus grunted.

Celer sighed. 'What a waste. And now I'll make you hurt all the way into the netherworld for the trouble you've put us all through.'

'Talk, talk, talk,' the young praetorian said in a bored voice, though he treasured every moment of the tribune's diatribe. Every sentence bought extra time for Senova. He almost looked back over his shoulder again, but decided not to. No point in drawing attention to the others unless he had to. He stretched his neck and rolled his head, loosening the muscles.

'Very well. I understand that you were once an excellent fighter. I'm willing to bet that the stripes I put across your back are impeding you somewhat. I'd wager it was an uncomfortable ride from Potaissa.'

Rufinus said nothing, simply standing with blades at the ready.

'Let me see what you have,' Celer said. Rufinus stood still. He would not play the tribune's game. Besides, every moment gained was time for Senova and Luca. Celer frowned. 'I'm sure it's not fear or reticence holding you back. Never mind.'

His lunge came so fast that it nearly did for Rufinus there and then. The sword flashed out at neck height and Rufinus was too slow bringing up the blades to block. Instead, at the last moment, he leaned to the side, the sharp edge whispering past his throat, pulled back expertly before the officer opened himself too much to a counter strike.

Rufinus cursed himself. Was it that the tribune was too fast, or that Rufinus was too slow? He should have parried that. He set his expression in a stony snarl and beckoned Celer with his pugio. The tribune snorted a laugh.

'If that's all you have then this will be a poor show, praetorian.'

Rufinus prepared himself and this time, when Celer swung, he managed to bring the blade up and turn the blow aside. The result was telling, though. The tribune recovered his swing in a heartbeat and brought the blade back round in another slash from the other side. Rufinus managed to get the pugio in the way, but his back was afire with pain from the sharp movements, and the clash of blades had sent shockwaves up his arms and into his shoulders. He was staggering now, the battle clearly lost in its opening moments.

Celer recovered. 'I will allow you time to breathe, Rufinus, since this could be over all too quickly.'

The young praetorian grunted and lunged.

A month ago, in full health, Rufinus would have driven home that blow and despatched the tribune, even turning aside any potential parry with the dagger in his left hand. But he was exhausted. He was in pain – *so much pain* – and he was weak from it all. His lunge was on target but lacked power and drive, and Celer knocked it aside with a disappointed expression.

'How sad,' the man sighed, 'to see a good warrior in such poor condition.'

'Piss off.'

'Foul language and invective are redolent of a base mind, Rufinus. This is why you would never make an officer. You are not suited to it.'

He lashed out with astonishing speed, his gladius striking Rufinus' own sword just below the hilt. The blow was hard and unexpected, and Rufinus almost lost his grip on the weapon, his knuckles vibrating unpleasantly. He tried to bring the sword back for another blow, but the tribune was there again, instantly. Pirouetting like a dancer, Celer brought his gladius round once more and hit the praetorian's sword again at the hilt. His hand already numb, Rufinus tried to maintain his grip, but the shock was too much and his fingers twitched, the sword falling away from his aching hand.

'That is a rather poor sight,' Celer sighed. 'I think Daizus over there is hoping that I will tire, or that you will win so that he can have a go at you himself.' The tribune smiled over his shoulder. 'Apologies, centurion, but I think Rufinus is mine today.'

The young praetorian, desperate now, knowing his main hope had been dashed with the loss of his weapon, held up his dagger defensively, casting his gaze down in search of the fallen sword. He spotted it with dismay just as Celer danced over to it and hooked his foot under it, flicking it away across the dirt towards his cavalrymen.

'What hurts most, Rufinus? The back or the knowledge that you failed?'

'Don't you ever get tired of your own voice?'

Celer gave a weary shrug and leapt forward with a flurry of blows. Rufinus was hit by a wall of panic. His pugio came up and he knocked aside the blade twice in the manic attack, but he felt the blade scoring painful lines across his flesh in half a dozen places before the man ended his assault with a single blow across the back of Rufinus' hand, cutting to the knuckles. The dagger fell from agonised fingers, and Rufinus staggered back as Celer came to a halt, kicking the pugio away to join the sword.

Rufinus was unarmed and a quick glance down showed that he was also running out of space.

'To some extent you thoroughly disappoint me, Rufinus. Clever and skilful enough to drag me all the way here from Potaissa and evade capture at every turn. And you killed two scouts. And two of my men are back in Commodava a pale grey colour and unable to stop vomiting. I don't know how you did it, but that has to have been your doing. And yet here we are at the very end and you have nothing. Even the recruits you trained at Drobeta could put you down now without breaking a sweat.'

Rufinus made his last try. It was a feeble attempt, but he was unarmed and desperate. He threw himself at Celer. The tribune stepped out of the way with ease and Rufinus staggered and fell to his knees in the dust, yelping as he felt stitches pulling free again in his back.

'How sad.'

Celer beckoned to Daizus and handed his sword to the centurion, who passed over his vine staff of office in return. Rufinus, tears in his eyes, back on fire, gasped where he knelt, but a moment later a whole new wave of pain broke over him as Celer drove the point of the iron-hard stick into his spine.

He screamed.

Celer nodded. 'Had I the time back in Potaissa I would have made your back a work of art, praetorian.'

Rufinus growled and struggled, trying to find his feet.

345

'Gods, but there's fight left in him,' Celer laughed, clapping his hand on his leg in delight.

The young praetorian, gasping, agonised, pulled himself up straight, though the pain was intense, and he staggered backward some way.

'Beware, Rufinus,' the tribune smiled. 'You're very close to the drop.'

And he was. He had staggered back to the edge. Rufinus looked around. It took him a moment. Senova and Luca were at the bottom now, with Atalanta and Acheron. They had paused, watching in rapt horror the action on the top of the escarpment.

No. It wasn't over. Rufinus turned back to the tribune and grinned.

'You still have some fight in you, praetorian?' Celer mused. 'You surprise me. But I'm bored of this now. And I'm sick of the wilderness that you've dragged me through. I long for a hot bath and a good wine. What would you prefer: the sword or the cliff?'

But he was smiling and held no sword. Celer took a step forward and Rufinus took a matching step back away from him. The tribune grinned. No more words, though. He stepped forward again and jabbed with the vine staff. Rufinus stepped back out of the way again, right to the lip of the escarpment. He had to be strong. Probably the *last* of his strength, in fact.

Celer jabbed, smiling, prodding Rufinus out into space. The praetorians foot slipped on the edge, mud, dust and gravel skittering away behind him down the steep slope. The fall would undoubtedly be fatal. Either he would fall clear out and bounce a few times on the way down, or he would simply slide down the slope, the rocks and gravel tearing the flesh from him on the descent. Either way, in Rufinus' condition it would be miraculous if he survived it. Better to make it fast and not scrape off his flesh.

He felt himself going, the vine stick coming in for a final prod. As it neared, though, he grabbed it tight. Celer's eyes narrowed into a frown and then widened in surprised

346

realisation as Rufinus pulled on the stick with all the strength he could muster. As the young praetorian pushed with his left foot and toppled backwards, the tribune, jerked from his feet in shock, came with him.

The two men sailed out over the edge, the vine staff falling away unheeded as Celer shrieked in panic. Rufinus was silent as the grave as he gripped the tribune, wrapping his arms around him as they fell.

He'd not *quite* achieved his goal. He'd pushed off from the edge with one foot as they fell, trying to launch into a spin. It had partially succeeded, so that when they first hit the jagged slope they did so on their sides, rather than Rufinus being trapped beneath Celer, ruined back exposed to the rocks. Instead, he felt his arm shredded by jagged stones. Celer honked out his panic, struggling, but Rufinus had only one goal now: hold on. His grip tightened.

The second bounce missed Rufinus entirely and instead tore the voice from the tribune as it winded him, breaking ribs and tearing away leather and linen and flesh in equal quantities. Their twisting had almost completed, and Rufinus was now on top.

The next thud tore Rufinus' leg with sharp rocks but battered Celer beneath him all the more.

They landed at the bottom with an unpleasant and very terminal crunch.

Rufinus wondered if the boatman would come for him without a coin under his tongue. But he felt utterly broken and there was no hope of retrieving a coin. He lay there, breathing in sharp, ragged gasps. Celer was beneath him, and beneath the tribune just hard, unforgiving rocks. Rufinus had heard the breaking of dozens of bones in that massive crunch as they struck, and knew most of them to have been Celer's. Not all, though. There was a sharp pain in his own ribs. He couldn't feel either leg. His left arm was definitely broken. His right was numb, and might well be. Those two limbs had hit the rock first, still wrapped around the tribune.

Celer was dead. There was no doubt about that. The man's face was pulped where it had struck the rock and, curiously, Rufinus could see among the hair what he presumed to be brain. But he himself was not in a much better state. He could not even lift his head, and his voice seemed to be nothing but a whisper. He closed his eyes and felt agony and exhaustion claim him. With luck he would expire quickly and not just lie here in conscious pain to be eaten by passing scavengers.

He thought he must have died, then. It was suddenly all so quiet and dark and peaceful. Then there was a sudden agony in his neck and head and he blinked his eyes open. All he could see was blood. It was in his face and all over his head. He couldn't wipe it clear. Couldn't move. Blinked again. A shape above him.

Senova.

Gods, woman, you should be running...

But she wasn't. She was kneeling by them. Then there was the most horrendous wave of pain as she dragged him off the tribune by the shoulders. The sheer torment was too much and Rufinus passed out again.

He must have been gone for only moments, but he blinked awake to see Senova above him, cradling his head, wailing and crying. Damn it, woman. *Run.* Leave me and run! But she wasn't. She was wiping all that blood from his head. Then she was looking away, up the cliff and calling someone a bastard.

He heard distant argument. *Focus. This was important.*

He could hear them.

'...go down and deal with them all.'

'Fuck 'em.' Daizus' voice. He would be the ranking officer up there now.

Senova was calling him some very unpleasant and colourful things as she shouted up, some of which Rufinus didn't know but recognised as Briton curses she used when things broke or she stubbed a toe. Then she was wailing again and rocking back and forth, clutching Rufinus' bloody head.

Even in his moments of demise, Rufinus found himself feeling slightly nauseous and wishing she would stop all this swaying.

'The tribune…' someone said at the top.

'Is dead,' Daizus snarled at the man. 'Just like the praetorian with the broken head. It's just a woman and a boy now. Not worth the effort. I'm not taking on that bloody dog for them.'

Rufinus groaned and shifted slightly.

'Lie still, idiot,' hissed Senova, still rocking sickeningly back and forth.

'What?'

'They're going,' she whispered, then let out a huge wail of grief.

Rufinus lay there for some time, feeling queasy and weak. There was a stench of latrines, too. He realised with distaste that in death Celer had soiled himself right beneath Rufinus.

'They've gone,' Senova said finally. Rufinus made to rise, but she held him down with a grip like iron around his blood-soaked head. 'Oh no, you stay right there while I cry about my dead man at full volume for a good hour yet.'

'What?'

'They could easily come back just to check. And they'll be expecting to hear my grief all the way down the mountain. You lie still and rest until they're long gone while I play the grieving widow.'

'I'm not dying?'

'A few broken bones maybe. Nothing remotely fatal, I think.'

'But all the blood? At least I need to bandage my head before I bleed out.'

Senova shifted slightly, moving her arm into his field of view. She had cut a jagged rent in her forearm a good hand-width long. Blood was pouring profusely from it.

'What in Jove's name?'

'Had to make it look convincing,' she said, then let out a huge wail of anguish that bounced from tree to tree across the valley.

'You,' Rufinus said in wonder, 'are a very devious woman.'

'Be grateful for it,' she replied, then tore a piece of cloth from her tunic hem and began to mop and wrap her arm. 'We've got proper dressings and unguents, but I'd rather not bleed out before we can use them.'

Rufinus chuckled, but the effort was too much, and he passed out again.

XXIV – Into the unknown

They waited a full hour in that position, with Rufinus lying still and Senova cradling his head and wailing. Luca began to get bored after a while and started poking around, while Acheron kept sidling up to Rufinus and nudging him with his muzzle, confused and concerned. Finally, when Senova decided the cavalrymen and Daizus must be long gone, she helped him to a rock where he could sit. She then emptied everything she needed from the kit bags and set about stitching and binding her arm, then tending to Rufinus' injuries with the same offhand lack of sympathy as a legionary medicus.

In the end, it turned out that Rufinus was slightly more seriously injured than Senova had estimated, but still nothing was potentially fatal. Broken left arm – splinted and slung with all the care and attention of a blind wrestler with a twitch. Three broken ribs – deemed safe to leave and would heal in their own good time. Sprained wrist – stop messing with it. Endless scrapes and cuts – stitched like a sailmaker with a needle that felt like a javelin and thread that resembled a ship's hawsers. She would never make a surgeon, but Rufinus had to admit that she patched him up remarkably well for a woman with no medical training at all.

Then they moved. Slowly, and with Rufinus grunting and yelping on every other step. Senova and Luca helped him up into Atalanta's saddle straight away, accompanied by cries of pain and a lot of swearing. He rode a whole three horse lengths before it became clear that with his broken ribs and various pains riding was simply impossible. Plus, with a broken left arm and sprained right wrist his handling of the reins was slipshod at best.

So Rufinus became a pedestrian once more, and they moved on across the hills, the slowest any of them had ever travelled. The sun was already low by the time they had settled into a pace and they only managed one mile before making camp for the night, cold and uncomfortable in the forested valley. They followed Scoris' instructions and by late the next day they had travelled a grand eight miles, passing that high cliff and the disused mines, arriving finally as the sun slid from the sky at a small village that had to be the Coido of which Scoris had spoken.

Rufinus had been staunchly against going into the village, reasoning that they were still too close to Commodava and Daizus to risk being remembered, even in a native village. Senova blithely ignored him, as she had done most of the day, given that his level of grumbling and complaint had steadily risen over the hours.

She left Rufinus sitting on a log with Luca and the horse, and wandered off on her own, with only Acheron for company and support. Rufinus sat and fretted, complaining at Luca about everything that popped into his mind and periodically sighing or yelping at his movements. Just as he'd become convinced she'd been raped and eaten by some mindless yokel and rather selfishly begun to wonder what he was supposed to do without her, Senova returned.

She was very pleased with herself and was full of news and information.

They were no longer in Dacia. The villagers *considered* themselves Dacian and spoke the language, but they said they paid no tax to the empire and had seen only an occasional Roman trader in years, let alone troops or settlers. The village had a tavern which had one room they let to travellers and which was free. Best of all it had a bath tub, to which Senova was rather looking forward. They would have beds and hot food for the first time since Rufinus' arrest. She had managed to converse enough to confirm the next few days' route through the mountains, which would apparently become easier quickly. She had negotiated for replacement animals – Rufinus started to argue at the price she'd agreed but she simply ignored him and talked over the top. They would have three more beasts and would be able to travel comfortably. And she had acquired a medicine for Rufinus.

This latter both intrigued and worried the young praetorian.

'Poppy juice? You know I can't take poppy juice. Remember what happened before.'

Senova rolled her eyes. 'Do you believe even for a moment I would let you do that again? No. But this isn't poppy juice anyway.'

'What is it then?'

'I don't really know. I got it from a witch.'

Rufinus stared in horror at the vial, whose contents looked rather like swamp water. 'I don't think that's a good idea. A witch you say?'

'I think that's what they were calling her. She had a shrine to Hecate, and I remember you saying she was a witch goddess.'

'You want me to drink swamp water you bought from a barbarian witch?'

'Be quiet and drink it.'

Rufinus took a sip and made a sour face, though in all honesty it was nowhere near as unpleasant as he had expected and actually left quite a sweet, spicy taste on the tongue. He waited, running his tongue over his teeth and preparing to tell her how pointless it was.

He woke several hours later, with a slightly giddy feeling and a fluffy warmth throughout his body, in a comfortable bed in a warm room, with a plate of now-cold meat and vegetables on the table beside him. Miraculously, for Dacian food, it seemed to contain no knuckles or hooves, and he devoured it with gusto and considerable difficulty, hissing with pain as he used sprained wrist and broken arm. He washed it down with lightly watered wine. The brew proved to react strongly with his new medicine, and the next time he awoke it was light again, and he was sprawled across the side of the bed, wearing what was left of the late dinner, the plate upside down on the floor.

Senova had slept in the chair, judging by the blankets draped over it, and Luca on a rug, allowing the injured Rufinus full rein to collapse all over the bed. There was no sign of anyone in the room that morning, and Rufinus grumbled and muttered as he lay and floundered in pain. In the end, with some effort and yelping, he managed to use his right elbow to lever himself up from the bed, ribs shrieking in pain. He looked down at the Dacian scout's tunic he had been wearing since Commodava. It was covered in dry gravy and blood and smelled like a sick animal.

When Senova finally put in an appearance he was in dire straits, having decided to change clothes and got himself thoroughly tied up trying to remove the tunic over a slung arm and with no fully working limbs. She rolled her eyes and shook her head, but helped him unsling the arm and change out of the tunic.

'Where's my good red one? It's about time I changed back.'

'It's packed for the journey. Wear these,' she commanded, picking up the pile of clothes she had brought in and displaying them for him. They were drab and horrible. Barbarian clothes.

'No.'

'Put them on, Gnaeus. We're descending to Roxolani territory and legionaries are as welcome there as in any other Sarmatian land. Praetorians no more so, I imagine. Your equipment and armour is all safely packed away where it won't bother anyone. You'll wear Dacian clothes and keep growing that fuzz until it looks more like a beard. Everyone has beards and you'll stand out if you don't. By the time we get down to the Roxolani lands beyond the mountains it will have grown a bit and you'll blend in.'

Rufinus tried to argue but it was like trying to persuade the tide not to come in, so in the end he gave up and went back to his constant grumbling. He was taken from the tavern out back and given a hasty breakfast of bread and butter in the morning sunlight while Senova made the last checks. He grumbled about everything and pointed out what she'd done wrong as a matter of course, though in truth she'd done a remarkable job, and certainly as good as he'd have managed. She had purchased three beasts: one mountain pony that looked hardy and strong, and two mangy-looking donkeys. One of these was loaded with pack, as was Atalanta. Luca saddled the other donkey and Senova patted the pony.

'I call her Damara.'

'I take it that's some weird goddess from your homeland,' he grunted unkindly. She ignored him and went around to the back of Atalanta. Rufinus noticed now the travois attached to the horse's tack. 'That's for me?'

She nodded.

'I'll get shaken to bits on that.'

'I live in hope,' Senova snapped, 'that one day you will stop grumbling about everything and express a little gratitude to those people who saved your life and are looking after you.' He fell into a sullen and rather ashamed silence as she went on, narrow-eyed and acerbic. 'You cannot walk the journey to the sea, because at the rate we have been travelling we will all have died of old age before we see the first ship. You cannot ride, because of your wrist, arm and ribs. We tried that. Unless you intend to float across Roxolani lands, and the rivers in the mountains are not navigable, by the way, this is the only option. And I have done what I can. We have nailed a number of small wooden battens to the lower edge that Luca hopes will act as a sort of makeshift suspension and cut out the worst of the bumps. I have six great big fleeces that will cushion you and keep you warm. We have nailed an extra batten across the bottom for you to rest your feet and thereby not slide off as we travel. I have looked into all alternatives. There are no wagons or carts in the village, let alone ones for sale, and it seems unlikely we will find one as we travel in the mountains. The villagers in this area don't travel far and there's no real farming, so they don't generally need carts. The Roxolani are nomads and seem to use them from what I understand, but that's when we get down to the plains and we can't guarantee they'll want to part with one. If we find one on the journey we will try to buy it, but in the meantime, you travel on this. Oh, and I tried to see if I could rig up some kind of net sling with Luca instead, but I can't get the locals to understand the idea and we can only get two lengths of rope anyway. Since we want to get moving and out of these mountains as quickly as we can, Luca and I have done what we could. Now wrap yourself in this,' she thrust a huge fleece at him and laid several similar on the travois, 'then climb on, and the next complaint I hear out of you, we will tip you off the thing and leave you behind.'

Leaving him staring in distress, she moved around the other side of the hardy pony and climbed up. No saddle, Rufinus noted, just a blanket and reins like a barbarian. He crossed to the travois, eyed it suspiciously, and climbed onto it, not daring open his mouth even to hiss in pain. Luca appeared from somewhere, unstoppered the vial of swamp water and tipped a healthy dose into Rufinus' mouth, waiting until he swallowed it and then moving off, returning moments later with another fleece which he tucked around the recumbent praetorian and then secured him to the thing none-too-gently with a rope. They moved off. Rufinus actually felt warm and comfortable until they hit the first cobble. The second one made him yelp. He was blessedly unconscious by the third.

He awoke with the sun just dipping beneath the horizon, stomach growling and head pounding. He opened his mouth to complain about aches and pains and quickly thought better of it. They stopped for the night in a small village not unlike the one higher up, but already they had clearly moved through the highest peaks while he slept, and the valley sides here were lower and more forgiving. Rufinus felt a huge wave of relief when Senova, having been into the village, returned and announced that she had bought a cart. They made their way to a barn that she had negotiated as accommodation for the night and as Rufinus collapsed in the hay, Senova lit a small fire outside and cooked goat stew. Rufinus tore through the stew and the bread she served with it like a starving wretch, thanking her profusely and apologising for his earlier behaviour. She smiled and let him off, announcing that the pain had clearly made him 'out of sorts.'

They slept well and warm, and together. The next day she laid him in the cart among the fleeces. It would have been a lovely journey had Acheron not claimed ownership of the fleece bed and curled up on it, forcing him to make room. Twice during the journey Rufinus let out a blood-curdling scream as Acheron, in deep sleep, dreamed and kicked out rhythmically at Rufinus' wounded frame.

Still, it was a marked improvement on the travois. They moved rapidly that day, stopping periodically and letting the horses rest as required, and the miles were eaten up as they descended the valleys on the eastern side of the Carpates into the foothills. At least it was sunny and warm.

Three days they moved down from the hills, the valley gradually flattening out and delivering the road and the small rocky river they followed onto the plains of the Roxolani. The last two days there had been no villages and no sign of human life in the hills, and they had camped in the wild. Rufinus was rapidly becoming bearded once more and was twitching to shave it off, though Senova would not let him. When the pain got too much she would let him have some of the witch's swamp water, though she was sparing with it, and with good reason.

Rufinus resigned himself swiftly to being a patient and taking care with his recovery. He knew from long experience in both the army and the boxing ring that ribs and arms could take over a month to heal, perhaps two if they were bad. These breaks, he reasoned, were not too bad and with his excellent record of recovery, he should be fine within the month. It had already been five days, and some calculation as he bounced along in the cart with the map led him to the conclusion that there was still a hundred miles to travel across the flat land to the great Danuvius and Roman territory beyond, and perhaps fifty miles from there to the coast. At the rate they were travelling, and barring potential delays, he reckoned twelve days would put them at the Euxine Sea. He would have been convalescing for two weeks then, and should be well on the mend. By the time they took a ship, he would be considerably more hardy and mobile.

The next day they camped on a flat, featureless plain in the loo of the cart, using it as a wind-break. The road had petered out quickly on the flat and the river turned and marched off southwest. The terrain here on the plains was utterly different from everything Rufinus had experienced so far since arriving at Drobeta. An endless sea of grass, the Carpates range gradually diminishing to a hazy blue line on the western horizon. Lakes and rivers were scattered about the great flat land.

The encounter came on the second day of travelling the plains. There were no roads here. The Roxolani, like all the wild, non-Romanised Sarmatian tribes, were seasonal nomads. Cassius had explained it to Rufinus on their long journey into Dacia. The Sarmatians lived a permanently mobile life, creating a settlement of great heavy tents wherever the weather and the season required them to be, and then packing up and moving on as needed. Thus there were no permanent towns or villages and, with no such settlements, there was no need for roads to connect them. Consequently, they relied on the sun and Senova's sense of direction. Each morning, they would note east as where the sun rose and Senova would pick the most notable landmark, of which there were precious few – a hillock, a tree, a cairn – and would make for it, then note the next landmark in the line and make for that, and so on. Gradually they trundled east across the great grassy sea.

The cart was bumping and rolling, Rufinus complaining silently in his head where Senova could not hear. It was mid-afternoon of the eighth day out of Commodava, and the first sign of potential trouble came from Acheron. The great black hound had been curled up in the fleeces beside Rufinus, taking up plenty of room, but suddenly an eye opened and an ear pricked up. A moment later he was bolt upright, alert, a low growl starting in the back of his throat.

Rufinus, startled by the change, pulled himself painfully up to a seated position and looked out in the direction of Acheron's gaze. He heard the Roxolani before he saw them. It sounded like distant thunder, like the rumble of an avalanche. Then, finally, the tribe hoved into view. Hundreds of horses, bearing riders of all ages and both genders. Rufinus peered at them with interest. Almost half the women were armed with spears and swords and bows like any steppe warrior. Behind them, the rest of the horses were being led as spare mounts and, behind *them*, a slew of wagons, each one packed with the great tents they moved from region to region and all the things needed for their next home. More riders came along, then, herding cattle at the rear of the mass with outriders here and there watching the surroundings for potential danger.

Half a dozen of the Roxolani broke off from the main group and made for the small party of travellers. An impressive man of powerful build with shaggy brown hair and a thick beard pulled out in front and dropped into an easy trot alongside them, a spear gripped tight in his hand, eyes curious and questioning rather than suspicious or angry.

He barked out a question in some strange tongue that sounded like a man trying to swallow a mouthful of pebbles. Rufinus watched with nervous curiosity as Senova edged her horse toward him. She threw the man a greeting in what Rufinus recognised as her native Britannic language. The man looked dumfounded but curious, and Rufinus smiled to himself. She was putting him at ease. The Roxolani might have no idea who she was, but they knew Romans and they knew Latin, and she had established at the outset that they were not Roman. Fortunately, Rufinus did not appear to be required.

Roxolani women could be warriors and leaders, apparently, and so Senova commanding this small group raised neither surprise nor disapproval from the man.

Rufinus watched and listened as the pair entered a long and very complicated exchange. The nomad clearly had no idea what Senova was saying, and likewise she was oblivious to the man's words. Rufinus was in an even worse position, having no idea what *either* of them were saying, and listening was starting to give him something of a headache. Gradually, though, as the two groups kept pace, heading east, the two of them seemed to start communicating with gestures and tone more than words, and Rufinus gave up, lying back among the fleeces and leaving them to it.

When they stopped at the end of the day, the sun beginning its descent, they were still with the Roxolani, though Rufinus and Luca had been left rather to themselves as Senova had ridden alongside the tribe's spokesman, conversing in their weird manner. Finally, the cart rumbled to a stop and Rufinus sat up with difficulty once more to see that the nomads had gone back to their people and begun unloading their wagons for the night. Senova had ridden back to join Luca and Rufinus.

'What very pleasant people,' she said quietly, trying not to let the Latin be heard in the distance where the tribe were busy working.

'We're staying with them tonight?'

Senova nodded. 'Aldas was concerned that we might fall foul of marauders. There are apparently dangerous cattle raiders in this area and we're very lucky that the tribe were passing through. They tend to avoid the area because of the dangers, but it seems the women can't take a man until they've killed three people and the chief's daughter is one short, so she's hopeful for trouble. They are travelling to their summer pasturelands that lie in the east near the big river, which I presume means the Danuvius. His tribe will escort us safely as far as the river, which means we'll almost be in Moesia, yes?'

Rufinus blinked. 'Yes. That's astounding. I'd not imagined Sarmatians being quite so welcoming. They don't have that reputation. The big cannibal one at Lucilla's villa was not friendly.'

'Tad was something of an exception,' she replied. 'It seems the Roxolani have a tradition of hospitality. We will share their great huts and eat and travel with them. But don't let them know you're Roman. We were right about that. Your people aren't very popular here. Trajan annexed the place briefly, it seems, and left traces of forts here and there, but they didn't take kindly to it.'

'So who does he think we are?'

'No idea. We couldn't work that bit out. I pointed north and made swimming motions. He probably thinks we're some sort of Germans. But the important thing is not to let them see any Roman kit and not to speak Latin.'

'Conversation's going to be fun for the next few days, then.'

'No conversation. I've got them convinced you and Luca are mute. Not a word until we're in Moesia, or we probably break some hospitality rule and end up dead.'

It was a peculiar evening, and one that Rufinus had no wish to repeat, though it seemed he was doomed to do so several times yet. The Roxolani were swift and efficient at setting up their camp. Their huts were giant circular things made of ropes and leather and fleece, thick against the cold winds of the plains. They lit great fires using the scarce dead wood they had collected on the journey, augmented with ancient, dried horse turds they carried in a purpose-designed cart. The smell was eye-watering and Rufinus wondered how many nights it took to get used to the reek of burning poo. A lot, he suspected. They ate a meal of roasted miscellaneous meat without bread or vegetables. Senova had asked what the meat was, and the nomad turning the spit with huge chunks of meat dripping fat into the fire pointed at the horses. Rufinus felt a dip in his appetite then, but it seemed horse was all there was on offer

361

and eventually hunger won out and he tucked in. It was surprisingly tasty in the end, and Acheron was given a sizeable portion of horse into which he tore with a vengeance. Rufinus was then passed a cup of something yellow and gloopy. He eyed it suspiciously, but everyone seemed to have one, from old men to women to children, and they were supping it down so Rufinus tried it.

He gagged. It had a fiery burn and yet tasted like very old milk and smelled like feet. He tried to pass it back, but some grinning lunatic insisted that he drink it. He did so, wishing he was allowed to speak so that he could express just how horrible this was. He smiled weakly and held the empty cup out for the man to take away, but the nomad just grinned and refilled it.

The music began then, if you could call it that. A drum was produced and rhythmically beaten, and a man started playing some sort of horn attached to an inflatable bladder that made a sound like a bovine being fatally squeezed. Rufinus looked forward to a long and troublesome headache, which came on leaps and bounds when two of the woman started to sing with a sound like a cat being shredded. His spirits sank as he saw Senova stroll over to the two women and crouch next to them, mimicking their dreadful caterwauling.

Soon, when the meal was done, the young men and women began some insane game that involved leaping through the flames and only occasionally missing and catching fire. He turned to Luca for a comforting presence only to find that the lad had vanished, and spotted him eventually joining in the fire-leaping, still playing the mute but grinning like an idiot. Once more Rufinus wished *he* was not a mute so that he could call the young idiot back.

He slept well that night, though, in the warm giant tent with a dozen of the tribe and his own companions. The belly full of meat and the several cups of what he surmised must be some sort of fermented milk product helped. They woke early the next day and Rufinus had to fight to stop himself saying good morning to Senova in the public life of the communal tent. In less than an hour, the whole settlement was packed and the tribe moved on, with Rufinus bouncing around in the fleece-lined cart once more and Acheron taking up too much space.

The day was excruciatingly dull. There was nothing to see but lakes and grass and a few occasional lonely looking trees, Senova rode with two warrior women, laughing and exchanging stories as best they could, and Rufinus and Luca were left to clatter along in enforced silence until the end of the day when the whole ghastly experience of a Roxolani evening was repeated. Once again Rufinus forced himself to eat the meat, failed to opt out of the thick milk drink, and had to listen in tortured silence to the grim shrieked song and the honking bladder-horn while young men attempted to immolate themselves for fun.

For seven days they repeated the procedure, and Rufinus found himself lying, stupifyingly bored, in the cart during the daytime, dreading the coming evening and running over every word he could think of, wishing he could say even one of them out loud. He repeated them over and over, thinking of the most complex words he could and stringing together sentences of them, increasingly concerned that when he was finally allowed to speak again he'd have forgotten how to.

Fifteen days out from the fort of Commodava and the last Roman building Rufinus had seen, they finally reached the Danuvius. The Roxolani who, though Rufinus had loathed much of his time with them, had proved to be genuine and friendly, delivered Senova and her two mutes to a small settlement by the river where a ferry had been set up. On the far bank, a fort sat glowering at the barbarian world. Rufinus almost cried at the sight of a Roman wall with a settlement clustered around its base. Senova thanked Aldas for all his help and tried to offer him coins or other remuneration, which he flatly refused. With a wave of farewell, the Roxolani went off downstream, heading for their summer camp site.

Rufinus looked at the ferry. They had done it. In truth, *Senova* had done it. Rufinus had saved them from Celer and his men, but Senova had kept them alive and seen them safely through a hundred miles of barbarian lands with just her wits and good humour. And now they were safe. One short ferry ride and they were back in the Roman world. The coast lay maybe fifty miles from here and then... who knew? That was something to discuss. First, though, into Moesia Inferior.

XXV – Whither now

They crossed the Danuvius that afternoon as the sun slowly slid into the western haze. The tiny hamlet on the near side smelled of fish and waste, both animal and human, but nothing could strip Rufinus of his relief, and he actually smiled as the small boat slid out into the brown-green water and the expert ferrymen rowed for all they were worth, angling across the current. Acheron stood at the prow, hair wavering in the strong wind blowing up the river. Rufinus noted how, now they were away from Dacia and the mountain peoples, the general nervousness around the big black dog was back. People did not fear bears here, and therefore did not need to keep a dog that could kill one, so they were not used to such animals. The men of the boat kept nervous eyes on Acheron throughout the trip.

Durostorum sat waiting for them on the far bank. They'd not known precisely where on the great river the Roxolani had left them and, when the ferrymen told them the name of the place and Rufinus consulted their map, it turned out that they were a lot further south than Rufinus had expected. He had been planning to cross at Capidava or Sacidava and make for the port of Tomis where there would be plenty of ships, though the danger of being in the provincial capital unnerved him a little. Instead, though, they were some thirty to sixty miles upriver. Never mind. Nothing was going to destroy his relief. They would work it out.

As the boat slipped toward the southern bank and the first soil of the Roman world for many days, Rufinus reappraised his impression of Durostorum. He had spotted the strong walls and a small settlement, but what he'd actually seen was just the port area stretching down to the water. Durostorum was a lot larger than he'd realised, stretching out beyond the fort high on the river bank. It was something of a thriving town or small city, in fact.

'What now?' Senova said, and Rufinus pursed his lips in thought. It had been so long since he had spoken more than a few whispered words that he found speaking aloud odd and uncomfortable. Moreover, Senova had taken charge over the entire journey across the mountains and plains and it also felt odd to be asked an opinion.

'We check and see whether the locals are looking for us,' he replied. 'If the governor *is* in league with Albinus, then word could already have reached this far by courier. If so we need to be extremely careful.'

'And this is not where you thought we'd cross.'

'No,' he admitted. 'But that doesn't matter. We can still get to the coast easily enough.'

The boat docked and they paid for their passage with medium denomination old coins that would attract no undue attention. Leading off the beasts and with Acheron gathering nervous smiles of relief as he left the lives of the ferrymen, they arrived in Moesia Inferior. A small inn called the *Bartered Goat* stood not far from the dock and Rufinus directed the others to the place to secure a room for the night. Better they weren't seen together up in town or by soldiers until they knew what they were facing.

As Senova and Luca dealt with the accommodation, keeping Acheron with them, Rufinus wandered up into town, confident that with his native clothes, shaggy hair and beard, he would not look like a man any soldier might be watching for. He skirted the fort and wandered around the town, purchasing a few small oddments of food and bagging them up one-handed. His left arm was still held tightly to him with the stinking sling, but his left wrist had almost entirely recovered, and his ribs now only pained him when he bent too low or twisted suddenly.

Finally he found what he was looking for. A mansio sat on the main road that ran along the river's southern bank. Within, as well as the staff, were two soldiers looking travel-worn, one courier tucking into an evening meal and a wealthy nobleman and his wife engaged in quiet conversation. This was a risk, but a calculated one. He watched the soldiers suspiciously as he crossed to the mansio's owner at the counter. A native might well be suspicious of soldiers, so the soldiers probably wouldn't think the reaction odd.

'We don't serve just anyone,' the owner said in a rather snooty tone, looking Rufinus up and down. 'This is a mansio, not an inn. You need official paperwork or a lot of money.'

Rufinus nodded and spoke, keeping his voice deep but loud enough, and trying to inflect his Latin with a good dose of Dacian accent, on which he felt like something of an expert after his travels.

'I've got news on Rustius Rufinus. I seen 'im.'

The mansio's operator sniffed, one eyebrow ratcheting up a little. 'Who?'

'The *praetorian*,' Rufinus hissed, still loud enough to be overheard by the soldiers nearby.

'I have absolutely no idea what you are talking about,' the man said in a tone laden with distaste. 'Now unless you have appropriate documents, which I find highly unlikely, then I would ask you to leave this establishment. You emit a serious odour of horse dung.'

Rufinus backed away, watching the soldiers as he left. Neither of them leapt up to arrest him. In fact they looked relieved that he was leaving. He emerged from the mansio and sighed, grinning. He was about to return to the inn with his news when he spotted a welcome sight just a little further down the road. Senova would worry if he was too long, but still...

He opened the door to their room in the inn an hour later to find Senova pacing back and forth in irritation and worry. She rounded on him with a jabbing finger and her eyes narrowed dangerously.

'Did you have fun?'

Rufinus shrugged, which still hurt a little and made him twitch. He stood in the same clothes as before, but his hair was short, his beard gone, his skin scraped and scrubbed clean, a new dressing and sling on his arm.

'I happened to pass a bath house which had a physician's shop open inside. I figured that I needed the wounds looking at as soon as possible, so I called in. The man reckons another six or seven days and I can probably lose the sling. Healing really well. And he thinks the ribs are about there too.'

'And you hate the beard,' she said archly.

'That too,' he admitted.

'I take it we are not being sought then, since you have been busy lounging around in the town's bath houses?'

Rufinus smiled. 'I tested the waters in the mansio. They're not looking for a praetorian or a man called Rufinus, and there were two soldiers passing through on the main road who never blinked at the name. It seems that Moesia Inferior is safe ground.'

'Good. And good news about your arm. If you ever abandon me like that again without warning I will be tempted to break the other one.'

Rufinus sighed. Unprecedented freedom and legal status had changed the meek Senova, as he'd noted on the road to Dacia, but this time in Albinus' province, and in particular the flight from Commodava, had given her a level of independence and authority that she was clearly going to maintain from now on. He considered the very real possibility that, if she continued to lose any sense of deference or respect at the rate that seemed to be happening now, soon she'd be talking down to the emperor.

He grinned. Now *there* was a thought.

'What are you smiling about?' she snapped.

'You, Senova. You know, I think I love you.'

'*Think?*' she said in a dangerous tone, which just made him laugh all the more.

They awoke the next morning to a world that had clouded over and settled in with constant drizzle, but it did little to dampen Rufinus' spirits, and his newfound enthusiasm seemed to have infected the other two as well. They broke their fast at leisure, Rufinus clean and neat, dressed once more in his red military tunic. By mid-morning they departed Durostorum and heeded the instructions of the innkeeper. The main arterial road followed the bank of the Danuvius all the way to the capital and major port of Tomis, and they would follow it for some distance, though over the previous evening Rufinus and Senova had settled on a different plan.

While it appeared that they were not being sought in Moesia Inferior, it was still tempting the Fates to head to the city in which both the governor and procurator lived. If word of the praetorian had reached *anywhere* in Moesia, it would be that city. Of course, Senova had pointed out, if Daizus had reported what he saw back to Albinus, which he most certainly would have done, then Rufinus would be presumed dead and of no further interest. Still, Rufinus knew Clodius Albinus and he wouldn't pin all his hopes on that – the man was devious and careful. Despite the turnout of events in Dacia, Rufinus could still feel the influence of Fortuna over their journey and, having been delivered somewhere other than expected by chance, he was content to trust to this change and forego the great port of Tomis. They would, instead, make for the lesser provincial port of Callatis, avoiding the dangers of the governor's city.

They followed the river in the drizzle on a road full of other travellers both rich and poor – many more of the latter – for more than twenty miles, arriving at the town of Altenum, nestled on the south bank beneath another fort. Altenum hosted a small naval station of the regional fleet, the c*lassis Moesica,* so the party of travellers stayed on the landward edge of town in a pleasant little local inn, keeping clear of both soldiers and sailors just in case. They arrived sodden and chilled to the bone and spent the evening by a fire drying out and listening to local music that Rufinus declared 'provincially cacophonic' but which Senova rather liked.

The next morning they set off once more and turned away from the river, heading southeast for the city of Tropaeum Traiani and the coast beyond. The rain had let up some time during the night but struck again mid-morning at a time when the travellers were in the most exposed territory possible. Despite the shortness of the day, they stopped mid-afternoon at the next town for the sheer convenience of having baths and comfortable inns. They shivered their way into town, cloaks saturated, hair plastered to skin. Senova was interested to find, in what seemed to her, to be a rather out of the way location on a more minor road, a fairly grand and well-fortified city with some impressive monuments.

'It's a statement,' Rufinus replied. 'Back when Trajan fought his first campaign there was a massive battle here, nearly ninety years ago now. Dacians and Roxolani against several legions. Trajan won, of course. Trajan *always* won. The city was founded in memory of the victory, even the place's name: Tropaeum Traiani. Trajan's trophy. Look.'

He gestured up to the hill opposite the town and Senova followed his gaze to a grand, white edifice on the peak. A glowing drum of stone with some complex sculpture atop it.

'That's the trophy the place is named after.'

'Romans,' sniffed Senova. 'You're not the most gracious of winners, are you?'

It stopped raining briefly again at Tropaeum Traiani, though the sky was still dull grey and the weather cold. They spent a comfortable night and then set off in the morning as the clouds decided to open once more and water the world. The landscape here became rolling green hills and fertile valleys, and they turned off even the lesser Roman road now, since that here veered north again to head for Tomis. Instead, they followed a native road of dirt and cobbles with a half-broken wooden sign suggesting that Callatis was forty miles from here.

The road was slower going and though Rufinus had hoped to press on and reach the coast by sunset, the combination of road surface – or lack thereof – winding route, terrain and constant requests for a halt meant that there was clearly no chance of that. They stopped for the night in some tiny native hamlet without a name, where there was no inn, but a friendly farmer donated his barn and invited them to his family meal. The night was pleasant and easy enough, and they dried out fast enough, setting off the next morning into the ever-present rain with lighter hearts.

One more day.

They reached the Euxine Sea the next afternoon, and Rufinus ran through some calculations in his head. He made it sixty six days since they had crossed the bridge at Drobeta and entered Dacia. Over two months. He might be wrong, of course. He'd been quite turned around temporally between the endless marching, time spent in captivity and then journeying half-conscious at best for the latter part. But that would make it sometime in mid Junius now. Should be quite warm, though present conditions suggested otherwise. But at least it was the height of the sailing season and there would be plenty of ships.

The sea was hard to make out. The sky was grey and wet, the town was grey and wet, and much of the land was grey and wet, so the sea sort of blended in all too well. Callatis was a smaller port, more like some of the ones Rufinus had grown up with in Hispania: Barcino and Baetulo, for example. It sat on a bluff, all wet gleaming stone and shiny tile roofs, walled and filled with tightly-crammed housing. The harbour itself sat off to the south on lower land, and was thriving. Ships filled most of the jetties and others were coming and going. Rufinus was pleased to note both fishing vessels and private traders but none of the grand vessels you'd expect to see if the Moesian fleet were in port. Good.

With plenty of daylight left, they found a comfortable inn on the southern side of the town, close to the port, and left their horses in the stable while they made their way down to the waterfront. In many respects, Callatis was much the same as any other port. The inns became dirtier and more raucous the nearer they came to the water. Lewd women called out things that made Rufinus blush. Two sailors were engaged in beating seven shades of shit out of each other in an alleyway. A dog was busy eating a purloined fish. Crates, barrels, boxes and coils of rope seemed to be stacked everywhere in a haphazard manner.

Rufinus peered along the lines of vessels and then made his way, with the others in tow, to the port official's offices. Acheron managed to acquire a stinking fish corpse from somewhere on the way and was carrying it as they entered. The smell of fish had been pretty intense outside but at least somewhat suppressed by the rain, though in this enclosed space Acheron's rotting prize reached a new level of eye-watering. As they made their way in, Rufinus could see mouths opening to complain until they caught sight of the dog from which the odour arose and hurried away, bulge-eyed.

A clerk waved them over as they entered the public enquiry office.

'Sailors or passengers?'

Rufinus frowned, looking at his companions and wondering in what odd world Luca and Senova might be mistaken for Sailors. 'Passengers,' he said in a baffled tone.

'Destination?'

'Ultimately Rome,' he said, though he'd not settled on that yet, in truth.

The clerk tutted and ran down the pile of tablets representing the ships in port, setting some aside.

'Ready to sail in the morning? Do you have animals? Cargo? Any other special requirements?'

Rufinus nodded. 'Yes. Four horses and a dog. No. No.'

The clerk simply tutted again and pushed away more than half of the ships from his pile. Another pass and he rejected more. Eventually there were two tablets remaining before him.

'Nothing in port that's Rome-bound and has room for animals. You won't contemplate selling the horses before travel?'

Rufinus and Senova both shook their heads.

'Very well. The best I can suggest is either the captain of the *Isis,* out of Alexandria, or the *Pinnata* from Athens. The Isis is bound for Rhodos next, where you could pick up another vessel. Plenty of ships dock at Rhodos going in all directiona. The Pinnata is heading back to Athens, though he might be expensive for the animals and he might not have quite enough room. Isis is at jetty twelve. Pinnata is at four.'

Rufinus thanked the man and led the others out again. 'I have no idea where those places are,' Senova said as they emerged into the rain once more.

'Rhodos is an island off the Asian coast, more or less south of here and on the way to Aegyptus. Athens is in Greece, on the way back west. That's our best bet, even if it's more expensive. As long as he can fit us in.'

The others deferred to his decision and they sloshed through the puddles of the dock-side down to the fourth jetty, marked well on a sign at the end. The Pinnata was a good sized vessel of old-fashioned Greek style. It was in fine condition and had been recently repainted with a pair of great white wings arcing back from the bow along the sides. Men were busy rolling barrels up a plank and onto the deck in pairs with a great deal of effort and no small amount of invective as they slipped and slid in the wet. Rufinus approached the ramp and stepped back in sudden alarm as a barrel broke free of the men's grip and rolled back down, almost knocking him flat.

'Watch what you're doing, morons,' shouted a voice from above, and a big, red-faced and bushy bearded sailor appeared at the rail, waving his arms. 'If one of those barrels goes in the water, so do you, with an anchor tied to your neck.'

His gaze strayed from the work and alighted on the small party.

'And what can I do for you?'

'I'm told you might have room for us and our four horses as far as Athens?'

The man huffed irritably and brushed back his wet hair, blinking away the water in his eyes. 'Just about, I reckon. It'll be cramped, though. And it won't be cheap, neither. Animal fodder is at a premium at the moment, and I'd have to devote one of my lads to keeping them fed and cared for. Hope you're not on a tight budget.'

'We'll manage,' Rufinus answered.

'Journey takes fourteen days,' the captain announced, as though trying to put them off. He might indeed be doing just that, since his eyes kept narrowing and flicking to Acheron, who lay on the wet boards of the jetty consuming the last of his stinking piscine treat. 'Twelve hundred denarii for the lot.'

Rufinus sagged. He'd expected it to be expensive, but that was quite something.

'Can we afford it?' Senova asked quietly.

'Yes,' Rufinus sighed. 'But it will wipe out most of our funds and only gets us as far as Athens. Still, from there we're well away from Dacia and can probably travel by land. And we don't have much choice.' He glanced sidelong at Luca, who was busy watching a gull standing on a wooden post. 'If we left the boy and two of the horses it would be half the price at most.'

'No.'

'Senova, the boy is the property of a legion. If he gets caught and that comes out he'll be killed for running away, and we'll get similar treatment.'

'If the legion was still interested in Luca they could have taken him back at any time until Potaissa. In fact, Daizus could have claimed him in the mountains after you died. No. Luca is with us now. And if we move on foot from Athens we'll still need the horses.'

Rufinus rolled his eyes. 'If we sold the horses we wouldn't *need* to move on foot. We could afford another ship.'

'The answer is no.'

Again, Rufinus sighed. He still had papers in his bag from Cleander that could secure him accommodation in mansios, in theory, but he doubted orders for him to travel from Rome to Dacia would get him far while he was in Greece and going the other way. And it wouldn't cover Senova and the boy anyway.

He looked up at the captain. 'A thousand and some work on the passage?'

The man gestured at his slung arm. 'Fat lot of good you'd be.'

'I meant the boy.'

Senova glared at him, and he sagged again. He was sure he could negotiate if only Senova weren't so damned protective over her pet slave boy. 'Twelve hundred, then. You sail on the morning tide?'

The captain nodded. 'That we do. I need you here with all animals and kit by dawn. And the money, of course.'

They returned to the inn and settled in for a meal, with Rufinus counting out each coin for payment with a dejected sigh.

'We will manage, Gnaeus. When we get back to Rome we will have your wage with the Guard.'

'If I get it,' he grumbled. 'News of my demise will reach the praetorian fortress long before I do. Even if I'm reinstated and all goes back to normal, given the speed of the bureaucracy I'll be a grey-beard before I get any more pay. Senova, I'm stumped.'

'Why?'

He leaned back in the chair and took a deep breath. 'I failed to come away from Dacia with any evidence since Celer took it off me. I'm been coasting ever since on the notion that the accusation alone will still carry some weight, but the longer we go on the less convinced I am of that. After all this trouble and pain and struggle, I'm no closer to stopping Cleander, no closer to helping Publius, and no more likely to save the family property from my father's position-seeking madness. I am looking at potentially being broke, I am slightly more disfigured, I've acquired a runaway slave that could get us into trouble, and I might not even have a livelihood any more, since I am officially dead. And if I suddenly come back to life, I'll attract the attention of one of the most powerful men in the empire who currently thinks I'm safely dead, but will do his best to make it true at his earliest opportunity if he discovers I'm not. Essentially, this past two months has only served to make things a little bit worse.'

Senova chewed her lip thoughtfully. 'I believed you were brightening up after all that grumping in the mountains. We got *away*, Gnaeus. We're back in your precious empire. We can afford to get as far as Athens in reasonable comfort. You have Atalanta and Acheron, and me. And in Rome we still have friends. Cestius and Pompeianus, for example. Fortuna has brought you through the worst of times – you still need to set up that altar, by the way – and delivered you here with us. She will see you the rest of the way. And if she falters, Brigantia will protect you, since you're with me.'

Rufinus gave a humourless snort and then sank into silence.

'What names shall we travel under?' she asked, brightening again.

'What?'

'Well it would seem dangerous to use our real names, just in case. They'll go on manifests and these ships could dock in port anywhere. Maybe even somewhere our names are known. We should adopt a pseudonym. Like spies.'

'You're mad, you know that?'

'I could be Astarte, an exotic dancer from Syria.'

'You look about as Syrian as my left foot.'

Senova nudged him. 'It's true though. We need new names for now. Just in case. Something we'll remember, too.'

Rufinus had been idly ruffling the hair on Acheron's back with his good hand and he stopped, looking down. 'Then I'll be Aulus Junius Dionysus.'

'Who?'

'Dis. The frumentarius who owned Acheron before me. You remember Dis.'

She shuddered. 'I don't like to think on dark days like that.'

'But Dis was not what he appeared. He was a good man. I shall be him. Aulus Junius Dionysus'

Senova frowned. 'Very well, if we're playing people we know, I shall be Septimia Apera.'

'The girl you met in Porolissum?'

'Yes. Lovely girl. I shall be her.'

'Alright.' Rufinus sagged again, and Senova frowned her irritation. 'While you're wallowing in self-pity, try and remember that there are always positives. I love you, for one, Gnaeus. With that she left the room and went for a short walk with Luca around the southern edge of town and down to the water. When she returned an hour later, she found Rufinus in their room and her eyes widened.

'What are you *doing*?'

Rufinus hissed in pain as he gripped the window sill with his left hand and tried to put his weight on it. It held for a moment and then he fell back with a yelp. She snatched up the sling from the bed and hurried over to him, but he waved her away with his right arm.

'Putting myself in the hands of the gods,' Rufinus said. 'Enough moping. You were right about a number of things. Fortuna *has* watched over me. But the gods always favour a man who tries. The physician back in Durostorum said six days for my arm.'

'*Six or seven you told me.*'

'Well, yes. But it's been four now already. I'm about there. It's healed. It can hold my weight. The only reason I fell was because the muscle's atrophied after all this time. I'm going to build it back up. No more sling. No more slouching and grumbling. Luca and I are going to work some of the passage to Athens. I'm sure I can negotiate with the captain. He needn't put a sailor onto looking after the horses. Luca can do that. And I can do a few things. And we'll sell the two donkeys – just take Atalanta and your Damara. With the money we'll save on all that, we'll be able to take a second ship from Athens to Rome. I still don't know what we'll do when we get there, mind.'

'We will set up an altar to Fortuna,' Senova smiled. 'A big one.'

'Right. I am going to try and sell the two donkeys. You re-pack and get rid of anything we don't need.' He turned to the boy in the doorway behind her. 'We're taking new names for the journey. I'm Aulus Junius Dionysus and this is Septimia Apera. What was your original name?'

'Luca,' said Luca.

'No, not your slave name.'

'I was born a slave.'

Rufinus shrugged. 'Well they won't be looking for a Luca, I guess. Alright. Let's get ready. On the morning tide we wave goodbye to Dacia and Moesia and head for the civilised world again.'

378

XXVI – Encounters unexpected and paths
to be forged

The civilised world turned out to be noisy, busy, smelly and headache inducing, especially after so many days at sea.

The journey had, in fact, taken only thirteen days due to a constant improvement in conditions as the sky cleared with every mile that slid beneath those great painted wings. Rufinus had negotiated and secured three hundred denarii off the price with the loss of the two donkeys and the agreement that he and Luca would look after the animals, *all* the animals, which included two more horses belonging to a trader from Axiopolis who was heading to Athens with a small group of dull and squint-eyed men to set up a new factor for his business.

Fortunately for Rufinus and his companions, the businessman was far too occupied and self-absorbed to take any interest in the strange party with whom he shared the ship, and at every night's stopover they disappeared to work on facts and figures. Rufinus' own condition continued to improve throughout the journey too, and by the time the ship had round the southern point of Euboea he was exercising every morning, building his muscle tone once more. He could lift, carry and jump. He'd even planned to challenge a fellow on the crew who fancied himself a boxer but, having mentioned the fact at the evening meal, the things Senova called him for the idea changed his mind. Reluctantly, he acknowledged that he probably wasn't quite ready to start fighting again. Soon, though.

There had been tense times over those thirteen days, too. Numerous times Rufinus had forgotten to answer to his pseudonym, and Senova had soon told everyone he had only partial hearing to help cover for the repeated oversight.

Inevitably, the crew had enquired as to their passengers' lives during those evening socials on layovers, and Rufinus had developed a somewhat complex history for Aulus Junius Dionysus who, as far as the crew of the Pinnata were concerned, was a citizen from Hispania who had suffered critical money troubles years ago and had sold himself into a gladiator school to pay his debts. He had ended up a free man, and with a small fund to his name, in Moesia, where he had met his lady friend and enticed her to return west with him. Every time he embellished and his story became slightly more fanciful, he would receive a surreptitious kick under the table from Senova. *He* thought he'd done quite well, since he needed to explain away his foreignness and excessive scarring somehow. Senova had been smooth and calm, revealing a Pannonian origin and leaving her home in Singidunum when her man – a soldier – had been killed, seeking a new start somewhere else. Luca had played their slave well, naturally.

It was a time of healing for Rufinus in more ways than one. His ribs stopped hurting, his arm became strong again and his muscles began to return to their former condition. But also, being ever further from the reach of Clodius Albinus and his cronies and the province that had almost broken him brought an increasing lightness to his heart. And though, at night and when alone, Rufinus still suffered pangs of worry and even panic about Publius and what lay ahead in Rome, Senova seemed to have some magical ability to wash away his cares with a touch. Their relationship became ever closer, and Rufinus had found himself thinking of Luca as perhaps something of a pet. Not a child of his, but at least someone whose welfare he cared about.

All in all, things had improved immeasurably for Dionysus and his woman Septimia Apera as they reached Greece. Civilization.

Rufinus had never travelled to the east before, spending his time in Hispania or Italia or on the northern borders. He had always thought of it as an exotic place, a hotbed of learning and thought and invention. His father, the sour old bastard, always called it a degenerate hole, but *his* opinion was always to be taken with scepticism, especially since he'd never been there either.

'Athens is not what I thought it would be,' he said to Senova as they leaned on the rail of the ship and watched the great port seething with life sliding toward them. Senova's eyes were wide with wonder, but to Rufinus it looked like any great city's port, not the marble land of wonders he had expected.

'That is not Athens,' noted the merchant, standing impatiently nearby.

'What?'

'That is Piraeus, the port of Athens. A little like Ostia and Rome from what I understand. The two are connected by long walls. It's about five miles to the city from the port.'

Rufinus nodded. He recalled hearing about Piraeus and the walls somewhere. One thing was certain, though: it was busy. Busier than any port he had ever seen excepting perhaps Ostia. Ships of every size, type and nationality sat at the jetties, manoeuvred around the harbour and slid in and out between the great, reaching, welcoming moles. The sailors did all those arcane things sailors did with ropes and sails and bits of wood, and the merchant ship slipped into the calmer waters of the harbour with ease, passing a Cretan ship in the process, whose crew shouted greetings and lewd suggestions about what might await the new arrivals in port.

'Are we going into Athens?' Senova asked quietly.

'Not sure,' Rufinus replied. 'I'd certainly like to see it, but what matters more is securing the next stage and heading back to Rome. There should be plenty of opportunity for that. There'll be loads of ships between those two cities. Before we decide, I think we should visit the port office and see what we can find out.'

Senova nodded and the pair fell silent as they watched Piraeus closing on them.

The Pinnata ran across the jutting ends of numerous jetties and began to turn more sharply than Rufinus had anticipated, the passengers holding on to the rail as the spray hurtled up into the blue. The praetorian's breath caught in his throat. The jetty for which they were making sat neatly between two ships that made him nervous on sight: a trireme bearing the same sails they had seen on the local fleet on the Danuvius, and a great warship with sail markings Rufinus had seen before plenty of times – the insignia of the Misenum fleet back in Italia.

He tried to steady his pulse. Athens was one of the great cities of the empire and a hub for trade and politics and the military. Warships from both east and west would have a thousand reasons to be here. Still, he found himself sweating nervously as the merchant vessel slid into its assigned position between the two military ships.

He waited impatiently, nervously, near the bow with the others while the horses were brought up, along with all the gear, and the ramp was run out to the jetty. Sailors tied ropes and secured fittings and it seemed to have been an age when the ship was finally considered docked and the passengers were allowed to disembark.

Unlike small Callatis in Moesia, this place was not so easy-going with arrivals and departures, and Rufinus could see soldiers on duty in various positions around the port, and virtual cohorts of clerks and functionaries strutting around the place on missions of word and parchment. A man in a neat tunic and cloak with oiled, curly hair and a face like drooping candle wax waited on the dock with a tablet and two assistants. As Rufinus skittered down the ramp, leading Atalanta and with the others following on close behind, the official stepped forward, his jowls wobbling around beside his fat, fleshy lips.

'Place of origin?'

Rufinus frowned. Presumably the man meant where they boarded the ship rather than his home. 'Callatis, Moesia'

'Inferior,' he announced. The man nodded, jowls rolling again, and scratched something on his tablet.

'Size of party?'

'Two adults, one boy, two horses and a dog.'

The man ignored the details and scratched 'III' on his tablet.

'Names?'

'Aulus Junius Dionysus and Septimia Apera, and the boy is our slave, Luca. I don't suppose you want the names of the horses and dog?'

The man gave him a long-suffering look and scratched slowly away. Rufinus watched impatiently, the merchant standing tapping his foot and waiting behind them on the ramp as the official made a mistake and had to flatten the wax and start again. Some sort of commotion was going on aboard the great warship to their right and Rufinus was starting to feel distinctly nervous standing here and waiting.

'Is that it?' he asked as the man was still finishing his writing.

'I have to check a few things,' the man said in a bored, officious voice.

'Go on, then.'

'Have you travelled through Armenia, Parthia or Arabia?'

Rufinus rolled his eyes. 'Dacia and Moesia, and no, we have not brought back plague.'

'Have you...'

'Hold,' called a voice from above and Rufinus' blood chilled as he looked up to see a man in a senior naval officer's uniform at the rail of the warship.

'Yes?' the official replied.

'Send that man and his party up here.'

'That is most irregular,' muttered Jowly.

'Nevertheless, you will comply,' the officer said, coldly, and then turned to Rufinus. 'Master Dionysus, please be so good as to come aboard the *Fortuna* with your companions. You can leave the horses and dog, though.'

The officer indicated a steep ramp up to the warship. Rufinus felt panic gripping him. In a way, there were several things he should be grateful for. It could have been the *Moesian* ship that had summoned him, which would have made unpleasant sense, after all, and the fact that the Italian vessel was named for that same goddess of luck as had been sheltering him all the way across Dacia commended it somewhat. Still, recognition from an official or military source of any sort boded ill.

Senova shuffled up close to him, with Luca dogging their steps and Acheron at heel too, the official's assistants holding the two horses' reins uncomfortably as he moved on to the impatient merchant.

'What is this?' Senova hissed.

'I wish I knew.'

'How is your arm now?'

'If you're about to suggest I take on a warship full of sailors and marines, I think you must have been drinking that medicine from the mountains, or maybe Cassius' fruit spirit.'

'What if it's Cleander?'

Rufinus shook his head. 'The chamberlain won't leave Rome.'

They climbed the ramp with trepidation and in a sweat, and the officer bowed his head as they reached the top. 'Master Dionysus, and the charming *Septimia Apera*. I cannot allow the dog on my ship, though.'

'No dog, no us,' Rufinus said flatly, and the two men regarded one another silently, engaged in a battle of wills.

'Very well, but it must remain under control. Follow me.'

The man led them aft to where a sheltered cabin sat, a luxury missing from most warships and only feasible because of the sheer size of the Fortuna, with its five rows of oars. The door stood open and the interior was dim. Rufinus and Senova shared a worried look as the officer stopped beside the door and gestured for them to enter. Rufinus moved inside first, his form blocking out the light from the doorway, the others moving forward behind him,

The room was done out as a sleeping chamber and office combined, and its sole occupant sat at the desk, peering toward the door in an oppressive gloom. Rufinus could just make out a curled beard and similarly curly hair. He drew an involuntary sharp breath for a moment, for the figure looked worryingly like Clodius Albinus. Then Rufinus stepped aside and the light from the doorway illuminated the room a little. Rufinus stared in astonishment.

'Interesting,' Lucius Septimius Severus, Governor of Gallia Lugdunensis, said quietly, rising from his seat. 'And most curious.'

Senova slipped into the room, Luca and Acheron completing the group. Severus reached behind him and opened the shutters of the window, raising the light level considerably. Rufinus was still staring.

'Here am I attending to a little administrative work in my cabin and I hear, against all expectations, my daughter disembarking the ship beside me. I have my man send for the new arrival in curiosity and, though I don't recognise the woman using my daughter's name, I find her companion to be most unexpected. Guardsman Rustius Rufinus. And under an assumed name also. Fascinating.'

Rufinus was shaking his head. 'I… this is not how it looks.'

'I am intrigued as to how you *think* it looks, Rufinus.'

'Well, travelling under a pseudonym, Governor, and using your daughter's name.' He shot an accusing look at Senova, who replied with a silent '*how was I to know*' glare.

'I believe I am watching the Fates at work, Rufinus. I had heard that you had something of a run-in with that oily snake Cleander. Did he not send you into exile, I hear?'

Rufinus felt a strange easing of tension. His few encounters with this man over the years had led him to the conclusion that Severus was perhaps a dangerous man, but a very forthright and straight one. Not one of the serpents of the court. He had no love for Cleander, and that Rufinus knew, and he suddenly had a flash of memory from Dacia. Senova had told him that Severus hated Clodius Albinus, words that had come directly from the mouth of the man's daughter.

'The enemy of my enemy,' Rufinus said quietly.

'I'm sorry?'

Rufinus shook his head. 'Thinking aloud, Governor. About trust, and honesty, and where people fit in the great game of Roman politics.'

'A complex subject, and one that is more suited to an evening of wine than a chance meeting on a warship, Rufinus.'

'But that's just it, Governor,' Rufinus said his eyes lighting up. 'You're wrong. This isn't the work of the Fates. This is Fortuna pure and simple. She has watched over me for months in a hostile land and now she comes to me in the form of a ship and bearing an unexpected opportunity.'

'You speak in riddles, Rufinus,' Severus frowned.

'I had begun to think there was no one left to trust. That only my friend in the frumentarii and General Pompeianu could be relied upon. But I was wrong. There is you.'

'The way you are talking sounds worryingly treasonous, Rufinus.'

'No, Governor. No, it isn't. *Far from it*, in fact. Can we talk privately?'

Severus frowned for a while and finally nodded. 'After?'

The officer outside ducked his head though the door. 'Governor?'

'Close the door and move your crewmen out of earshot of the cabin, if you would.'

The man did not look happy, but saluted and retreated, shutting the door and calling to the few sailors working nearby. Once silence reigned, Severus lit two lamps and closed the window shutters once more, plunging the cabin into a golden gloom.

'Note the unprecedented trust I am placing in you, Rufinus. I should, by rights, have a number of lictors around me, ready with their axes in case of trouble.'

Rufinus nodded. 'Governor, I have been in Dacia and I have such a story to tell you...'

Severus sat in the lamp light and listened to Rufinus' tale in rapt silence, never interrupting, reaching out after a while and pouring wine for them all, gesturing for Senova to be seated. Periodically he nodded, or winced, or shook his head. Finally, Rufinus slumped back in his chair.

'So we took ship from Callatis thirteen days ago. Even though there was no indication that the local governor was part of Albinus' web and that we were being sought, we thought it best to use assumed names. I used the identity of an old acquaintance in Rome, now dead, and Senova here took your daughter's name. And here we are, on the way back to Rome to try and confront Cleander with the information, get Publius freed and reinstate myself in the Guard. I remember you, Governor, from meetings at Pompeianus' villa. You always seemed to have the right interests at heart. I hope I am not mistaken.'

Severus nodded again and took a sip of his wine. The way he threw back his head to drink, combined with that impressive hair and beard gave the impression that the man ought to have let out a roar. Rufinus frowned. Cleander: a snake. Commodus: a peacock. Albinus: a weasel. Niger: a dog on its back.

Severus: a lion.

There was something about that impression that stuck in Rufinus' mind and he couldn't shake it.

Finally, the governor leaned forward on the table and steepled his fingers. 'You are in a very strange position, my young praetorian friend. You know potentially empire-shaking secrets, yet with no evidence. You have unsolvable problems to solve, and seem to have navigated the most incredibly dangerous currents and yet come out floating and with a following wind. *And* you seem to have failed to note

Praetorian: Eagles of Dacia

specifically in your precis the one factor that I would consider of prime import.'

'Governor?'

'You're *dead*, Rufinus. I suspect you will be surprised how many options that opens up if you work things out correctly.'

It was the turn of Rufinus' eyes to narrow now. 'Sir?'

'The men who you exposed are not hunting you, because you are already dead. Any trouble still hanging over you in Rome will dissipate. Even your brother, I think, will go free.'

'Free?'

'Cleander is a methodical man. Your father is busy lobbying for position back in Rome. I've met the man. He has your ambition but not half your wit. Cleander has no need to keep your brother if you are out of them picture. Keeping him as a ward of the court is a very expensive business and now totally unnecessary. Equally, disposing of him would risk raising questions as to his fate. No. Cleander's simplest choice is to send Publius back to your father. That way your father will stamp on any resistance from your brother, because he won't want anything to interfere with his social climbing. No, Rufinus, I think your death will have simplified things in Rome.'

Rufinus boggled. It was so clear. The man was right. A carefully-worded letter to Vibius Cestius and he could check, but it seemed so likely. As an unnamed corpse, a ghost even, Rufinus was safe and his friends and family would be safe too. He felt a sudden jolt of responsibility.

'But I cannot simply hide and let the world go on around me, Governor. Pompeianus was right: once you start to play the game, you can't stop. Even when you win, you just have to play the next match. Dead or not, my duty is to the emperor, and that duty is to find a way to bring down Cleander. And also to find a way to stop Clodius Albinus preparing to take the throne. I cannot *imagine* Rome under his rule.'

Severus shrugged. 'Forget about Albinus for now.'

'But he is manoeuvring for the throne.'

'Rufinus, *everyone* is manoeuvring for the throne.'

A sudden panic shot through him. Surely not? He had just revealed everything to this man.

'My duty is to the emperor,' Rufinus repeated, stern faced and straightening. 'To Caesar Marcus Aurelius Commodus Antoninus Augustus, emperor of Rome.'

'For gods' sake, Rufinus, relax. You'll do yourself an injury. Don't panic so. I am loyal to the emperor. As loyal as any subject and a damn sight more than most. I have no intention of revolting against him, but then neither has Albinus. Nor Pertinax or Pompeianus or Julianus or any other player of the game. But Commodus has no heir in place and he is becoming unpopular with the senate and the powerful families in Rome. It matters not how much the people and the army love an emperor if he angers the nobles. Ask Caligula. Or Nero. Or Domitian. No one with any sense is moving against the emperor, but we all intend to be ready when the time comes, because when the emperor falls without succession there will be a feeding frenzy the like of which you have never seen. It is useful to know about Albinus, and about Niger, and all their web, and that information will be invaluable at some point. But for now it is just that: information.'

The beast was roaring again, and Rufinus felt an odd thrill at the knowledge that, while men like Albinus were vying for power, and Cleander still slithered about in Rome, there were still lions like Severus in the empire.

'Cleander, though,' Rufinus began.

'Cleander must fall – you are correct on that count – but it will be difficult, and will not be a quick job. Plans must be put in place and carefully executed, unless those responsible wish to be carefully executed themselves.'

'Then what do I do?' Rufinus sighed. 'I am nobody. Not a praetorian. Not anything. I'm a ghost.'

'You don't have to be nobody,' Severus said with an odd smile.

'Governor?'

'Join me, Rufinus.'

The young ghost frowned. 'How? When? Where?'

'The *how* is easy. Choose a name. This Dionysus, even. Within a week back in Rome I will secure you documents legitimising you. The *when* is now. I will always find a place on my staff for clever and honest men. You will be useful to me and, believe me, I can be useful to you. The *where* is more complex. I am bound for Emesa, and I am in something of a hurry. I am seeking a match with a certain noblewoman of Syrian origin, but as soon as that agreement is reached I will be returning to Gaul. There is still something of a mess there following Maternus' uprising. Come with me. To Syria. To Rome. To Gaul. We will think upon the coming months and plan the downfall of Rome's wicked serpent.' The governor smiled. 'Your lady here, too. And your slave. And even that thing,' he added, pointing at Acheron who stood quietly beside Luca near the door. 'What do you say?'

Rufinus shook his head in wonder. Fortuna. The altar he was going to have to devote to her would need to be the size of a house at this rate. But this lion of a man could be the very one to make a difference. To change things. To repair Rome.

He smiled.

'Yes,' said Rufinus.

THE END.

Historical note

Praetorian 3 is both *about* a journey and *is* a journey in itself. I first devised the plot immediately after completing the second book, but I knew that if I were to try and write this with any hint of authenticity I would have to travel Rufinus' route, smell the smells, climb the slopes, listen to the sounds and feel the sun and rain. Time and financial constraints prevented the research trip for some time and so the book was delayed by more than a year. I'm glad I waited. Some of the locations and scenes in this book that I love most would never have been written had I not experienced Romania. I urge you to visit (more on this matter at the end of the note, which holds a *key* for you!).

The plot of the book is my own devising, based upon a few known elements, unlike books 1 and 2 which were based heavily around solidly documented events (the plot of Lucilla and the downfall of Perennis.) All I had to work with for this was a brief note that Clodius Albinus and Pescennius Niger commanded together in Dacia during an otherwise unrecorded altercation. The timeline is a little confused, and there are Sarmatian incursions, local risings and a revolt of the gold miners. I have simply slipped these events into the plot in such a way as it builds a plot for Rufinus to unravel. And yes, I know he seems to have lost again (he was somewhat dejected at the end of book 2) but looking a little deeper, he has actually emerged in a strong and unexpected position with a powerful ally. This was necessary and lays elements of two books yet to come.

Each of the Praetorian novels has explored a theme to the backdrop of a new location. The first was set largely in Rome and environs with Rufinus as something of a young fish out of water, learning the hard way the rules of Roman political shenanigans. The second explored darker themes of addiction and revenge among the Danubian provinces. This third has been a journey that has explored relationships and changed Rufinus in subtle ways.

A little something on locations is needed, I think, though I'll skip most of this and you'll see why later.

The Savus marshes through which Rufinus and Senova pass in the first chapter are now gone. At the time of the geographer Ptolemy, the Savus became a huge marshland before emptying into the Danube and it would have been the same in Rufinus' time. The marsh was drained in the later empire and reclaimed, partially by the emperor Probus who ordered a canal dug in 282. My image of the ancient Savus marshes is a recreation of the Dyfi wetlands in North Wales, which contains much the same flora and fauna as would have been visible there.

Apulum (modern Alba Iulia) has been much covered with later building (though some of that is phenomenal and historic in its own right. Alba Iulia remains one of my favourite places I visited and is the home to a Roman festival and the re-enactment group Garda Apulum. Their centurion, Ciprian Dobra, guided us around the Roman remains of the city and has since acted as a great source of information on Roman Dacia and in particular the gold mining. More of this later, too.

Much of Romania's Roman heritage is well cared-for, and there really is quite a lot. The beauty of it, as a Roman historian, is that Dacia was only a Roman province from 107 until 275. Living in Roman Britain I often bemoan the fact that we have remains from only 367 years of occupation from an empire that lasted 2 millennia. Romania only has 168 years' worth. But that means that much of what was there in the early days was there at the end and vice versa. Certainly for a visitor somewhere more or less halfway through the province's life, things were very much settled and existed by Rufinus' time.

Commodava (Cumidava) is an interesting site in that respect. I had, prior to writing, seen the fort mentioned as part of the Severan refortification of Dacia's eastern limes. On further research, I have found it suggested that it was part of the original Trajanic system. Somewhere in between, while in nearby Brasov I found a source that suggested that the site, and indeed the entire frontier, was actually already being reworked in the Commodian era as a response to the various invasions the place had suffered. This source also suggested that rather than the 'Cumi' being a Latinisation of Dacian 'Comi', the site had originally borne another name and that Cumidava came from Commodava, named for the emperor who reworked its place in the system. One thing is certain: Cumidava existed in Rufinus' time, but had not yet acquired its stone walls. At this stage it was still a turf and timber frontier fort. A work from Durham University (http://etheses.dur.ac.uk/3957/1/3957_1473-vol1.pdf) sites that Cumidava has produced evidence of a 2nd century occupation phase. This is somewhat supported by

"Pending excavations, the date of its construction can only be guessed at. The general assumption is that the Limes Transalutanus was constructed around 200 A.D., and abandoned by the middle of the 3rd century. Even without excavation, the traces found at certain camps (Săpata de Jos, Urlieni, Băneasa) of two forts, side by side, indicate two construction periods, for it is unlikely that they would have been in use simultaneously. This suggests that the camps in the outer line were used for a longer period of time, and that they may have been constructed before 200." from http://mek.oszk.hu/03400/03407/html/13.html. I have therefore chosen to go with this.

A mention of dates, too, needs to be made. It is commonly noted that Niger and Albinus held their commissions in Dacia around 182-183, or possibly 184. There is a suggestion of an insurrection in 185 and the miners' revolt in 187. Dating these events accurately is something of a headache, especially given that Herodian, Cassius Dio and the Historia Augusta generally disagree with one another and are often anecdotal. From

http://mek.oszk.hu/03400/03407/html/16.html we find:

"During Commodus's reign, unrest and disturbances were rife among the people of Dacia. The causes were many: fifteen years of devastating war, the plague, the inadequacies of military defence and public security, the slow pace of reconstruction, economic difficulties, and progress toward urban self-government that was slower than in other provinces. It is briefly noted in the Emperor's biography that a local revolt broke out in Dacia around 185. There is no indication that indigenous Dacians participated in the insurrection."

There is a list of the Legates of the 13th Gemina in Alba Iulia, which Ciprian Dobra helpfully showed me, which has the post held by M. Valerius Maximianus 181-182 and C. Caerellius Sabinus 183-185, then a gap until M. Herennius Faustus in 190. In my reasoning, since Niger and Albinus would need to command the two legions in Dacia for the campaign that is recorded it could not be between 181 and 185, and would have to be after that. I am therefore unrepentant in setting my campaign in that gap. Plus it fits with Rufinus' arc. And any other dates that have been tweaked a little have only been done so as to help the story. Incidentally, while it seems almost beggaring belief to 'bump' into Septimius Severus in Athens, he is historically attested at this time travelling to Syria to woo the woman who would become his wife and future empress. And boy, does it segue nicely into my plan for book 4 which, you will hopefully be pleased to hear, will finally deal with Cleander.

I will hold my hands up in a mea culpa to one unit being moved for the simple reason of story. The Numerus Germanicianorum are based in the book at the fort in the place now called Buciumi, which was almost certainly the ancien fort of Bucium. In fact, the Numerus were apparently based a the unnamed fort at modern Bucium. I could in fairness hav rejigged the plot and used a different unit, but that Numeru was in operation somewhere in Romania probably throughou the existence of Dacia province in several locations and during times of war, Roman units – especially scouts – moved a lot, so I am really rather unrepentant. Narcissus and his men were fun.

There will, as I hinted earlier, be a book 4 (and possibly more yet) and it is scheduled for late 2018. But as an extra note you may be aware that my first novel with Orion (Caligula) is released in March 2018. Well, the second novel in the Damned Emperors series (2019) will be Commodus, and will deal in some detail with the life of the emperor I have touched upon in this series, so if you're concerned that I'm skating around the life of that Herculean emperor, then remember that it will be thoroughly covered in a whole separate novel in due course.

Finally, before I run off and write something new and also exciting, there is one thing I need to give you. I mentioned a key earlier. As I wrote this book, I continually penned a page on my blog that follows Rufinus' journey (and therefore my own research trip) with plenty of photos, for you to have a look at and perhaps see something of what you've just read.

Visit https://sjat.wordpress.com/eagles-of-dacia-rufinus-journey/ to experience more of Rufinus' travels. But I would ask you not to advertise this page and to keep it as our closed little secret, lest it spoil the novel for those who haven't read it yet. In terms of what Rufinus (and I) saw, this webpage is more or less the second half of the Historical Note.

I hope you enjoyed reading Praetorian III as much as I enjoyed writing it. Rufinus will return, while, for now, I change centuries and work on something new.

Vale,

Simon Turney,
November 2017

If you liked this book, why not try others by S.J.A. Turney

Interregnum (Tales of the Empire 1)

(2009) *

For twenty years civil war has torn the Empire apart; the Imperial line extinguished as the mad Emperor Quintus burned in his palace, betrayed by his greatest general. Against a background of war, decay, poverty and violence, men who once served in the proud Imperial army now fight as mercenaries, hiring themselves to the greediest lords.

On a hopeless battlefield that same general, now a mercenary captain tortured by the events of his past, stumbles across hope in the form of a young man begging for help. Kiva is forced to face more than his dark past as he struggles to put his life and the very Empire back together. The last scion of the Imperial line will change Kiva forever.

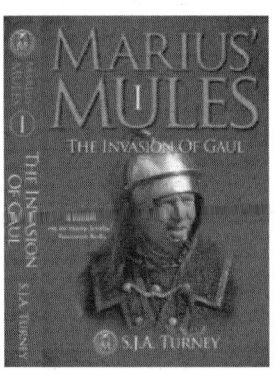

Marius' Mules I: The Invasion of Gaul

(2009) *

It is 58 BC and the mighty Tenth Legion, camped in Northern Italy, prepare for the arrival of the most notorious general in Roman history: Julius Caesar.

Marcus Falerius Fronto, commander of the Tenth is a career soldier and long-time companion of Caesar's. Despite his desire for the simplicity of the military life, he cannot help but be drawn into intrigue and politics as Caesar engineers a motive to invade the lands of Gaul.

Fronto is about to discover that politics can be as dangerous as battle, that old enemies can be trusted more than new friends, and that standing close to such a shining figure as Caesar, even the most ethical of men risk being burned.

The Thief's Tale (Ottoman Cycle 1)

(2013) *

Istanbul, 1481. The once great city of Constantine that now forms the heart of the Ottoman empire is a strange mix of Christian, Turk and Jew. Despite the benevolent reign of the Sultan Bayezid II, the conquest is still a recent memory, and emotions run high among the inhabitants, with danger never far beneath the surface.

Skiouros and Lykaion, the sons of a Greek country farmer, are conscripted into the ranks of the famous Janissary guards and taken to Istanbul where they will play a pivotal, if unsung, role in the history of the new regime. As Skiouros escapes into the Greek quarter and vanishes among its streets to survive on his wits alone, Lykaion remains with the slave chain to fulfill his destiny and become an Islamic convert and a guard of the Imperial palace. Brothers they remain, though standing to either side of an unimaginable divide.

On a fateful day in late autumn 1490, Skiouros picks the wrong pocket and begins to unravel a plot that reaches to the very highest peaks of Imperial power. He and his brother are about to be left with the most difficult decision faced by a conquered Greek: whether the rule of the Ottoman Sultan is worth saving.

* Sequels in all series also available

Printed in Great Britain
by Amazon